Queen's Park to The Elephant

D1825465

This book is dedicated to the memory of Phyllis Hogan and Andrew (you'd have liked this one mate).

A journey taken every day, often the same people sitting there in the carriage that you've claimed for yourself, it's yours and these people are being allowed to share it with you. Looking at insurance and holiday adverts above the person opposite. Eye contact is a glimpse in to their soul and they're not going to give you that, who knows what they'll give away? The person who gets off the train at that obscure stop which you know nothing about, what's there? Who even lives there? Why does that old Chinese lady live in Warwick Avenue?

Cities are big places, you know barely anyone, those you do know, their lives are no longer interesting because they've told you a thousand times about that time they went to India to find themselves while dropping acid with washed out hippies. So cool, man! they probably never went anyway. Cynicism, why do you have to be so cynical? That guy over there, holding his sleeping bag, tattered trousers, big beard and a bright red jacket, he doesn't look like he belongs, he sticks out, I bet he has a proper story to tell.

Oxford Circus, the tourists pour on and off the train, excited little kids with their mothers secretly hoping that mum is going to buy them something nice, already planning what they'll do with their new toy when they get home, the chance of disappointment buried deep at the back of their minds because for the next couple of hours they'll be living in hope, hope for the simplest of things. Like when you were a kid, when your mum used to take you to Oxford Street so you could look at the shop windows and the lights and the thousands of big red buses, and the people, so many people. You're envious of that kid, a day living the innocence of childhood again would be the greatest Christmas present.

It's enough to make you smile and remember that it isn't all doom and gloom and the world isn't about to end because that's all the television and your friends on social media are telling you. It's a great place to live, you should have got off at Regent's Park and taken a trip to the zoo, it's a long time since you've been to the zoo. They've got a new panda apparently. You could nip over to Madame Tussauds while you're there as well, you've always wanted to meet William Shakespeare, lose yourself in your own little world, recapture the imagination that's been lost in a world of facts and information overload.

All the sights and sounds, without the people there'd be no sights and sounds. Cities and towns and villages across the world, it's the people who make them. Even the ticket inspector who stopped you yesterday and told you you had to pay a fine because you'd bought the wrong ticket, you're still wishing ill upon him now, the thought of him makes you furrow your brow, I wonder when he went home did he give me a second thought? I doubt it, there's no conscience for the wicked. I bet he's doing the same thing to another misfortunate right now, he'll be enjoying it too.

That uncle of yours, the one who lives in Kilburn, the Irish fella who came over on the boat years ago, long before your mother, I bet he'd have told him where to go. You should go up and see him soon, it's been a long time since you've sat in the bars of County Kilburn with a pint of Guinness, the soft voice of uncle Mickey telling you stories that make you laugh, pints flowing, songs of rebels and fields in the background.

People get up, careful not to bang into someone else, fear of confrontation, fear of exposure. God forbid someone interacts with them. Your little dream well broken as the doors open and the rush up the stairs to the world above begins. The Elephant and Castle, there aren't any elephants, and the castles are bright pink. All change please, this train terminates here, all change. Queen's Park to The Elephant, sixteen stations, sixteen different people all with tales to tell.

Queen's Park – You're Turning into One of Them

Queen's Park, an area of West London, mostly known for its park and gentrification

"Hugo, darling, please don't throw the books on the floor or the man will ask us to pay for them."

Hugo picks another book out from the shelf and throws it on the floor. Mummy looks at him, looks at me with a shrug of the shoulders. 'What can you do?' I know what I'd do to the little fucker but I'd end up in the nick across the road. Mummy grabs him by the hand and pulls him out of the shop, Hugo looks at me with menace in his eyes as he drags his feet, a final 'fuck you!'. Fuck you too, Hugo, I hope mummy goes home and finds out daddy has been shagging the Belarussian nanny while she drags you around 'quaint' little bookshops.

The books are all over the floor, I place them back on the shelves, they don't seem to be damaged. I reckon I should just ban kids from coming in here, all they do is cause grief and try their best to wreck the gaff. I flip the sign on the door so it shows the shop as closed and lock the door. Someone walks up and pushes the door. It's locked you clown! They look at me with pleading eyes, I can't be bothered, I mouth 'come back tomorrow', he rolls his eyes and walks off, doubt he'll be back. Why come now? You had all day.

I sit down at the back of the shop and light a fag, inhaling deeply and then slowly letting the smoke out. I've been testing myself, trying to see if I can go from lunch until close without having one. It makes them taste better. I feel the tension slip away, maybe poor Hugo isn't such a bad kid after all, I should have opened the door for that fella too. This not smoking business might be doing me more harm than good. Smoke them and they're killing me, don't smoke them and I hate the world and wish life changing events on small children I don't know.

I stand by the door to my office and look out at the shop, it's one of them old bookshops that you don't really see anymore. Books on shelves stacked top to bottom, the bookcases are arranged in no real order, walking around the shop is like navigating a maze. Some of the books would probably fall apart if you took them out. If someone does pull one out and it falls apart it'll be an extremely rare and expensive book that's not available anywhere else. You'll have to pay for it mate, sorry but it's irreplaceable.

I look at my watch, I've got to make it to that small gig for eight. I've been looking forward to it all week, ever since Johnny rang me up asking if I could do it. It's in some small bar down in south London. I don't really like going down there, different breed of people ain't they? He told me it was for a bunch of students who like to see themselves as purveyors of social justice and I need to be careful with my material. I've had a good think about it and they'll be in for a good night.

I walk down the road and over the bridge which Queen's Park station sits on, it's like crossing an invisible boundary. Leaving the little coffee shops, organic food shops, oh and my little book shop, on one side for high rise tower blocks and the riff raff that they're scared will drive the prices down on their little investments if they cross the bridge and sully their little enclave in north west London. They've even started giving these places new names, like north Maida Vale, it ain't north Maida Vale, it's Queen's Park, South Kilburn at a push. It's all money though ain't it? The estate agent isn't going to have a crisis of conscience and think changing the names might hurt the feelings of people that live in these areas.

I open the door to the flat, a nice two bedroom in an 18 storey building. I push past the boxes of books stacked up against the walls. I need to find somewhere I can store them, my flat looks like one of them hoarders' places. I fall back on the sofa, have a rest before I get ready to hit off to the other side of the city. What am I going to do with this shop? Ten years I've had it, it wasn't the same place ten years ago, not that it wasn't nice, it's always been nice around there but not like it is now. Different kind of people that have just popped out of nowhere.

One day I was walking down the street past chicken shops and best buys, the next it was Peruvian coffee bean shops and art shops. My old man had the shop for years, when he died he left it to me even though I never had any interest in it. I don't read books, well I never used to, I do now because no fucker comes into the shop and I have nothing better to do. Quite well versed in Greek philosophy these days, I like a bit of Socrates, nothing like sitting in a Queen's Park bookshop on a Monday afternoon pondering the true meaning of justice. The problem with the shop is, no one comes in anymore. I rarely sell a book. You get mummy and little Hugo but all they do is look, they don't buy. I don't want to let it go for my old man's sake but I can't keep it up if it ain't making any money.

What I love is comedy. It's what I've always wanted to do. I mean, I do it now but it's not serious, I do a few gigs that Johnny sorts out for me but I want to make some proper money out of it, go on tour all of that. If it wasn't for the shop I'd be on my way to getting somewhere with it. I let out a deep sigh, even if it was making money I don't think I'd want it. It's boring, the customers, they aren't my kind of people, you can't really have a good chat with them. They come in all cheerful then when they hear my accent their attitude changes. It's not like I'm a 'clean your chimney guvnor' type person either.

I put my shirt and trousers on and grab a beer from the fridge, quick one before I go, helps with the confidence. I neck half the bottle as I look out the window. It's a beautiful summer's evening, the sky still a dark blue colour, people downstairs standing around chatting with friends, kids still out playing, chasing each other around the bottom of the flats. I spot a middle age man on one of the balconies, he pulls a water balloon from a plastic bag and throws it down at the kids. They dance around underneath him as they try to dodge the water, laughing, the man laughing as well. Wish I could join them.

The old fella next door is sitting outside his door dressed in shorts and t-shirt, sitting on an ancient looking deckchair. The floor we live on has only a small window on the landing.

"Hello, George! How's things? Enjoying the weather? Got my nice little spot here by the pool."

"Beautiful ain't it? Mind you don't fall in the pool, Alfie."

"Oh, don't worry about that. Betty is a great swimmer, she'd never let me drown!"

Betty's his wife. She's been dead for two years.

"Okay, mate. I've got to go, got a bit of work down south London."

"I'll pop into the bookshop next week, there's a book I want."

"No problem, Alfie."

He's not going to come to the bookshop.

"George, could you get me a pint of milk on your way home?"

I can see into his kitchen from the open door, there's a two pint bottle of milk sitting on the counter.

"I will Alfie, might be a bit late when I get home though so I'll drop it into you tomorrow."

"It's okay, I'll be up, don't worry about disturbing me. You can have a nice cup of tea when you've finished work."

"See you later, Alfie."

I'll probably be wanting more than a cup of tea when I've finished tonight. Better not forget his milk or I'll never hear the end of it. The geezer on the balcony has ran out of balloons and is now throwing buckets of water down at the kids below. All of them are drenched, not trying to dodge the water now but trying their best to be underneath it as it falls from the balcony above. Sometimes I think I'd give a day of my life away just to be one of them kids for an hour. That's just nerves though, every time I go to do a gig I'm always thinking about ways to escape. Nerves, I hate them.

There are only about fifty people in the room, sitting there waiting for me to start. Some of them are holding pints in their hands, others gazing at their phones, bored with their company, or telling their friends that they're watching a comedy show even though they are barely taking any notice of it.

"We're always using our phones these days ain't we? I mean we go out with our mates but then spend half our time talking to people that ain't even there. I was down the pub the other night and my mate ordered a pint then he took a photo of it and posted it on Facebook with a caption 'First of the night!' Who gives a fuck? Half the country are out having a pint! What makes you so special. It got worse after that. I was standing outside the pub having a burn when the geezer standing next to me got hit over the head with a bottle, then his mate starts filming him on the floor spark out. Doesn't call an ambulance, don't try and sort the geezers who've just knocked his mate out, nope, he films his mate knocked out on the floor. Then an ambulance turns up, geezers still filming by the way, put him in the back and take him off to hospital. His mate doesn't go with him, he turns to me and goes, 'I'm going to get a loads of likes for this one.'

You put on this sort of cheeky chappie persona, someone who lives life on the edge, bit of a wideboy and they're eating out of your hand. Reality is, I just sit in a fucking bookshop all day thinking these things up. These people standing in front of me are the sort of people that come into the shop, pick up a few books and never buy anything. I'm standing here, smiling, telling jokes, laughing along with them, but I fucking hate them. Is it rational? No, most of them are probably good people who'd wish no harm on anyone.

At the end of the show Johnny comes up to me with my money.

"Listen mate, I've got something coming up soon. Me and another geezer I know were thinking about taking a few local comedians on a tour of the country. Money won't be great but it'll be exposure. You fancy it?"

"I'll definitely have a think about it."

What am I going to do about that the shop? This gives me the excuse I need to close it, I'll sell it, they can probably turn it into a coffee shop or something. It'd give me a bit of money to relax for a while too. Sounds like a good idea.

Alf is still sitting outside on his deckchair even though it's almost midnight.

"See you didn't fall in the pool Alfie. What you still doing out here at this time mate? Come on, we'll go inside and make a cup of tea."

"Okay, son. Your dad was a good man, you know that? Really loved this place, loved his little bookshop too. He'd have been devastated if anything ever happened to it."

Where's he got all this from?

"I know that Alfie. Nothing's going to happen to the bookshop."

Alfie's living room is like stepping back 30 years. The carpet's purple, the wallpaper is dark with flowers on it, the curtains yellow.

"Open that cupboard over there, boy. There's a bottle of whiskey I've been saving."

"What? You want to drink it now?"

"Yeah, come on, we'll get pissed."

"Go one then you silly bastard, I'll have one with you."

I pour us both a drink, handing Alfie his. He lifts his glass and nods his head.

"You know what George?"

"What's that mate?"

"I don't mind the gays really."

"What?"

"The gays, I don't mind them. I remember once, a long time ago, we had a friend, me and Betty. Right good looking fella, he always used to go down the west end in nice suits. Betty always used to ask him why he didn't have a nice girlfriend. Turns out he was a raving iron."

"You can't call people 'raving irons' Alfie."

"Oh! I know that."

"Are you trying to ask me if I'm gay?"

"No, I know you're not gay. If you were gay I wouldn't care anyway. This fella, he didn't care what anybody thought. He just got on with his life. You have to remember back then people thought the gays were evil, there was something wrong with them. You care too much what people think about you George."

"How have you come to that conclusion? I stand up in front of a crowd every other night and tell jokes. If I cared what people thought I wouldn't do it."

"It's just you telling yourself that George, it ain't real. You're lost and you don't believe in yourself."

"What are you telling me this for?"

"I know you're struggling, son. You think I've lost my marbles, that I don't see things. Sometimes, when you get to my age George, you need to pretend, you've got to use your imagination. Don't waste your life wondering what the right thing to do is. I always said to your old man that I'd make sure you were okay. At the moment, I don't think you are. You hate that shop, don't you?"

"I don't hate it Alfie, it just ain't me, it's not what I'm about."

"What are you about?"

"I haven't got a clue, but sitting in a bookshop all day isn't it. It don't make anything anyway, I'll have to give it up at some point or I'll end up bankrupt."

"It's changed a lot 'round here. Not that it's all bad! When I was a kid they always used to say 'You gotta look after your own'. Who's your own these days? It's all about money. I used to love going for a stroll up over the bridge. What's the point in me going there now? They've closed the pub. Turned it into flats or something. I used to love going for a drink down there George. I ain't going to be sitting outside one of them coffee shops drinking coffee."

"That's the way it goes though. Things change. You're right, it is about money, that's not a bad thing is it?"

"You seeing any of that money, George? Someone will want to buy that gaff off you soon and they'll turn it into a coffee shop."

"They'd be doing me a favour if they did. I'd love the money, go and do what I want and be able to look after meself. I'd still come 'round and see you, not like I'd just disappear."

"You'd better get off, you look tired. Just remember, George, look after yourself, don't worry about things. Do you want to be part of something you hate?"

"See you later, thanks Alfie."

What does he mean do I want to be part of something I hate? Jesus, I thought the old fella had lost his mind years ago and now he's wrecked my head more than any of them philosophy books I've been reading. I don't think I can even sleep at the moment. Might as well go for a stroll.

It's mad how your whole life you're always thinking what your parents think. The old man always let me do what I wanted, the only thing he wanted me to promise was to look after that shop. Now I think about it, he didn't really let me do what I wanted did he? I mean, I'm tied to that shop. He was going to die at some point so I had no choice but to keep the shop in mind. I couldn't go off and do my own thing.

I wonder what mum would have thought? I don't really remember that much about it. When she died I was only 6. Maybe the shop was just a way for the old man to keep me around, he was scared that he'd lose both his wife and his son. One of the only memories I have of mum is going to the park on a Saturday morning, we'd go into the shop first and dad would give me a couple of quid to take to the sweet shop. Then we'd go to the park and she'd sit on the bench reading a newspaper while I kicked a ball about. Sometimes she'd take me to the café and buy me a can of Coke. It's all I really remember, it must be something to do with suppressed memories, I try to think back but most of it is just blank.

I walk up over the bridge and cut down the side road, past the police station and towards the park. The spikes on the railings aren't enough to put me off jumping over. We used to come in here during the winter when I was a kid, smoke cigarettes at the back of the park. It was stupid because we'd hide in the bushes but make as much noise as possible. Anyone passing by would know someone was in there, no one ever bothered us though, we were harmless kids. That was when I realised I could make people laugh. I loved seeing my mates rolling around laughing, not having a care.

Some people say that comedy is an escape, people use it to escape something. I don't really see anything that I'd be escaping from. Yeah, I lost my mum and it hurt me but the old man was always good to me, he worked hard and he used to come home late but he made sure I was looked after and he still made time for me even when he was at his busiest. After mum had gone it was him that used to take me down to the park on a Saturday, he'd shut the shop in the afternoon and we'd go and play pitch and putt together. That's why I feel like I owe him something. He held it together, made sure I had the best life I could have.

There was that day he took me up to Kew to see the plants and the flowers. I used to love the smell of the train station, when that smell of diesel hit my nose on the platform I knew I was going somewhere different, somewhere exotic. I'd be watching out the window as the train sped through west London. Looking out at nothing much, trying to catch a glimpse of something, I never knew what it was that I wanted to see, just something different, something that you didn't see where you lived. Only five miles from home but it was like being in another part of the world.

The park is silent, not a soul about. I walk over to where the pitch and putt is and walk around the small course, remembering the times we used to play. I don't have any bad memories, there weren't any. I'm walking and I feel like I should feel sad, wanting someone who isn't here to be here now but I'm not, I'm smiling. I'd better get back, the sky is starting to turn that light blue, reddish colour it does on summer mornings as the sun starts to rise. It's going to be a long day.

"I wonder if you could tell me if you have this book?"

"I'm not sure, I'll look it up for you, just give me two minutes."

"Thank you! You have a fine bookshop here. How long have you been in business?"

"Must be nearly 30 years now. My father opened it and I'm looking after it now. We don't seem to have the book in stock but I can order it if you want it."

"I'll order it. I'll have a bit of a browse around if you don't mind?"

"Of course not, take your time."

The fella wanders off around the shop. I can hear him muttering to himself every now and again, even the occasional gasp of amazement, at least someone likes the place.

"I'll be back next week to collect the book. You really do have a fascinating little shop here, you don't see many like it anymore."

The door flies open almost knocking the man on his way out.

"Hugo, you little bastard! I told you if you don't behave we won't be taking you away on holiday. You can stay at home with Svetlana."

Fucking hell! He really does have a Belorussian nanny! I bet daddy is pleased.

"I'm so sorry, he really does like your bookshop for some reason. He's just a bit, you know?"

"Naughty?"

"I'm not sure naughty is the right word. He's awfully clever and I think it affects his brain. I think overenthusiastic is probably the right word. Now come on Hugo! We must go, leave the poor man in peace."

If I wasn't going out tonight I'd have had the hump with Hugo but I'm in a good mood, first time I've been out in a long time. Going to go down the pub with a few old friends. I don't see my friends anywhere near as often as I should these days, maybe that's half my problem. Let's get out of this place!

Alfie's sitting outside his door reading the paper.

"Remember what I said son, don't be walking around with your head up your arse all the time. Get yourself a nice girlfriend. She can look after the shop for you then."

"I'm okay on me own Alfie."

"You sure you're not bent?"

"See you later, Alfie, I'm off to the pub."

"Have one for me, long time since I went down the boozer…"

No way am I having Alfie tagging along with me while I go to the pub. I put my hand up and wave him goodbye. I can hear him singing to himself as I wait for the lift. It can't be easy for him being on his own like that. I'm on my own too, I never really thought about that. Fucking hell, I don't want to end up like him, an old man all on his own, sitting outside the door waiting for the neighbour to come home so I can grab a two-minute chat.

The pub ain't how I remember it. I've not been in here for years. Loads of people are standing outside smoking, it's a nice evening but the point of a pub is its atmosphere ain't it? There just doesn't seem to be much of one when most people are outside, only coming in to grab a couple of drinks then rushing out again. The carpets have been replaced with wooden floors as well, it feels new, hollow, not the same place it used to be.

"Long time since I've seen you in here Georgie boy! How's things? What can I get you?"

"I'll have a vodka and coke please, Terry. Yeah, long time. It's changed ain't it?"

"Got to move with the times. Was thinking about turning it into one of them gastro pubs. Somewhere people can come and get something to eat."

"Yeah? You going to do it then?"

"I don't know, been offered quite a lot of money for it and I'm seriously considering taking it. I've been here a long time, I love it but it's hard work. You don't get all the regulars in here like you used to either."

"Be a shame to see you go. I know I don't come in much anymore but it's nice to know this place is always here. Who wants to buy it? What are they going to do with it?"

"What do you reckon they'll do to it?"

"Flats..."

"Yeah, that's the rumour anyway."

"Fucking hell, will be there be anywhere left to go and have a drink?"

"We'll all be drinking at home on our own in a few years mate."

"You're the one selling it."

"I can't turn down that kind of money, I'm going to get rid of it at some point anyway, would you say no?"

"Fuck knows. Probably wouldn't, don't see any developers coming to buy my little shop."

"People will live in a cupboard these days mate."

"Speak to you later, Terry."

Mark is standing by the pool table talking to some woman that doesn't seem all that interested in what he's saying to her. We went to school together, he lived two floors down until he moved away when he was 18. He was one of the boys that used to jump over the fence of the park with me. We used to call him Tin Tin because he would spike his hair up at the front.

"Here comes the comedian."

"All right mate?"

The woman he was talking to slips off, looking relieved to get away from him.

"I didn't think you'd come. You're like a hermit these days."

"I don't have the time. It's easy enough for you to say that, all you do is sit around all day doing fuck all."

"I'm an antrepreneur."

"It's entrepreneur and you haven't got a fucking clue what it means."

"Jealousy is a bad thing, George. You're getting bitter in your old age."

"Where's Pat?"

"Dunno, he was here a minute ago and then he went off somewhere. Might have gone to the bookies, reckoned he had a tip for some horse."

It's like no time at all has passed. The same people doing the exact same things they were doing ten years ago. They just look a bit older. No one really gives a fuck what you've been up to though do they? No one asks, how's life? How you coping without your old man? Do you miss him? Do you think the loss of your mother when you were a child had a deep psychological impact on you and do you use comedy as a means to avoid dealing with it? If I gave you £100,000 right now, would you run away? Yes, yes, I would.

Mark is going on and on about some new scheme he's got up his sleeve. It sounds shit and I'm not really listening. I know what's going to come, he'll ask me for money and guarantee a massive return on my investment. I'll laugh and decline and then that will be the end of that; until next time I see him and he's got another scheme that he's plotting.

As I'm listening to him talk nonsense I look around the pub. There are two fellas playing pool and another two waiting next to them to finish. I recognise the two that are waiting, they live in the block opposite mine. One of them is Alfie's nephew but Alfie doesn't have anything to do with him. They're talking to each other and laughing, the two playing pool look as though they are starting to get annoyed, they must be talking about them. The taller of the two playing the game is taking a shot, he suddenly stands himself up from the table, I can read 'fuck off' from his lips.

Alfie's nephew laughs loudly and hits his mate on his back. Two clowns looking for trouble. I walk over to the table leaving Mark selling his pitch to some other fool I've never met before.

"You all right Nelson?"

"All right, George! Just having a laugh mate. These two can't take a joke. Shouldn't be in here anyway, it ain't their pub, we've been coming here for years, now every time we come in, there's someone on the pool table."

The two playing pool look across at me and then at the other two.

"They're just having a few drinks and a game of pool, there's no need to start on them."

"Who the fuck do you think you are, George? Don't come over here telling me what to do."

17

"I ain't. I'm just telling you to leave it, it'll be more trouble than it's worth."

"You always were a prick. You know no one thinks you're funny? Everyone just laughs because they feel sorry for you. You ain't no different to these two anyway, you were never one of us. You and your old man and his shitty little bookshop. Who reads books? I bet you're fucking loaded and you've never done anything for anyone."

"Seen Alfie recently, Nelson? You always were a horrible cunt, it's no wonder he wants nothing to do with you."

In the hospital. There's blood all over my shirt, ruined. It ain't my blood though. Mark ran over and Nelson pulled out a blade, got him in the leg. They reckon Mark's going to be okay but it was a bit touch and go. As soon as he cut him he ran, the old bill keep asking questions. What am I going to say? I ain't going to grass him up. It's a loyalty that's ridiculous, I have no feelings towards Nelson, there's nothing that bonds us but I ain't going to do it, I just can't. If Mark'd died would I have? Probably, but he didn't die.

"You can go and see Mark for a few minutes now, sir. Not for too long though, he's not had the best of evenings has he?"

"Thanks, my evening has been delightful too."

I don't know what to expect as I walk past curtains of sick people, some of them clearly not very sick at all. Is he going to be annoyed at me? Why the fuck did he come and intervene. I don't think Nelson would've have cut me, he knows I look after Alfie and as much as he doesn't give a fuck it does give him something to keep in mind. I ain't got many friends left, I hope this it ain't going to ruin my relationship with the ones I do have. Fuck's sake.

"You're not looking too bad considering..."

"I nearly done him George, I've wanted to do him for years. If the sneaky bastard hadn't had a knife I'd have thrown him all over the pub."

"It was stupid. Stop talking shite."

"What? I could have saved your life and you're here giving me grief! Thanks George, thanks a fucking lot mate. No 'thanks Mark, you're such a good friend, I hope you get better soon'."

"He's a lunatic, you know that as well as I do. He wouldn't have done me because of Alfie."

"He doesn't give a fuck about Alfie. What's wrong with you? You're different these days George. Spending too long on the other side of that bridge is turning you into one of them."

"One of who?"

"One of them Notting Hill, 'I want to live somewhere a bit edgy, but not too edgy because I might get stabbed' wankers that go into your shop."

"No one comes in the shop Mark. Apart from some little fucker called Hugo and his mummy who's drugged up to the eyeballs on antidepressants. I'm lucky if 20 people come in there a week. I'm just trying to make a fucking living like every other wanker. At least I ain't sitting on my fucking sofa thinking up stupid plans that ain't ever going to come to any fruition and signing on every couple of weeks because I can't be arsed to get a proper job.""

"Touched a nerve have I, George? Bit too close to home?

"What do you want me to say? Yeah, I love my little bookshop, I love spending my lunchtimes sitting outside coffee shops sipping lattes and eating muffins. Look at me, I'm the same person I've always been. Why you so envious anyway?"

"I'll tell you why, George. Every couple of weeks I have to walk into an office and sign a piece of paper. The woman treats me like a complete cunt. She looks at me as though I'm scum of the earth. All I'm trying to do is get a job. I don't sit on my sofa all day. I go in and out of shops looking for application forms but they never get back to me. Years ago I could have walked into a shop and had a job no problem. I don't fit the profile now. Do you know how demeaning it is? You don't get it George because you've never had to do it, you were lucky, you had a touch with that shop. I fucking resent you and I shouldn't because you've always been good to me. I was lying there five minutes ago thinking he could have done me a favour and killed me."

"Laters Mark."

Have a I turned into one of them? Of course I haven't, how could I have. You know what, even if I had what does it even matter? All I want is a decent life, to live comfortably. If he can't get that for himself that's his own fault. If he's thinking like that he ain't ever going to get anywhere anyway. I've got no love for this place anymore. Everyone seems to hate and resent each other, it's madness.

Walking along the canal I wonder what it would be like to have one of them canal boats, live in there, go where I want. Where does the canal go anyway? I don't want to live somewhere shit like Birmingham. Maybe find a nice little spot in the countryside, moor the boat and live a life of peace and tranquillity. I could start growing my own vegetables and all that game. They'd really think I'd turned into 'one of them' then. It'd be a laugh living on one, get a few beers on a Saturday night, get pissed by the side of the canal.

Maybe Mark is right. I don't understand what it's like. By virtue of my dad owning that shop I've never had to go out and look for a job. I've just seen him as some chancer that's been sat at home for years doing nothing. Alfie was right, all them schemes he comes up with are just ways of giving himself a little bit of hope. If you're getting knocked back all the time you're going to give up at some point. Confidence isn't unlimited. I'll sell the shop and take him with me on my canal boat, he can look after the vegetables, I'm sure he'd love that.

"You seen the newspaper this morning, son?"

"I don't read the newspaper, Alfie. What's the matter?"

He's sitting there looking intensely at a broadsheet newspaper, I've never seen him read a broadsheet.

"Your shop, it's in the paper."

"What? Why?"

"Apparently it's a 'treasure trove of books in the lovely little area of Queen's Park, North West London'"

"Who's written it?"

"No idea, never heard of the geezer."

"What else does it say?"

"Just that it's a nice little bookshop in Queen's Park, the owner is a very helpful local and it's a 'hidden gem'."

"Okay! I don't really know what to say."

"Here, I'll give you the paper and you can have a read yourself."

"Nice one, anything you need when I'm on my way home?"

"Just a bottle of champagne."

"What do you want a bottle of champagne for?"

"To celebrate!"

"Laters Alfie."

All sorts are things are going through my head now. There could be queues of people waiting outside the shop, I mean it's been in one of the biggest national newspapers. There might even be other journalists that have turned up to see what it's all about. My head is spinning, how has all this happened? I need to go and get a coffee first. I'd have a drink but it's too early! As I pass people in the street I keep thinking they're looking at me, they know who I am. Don't be stupid! Most of them won't even have read the newspaper. Keep your head Georgie boy. I didn't even want the fucking shop yesterday!

I grab my coffee and walk down towards the shop, lifting my head to see if I can see anyone outside, no one there. It's a bit early yet though ain't it? Most people wouldn't have read the paper, let alone decided to come down here and have a look. I'm sure this afternoon will be when people start to turn up. I need to have a proper read of the article when I get in. I wonder who it was? It can only have been that geezer that ordered the book the other day, must have been him, he looked quite well to do, kind of geezer that'd be a journalist.

I sit down at my desk, still no customers, not even one person has come in. I thought some of the lads from the estate might have come down, probably wouldn't read *that* paper though. Saying that, they'll more than likely not want anything to do with me given the way Mark was going on the other night. Fuck them.

The article talks about how there aren't many of these kinds of bookshops around anymore, how we should be supporting local businesses like this. I can't believe we've ended up in a national newspaper. I sit back and let out a long breath. I wish the old man would have been around to see this, it'd have made everything he worked for worth it. It's still worth it, but I just wish he'd been here to see it.

It's 3 o'clock and there's still no one come in. Usually there's one customer at least but so far there's not been a single person. Fuck's sake. I was imagining hoards of people wondering around the shop and buying books. I was going to get a big bottle of champagne and me and Alfie were going to sit on the landing and get pissed. Not even Hugo and mummy have turned up to say they were one of the first to discover it! Silly cow. I'm definitely going to get a 'No Children Allowed' sign for the shop door now, that'll show the little bastard to not show up on the day. I was even going to give him a free book.

The phone's ringing. It's Johnny. Fuck! I'd forgotten about that tour he was on about.

"George, how's it going? Listen you still up for this tour we've got planned?"

"When?"

"Going next week, mate. I've got a few other comedians, we're just going to take off and try our luck blagging shows in pubs and clubs. Don't know about the money, it could be a bit hit and miss. It'll be a good laugh though, you never know who might see you, chances like this don't come around often mate! I know you want out of that place as well, don't let me down here."

"What if I join you in a couple of weeks?"

"Sorry mate, if you don't start off with us there's no joining later."

"Well that's a bit stupid ain't it?"

"That's the rules Georgie."

"What day you going?"

"Monday morning. About 8 o'clock."

"I need to think about it, something's come up."

"All these years I've supported you George, don't let me down now…"

"Don't start that emotional blackmail bollocks, if I'm coming I'll let you know. If you don't hear from me I ain't going."

"Live your life, Georgie, you're only sitting there wasting it…"

"Bye."

What do you do? Chase your dreams? Is it really my dream though? People will say you can always come back, you don't have to give the shop up. If I leave, I don't want to come back. It ain't like the memories here are horrible and I hate it. I don't hate it, I just don't want to be here, the place has changed, it ain't the same place that I remembered walking around as a kid. The people have changed, the community has changed. It's like it's all been diluted, it's become this diluted mix that is dull and can be found anywhere. What if I they decide to knock down the flats? Then what?

Why can't I just fit into it though? Just become part of this new world, one where everyone is supposed to be doing well for themselves and those that ain't are just ignored, put in a corner, pretend they're not there. It's like I leave in two different worlds, and I don't like either of them. Would I miss it all though? Yeah, I would, sometimes the idea of doing something is a lot better than when you actually do it. I'm trapped, but I'm not sure if I want to escape or not.

"Where's the champagne, son?"

"Not a single person turned up today, Alfie. It ain't going to make any difference."

"I always thought you were quite bright, George. What did you think? Half the world was going to turn up at the shop today? Clear you out of books?"

"No! One person would have been nice, though!."

"They'll come."

"I'm not Kevin Costner building a baseball pitch. You were telling me to leave the other day."

"I wasn't telling you to leave, I was telling you to do what makes you happy and not care about what other people want you to do."

"I could leave next Monday if I wanted to."

"What with your merry band of comedians? That'll be a laugh a minute and it won't be the jokes you're all telling that'd be funny."

"Thanks, Alfie."

"I know what happened with Nelson. Thanks for not telling the police."

"Why? It's not like he ever comes and sees you is it."

"He's still family, he's a horrible little bastard but I don't want to see him locked up."

"That doesn't make any sense Alfie."

"Of course it makes sense, maybe you just don't understand."

"Don't you start with all that 'don't understand' bollocks. I'm off to bed."

The God's honest truth is, I don't like what this place has become. I don't like that all my mates hate me because they *think* I'm successful. I hate that it's changed so much that my old man wouldn't recognise it anymore. I hate it that Alfie can't go and have a pint with a few of his mates because there ain't anywhere for him to have a pint. I hate that I'm starting to hate my own friends. Happy? I ain't happy.

I throw my bag on the bed and start to pack my stuff. I can't be bothered with this anymore, sometimes you've just got to cut your loses and go. It'd have been easier if the decision was taken out of my hands but it hasn't. I ain't coming back to this gaff, I'll sort it all out when I'm away. I sit down at the coffee table and start to write Alfie a long letter, but what can I say that the silly old bastard hasn't already said to me?

Alfie,

I'm off, mate. Thanks for everything, I'll be back to see you soon. I've put the key to the shop through the letter box, might need you to sort some things out for me.

Look after yourself and don't go falling into that pool.

Georgie Boy

See you later, Queen's Park, time to move on.

Kilburn Park

Kilburn, affectionately known as 'County Kilburn' and home to a large community of Irish

Mikey's pissed and Patrick doesn't know where he is. Pints of Guinness, packets of John Players, broken bottles and fallen men. The sound of music from far away, a boat across the sea, a bus from Holyhead reaching the pub in county Kilburn. The fallen men moan and groan as they lay against their bar stools, singing along to songs they don't know the words to. A burly man, as big as a bale of hay lifts them both by the collar and out the door they go. No one looks, merriment carries on without a distraction.

"I told him! I told him! Jesus every day he's in here pissed!"

"Ah sure, what can you do! The fucker'll only go down to the Old Bell and be there until the morning. You can't keep a man from his Guinness."

"Will you go home in the summer, Johnny?"

"I'll tell you now, I don't know for sure. We'll see what the summer brings and then we'll make a decision. Sure we've months to go yet."

"The mother'll be missing ya!"

The mother. Tall and big, she'd fling a cow around the field if she had to. No man would mess with that one. I can still see her as I walk home from school, waiting by the wall, the wooden spoon in her hand. I look for a wall to jump or a field to escape through. That would only make it worse though. I submit to my fate, the weasel faced teacher on the bike had beaten me home, told my mother stories of how I'd been naughty, been pulling girl's hair and giving him lip. Not a word said as I walk in the door, the mother following behind, my brother in the corner laughing, the weasel faced fucker looking self-important as he drinks a cup of tea and eats some cake.

It stings, but I won't scream, not with that bastard here. He'd enjoy it. My little brother would enjoy it too, he'd tell tales just to hear me scream. I pull up my trousers, a frown on my face that only a little boy in trouble can make. Back to the kitchen with still not a word said. I can't sit down because it'd hurt, I'm not going to give them the pleasure of seeing that.

The bastard tells my mother all the good he's done since he's become our teacher. The mother nods, she doesn't like him either, but he's some bigwig in the church and she wouldn't want to upset the church. God himself might turn up at the door and curse the farm with locusts and pestilence. A plague would wipe out the weasel so perhaps it'd be a good thing.

"You're daydreaming there again, I'll get another pint, do you want one?"

"I will."

The air is thick with smoke and the smell of spilt beer. The old fella sitting on his own is singing to himself, songs and tales of glory. A story could he tell, most of them not true but then who tells a true story these days? Shouts over another pint, free Guinness for his tales, he'll never buy another drink before he dies. A young lad sits in front of him with two pints. He gazes into the distance behind the young fella, looking back over the sea and back through time. Or just looking at the picture behind the bar, racking his brain, there can't be that many tales left to tell, he's told most of them. If the tales are gone he'll be gone, no more free pints.

"Look at Mikey over there chatting to your one. Jesus, she'd eat him alive!"

Mikey, Mikey. A small fella, where he's from nobody knows. Just turned up one day, ask him where he's from and the subject changes. The weather, the price of fags, how many pints he had last night. Pissed as usual, chatting to some woman. Usually they take no notice of him. Too small, always drunk, how could you ever take him back to your mother? He's not changed his clothes since he turned up. He's giving a spiel to this one, she looks interested, I'd say there wouldn't be too many interested in her.

"A good woman would sort him out and Jesus she's a fine woman. She'd knock seven shades of shite out of him if he tried any of his carry on."

"I heard a rumour that he's an American."

"An American? How in the fuck would he be an American?"

"A con man, a shyster, sure he's only putting the accent on. Came over on the boat from America, someone said he murdered a man over there."

"Will you fuck up! He couldn't murder a fly."

The music gets louder, dancing and merriment, falling over and silliness. The curtains are down, not that they make an ounce of difference, anyone with a bit of sense would know it was a lock in.

"Were you good at school, James? You look like the kind of man who was good at school."

"Jesus no! The teacher hated me. Ferrety looking fucker, I'd love to find him and put him in the foundations of one those buildings we're putting up."

Walking down the road to school. A cow or a sheep or even a butterfly would distract me, even a flower if I thought it would look nice in the hair of my darling Aoife. Oh Aoife, she's ruining my schooldays. I smile at her as I walk through the door, she doesn't even look at me. Far too below her, poor people, not the sort of boy one should be mixing with when they have aspirations of greatness, they'll bring you down to their level and you'll be cleaning floors for the rest of your days.

There was no girl in the world more beautiful than Aoife though. Her friend is the nasty one, has an evil eye, she'll look at me and I'll spend the night awake frightened of what curse she's put on me. I'd look at Aoife but do it quickly because she'll know, the red headed one, Sally Murphy, she'll be waiting for our eyes to meet so she can wish some evil upon me. Then the teacher will give me a clip around the ear and lecture me on the evils of lust, the only place for such people as myself was Hell.

The cow, the flower and the butterfly have made me late so that's another clip around the ear. They all laugh. Slinking into the sit, my ear stinging, I wish I could kill the bastard! Jesus if there's a God come down and punish him for his sins.

"If you don't learn your Irish you'll be staying back another year and your mother will be the talk of the town! You wouldn't want that now would you?"

Fadas and bhs that sounds like vs, how does a bh sound like a v? No fucking use anyway. Chanting and noise that means nothing, what's the time? Surely it's time to go home?

"I'd never have thought that now! Jesus, you were the naughty one?"

"I wasn't the naughty one. That bastard just hated me."

"What happened to your one?"

"Which one?"

"Your one! Didn't you say you were in love with her? Aoife?"

The day before I'm to get the boat over to England. Brothers and sisters fussing, telling me to be careful.

"You never know what those heathen English will do to ya! Mind your money on the boat too!"

I was the first, the first to go over. The mother is crying, she wants me to go, but she has to cry because if she doesn't cry what kind of mother is she? And what would the priest think? They've given me a fine feed, big pork chops with spuds and carrots and peas and gravy and sprouts. The best meal I've ever eaten. The sisters were crying now too, Jesus would they ever shut up!

"Will you go to town for one last drink before you head over?" says the brother. "We'll go for a drink or two, or three or four, fuck it we'll get pissed, who knows when I'll be back." The mother is roaring now, the handkerchief isn't wet, dry as a bone. Off down the road to town. Dark, no butterflies or flowers to distract, the moo of a cow, but cows don't interest me anymore, I've seen enough of them fuckers. The pub is packed, what are they all doing here? They're not here for me anyways. Dancing and drinking, singing if they're able or not.

Sat in the corner there she is! In the pub? Surely that's a sin? No such lady would ever be seen in a pub like this! Stone faced, not impressed with the rabble, eyes roll as they all make fools of themselves. Tomorrow they'll be sick and their heads will be sore and they won't know what it was they did the night before. Never would she do such a thing, yet here she is mixing with the rabble, not mixing, watching, but why would she be here? Tomorrow morning it'll be off on the boat, I'll never see her again.

Oh that hair, the beautiful black hair and the blue eyes. She's a princess among paupers, they don't deserve to be in her company. The red head, she'll be here somewhere, they're never not together. Her protector, putting spells on anyone that looks at her, making sure a glance in her direction is enough to send them to the priest the next morning. I can't see her, perhaps she's dead? That'd be a fine going away present. Jesus, you shouldn't be thinking like that! There she is! The red head! She's pissed!

No evil curses tonight. A smile never seen before, her eyes are only full of joy and lust. Lust? Jesus, she'd want to be careful with thoughts like that. Your man from the school will be down quick enough to condemn her to a life of reading the bible, being a good woman, knowing her place. She's looking at me, fire in her eyes. I should have stayed at home with my mammy, she's turned into a witch, a temptress, she's looking to corrupt my poor innocent soul. I take my pint and turn to the bar. She's going to defile me, and Aoife! Jesus what will Aoife think?

She's gone! My princess, the one I've never said a word to, the reason I went to school, the reason my ears would sting every night when I got home. She's gone and she'll probably never be seen again and all because of that red headed hussy! I'll go to the priest before I go! Our Father, forgive me for I have sinned. Are those even the words? Jesus, I don't know! I've spent too much time in the church daydreaming. Forgive me father for I have sinned... that's the one!

Now she's standing next to me. Her hair, never have I seen a colour so red. The eyes, the eyes are demented, the woman has gone mad. There's no evil in there now, just pure lust, and madness and the urge to defile me. Oh God! I really should have stayed at home with the mammy and the sisters and they could have all cried together and then they'd go to bed and I'd be on the boat and there'd be no defiling at all. A drink, she wants a drink. Hasn't she enough in her? Another drink and there'll be no stopping her. Sally Murphy, the devil himself has turned up in this town and corrupted you.

The drink is flowing, she's not so bad after all! A fine looking woman, never noticed before. Swinging me around the floor, clapping and laughing. There's no evil in her, all sweetness, goodness, how could I ever

30

think such beautiful woman would ever put a curse on me? The boat tomorrow, what time does it leave? I could stay, marry her, lots of kids with red hair running around. The mammy would probably cry even more if she thought I was staying. What did I ever see in your one? What's her name? Aoife! She was just a mistake, a product of misguided childhood. I never saw which one was the fairest, the flower just waiting to be plucked.

She's always loved me she says. From the moment she first saw me at school she knew I was the one, we were going to have lots of babies together. Another drink, I could stay another week anyway, put it off, could go over anytime I like. There's nothing wrong with being defiled either. The pub is almost empty, old men staggering out the door, still singing, falling out into the empty streets. The debauchery of the night is over for them. She grabs me by the hand and down the road, into a field.

The clothes are coming off, her eyes are wild. I'm shaking, frightened, excited. Her mouth is filthy, how did I never see she was such a woman. Two figures peering over the wall! The sound of a gasp, something hitting the floor. A scream. Oh fuck! It's the sisters. Sally tearing off into the darkness of the field, she'll be forever tarred! The mammy is on the floor, making the sign of the cross, "Oh lord please forgive my evil bastard of a son and his wicked thoughts and deeds!" "That poor girl", they say to me, how could I do such a thing to such an innocent. A hand across my head, one more stinger before he goes across the seas.

"Ah Jesus! If it was me I'd never go back. What happened to your one? Sally? I'd say she ran away too."

"She's married. I was the devil, the man possessed by the evilness of lust, I'd corrupted her and she was forgiven."

Your man telling the tales is looking into an empty glass. Get him another! The fella going to the bar rolls his eyes, he's nothing but a charlatan. The young lad sitting with him is wide eyed, dying for another story, another pint for the storyteller too, he'll have a whiskey as well, he's in the company of greatness, this man should be writing books and making millions. How did he ever end up on Kilburn High Road on a Saturday night?

"When you first came over I didn't know you did I? I'd never see you in the pub."

"No, I'd just go home. I didn't know anyone and I was still shy."

There I was standing at Euston station, not a fucking clue where I was going. Cars everywhere, a new world, everybody rushing about. What's their hurry and where would they be going at six o'clock in the morning? A piece of paper in my hand with the address. Some fella I was told to see. O'Malley, and an address in Kilburn it had written on it. The buses, all going to some place or other but not where he wanted to go to. "Excuse me Miss? How do I get to Kilburn?" No reply, she walks on, not looking back, there's no telling what the wild Irishman might do to her. "Two stops on the train mate," says a little lad selling newspapers.

Cambridge Road I'm looking for, this place is a fucking maze. I'm self-conscious, everyone is looking at me, they know I'm fresh off the boat. Maybe I should go back, go back to Sally Murphy and have lots of babies, they'd forgive all my sins if we were to get married. Sally's madness was a message from God, I was to stay at home and not go over to this God forsaken place full of heathens and wild people, but I'd ignored the message, please forgive me for my sins!

There's a fella standing at the door, he looks just like that bastard, ferret faced teacher. Skinny, weasel-like, it's O'Malley, it has to be. O'Malley looks me up and down, sizes me up, snorts and takes me off up to my new room. A bed, a table and a light. O'Malley likes rules, I'm not to come back late, I'm not to bring anyone back with me, if I'm late with the rent I'll be out on my arse. He hopes to see me at church too. I thought they didn't go to the church here? If I break anything I'll be paying for it. I look the room up and down, there's nothing to break. O'Malley mutters to himself and goes.

"I knew that fucker, he was a horrible old bastard. Why'd you stay in one of his rooms?"

"Where else had I to go? I didn't know anyone. Jesus, he *was* a horrible old bastard. Whatever happened to him?"

"Pulled him out of the canal one night, someone threw him in there they said."

"Best place for him, I hope they tied that fucking iron bed he had in that room to him too."

"We'll have one more shall we and then we'll walk home."

"Go on, we'll have one more."

The bar is empty, the stragglers, the last few dregs, the ones who have nowhere to go and the ones that don't want to go home. Home to arguments or to no one. The chat is less, drowning their sorrows, the storyteller with his audience of one who's bored, listening so as not to offend, his glass is empty but there are no takers for another pint. The walking stick in his hand, one more tale and time to go, slow walk home to his little room, there's no one to listen there.

"Do you ever know where he came from?"

"Who? The murderer?"

"No, the fucking storyteller! He appeared one night and he's been here since but he doesn't seem to work."

The job was easy enough to find. Money and food, homesick though, dreams of Sally and Aoife. Dreams of marrying the mad one and then running off with the beautiful one. The pub is empty, a quick pint after work then back to O'Malley's room. They were knocking them down soon, the whole road, O'Malley's little racket would be gone. New buildings they'd be putting up, walkways in the sky or some shite like that they were saying, a new way of living, everyone would be happy, no need to worry anymore.

"A pint and a whiskey!" says the fella at the bar. He sits down next to me, no invite from me, only his own. He talks and talks, talks shite, nonsense, these fellas have too much to say. Hard up the fella reckons, what's he buying pints and whiskey for so? Waiting for the catch, waiting for him to ask for money or another pint. Nodding my head as the fella talks, preparing my exit, out the door and up the Edgware Road, better to be in that pokey little room than listen to this madman.

Colourful life the fella says. No one's lived a life like he has, seen the world, sailed the oceans, walked in jungles, climbed mountains. He's only a little bit older than me, how the fuck would he have done all this? You'd never believe who he'd met, there's not a man in the world that has done all he's done! Shite! His pint finished in a couple of gulps, the whiskey down the hatch too, more shite, worse than before, the drink has got to him, stories that can't be topped are being topped by this skinny little man who looks as though he'd have trouble finding his way home.

"You'll buy me a pint won't ya? We'll get pissed and I'll tell you stories like you've never heard before." *Fucking stories is all they are.* "It's been a hard week, the mother died after me sister ran away with a Jamaican man. You know how it is, we all have to stick together." *I look for the exit, the man has already waved to the bar man, pouring the two pints and two whiskeys. Oh for fuck's sake, drink them quickly, maybe he'll fuck off then and bother someone else.*

"Did you get the boat over?" he asks.

"I did."

"Jesus, it's a long old journey."

"It is."

"Not as long as to America though, that's some journey, I bet you've never done that journey have ya?"

"I haven't."

"It wasn't that long ago I was there. You sure you've never been to America?"

"I've never been."

"Well you're missing out, you should go sometime. The women over there, unreal! They like an Irishman too. Well I lived in New York, beautiful place. One day I was sitting drinking a pint in a bar and you'll never guess who walked in the door?"

"Who?"

"John Kennedy."

"Will you ever fuck off!"

"As sure as you're sitting there now he walked in the door, ordered a pint of Guinness, drank it in one go and walked out again."

"I'm surprised he never shook your hand."

He didn't but do you know who did shake my hand?"

Father forgive me for my sins...

"So where did he come from?"

"How would I know? I don't think he knows where he comes from himself!"

"Did you buy him another pint?"

"No, I pretended to go to the toilet and climbed out the window."

"The best way."

"We'll go now will we?"

"We will."

The high street is empty, broken glass on the streets, a lad asleep against a shop window. He'll wake in the morning and not know where he is, somebody's probably wondering where he is. It must have been some night! He won't be doing that again. He might catch hypothermia, there was a fella who went out for his birthday last year, fell asleep on the bench, they found him in the morning, dead. Happy birthday! At least he went out with a good birthday, he'll be telling that story up in heaven.

It's still only one. He has a thirst still, not ready to go back to the room, wide awake, he'll only be thinking, always thinking. Over and over everything he's already been over tonight, the beautiful Aoife, the mad Sally. Should he have gone home? No, go home and it'll be the mammy and the sisters nagging him, get married, have kids, you can't be going to the pub, you're a responsible man now. Here there's none of that, do what you want, spend your money how you want, write them a letter, tell them streets are paved with gold and you're rich, tell them what they want to hear, never harmed anyone.

"We'll go for a pint in The Bell, sure there's no point going home yet, the night is young."

"I've a wife to go home to."

"She'll not miss you, she'll only be sleeping."

"You tell her that in the morning when she's chasing me around with a saucepan."

"We'll only have the one."

Tap, tap, tap!

"Who is it?"

A smile and the door opens.

"Come in lads, not seen you in a while. Where have you been drinking these days?"

Bodies on the floor, the pub you shouldn't go into, the one they warn you about. Those fellas you see asleep on benches and drinking from a bottle in the morning, they're the kind of fellas that come in here. Harmless, they're only bothered with their drink and the bar man is only bothered with their money. No music in this place, drink, drink and more drink.

"Had you many in tonight?"

"A few, it's quiet enough."

Sticky floor, a man asleep on it too. Just left there until the morning, he'll wake up and then he'll have a drink and then go on his way. He has the money so what's the point in sending him away, he could die on the way home and then he wouldn't be back tomorrow. You've to be clever in this business. The two take a seat in the corner, far from the rest of them, segregation, the beyond help and the looking for one more drink before the night is over divide. The fella on the floor punches at the air in his sleep, fighting, he's better off fighting in his sleep because he looks as if he'd be blown over by a gust of wind.

"How did you meet the wife? She's a good woman."

"Ah Jesus, I've no tales of Aoifes and Sallys. I'll tell you how I met her though."

The shop was closed, dark inside, no one there at all, me peering through the window.

"Who are you looking for?"

The biggest man he'd ever seen in his life standing in front of him. Menacing, arms and fists ready to put him in the hospital.

"Just wanted to buy something but I see you're closed, I'll be back tomorrow."

"You won't be back tomorrow, and if you do come back tomorrow you'll be sleeping in the cemetery tomorrow night."

"Well it's the closest shop you see, and well there's nowhere else to go."

The big man looks up and down the road, there's plenty of shops.

"Well you come back tomorrow and then I'll break your nose and we can call it quits."

Those big lads always thinking they can push people around. I'll teach him a lesson tomorrow. He can't stop me coming into the shop. The size of him though, he'd break me in half. Does she know her brother wants to kill everyone that looks at her? I see the way she looks at me when I come into the shop, shy, but I'm shy too. 'Hello, hello, hello', that's about all I can say, never anything more than hello. Even the 'goodbye' doesn't come out, just a nod of the head, a silly smile, she probably thinks there's something wrong with me in the head. There is something wrong with me in the head, I can say no more than 'hello' to a woman.

They gave me one of the new flats. All strange, big square windows, a balcony too. I don't like the balcony, I could fall off it. If I was to fall off there'd be no going home and there'd be no one to look after the cat. I'm too soft! The cat, everyday outside the door, 'meow, meow, meow!' A bowl of milk, a little bit of cheese and it's moved in. Sitting on my favourite chair, I can't move him, sure he looks so comfortable and if I move him he'll be upset. He's company though, great company. Great chats we have, 'meow' is his only answer.

You can hear the neighbours, talking and chatting away. Your man comes home drunk and there's no chatting. Shouting and saucepans and plates smashing and crashing are the only sounds. The cat under the bed, my head to the wall, I wouldn't say I was nosy just a bit curious. The next day, your man has a black eye and your one is smiling. Only one winner of that fight, no drinking for him for a little while.

Butter and milk and a few eggs. Need a good breakfast, best meal of the day, if there's no breakfast you won't be doing anything. My mother always said that. A smile when I come in the door, all I can give is a smile, no 'hello', she'll think a smile is rude, I've no words, I could have said hello too. Did she smile back at me? Butter and eggs. Oh Jesus! The brother is out the back, menacing, I told you not to come into the shop his eyes say. I'm too young to have a bent nose. Butter, that's what I came for. She smiles!

"Anything else?"

"No, no, just the butter, you can't beat a good breakfast."

More than hello! The Gods are looking upon me today!

"Jesus you were an awful eejit."

"I'm still an eejit now."

He's coming, he's seen me, he wants blood, I can see it. I wanted eggs too and milk, I've no milk to make a cup of tea.

"I told you not to come in here. Every day you're in here and I know why you're coming. You stay away from her, she doesn't want anything to do with you."

"Will you shut up and go back out there?"

His eyes turn to a puppy's, he's scared of her. A look at her and he's a puppy, a look at me and he's a man possessed. I'd better go, I'll borrow a cup of milk from your man next door if he's still alive.

If I were to go off the balcony would it hurt? The fucking cat though, I can't be doing that to him. It's a long old way down. Will you stop talking about throwing yourself off balconies and cop yourself on you fucking eejit. You talk to a girl and you're suicidal, where did they get you from? True, it's a bad idea, suicide I mean, that's the end isn't it? No coming back from that, no rising from the dead. The old English girl that lives down the way, she says she has a ghost. An old fella she says, makes himself a cup of tea at night and then disappears. It's bad to be old isn't it?

I can go back to the shop, ask her out, take her to the cinema or take her to a dance. Take her to a dance? That'll not do at all, there's some bad lads in those dances and they'd be taking her off me. I'd be standing there, saying nothing but 'hello' and they'd come over with all the chat. 'How are you? Would you like to dance? Will you come home with me tonight? Will you marry me?' That will be that and I'd have no one but the cat. I'll take her for a cup of tea.

"Would you like to come for a cup of tea?"

"A cup of tea?"

"Yes, a cup of tea."

"You know how to treat a lady."

"Will you come with me?"

"I'll go with you, don't mind him in the back he's all bark and no teeth he won't touch you."

"When will we go for a cup of tea?"

"When would you like to take me?"

"I'll take you when you want to go."

"Well that doesn't help, but this evening when we close the shop."

"Grand, I'll be waiting for you."

I see the eyes on the big fella turn towards me, he's doing me some damage in his mind, I'm being thrown all around the shop, bottles over my head. I nod at him, he sneers. I'm going for a cup of tea!

"You took her for a cup of tea?"

"Where else would I have taken her? We're married now so it worked!"

"None of the lads at the dance took her off you so."

"Well they tried."

"What happened to the brother? I don't remember him at all."

"A bigger misfortunate there's never been."

Married life, work, home, sometimes the pub. All the whistles and bells, kids and Sunday dinners at home. The mother at home was delighted, her son had done her proud, rich and now a wife she could show off.

Still the evil eye from the brother. Sunday dinner, sitting there talking, talking shite, just making conversation. Staring, he's killed me a thousand times over with his eyes, different ways, over the balcony, in the canal, probably poisoned the spuds too, it might make them taste better, a nice spud before I go and sleep with the rest of them in graveyard. 'Ah sure, he's harmless,' she would say, 'he'd never hurt you, he's just a bit protective'. Away with the fucking fairies I'd say!

"I'm getting married" he says.

"To who? You never leave the shop only to come here? Where's she from?"

"She's from Italy. A good Catholic girl, her father makes shoes in the West End, good family."

"How have we never met her?"

"Why'd you have to meet her?"

"Well we don't but it'd be nice to see your girlfriend before you get married."

"Well you'll have to wait, she works a lot and she hasn't much time."

"How'd d'ya meet her?"

"Never mind how I met her."

"Have you told daddy?"

"No."

"You'd better tell him."

"I'll tell him so."

I always thought he was a bit thick, but Jesus I don't know how he gets out of the bed in the morning.

Still no sign of the Italian one, the wife is excited, making plans, flowers, she's going to make the food for a party after. A book she bought on the table, 'Italian for Beginners', running around the kitchen 'Buon giorno , buon giorno!' Jesus I hope this lass is real. The father was delighted, couldn't wait to meet her, talked about her all the time. Maybe they'd all go to Italy on holiday, he'd have to mind the skin though, wouldn't want to be getting burnt. Do they eat spuds out there? I don't know, ah they must do.

They had to find a tailor, your man was big as you well you know, a massive fella, and well it wasn't easy to find a suit. They'd walk into the tailor and the fella would take one look at him, busy they would say, don't think they have the time before the wedding, perhaps the lad down the road would be able to do it. The lad down the road would have the same story, 'busy, awful busy', not sure he has the materials either. Well, didn't the brother cry! Came home to the shop, and bawled like a small child. I didn't know where to look. I'm a bad person, but I enjoyed being a bad person that day I can tell you.

The day came, a suit had been made, not that it fitted him, but what can you do? The man was to get married and everyone was happy. She arrived. Jesus I thought she wasn't going to come, I said to the wife the night before:

"Don't be surprised now if your one doesn't turn up",

"Why would she not turn up?"

"Well you know what these foreigners are like and also there's the small matter that we've never met her and I've been thinking about it and I don't think she exists."

"Joseph McCarthy if you ever say such things about my brother again I'll throw you out of this house and I'll never speak to you again!"

She was beautiful, never seen a prettier girl since. How did this fella manage to get himself a woman such as her? The wife looked at me.

"I told you she'd come! You're a bad minded bastard Joseph and we're never to have such talk in the house again, he's your brother now too and this beautiful lady is your sister and you're to treat them with respect."

"And where's her family? There's none of them here!"

"They'd to go to a funeral. Back to Italy."

"You don't think that's a bit strange?"

"Did you listen to a word I just said?" You'll be out that fucking door and you'll be living on the streets like that old fella that drank the bleach and died."

"I'd better shut up so."

Drunk I was that day, I don't think I've ever been so drunk. Dancing on the tables, singing and dancing, danced with the brother and he was smiling, I'd never seen him smile before. He shook my hand and told me he loved me and he'd never entertain the idea of poisoning my spuds. We're going off on holiday to Italy together and he'd open a business in London and I'd be the first person he'd be asking to help him build the new shop. Never a better friend had I had.

A week later and he turned up at the door, crying, blabbering, neither of us knowing what he was saying. 'Gone!' he was saying, I knew it, I knew it, she's gone, I'm only a stupid idiot. The wife gave me a look, don't you say a word or over the fucking balcony you'll go. An hour he sat there without a word. Me staring at the ceiling, the wife sitting there with an arm around him. Jesus, he's still wearing the suit. You'd think she'd have washed it for him before she ran away. Another look from the wife, special powers she has, knows what I'm saying to myself in my head. I'd better shut up.

Your one, the Italian had left him. Two days after the wedding. He'd sat in the flat for three days waiting for her to come home and she never came. Her clothes and everything were gone and the eejit still sat there waiting for her.

"Some people are awful stupid aren't they? Where did she go?"

"I've no idea. We went looking for the father but he didn't exist, no one had ever heard of him. To top it all off, he'd been putting his money under the mattress and she'd taken the whole lot. For six months after that he lived with us and I was afraid to eat."

"And where is he now?"

"Ah, he went home, broken hearted. He married some woman back home and they've about 20 kids and they all look like him. I'll never set foot in that house, one of them is enough."

Only two left in the bar now. The barman is helping himself to the whiskey, the old fella on the floor has stopped fighting in his dreams but he's talking in his sleep. I'll find you, you bastard! Just you wait 'til I find you and I'll give you the hiding of your life.

"We'll have one more and then we'll go."

"You've been saying one more for the last four hours! You've not got a wife at home to kill you."

"You're late enough as it is, one more'll do no harm."

"You'll not be seeing me for a while after tonight."

"You know what I've been wanting to ask you for a long time Mr McCarthy?"

"What's that now, Johnny?"

"That time you were arrested, what did you do?"

"Oh Jesus, a terrible day that was. Cannabis!"

"Jesus Christ I never had you down for a drug dealer Joseph, awful things them drugs, what were you doing with cannabis?"

"We'll have one more and I'll tell ya."

We moved out of that estate, turned a bit bad, some dodgy lads hanging about. Drugs and people getting robbed and all that carry on. Well, we'd got ourselves a nice little flat and kept the shop. Same place we live now, Glengall Road. Gave up the old work and I'd sit in the shop.

43

own the High Road of the morning, I'd have my cigarette
e wouldn't let me smoke in the house and if I smoked in
now. In the door sniffing, the look and then I'd be in

Sitting there one day and a fella comes in. Never seen him before in my life. Long hair, stupid bracelets on his arms, a t shirt that'd gone almost yellow but I think it was supposed to be white.

"A hippy?"

"I'd say he was a hippy anyway."

"I don't like them hippy lads at all."

"You won't like this fella so."

Never seen a hippy before, but this fella would surely be one. Buying crisps, not just one packet, cheese and onion, salt and vinegar, what was there he bought. How can one man eat so many crisps, what does he be doing to be so hungry? I thought they never did a day's work in their life. Friendly but a bit weird. After the crisps he was looking for pop but we'd no pop until the next day when the delivery man came, always late that delivery man was.

"You look like you need to chill man!"

That's what he said to me!

"You're right there, I'm warm enough! I'd better be turning the heating off."

"No, you need to relax."

"Ah, no, I'm fine! Sure I sit here all day and do nothing only talk to the customers."

"Jesus, you really are an awful eejit!"

"What 'til you hear what he said next."

"You wanna make some money?"

"Well, I do well enough here so no I don't want to be taking on any extra work, I've already given up the old job and I don't think the wife would be too happy, you know how it is?"

"You need to tell your wife to mind her own business."

"That wouldn't go down too well."

"Take control man!"

"I'm well enough thank you! Now will you be wanting anything else or is that it?"

And off he went to do whatever it is that hippies do.

She wasn't too happy that this chap had turned up in her shop. You never know what these fellas do be up to.

"If you see that lad in the shop again you're to tell him we don't want his business and he's to go to another shop. Why'd you let him in the shop in the first place?"

"He looked like a nice enough fella, bit dirty but sure aren't the young ones all like that these days?"

Then the young one piped up, "Daddy what's a hippy?

"You go to bed!"

She's angry now and I'm not too hopeful of a dinner.

"Next thing you'll be going to them hippy festivals and you'll be smoking that cannabis and you'll go craiced completely. Only you Joseph McCarthy!"

"Your wife, she has anger issue, she does?"

"She's a lot of issues."

The bell over the door rings, thank Christ it's not him. All day I'd be looking at the door waiting for your man to come back. The old English woman, the drunk fella who wanted to know if he could buy a drink, the fella who couldn't speak English and shouted at me in some language I don't understand. No sign of him, I'm happy, I'll go home with a smile on *my face tonight, the wife will be happy and I won't be going to any festivals.*

"A bit like you and the red head, he could tempt me, you know what them fellas are like."

I'm about to close and doesn't your man walk in the door. More crisps he wants. My eyes are at the door and then back to him, Jesus if she walks in now that'll be the end of it all.

"I'm not to sell you anything and I'd be grateful if you'd go to another establishment to buy your wares!"

"Come on man, just a few packets of crisps and I'll be gone."

He wanted them crisps awful bad so what can you do? You can't let the man starve even if he is a hippy.

"The wife would have your bollocks on the chopping board."

"A chance I took."

"You really need to take control man, you can't let someone run your life like that."

"What are you talking about?"

"Your wife, man! She told you not to let me in the shop."

How does he know that?

"Well I suppose she did but she's a bit suspicious of people she doesn't know."

"Tell her how it is man, you need to lay down the law and tell her you can let anyone in the shop you like."

Jesus, I'm thinking, he's right, too long have I been scared, I'll go home this evening and I'll let her know who's boss, these hippy lads aren't so bad after all.

"You've no sense at all have ya?"

"You've to stop telling me who I can and can't let in the shop and you're to let me go to the pub when I like and if I'm home late you're still to cook me a dinner."

Well Jesus, Mary and Joseph I've never seen anything like it in my life. The kids were put in their room. Pots, pans, rolling pins even the dinner. Me behind the chair and then she'd come closer and the window was looking an option. Then she got the knife, well I got down on my knees and I begged for forgiveness. I thought it was the end of me!

"Did she forgive ya?"

My clothes and photographs and my books. You know how I like to read? I love a good book. Out the fucking window, the whole lot, down on the street. There's me watching all of it go out the window, not a word was said. She sat down then and she put the knife down. She threw it all out with one hand, awful strong when she wants to be.

She sat down and she said to me, "Joseph if you want to go and live with the hippies you can, but if you ever come near this house again I'll chop your bollocks off and feed them to ya!"

"I don't want to live with the hippies, your man was hungry, what was I suppose to do?"

"You tell him to fuck off and if he comes in again I'll be down and he'll not be eating anymore crisps."

"So, I can stay?"

"You can stay, your clothes are outside. I know that, I'll go down and get them."

"Did your man come back again?"

"No, but then I got arrested."

"Ah, Jesus!"

Not a soul all day, sitting in the chair, shaking, praying he doesn't come through the door. Still if he came through the door I was going to give him a piece of my mind! Ding, ding, it was a policeman! What does this lad want?

"You know anything about drugs, sir? Drugs?"

"Yes, sir drugs."

"Well I know you take them when you're sick, your man next door had pneumonia and he had to take some drugs."

"Don't get funny with me sunshine!"

"I'm not being funny!"

"We arrested a man today and he said you kept his drugs for him."

Jesus, this doesn't sound too good.

"Do you mind if I take a look behind those packets of crisps?"

"No, no problem at all, have a look wherever you want."

Didn't he pull out a big bag of some kind of a weed.

"How did that get there? What is it?"

"You should be telling me that sir."

"The hippy was hiding drugs in the shop?"

"He was."

Oh Jesus, this is the end, what'll I do? If I'm in the jail they'll eat me alive. All sorts in there, and what will I eat? Big fellas, big as her brother, they'll love to see a lad like me in the jail. It might be a good idea though, those big fellas would be better than going home to her. The clothes are already on the street, I can hear them landing on the pavement. Thud! And my books, they'll be ruined. I can hear the paper tearing. Why did I ever let a hippy in the shop?

"You can leave now sir."

"I can leave?"

"You can leave, the gentleman has confessed to hiding drugs in your shop."

"Can I not stay for another hour or two."

"You want to stay in here?"

"Well if you wouldn't mind."

"Go sir!"

"I suppose she went mad did she?"

"She did. That's one for another night. We'll head home now will we?"

"We'd better be going, it's getting bright outside."

Short walk home, the Guinness and the whiskey warming the soul. Two friends ready to part ways, stories of old told, they could teach your man who met Kennedy a thing or two.

"You mightn't see me now for a good while, Johnny. She won't be happy."

"Good luck, Joseph."

Maida Vale – People's Republic of Maida Vale

Maida Vale is an affluent residential area in West London.

"Hi, I'm Timothy from the…"

"Fuck off, I've had enough of you people coming and knocking on my door."

They just don't appreciate me, they can't see what dire straits this country is in and they certainly can't see that me, Timothy Owen-Langley isn't the one to save them from their inevitable doom. I have a message, a message which they can't ignore but they don't want to listen. It amazes how stupid people of this country can be.

What I need is to find someone who understands the message, knows what I'm talking about, someone with intelligence but not too intelligent because that wouldn't do. Someone with too much intelligence would argue back and try to find holes where there are none. I could try schools but I'd end up getting arrested. Colleges and universities would be a good line of attack, they don't really understand the world yet but they're full of ideas and hope and that's what I need right now, someone with hope.

Knowledge is perhaps the greatest enemy we have today. When you take away knowledge people follow blindly, they see what you want them to see because they have no other choice. Now they have access to everything, they can look things up on their phones in an instant, they can go home and look things up on the internet. What you need is to make them angry, when they're angry they want vengeance and something to take all their frustrations out on and that's what I need, a target to make people understand.

My house is filled with pamphlets and books, none of which anyone wants to read. I even gave one to a friend to read and they just laughed, said it was a mess and that I should give up. I haven't heard from them since. You see, I'm trying to achieve something they said would never be able to be done, create a new country, a breakaway country. One in which the people believe they are in control of their own destiny, in control of what they do and what others do. The people's part of it is just an illusion, a way of making them believe. In my People's Republic it'll be what I say goes and no one else.

What makes me think I can do this? What makes me think I can start a revolution from the quiet little suburb of Maida Vale and watch it spread as fervour takes over the rest of London and they bend down before me, obedient and adoring at my feet, wondering why it had taken them so long to realise my greatness? I believe in me and my own superiority, I also understand people's inherent stupidity, how they are manipulated by greed and power and will do anything which gives them a sense of power and the ability to change their own destinies. I will stand before Westminster Palace and declare 'The People's Republic of London' and they won't be laughing then.

Who am I you might ask? It's a reasonable question given my inevitable rise to greatness. I was born in London to parents who were born abroad. I will not name the country as I do not see it as relevant. They were hard working people who did the best for me. I would like to say I am working class but I am not, my family name is a prestigious one and money has never been an issue which you can see by this beautiful house I'm living in. Four storey by the way, huge garden out the back for when I'm entertaining and entertain I do!

At school I was seen as a high achiever, always doing better than others, many teachers remarked that I had outstanding ability. I went on to one of the best universities, again, I won't brag by naming it but I'm sure you will be able to guess for yourself. I then went straight to work and made myself millions by the time I was in my twenties. What better person would there be to run a country? I doubt you could find one.

Come to think of it, there is a college just down the road. I think I will go there tomorrow, I think some of the teenagers will be very impressed with my literature. They're impressionable, they want to make a difference and they always believed they are being oppressed no matter what their situations are. If that doesn't work I'll stand outside the station and hand out some leaflets. All it takes is one person to notice before an idea starts to gain some traction and then it'll snowball.

I can just see it now. Me sat in a chair, ordering people about, telling them how best to run a country. I'll get the best people, some of my friends from university, they're clever but not quite as clever as me. Once I have the best people running the country no one will be able to complain because the decisions made will always be the correct ones, even if they are unable to see it. Some would call it a dictatorship, I however would say it is just guidance, we all need a helping hand and it's sometimes best if you don't question that helping hand, much like a mother.

That reminds me, I'd better call her or she'll not be very happy. Last time I didn't ring her she came marching around here and threatened to cut off some of my allowance. You see I don't need the allowance, as I've already said, I've made so much money it wouldn't make any sort of difference, however it would be an inconvenience, just for accounting matters. I must remember to let her know not to come around unannounced too, last time she came I had a visitor and not a visitor she would much appreciate, if you know what I mean.

Kids, I hate them. I suppose I'm still a kid but I won't be for much longer, only another two weeks and it'll be my 18th birthday. I hate college, I like doing the work, I've always liked doing the work but I hate the other kids here. They're not the brightest sparks around. I have two friends, one is a complete social outcast who hates people and is not afraid to let them know and the other is a maths genius who has no interest in people, the only reason he talks to me is because I gave him a piece of chewing gum once, I don't think he likes me or sees me as a friend, he just kind of hangs around with me.

I'd be lying if I said I didn't look at the other kids with envy sometimes. I see them talking about going out for the weekend and what their plans are and I think I wish I was doing that. My two friends barely leave the house when they're not at college and I can't just turn up at one of these parties they all go to. I'd probably get beaten up or something. It'd just make life harder. At the moment, everyone just ignores me, I'm a bit like an invisible person. Some kids get bullied and some kids have a thousand friends, I'm neither, I'm just there but no one pays me any attention.

How would it feel to be adored? I've often thought about this question on the way to school. Imagine being so loved and liked that people would do anything you say. A bit like that guy in North Korea, all his people love him, he can get them to do anything they want. North Korea is a bit extreme though, I mean just at college. I'd love to be able to walk in the doors one day and each person I pass says hello to me or shakes my hand. When they're going to parties I'd be the first person they ask and if people knew I was going to be there it would mean more people would go. Can't see that ever happening.

You know what? I think that's going a bit too far. I don't actually want my name in lights and people fawning over me. That's a bit too much, I wouldn't like that either. I just want people to acknowledge my existence. I mean, my mother and my father, they both know I'm here and they don't do anything wrong. They give me money and they help me with college work, they're not strict but I know my boundaries. It's just everyone else. I'm the kind of person who will say something in a room full of people and nobody will seem to have heard, they'll just keep on going, as if I've said nothing at all.

I've told mum and dad. They just say to not worry about it, my time will come and then I'll look back and realise I was just being silly. I'm not sure about that though, I think I'm doomed to a life of anonymity. I'll always be that one in the background whose name nobody knows and nobody all that much cares for. I suppose people will say I'm some sort of victim but I'm only saying how I feel, there's nothing wrong with that is there? Why shouldn't I say how I feel!

There's this kid who's suddenly turned up at college, I don't know where he came from, no one has said, he must have got transferred in or something and everyone loves him. He could say anything and you'll have people swarming around him, wanting to be his friend. He sounds like he's come from up north or somewhere like that. I've always thought they were a bit different the people form up there, not that I'm ignorant or anything, I like to think I know a bit about the world but they just have something about them. I suppose that's why everyone loves him, because he's different.

There he is now, standing outside the gate, smoking a cigarette, looking all cool. What an idiot. I bet if he was from around here no one would care about him. Why is my friend talking to him? He never speaks to anyone but me. Jesus Christ! Now he's even taking my friends, what an arsehole! I can't believe this. I need to do something about it before it goes any further, being popular is one thing, nicking my friends is crossing way over the line.

"Why were you talking to that idiot for?"

"We were just standing outside having a cigarette, he was standing next to me, that's what you do, you just talk to people."

"You never talk to people, why you talking to him?"

"What's the matter with you, all he was asking me was if there was anywhere decent to eat around here. I pointed him the way of that new Vietnamese restaurant that's just opened up."

"Look at you going to trendy Vietnamese restaurants, the chip shop too good for you now?"

"Would you like to go to the Vietnamese restaurant with me?"

"Is your new friend going too? You can stand outside there and smoke cigarettes too, you'd look really fucking cool then, you could smoke Vietnamese cigarettes, start a new trend."

"If there's one thing I ain't it's a trendsetter. What's the matter with you, you lunatic?"

"Sorry, just had an argument with my mum before I left college. She told me I should be going out more, that I don't make enough effort."

"I thought you said she was understanding of you being a loner."

"I'm not a loner, I'm just a bit introverted. Where's this restaurant anyway?"

"You seriously want to go to it? I've never seen you eat anything other than chips and sausages and all that other shite you eat."

"I'll give it a go, broaden my horizons and all that."

"Meet me after college and we'll go."

Ah! An afternoon stroll around Maida Vale. There's quite a few nice restaurants opened up recently, I must pop in and have a look when I have some time. I suppose this place is like a middle class paradise, pushing upper middle class. That's what I call myself, upper middle class. I do have a good enough understanding of the working classes though, I know what they really want, in fact I probably know what they want more than they do themselves. My friend Geoffery, who's going to be my health secretary by the way, says it's nice to live just a little bit away from the unwashed masses, you can still be close enough to appear to care but not so close you have to mingle.

Anyway, the plan for today is to have a nice little stroll, and then stand outside the college and hope to not get arrested, I'm sure I could drop a few names if I did get arrested although I don't quite know what they could arrest me for. Last time I tried this I was chased away by some thugs who probably couldn't even read. They said I was a racist, I'm not sure where they got that idea from, I'm most certainly not a racist, I'd never think anything of the sort.

I have my target in mind. I need to find someone who looks like they might be lonely, not many friends, probably in desperate need of a friend and someone who 'understands' them. There's no need to go heavy on all the political stuff, I'm sure that would put a person of their age off. I want them to feel like I care about what they have to say, that I'm someone who will listen to their voice and won't just fob them off. A college should be an easy enough target. I sound a bit like a mercenary, however needs must and children are the most impressionable of people.

Now, this kid looks exactly like the kind of person I want. He dresses differently to the rest of them, he's on his own, head down, doesn't want eye contact with anyone else. I would say he is waiting for someone but I seriously doubt someone who looks like him has any friends at all. Now he is looking at someone but it's with a look of hatred and disgust. That's what I like, someone with a bit of fire in them, you can't go half measures when you're going to start a revolution.

"Excuse me, would you be interested in looking at one of my pamplets?"

"No, I'm not interested."

"You've not even looked at it and you've no idea what it's all about."

"I know, I'm not interested. You're one of them religious freaks aren't you?"

"No, it's nothing at all to do with religion. It's about life my young friend and how you can go about changing the world you live in."

I can see his eyebrows rising a little bit. Curiosity piqued.

"So you're one of them political freaks then?"

"You know about politics? You seem quite an intelligent young man."

"I don't know much about politics, just that it's boring and that we can't really do nothing to change anything."

"What would you like to see changed?"

"I don't know."

"Of course you know, you just said you want things changed so you must know what it is you'd like to see changed."

"Well, I reckon people who are not from around here shouldn't be able to go to this college."

Jesus, I thought he was going to say something quite profound and he comes out with something as idiotic as this.

"I'm sure that's something which could be changed in the future. Why don't you take one of the pamphlets and have a good read of it."

"Go on, I'll take one of them and see what it's all about."

"You waiting for someone?"

"I was waiting for a friend but it looks like they're not going to turn up."

"That's a shame. I'll tell you what, there's a coffee shop just over there, how about we go and have a coffee, you look quite upset your friend hasn't turned up."

"Yeah, I'm not sure about that mate, I don't know you and to be honest I ain't really all that interested in your pamphlet, I'm only taking one so as to be polite."

"Look, one coffee, you can just walk out of the shop if you find me too boring."

"You know what, I could do with someone to talk to, as long as you're buying the coffee."

"Of course."

Far easier than I thought. Now all I have to do is persuade him to start doing some work within the college for me. That part might be a bit difficult seen as he doesn't seem to the most sociable of people, but it's not always the charismatic ones who do the dirty work.

I have no idea who this geezer is and to be honest he sounds like he's talking a load of shit. I saw the word 'revolution' on his pamphlet. Now I'm not the cleverest person around and I'm not very political but I can tell you now that there ain't no revolutions happening. It's a free coffee anyway and it might be a laugh. I'm pissed off because Boris never turned up, he must have thought I was joking about going to that restaurant. Why do people always let you down when you really need them to come through for you?

I saw that geezer from up north swanning around outside the gates as well. He really does think he's something. How can someone who didn't know anyone a couple of weeks ago suddenly go to knowing half the people there and thinking themselves as some kind of superstar. It's annoying me just thinking about the geezer. I wish there was some way I could get rid of him. Spite is a bad thing, I know that but I can't help it, no one ever tells you how to cope with your emotions, they just tell you what not to do.

Funny thing about this guy is he's really well spoken. I know there's a lot of posh people around here but I would have thought they wouldn't be too bothered about revolutions and all that bollocks. He looks like a complete weirdo if I'm totally honest with myself and the last thing I should be doing is going for a coffee with him. I wonder if anyone's ever taken one of them pamphlets off him before? I bet I'm the first idiot that has. Mum would fucking kill me if she knew. I know I'm 18 but she's still quite protective.

He's sitting across from me and talking nonsense, going on about how he knows what it's like to be me, and he was like that when he was a kid. Judging by the way he's dressed and the way he talks, he's got no fucking idea what it's like to be me or 90% of the people going to that college. God knows what made him think going to the college was a good idea, he's lucky he wasn't beaten up, I know some kids in there would love to rob him. Got a nice watch as well.

"So, are you like a leader of a party or something? What's it called?"

"No, no, nothing like that, I haven't quite got my own party. I'm just someone who would like to make a difference to the average person's life."

"Why you hanging around outside a college then? Why don't you go somewhere like the Job Centre or somewhere like that. Wouldn't that be better?"

"Yes, probably. You are quite bright aren't you?"

"I wouldn't say that but it looks like I have better ideas than you."

"I would say you're quite different. You find it difficult to make friends, is that right? People don't really understand you, they don't give you that chance you're looking for, don't listen to you when you speak."

"Sometimes, yeah. I don't know why, you know like, if I'm standing in a big group and I say something everyone just ignores me, it's like I ain't there."

"Why did you say you didn't want local people to go to your college?

"Oh, there's this kid that's just turned up at the college, he ain't from around here but he thinks he's a big man, everyone likes him, hang on his every word and all that. I suppose it ain't his fault, I'm just getting angry for no reason."

"No reason! Of course there's a reason. He's come to your college and he's taking away people who could have been your friends."

"Actually, I think one of my friends went to a restaurant with him this evening."

"See, you're not mistaken in your thinking."

"It doesn't matter. What's the name of your movement anyway?"

"The 'People's Republic of London'."

"You what? Are you off your head? You want to create a breakaway country? Fucking hell, I thought you was a bit mad when you come to the college but you need help you do."

"How would you like to know what it's like for people to listen to you? I'll give you some of these pamphlets and then you go and wait outside the job centre and talk to people."

"Listen mate, I come for a cup of coffee because I felt sorry for you, I ain't into all this, you'll need to find someone else. Thank you for the coffee, but I think you need help."

Completely off his trolley the guy. Form a country called 'London'! No chance that's ever going to happen. Where do these nutcases get their ideas from. Funny thing is, when I was leaving he was still smiling, like what I was saying to him was funny. Trust me to meet all the lunatics, it's my own fault for even listening to the guy, that's my problem, I'm too nice, I bet matey from up north isn't a nice person. People's Republic of London? Haha! What a nutcase, I might even have to tell dad about that one.

Well, it went better than I expected it to, as long as he hasn't thrown away that pamphlet. He'll come around to my ideas, of that I can be sure. The laughing was just him being uncomfortable, what I was saying was hitting home with him. I know deep down he believes it.

There was a poster up outside the college about some kind of election for a college representative. Never in a million years would someone vote for me. I should have asked that geezer for some tips. It would be funny though if they voted for me. I'd make people's lives a misery, they'd have to listen to me then. I wouldn't even know where to begin with it though. What are you supposed to do to make people vote for you? What would the position even entail? Nah, it's just a stupid idea.

I suppose everyone will be going out tonight. I wonder what they'd be up to? Probably in the pub and then on to some club and then someone they don't know's house. I bet they have a right good laugh. What is the real reason no one ever asks me to go anywhere? Is it because of the way I look? The way I talk? I ain't that different from everyone else. I bet Boris had a nice meal with that geezer tonight, I bet they had a right laugh as well. How could he forget about me? He forgets how I stand up for him when there are people trying to bully him. Fuck them anyway, I'll show them all one day.

Interesting, on the way past the college I saw a poster for an election at that imbecile's college. I wonder if we could get him elected. It won't be easy, he has no charisma, he looks like he's just woken up and then been put through a tumble dryer, he can barely form a proper sentence using correct grammar. Although, that might be to my advantage, someone who can speak to them, in their language. Yes, that's it! First the college and then it'll be the schools and then people will have to listen to me.

I hope he doesn't tell anyone about me, I'm not sure his parents would take to kindly to my influence. We'll have to come up with something which these kids want, it doesn't matter if they can achieve it or not, it just has to be something they really want. I say they, I mean some of them, there is of course going to be another candidate or two, we'll need to divide them. I'm going to have to use all of my genius for this one. My people's republic is looking closer and closer every day, I knew there would be no stopping me once I'd started.

I can't believe that geezer is running for this stupid election. What makes him eligible? He knows nothing about us, he's come from some other school in a completely different part of the country and thinks he knows what we want! Fucking hell, if he gets elected I'm leaving the college, I'll take a year off and go to a new one next year, it'd be worth it just so I don't have to see his smug face. Why would people vote for him anyway? I mean it ain't like he's got any real power or anything, all he'll do is talk to the teachers, they're the ones who will make the rules. It's bollocks!

Jesus, that geezer is sitting outside the school. I think there really is something wrong with him upstairs, it ain't healthy him hanging around here like this all the time. I hope he doesn't talk to me, I don't want nothing to do with him. Why did he have to come and talk to me? A thousand other kids here and I'm the one he chose. Oh fuck! He's coming over to me.

"I see there's an election at your college, ever thought about running for it?"

"You want to be careful hanging around schools all the time, you'll end up getting nicked."

"I'm not doing anything. How about the election then? Clever kid like yourself, you must stand a chance."

60

"I told you last week, no one talks to me, they all ignore me, why would they end up electing me?"

"They'll elect you if you give them something to elect you for. Imagine standing up in front of the whole college after winning? People will be cheering for you, they might even start chanting your name. You'll be famous around here."

"No, I won't. They'll forget about me within a few days. Anyway, I'd bet you a thousand pounds, which I haven't got, that I couldn't win that election in a million years. Now fuck off and leave me alone or I'll ring the old bill."

"If I get you elected, you'll never see me again, and if I don't get you elected you'll never see me again either. How's that for a deal? There'll be no need for the police, I'm just trying to help."

"I doubt you're just trying to help, you've got some kind of agenda in this. Go on then, tell me your secret, how would you get me elected?"

"Look at all these kids outside, what are they doing?"

"Talking to each other."

Jesus this kid is fucking stupid.

"No, what else are they doing, something they can't do when they're inside."

"Smoking!"

"Yes, smoking. Now, how many of them in that college smoke?"

"I'm not sure."

"You need half of the people in the college to vote for you right? I don't think half of them smoke. You need to tell them that you'll be able to get them a place to smoke indoors, out of the cold."

"Well, that's not going to happen because it's illegal."

"Yes, but you just keep telling them there's a way you can do it, there's some law or other you've been looking up, a loophole."

"Okay, and even if people are stupid enough to fall for it, how about the rest?"

"Free lunches."

"Well, that's not going to happen is it."

"I thought you were clever. You tell them you'll get them free lunches, it doesn't mean you have to deliver the promise."

"Look, you're calling me stupid, but when I start giving them promises which I can't achieve, the teachers are going to get involved and they'll just remove me."

"Don't worry about that part, that'll take care of itself."

"Yeah, listen, I'll have to think about all of this because to be perfectly honest with you it sounds fucking stupid. I don't even smoke myself why would they believe me?"

"You don't have to believe in it, you just have to convince them you believe in it. You have to remember, you're clever and they're stupid, if you think like that, there's no way you can lose. Just think about it, you'll be there in front of the whole college and they'll all be talking to you, telling you how great you are and you're the first person to listen to THEM."

I've got the forms from the college. I ain't going to fill in what he told me to, they'd stop it before I even got started. I've just said I'll represent students interests best I can in cooperation with the teachers. This is madness but I am starting to come around to the idea of standing up in front of the school, people chanting my name. I might even get my picture in the local newspaper. I don't know what he's going to be getting out of all of this, who cares at this point, I'll just be using him.

I knew he could be persuaded, I just knew it. See, it's the first step, it's the smallest of steps but things will be getting heard. Once he gets elected and people find out who was behind his campaign they'll want to interview me and I'll be able to speak to people, tell them what they want to hear. I know people will think I'm stupid and it's only a bloody college but you've got to start with the young ones, they're the ones naïve enough to think they can change things. It's so, so close now, I can't mess this opportunity up.

I've bought a couple of hundred packets of cigarettes, and I'm going to arrange one of my friends to come and serve food outside the gates. It'll all be for free for them, I've had to pay of course but they won't know that, and it'll be worth it for the end result. There's no way this campaign can lose, I'm a mastermind. The day they ignored me will be the worst mistake of their lives. Not that anyone has ignored me before, it's just a turn of phrase as you well know.

I don't believe this, he's turned up at the school with a black bag full of Marlboro's. If anyone sees me walking around with a load of fags I'm the one that's going to get nicked. I don't know where he's even got them from, they could be stolen for all I know, because all of this wouldn't have been cheap. He says he's going to be outside at lunchtime with some chef geezer he knows and they're going to be serving food. I'm sure you need a licence for that sort of thing, what if the old bill turn up? If they do I'm putting it all on him.

He says I've got to hand the fags out on the quiet, not let anyone know, especially the teachers. This is madness, what have I got myself into?

"Oi, mate, I've head you're giving out free cigarettes? You got any on you?"

"Yeah, yeah, take one. Give your mate a packet as well."

"Nice one mate. What's your name again?"

"Alex. I'm doing a speech about the election later, could do with the support, any chance you lot'll come along?"

"Nah, I ain't really into all that mate. I couldn't care less to be honest."

"I'm looking into some loophole that'll give you, I mean us a smoking room, you'll be able to smoke inside when it's cold. Free lunches as well, you won't have to spend any money on your lunch, imagine the money you'll be able to save."

"Yeah? Straight? Ain't the smoking thing illegal?"

"Yeah, but there's some loophole, I'm trying to sort it out at the moment but it'll all be sorted by the time the election is done."

"It is kinda cold outside. They don't want to listen to that though, all they care about is themselves, telling you smoking is bad and smoking is stupid and I'm killing myself. I get that, but it's my choice, who are they to take away my choice? Yeah, fuck that, I'll come along."

"Tell your friends about it. Oh yeah, there's free lunches outside this afternoon as well. It's good food, trust me, you won't want to miss it."

"Seriously? Yeah, I'll let people know."

"Don't be telling any of the teachers about the cigarettes, it'll get me in trouble and then you lot won't get a smoking room."

"Yeah, yeah, of course. See you this afternoon."

Ah fuck. There's so many people in this room. Have all these people come because I've been giving them free cigarettes and they're going to get a free lunch? I have to give him credit this all seems to be working. I'm up next, just waiting for this idiot to finish his little speech. It's a bit like a stand up comedy routine. That's all he's got, he just knows how to make people laugh, there ain't nothing else to it. I'm starting to think I'll be able to win this now. Though, I bet the teachers are going to step in at some point and put a stop to it.

He's still prancing about on the stage, telling them shite they want to hear, they're all laughing at him too the fucking idiots. I'm nervous, this is going to be a nightmare, I know I'm going to end up fucking it up. He didn't give me any advice either, just told me to go up there and talk nonsense but look like I know what I am talking about. It's going to get stopped, I know it is, it's fucking ridiculous. I should just walk out of here and stop making a complete fool of myself, go back to being Mr. Anonymous.

They're all there staring back at me, waiting for me to say something. I just heard a couple of giggle, fucking hell, they're laughing at me already and I haven't even started. Some of the people I gave the cigarettes too are at the back of the room, there don't seem to be too many of them, I told them I needed them to come and they've let me down, I've got no chance here, shot down in flames before it's all begun. My name in lights is about to come crashing down onto the floor and smash into smithereens never to be taken seriously again.

"Thank you for coming here today, to hear me speak. I'm really grateful for you coming, it really is nice. I know some of you will be wondering who I am and what I stand for. I'll tell you a little bit about that in a minute but first I just want to say that I think it's great that we can have an election in the school. I also want to thank the great teachers for giving us the opportunity."

I can see a few people rolling their eyes already, well I've fucked this up haven't I?

"The platform I'm going to run on is that I am going to give people a smoking room and free lunches."

The giggles at the front have turned to laughter.

"What you laughing at him for? He knows a loophole, he wouldn't say it if he couldn't do it!" A saviour from the back of the room.

The teachers are looking at me in amazement, not sure whether they should put an end to this or let it go on because it's amusing them too.

"Yeah, a loophole, I know a loophole. One of my friends, he knows the law really well, he doesn't go to this college but you've got to trust me, he knows a loophole. Imagine, when it's cold and all you people are standing outside cold and wanting somewhere nice and warm to stand you'll be able to come inside."

"What if we don't smoke, what you going to do for us?"

"Free lunches."

The whole room starts laughing, even the ones at the back who are supposed to be supporting me, some fucking support.

"How are you going to pay for free lunches?" One of the teachers is asking the question, he's trying to keep a straight face as he asks but he isn't succeeding.

"I'll find a way, don't worry about how, I just know I can do it. Before you all start laughing at me, imagine what you'll be able to do with all that money you save. You could buy all sorts of things, it's going to save you loads of money, trust me. My friend is working on the loophole as well, we'll know more about it before you lot go to vote. I know some of you

think this is funny, but just wait until the election comes around, the clever people will vote for me. You don't want to look stupid do you?"

Laughter, and a few cheers from the back.

"Oh, after this there's free lunch outside if you don't believe me. Imagine having that every day, it's good food as well, go outside and try it yourselves."

They've all made a mad rush to the door, even the kids that were laughing at me. Well that went a little bit better than expected, it seems giving away things for free works. I don't know what's going to happen when they find out I won't be able to do it all the time though. Oh shit, the teacher is coming over.

"What do you think you're playing at? You know none of the things you just said can happen don't you?"

"I'm just giving some people a little bit of hope sir."

"Hope? It's a college not a bloody national election."

"Everyone needs hope, sir."

"Don't get smart with me. I should stop all this right now. But I'm not going to. You know why? Because I'm going to let you make a complete fool out of yourself. No one is going to vote for you, you do realise that? For God's sake, a smoking room? It's illegal, you idiot, I suppose you'll get a couple of clowns voting for you but you'll not win it and if it ever looks like you will win, I'll put a stop to the whole thing. There's only two of you running for this and I want to make it look like there's a little bit of democratic process so as you all might learn something. Do you have license for that food outside?"

"License sir?"

"Yes, you need a license and a health and safety certificate."

"Yeah, I've got one."

"Let me see it then."

"I'll get it when I get outside. You should come and get some free food too, sir."

"No thank you, but I will come and get these certificates from you, now let's go, this should be fun."

More than half the college are fighting over the queue to get the food. I didn't think he'd turn up to be honest. It looks like the food is quite nice as well. What about this fucking certificate? There ain't no way he's got a certificate. A couple of kids pat me on the shoulder and give me a thumbs up with a mouth full of food. I look at the teacher smugly, he looks at me with disgust.

"This whole charade is going to backfire on you, you know that don't you? They'll be out for blood when they realise you're lying to them."

"I'm not lying to them though sir."

"Certificate!"

"Sir, do you really think you can break all this up yourself? If you stop them they're going to go mad, you know what they're like. Just let them eat their food and then it'll be all over. I won't do it again, I promise."

"I knew you didn't have a certificate."

"I knew you knew, do you think I'm stupid sir?"

"Don't get cheeky with me, if you pull a stunt like this again I'm pulling you out of this election before it gets out of hand. Another thing, the smoking room, not going to happen, there are no loopholes, you're outright lying, you're going to have to change this."

"Yes, sir! Whatever you say sir!"

This has worked out perfectly. They're all going to vote for him, he'll win it in a landslide. I'm a genius! I'm a genius! That teacher who was talking to him didn't look too happy though, he looks like he could become a problem, all of the teachers could become a problem if we're not careful, we'll have to think of a way to get around it. Money always talks, it'll have to be money, it's a solution I was a bit reluctant to use but as long as nobody finds out we'll be in the clear.

"Excuse me, are you a teacher at this college?"

"I am, who are you and why are you giving away free food?"

"My name's Timothy, I'm a local philanthropist."

"I've never heard of you. If you don't get rid of the food and the setup in the next ten minutes, I'll be calling the police. Why are you helping one of my students to try and get elected? I find it rather odd."

"I just like to help. You know as well as I do that these things are just a show, the boy is short on confidence and I thought it'd help him get a bit more confidence before he goes out into the big wide world."

"Really? Sounds like a load of rubbish to me. If you don't go, I will call the police and I if I ever see you around here again I'll call them."

"What will you tell them? I haven't done anything."

"You've not got a certificate for one thing."

"I do, it's in my car, I'll get it for you in a minute. In the meantime, I think we can come to a mutual arrangement."

"Such as...?"

"I'll give you this money, it's probably about a weeks wages for you, you can go and take your wife and children for a nice meal somewhere. Just let the boy run the election, no matter what he says. We both know it's nonsense but why take away his confidence now? Look at him, I bet you didn't even know his name before?"

They're all coming up to me after college, asking me questions, not even about this election, just normal stuff. Someone even invited me to a party. This is madness, I can't believe I've managed to pull it off. There must be a way to find a loophole, if I find a loophole it will really annoy the teachers and they really all will think I'm amazing. I don't know where to start though, I'll just wait it out, we'll see when it's all done, I might not win, I've got more chance than some of them think though. This is incredible, I'm changing the way everyone thinks! Funny, the teachers have left me alone the last few days, they must think I'm definitely going to lose.

Oh shit! Here's some of Northern boy's friends. They don't look to happy. I don't want any confrontation, why can't they just accept that I'm going to win? I can't wait to laugh in his face when it's all done. He'll leave, he won't be able to accept the shame and embarrassment, it'll destroy him.

"Why are you lying to them? You know you can't do any of the stuff you're saying you can. Why are you taking it so seriously anyway? It ain't like this is some big thing, no one's given a fuck in the past."

"What does it matter to you lot? Worried your friend isn't going to win?"

"He'll win because you're an idiot who no one likes. You're in way over your head here, just drop out and save everyone the grief. You're getting people all wound up! Look how they was at the lunch you gave away, you're going to end up causing some kind of riot."

"So what? They only want somewhere they can smoke when it's cold and eat for free. What's wrong with that?"

"It's not going to happen. You can't do what you're saying you want to do. When you can't do it, they'll all turn on you."

"Stop worrying about me."

"We're going to ruin your name, not that you have much of a name anyway. After this no one will ever want to be seen with you."

"We'll see."

I'm going to spread a rumour. Tell someone that Northern Boy is cheating, he's been offering money to people to vote for him, he's new here why should he be having any say in what we do? Once they realise that, he won't have a chance, I need to make him look like an outsider, someone who has no right to be involved in this. With any luck he might just go back home.

It's the day of the election! My plans for a breakaway country are slowly coming together and my boy is on the verge of winning an election. It's only a college mind, I must keep telling myself that, keep the old feet on the ground! The teachers have left him alone, they don't think he's going to win so I think they'd have left him alone anyway. He came out of college the other day and people were chanting his name, they must be stupid not to realise he is going to win! All you need to do is offer a bit of hope and a bit of an incentive and it all falls into place.

The box isn't really that full but loads of people have turned up in the assembly hall. I thought there would be more votes than this. The headteacher is pouring them out onto a table. He's not got much respect for this process has he? There's two other teachers, counting the pieces of paper. I bet they stitch me up, they're not going to let me win, I know they're not. One of them is talking to the headteacher now and they're both looking over at me. I think I might have won! They're not going to let me win though are they? They're going to sabotage everything.

I stand in front of the stage and start to clap, the kids in front of me look at me as if I'm crazy, but then some of them join in, now half of them are clapping along with me. They're not going to risk a riot, there's no way they can stop me! They start chanting my name, one of the teachers has gone to the front trying to calm them down but there's nothing he can do, they've gone mad, there'll be no controlling them, if I lose they'll wreck the place. Now they're chanting 'Smoking Room'! I thought most of them didn't smoke!

The headteacher is standing at the front of the hall, he's holding his hands up, getting them to quieten down. They become silent as he opens up a piece of paper. This is it, this is what it has all been about.

"I'm pleased to announce, Alex is your new representative. Any problems you have at college you can go and see him."

I've won, I've actually won, I can't believe it, I've achieved everything I've wanted. I've been recognised, people know my name, they've written my name on a piece of paper and now they adore me. One half of the room is clapping and cheering, the other half is leaving the room.

"Now let's see if you can leave up to your promises, not going to happen is it?"

I don't care, I never cared about what I said, I don't even care about that weirdo who helped me get elected. Fuck him, I'm going to call the police tonight and tell them some strange man keeps hanging around outside the college, I don't need his advice anymore. They love me and that's all that matters.

Warwick Avenue – Child of the Revolution

Warwick Avenue, home to Little Venice and lots of canal boats

My little boat, my little house. All painted in green with red around the sides. Flower pots on the top and my little teddy bear on the front. Wherever I go, Pang Pang bear needs to be there. A symbol of the life I left and the life I live.

I step off the boat and stroll along the canal. Little Venice they call it. I've never been to Venice. I can't imagine Little Venice is much like Big Venice! It's quiet though, it's why I chose it. My friends think I am crazy! Why would you want to live on a boat? Isn't it dangerous? What if the boat sinks while you're asleep? Funny how people always ask you the negative questions. Try it! I tell them, you'd love it! 'No! No', they reply, I could never live on a boat!

A couple pass by with two kids, one of them is dangerously close to the water. I want to reach out and pull him back in but the parents don't seem bothered. He picks up a stone and throws it into the water and laughs before running back to his father's side. A duck rushes to where the stone entered the water, it quacks loudly, disappointed, it's not food, just a stupid stone. The boy runs to the side again but this time his father grabs him just as he's about to join the duck for a swim.

Another question they're always asking me back home, 'Why don't you have any kids?', 'Why have you never met a nice man?' I like kids; I just don't want any of my own. I love my freedom. That's probably why I've chosen to live on a boat, eight thousand miles from home and family. The silly part is that I still haven't gone anywhere on the boat. My beautiful green boat sitting there, just waiting for an adventure but I'm too frightened something will go wrong. If I sink it, what will happen then? Where would I live?

I sit there at night, dreaming of floating through the English countryside. Me all on my own, watching the world go by. That's what they used to call me back home, 'a dreamer'. Dreamers are no good in China. Dreams will corrupt you and you won't be able to find a husband who has a good job, a car and a house. Without those three things, what's the point in life? So I left, and here I am, I'm the ill-disciplined child with the delusions of grandeur, thinking I'm better than everyone else. I'm happy and they're not.

A boat floats by, a small man with bright clothing standing at the back steering it. That's someone I envy, able to take off on his own, not worried about what will happen when he reaches a lock or if his boat will sink while he's passing London Zoo. People laughing at you as you desperately attempt to keep your boat afloat. No, it's okay where it is for the moment! Maybe one day I'll take it on a journey. One day! I wonder when one day will be?

The lady in the café brings my coffee over. I'm the only person here, everyone else seems to be enjoying Sunday strolls instead of Sunday coffees. On the opposite side of the canal is a lady flying a kite. Rarely do I see people flying kites here. My father used to take me with him when he flew his kite out in the fields next to our old house. Our home in the countryside, fields of orange trees, strange looking insects chirping, you could only hear them, you never saw them. The heat shimmering in the distance during those sweltering summer days.

"Little Liu, we'll go and fly the kite in the fields."

"But dad! It's too hot out there!"

"We'll stand under the orange trees, it'll be okay!"

"Always flying your kite!"

"Keep her out of the sun!", my mother would shout at him, unsure which of us was really the child.

The kite was red and blue. I never knew where he had found it. He came home one day shouting my name as he ran down the road.

"Little Liu! Little Liu! Look what I have found! Isn't it beautiful?"

I looked at him as if he was crazy. Off he rushed to the fields, the string from the kite dragging along behind him. He ran around the field, shouting because he wasn't able to get it to fly. From that day on, he was out there every day with it, eventually getting it to fly, like a small child taking enjoyment from such a small thing.

One day he was lost in his own thoughts as he flew the kite, usually he would talk to me, tell me about his mother and father or the mischief he would get up to when he was a child. Other times he would tell me about things I had no care for, I would nod my head and ask questions I thought would keep him talking and happy. That day he just followed the kite with his eyes as it floated back and forth in the wind, the background of the blue sky making it stand out, a tamed dragon enjoying a few hours of freedom. The day was hot, I looked into the distance looking for a speck of cloud which might bring the promise of rain, but there were none.

Behind the orange trees there was a small hut. I didn't know what was in the hut and I had never asked, it was just there. I assumed it belonged to us, and as curious as I was as a child, the hut held no mystery for me. It should have been a child's dream, a strange, empty hut in the middle of a field. Mystery and temptation to go and explore, but no, this curious child who asked her mother and father endless questions didn't care for the hut or where it had come from, even who owned it and why it was there.

On this day though, it looked inviting, my father was in his own world, the kite the only thing he could see, his mind occupied by unknown thoughts far beyond my understanding. The sun was hot enough to burn my skin and the cool looking old hut was calling out. I pushed open the door, I had no expectations, other children would have thought of ghosts and fairies, but I just wanted shade. The hut was empty, probably why no one had ever mentioned it, a bare floor and bare walls made of wood. I sat down by the door, took out my school book from my bag and began to practice my writing. I loved to write my name, one stroke by one stroke. Not all the children could write, but I could. My teacher would be impressed I thought to myself as I looked down at my neat handwriting. 小刘 Little Liu.

After writing it another fifty times, I always counted and it had to be fifty times, I looked over the small book and beamed with pride, my excellent handwriting skills were a sight to behold for my young eyes. I looked out the window, the red dot was still floating about in the sky. As I stood up I noticed a shape in the far corner of the room, hidden by the darkness. Now I was curious, what could possibly be in here? I looked again to make sure the kite was still in the sky, my father still outside, if he was there whatever was in the corner wouldn't be able to hurt me!

As I got close, I could see it was a teddy bear. It was old, its nose and one of its eyes missing. Its fur was covered in dust, I tapped it lightly and watched as the dust fell away, its brown fur became lighter. He looked sad and tired, his missing eye and missing nose must bother him. I put him back in the corner.

"Little bear, I'll be back tomorrow, you watch me write and I will make you happy again!", I told him happily, watching to see if he smiled. No smile, but I think he was happier.

"Little Liu! Little Liu! Where are you?", I could hear my father's footsteps passing the hut.

"See you tomorrow, little bear!"

Quietly I sneaked out of the hut and sat underneath one of the orange trees.

"I'm here!"

He looked at me in surprise, wondering how he had managed to walk straight past me.

"Why didn't you answer me?"

"I was writing! Look!"

"Very good! You'll be the cleverest little girl in the village! We should go! Your mother will get angry at me for taking you out in the sun for so long."

"Dad? What were you thinking about?"

"Nothing, Little Liu. Isn't the kite beautiful?"

"Yes, it's very beautiful."

It's funny how things can trigger your childhood memories. The woman packs away her kits and walks off down the canal and past my boat. I wonder if she noticed my boat? She made me remember something, I wonder if I had any influence on her? I doubt it. Her kite had taken me back to the Chinese countryside of my childhood, such a small thing opened such a beautiful memory. I drink the rest of my coffee and continue with my walk.

My father would love it here. He'd be asking so many questions. "Why's that man wearing shorts when it's so cold?", "Why does that man have such a big nose?", "Can they speak Chinese?", "Why do foreigners all look so funny?"

I would laugh at him and he wouldn't understand why I was laughing. He would think I was teasing him. He once told me a story of a foreign lady who had come to our village and every single person went outside to look at her. They didn't know why she was there. You couldn't get lost and end up in our village, it was too remote and foreigners were very rare then. My father shouted 'hello!' at her, the whole village erupting in laughter. The woman shouted 'hello!' back at him and then jumped on her bike and rode away, no one ever knew why she had been there. That was the one and only time he had seen a foreign person.

I climb the stairs from the canal up to the main road, walking past huge houses. Some would dream of living in them. I think some of my friends back home believe I should be living in one. They'd be too big for me, why would one person need such a big house. A little boy is outside one of the houses, kicking a ball and eating strawberries. His mother calls him from the doorway and he reluctantly goes back inside.

"Little Liu! Little Liu! Two of my buttons and a needle is missing, have you seen them?"

"Mama! I haven't seen them, perhaps granny took them."

"Always taking my buttons! Your father has to see the village cadre tomorrow and his jacket is missing two buttons."

I remember guiltily pushing the two buttons together in my pocket, hoping they wouldn't jump out on their own. Two buttons, they'd mean nothing to most people, you could just go to the shop and buy two more but back then we had very little and two buttons were a big thing.

"Little Liu! Go to town and buy two buttons, tell Old Wang I will give him the money next week, I don't have it now."

My face went red, she was getting credit from Old Wang, the shop owner.

"Go! Quickly! It'll be dark soon."

Old Wang. I hated Old Wang, everyone hated Old Wang. He was a small man who knew everybody's business. He would always be having tea with the cadre, telling him tales. I walked to the village as slowly as I could, hoping my mother would come from behind me to tell me she'd found two more buttons. I remembered it would soon be dark and I was more scared of the dark than Old Wang and even more scared my mother would discover it was I who had taken the buttons.

All the other shops were open and inviting. Mr Zhang with his small shop which sold some sweets and little toys, Mrs Xia with her shop selling vegetables and fruit. She was a plump lady with big red cheeks, she loved children but she had no children of her own. None of us kids knew why she didn't have children or even a husband. All the adults would talk about her in whispers.

"Little Liu! Come and have a strawberry, I know how much you like strawberries!"

She handed me a strawberry with a big smile on her face, her bright red cheeks shining in the sunlight.

"Xia, sister, how do you sew a button?"

She looked at me with suspicion, her smile fading away.

"Why can't your mother sew a button?"

"She's busy, collecting the oranges."

Her smile came back and she went into her shop to get a needle and thread.

"I don't have any buttons but you must do it like this. Be careful of your finger or your mother will blame me for showing you how to do it wrong."

"Thank you, sister!"

"Come back and show me what you have sewed, I would like to see! Now run along and do what you came to do, it'll be dark soon and you shouldn't be walking back on your own in the dark."

Old Wang's shop had a door, not like the other shops which you could just walk into. It was dark inside, he was sat as his little desk. I could smell the rice wine in the air, a funny smell, sickly sweet. As I shut the door he looked up and put some paper into a box and closed it, hiding it away. His nasty little eyes looked me up and down as I stood at the door, scared to speak. I put my hands in my pockets, playing with the two buttons, looking down at the floor, why did she have to send me to Old Wang?

"What do you want?"

"My mother said can she have two buttons and she will pay you next week."

"Two buttons? Does she not know there is a shortage of buttons?"

"I don't know."

"How is your father?"

"He's working hard in the fields and has to see the cadre tomorrow so she needs to sew some buttons for him."

"I know he has to see the cadre tomorrow. Does your father go to the city often?"

"Sometimes, but not a lot."

"Why does he fly that kite all the time?"

"He likes his kite. When he's finished in the fields he flies his kite and he tells me stories."

"Do you ever see any other kites?"

"No, I've never seen another kite."

"I hear you are able to write?"

"Yes! I can write two hundred characters."

"Be careful, being curious is a dangerous thing."

"Can I have the buttons?"

"I'll give you the buttons. Tell your mother if she doesn't pay me next week she will have to pay me double."

"Thank you, Mr Wang."

"Remember what I told you, being curious is dangerous. Little girls like you have no need to be curious."

I put the two new buttons in the other pocket so I wouldn't get them mixed up. Mrs Xia was still sitting outside her shop eating strawberries. She stuck her tongue out at me as I walked past her, her big red cheeks still shining, she bursts into a big smile, waving me goodbye as I walked out of the village.

The sun had disappeared behind the hills but I still skipped and hopped and stopped to look at things on my way home, happy I had two buttons from Old Wang and happy I was on my way home. Ahead of me in the dusty road I could see a figure approaching. I knew who it was even if he was far away, it was my father.

"Did you take the buttons from your mother?"

"Yes, I took them."

I could never lie to him, he would know when I was lying.

"Why did you take them? I told you, you must never steal."

"I liked the colour."

"Don't tell your mother you took them. Did Old Wang give you two buttons?"

"Yes, he told me not to be curious as well."

"Ignore Old Wang, no attention should be paid to such an ignorant man."

"Father?"

"Yes?"

"Whose hut is that behind the orange trees?"

"Your grandparents used to live in it, before they built the house we live in, in fact I lived in it when I was small."

"But it's so small!"

"Ha! You're spoilt that we have such a big house now! You are lucky you have rice Little Liu, that's all a person needs."

He took me by the hand and we walked home together as he told me the story of a rabbit who lived on the moon.

I sit on the deck back at my boat and open a beer. People pass by on boats, excited and tired children on their way back from the zoo. My neighbour waves as he walks past carrying a bottle of wine.

"Hi Annie! How was your day?"

"Good! Thank you! I just went for a walk along the canal, remembering being a child!"

"I like your bear by the way, he looks good as captain of the ship!"

Two days had passed and I still hadn't gone back to see the bear. Each day I woke up excited, thinking I might have the opportunity to go and see him. I lay awake that night, listening to the chirp of the insects, wondering how I could sneak out. Dad had not flown his kite since he had come back from seeing the village cadre. He had been very quiet, mum told me I shouldn't disturb him because he had too many things on his mind.

The next day, as I arrived home from school I could see there were some strange looking men in the house.

"Little Liu! Go and pick some oranges for me."

"I have to do my homework!"

"Go and pick the oranges, I will come and find you later."

I scuffed my shoes as I dragged my feet through the field, I wanted to know who the men were and why they sent me away. I can see the bear, I suddenly remembered! I opened the door to the hut, sitting there was the bear. I shook him gently, the dust falling off him. I tried to remember what Mrs Xia had taught me, taking the needle, thread and two buttons from my pocket. I wouldn't have to hide them any longer.

Gently I pressed the button over his missing eye, following her instructions. An eye and a nose. I bit the piece of thread, the eye and his nose sewed tight against his face. I held him up to the light. Now he had two eyes and a nose. He looked happier. I put him back down in the corner and sat next to him.

"You need a wash! Next time I come, I'll bring you some water and I can wash you."

I brushed his head, he looked very smart now.

"There are some strange men in the house and I don't know why. I think it's because of Old Wang. I really don't like that man!"

I'm sure I saw his head move in approval.

"I need to give you a name but I don't know what I should call you. Every night I think about it! You're quite fat for a bear so maybe I should call you fat bear. Pang Pang Bear! There you go, there's your new name."

I sat him on the small window as we both looked out, waiting for the men to go and my father to come. The clouds were coming, it would rain soon. I leant my face against the soft fur of the bear, his new eye still hadn't fallen off. I was pleased with myself. I'll bring him to Mrs Xia one day and she will be able to see what I have done. I think she'd like him too.

Another hour passed. The rain had come and gone, the air was cooler. I was angry, why hadn't they come to get me. Why didn't they come when it had been raining? They didn't know I was in the hut! I was hungry too. I hoped he would come soon. I took out my book and wrote the bear's name fifty times on a piece of paper. 胖胖. Still no one had come, they had forgotten about me surely, I had to go back on my own.

"Goodnight, Pang Pang! I promise I will come tomorrow and wash you, you will look even better once you've had a wash."

The air smelt strange after rain, a damp almost fruity smell. I skipped over the puddles of mud. The men had gone and my father was walking towards me from the house. He looked sad and tired.

"I'm sorry! Are you cold?"

"No, but I am very hungry!"

"Will you accompany me while I walk for a little while?"

"Yes, of course. Where's your kite?"

"The kite is gone."

He stayed silent as we walked. I wanted to ask him where the kite had gone but he didn't look like he wanted to talk.

"Little Liu, you are a good girl. I want you to do well in school and then you will be able to leave the village and go to the city."

"I would like that."

"Can I tell you a story? Are you too hungry?"

"No, I want to hear your story!"

"We'll sit here for a little while, the house is hot and the air is cooler outside."

It had got dark, I sat there waiting for him to tell his story. I looked up at the sky, it was filled with stars, one night I will take Pang Pang out with me and we can make wishes on the stars together. My father took my hand and held it as he began to speak.

"When I was just a boy we lived in that hut. Me and your grandparents. See these fields? A rich man owned them. They would spend all day in the fields, when they came home at night they were too tired to talk.

"One morning, my father took me by the hand and said 'YaoYao, we're going to the city'. I was so excited! I had never been. All I knew was our little village and it was even smaller then.

"He put me up on his bicycle and he rode and rode for what seemed like hours. When we arrived in the city I was frightened. Everywhere there were people, there were strange smells, food I had never seen before. I held my father's hand as tight as I could as we walked through the streets.

"We stopped at a shop and my father spoke to the man. The man didn't seem friendly, not like back home in the village where all the shopkeepers smiled."

"Not Old Wang!"

"No, not Old Wang." His face looked angry as he said his name. "The man took a teddy bear from the back of his shop and he handed it to my father. They argued about the price, finally my father gave him some money. I don't know where the money came from because back then there were days when we didn't have enough to eat. My father handed me the teddy bear, he didn't say anything, put me up on his bike and we cycled back to the village. The whole way I clasped the teddy bear so tight when I got back home my hands were white!"

"I think he gave it to you because he loved you."

"My father said very little, not like when me and you sit outside and talk and you accompany me when I go to fly my kite. He worked very hard and said few words, even to my mother. When we arrived home he sat me down on the bed and he said to me 'YaoYao, I say very little, but this bear is my heart.' Then he went and sat outside and I fell asleep with the bear in my arms."

It had to be Pang Pang bear, I thought to myself! He must know he's there!

"War came and went, one day the cadres came to the village and gave us land and the man who owned the fields disappeared. I married your mother and then we built the new house. I left the bear in the old house so he could look after it. Maybe I was ashamed too, ashamed that as a man I had a teddy bear. Don't ever be ashamed, Little Liu.

"One day I might not be here. When I'm gone, please remember the time we had, the simple times and the stories. When you are older you should go where your heart takes you. Your father is a simple and foolish man but you are neither."

He stood up and I followed him back to the house. I wiped a tear from my eye, I didn't understand, I didn't want him to leave.

I take another beer from the fridge. I wonder what he would have thought of it here? I don't think he would have liked it. Too many people, too different. His fields and his oranges would have been too far away. The food too, he would never have been able to cope. I can imagine his face if were to tell him they don't eat rice all the time.

A couple of men from the pub walk past the boat. They are both drunk but they are harmless, one of them pretends to fall into the water, his friend laughs at him and they carry on their merry way.

Each day I came home from school I went straight to the fields to make sure he was still there. I still didn't know what had become of his kite, instead he would walk alone among the orange trees. While he walked I would go to the hut and tell Pang Pang about my day. I would tell him that my father missed him and was sorry his eye fell out but he was a man now and he couldn't be seen with a teddy bear.

He was with Old Zhang when I met him on the road, both of them singing, staggering.

"Little Liu! Your father is a bad man!" I grimaced as he said it, I knew what that meant.

Every day at school they would tell us there were bad people and we had to take the right path. If we thought someone was taking a bad path we were to report them to the cadre. I could never report my father, besides, I knew he wasn't really a bad man. I could smell the rice wine as they swayed down the road.

"Old Wang has chosen the wrong path! A rightest! He has wrong thoughts!"

I felt my body go numb, he laughed as he said it. I looked around to see if there was anyone else about, anyone who could listen in. There appeared to be no one. Even as a small girl I knew what he was saying could be dangerous. I left them to walk back home, I continued to the village, I had Pang Pang hidden beneath my dress, I wanted to show Mrs Xia what I had done with the buttons.

Old Wang was stood outside his shop looking pleased with himself, his nasty smile spread across his face. Mrs Xia's shop was closed. His smile turned into a laugh.

"She's gone, that's why you shouldn't be curious."

I ran all the way home, my mother was sitting outside the house.

"Mama! Mama! Where is dad?"

"Asleep, he's drunk, leave him be before he brings more trouble upon us."

"Mrs Xia has gone."

She looked down at the floor and said nothing. I knew Mrs Xia wouldn't be back there were to be no more questions. I took Pang Pang back to his hut. Mrs Xia will never be able to see him. Poor Mrs Xia, I can only ever remember her smile and her rosy red cheeks.

"I'm only a little girl, Pang Pang. Why do people have to be so horrible to each other?"

He didn't have a smile that day, but he listened, as he always did.

"They don't teach us to write anymore, only to sing songs and to question the bad people. I just want to go to school and learn new things. Do you think I will be able to speak English one day Pang Pang? I would love to speak English.

"I'm worried for dad, he drinks too much and he doesn't look after the oranges like he used to. I found some on the floor today and they were nearly rotten. One day, when I leave for the city, I'll take you with me and we can live together, away from all of these people."

The next day, when I arrived home from school, he was waiting at the door for me.

"Little Liu! I'm so excited I nearly came to the school to pick you up and take you home."

"What's the matter?"

From inside the door he pulled out a kite. It was bigger than the old one, even redder too.

"They'll never be able to take this one from me, look how red it is! Not even Old Wang is this red!"

My mother came to the door and rolled her eyes, tutted and went back inside to cook the dinner. I hadn't seen him so happy since he had lost the last kite. Into the field he ran with the big red kite. I threw my bag down and followed him, running and laughing together. He picked me up in one arm as he flew the kite with the other. Dizzy, he fell to the floor with me in his arms, we lay there looking up at the sky laughing.

"Little Liu, whatever they tell you, you're not to believe it."

"Who?"

"Anyone! If someone tells you this is an orange you must look closely. If it's not a perfect orange then you must ask a question."

He has finally gone crazy, I thought to myself.

"How is my bear?"

"He has a new eye and a new nose and I wash him too. Sometimes he smiles and sometimes he is sad. I think he misses you. Why did you really leave him there? I don't believe you were ashamed, you run around the field with a kite like a fool, why would a bear matter?"

"Maybe you're too small to understand. Some memories are too hard to have near but you don't want them too far away. He was a reminder of simpler times, Little Liu. Times when what you said and what you thought didn't matter."

"Dad, please don't do anything stupid. I don't want you to go away."

"I won't, don't worry. It's not always what we do, it's what others say we do which causes bad things to happen. Who is your favourite person in the village?"

"Mrs Xia, but she's gone now."

"She was a good person. You aren't to listen to what they say, if you do you'd think she was a bad person. All she had was her heart, it was a good heart. She meant no malice to anyone. What you think is never wrong."

I was convinced he had gone crazy because I didn't really understand what he was saying.

"Help me pick up these oranges, I've not been looking after them."

We picked up the oranges as he told me of places he'd never been to and places he'd never be able to go to. The sun had set, the air was heavy. It felt as though you could reach out and grab it in your hands and mould it into shapes.

"Can I go and see Pang Pang before we go and have dinner?"

"Yes, I'll wait for you here. Don't tell your mother though, she would disapprove of you talking to a bear."

I opened the door to the hut, hoping Pang Pang would have a smile on his face. He was gone, I would have searched but there was nowhere to search, just an empty, dusty hut with nowhere to hide. Dad will think I've lost him! All these years he's stayed in this hut, away from the world and its dangers, safe, and now he's gone and it's because of me. Who knew he was there and why would they take him? I ran back to dad, he was lying down by the orange trees, looking up at the sky.

"The bear, he's gone!"

He turned to look at me, smiled a forced smiled and got to his feet.

"Come, let's go, your mother will be worried about us."

"Did she take him?"

"No, she'd never have done something like that."

We all sat in silence as we ate dinner. I looked at my mother to see if I could see some sign of guilt on her face, to see if she had stolen away my best friend. She just looked at me and smiled. I don't want to believe she took him but who else would have done it?

I lay in my bed that night, wondering why everyone was so cruel. Why had they taken him away? Maybe she found out I had taken the buttons, perhaps it was my own fault, I should never have stolen them. I could hear my parents whispering to each other, they sounded angry, like they were trying to make a decision but they didn't want me to find out.

I will never forget the dream I had that night. My father in the field, flying his kite, the bear propped up against one of the orange trees, watching him. I could see the rain coming, the wind was becoming stronger and stronger. I shouted out to him but he didn't hear me, the wind took his kite, I watched on helpless as he ran off into the distance chasing the kite.

The next day, I sat in the school listening to them argue and sing stupid songs I had no care for. I just wanted to learn, not listen to *them*; none of them had a good idea in their heads. Everything was good, or bad. There was nothing in between, if you didn't agree you were certainly bad. The teachers were gone and the children had taken over. We knew nothing and what we did know was of not much use.

Walking through the village on the way home, Old Wang was stood outside his shop, he called me over to him.

"Come into the shop."

"I don't want to."

"Do you want the whole village to know your mother owes money?"

I looked down at the floor and followed him into the shop, his feet were bare and dirty, he turned around with a smirk on his face.

"Tell your mother, she doesn't owe me anything. She can have the buttons for free."

"Why?"

"No why! I'm a good man who likes to treat people well. Now, go home!"

There was a reason he'd been nice to my mum, I knew that much. No, not nice, he was pretending to be nice. Even me, as a little girl, knew it wasn't real, he had done something or he wanted something. As I approached our little house I could see my mother sitting outside on the small chair.

"Old Wang said you don't have to pay money for the buttons."

"Little Liu, sit down."

I sat down in front of her, trying to think what I had done wrong.

"Your father is gone. He won't be coming back. You're not to talk of it either, especially not at school."

She stood up and put her hand on my cheek, rubbed it and then went back inside. It was the last I heard her mention my father. I ran to the little hut. The bear was sitting there in the corner of the hut where I had left him last. His fur had been washed, he looked as if he was new, born again.

"He's gone Pang Pang! I knew he would go but I didn't think it would be so soon. Where did you go? Yesterday I came and you weren't here! It doesn't matter, you are here now. Wherever I go, I'll always take you with me, you come and live in the house with me now. I don't care what she says. What will we do Pang Pang?"

I picked him up and walked back to the house, my mother was cooking. She looked at me as I came in the door, then at the bear. Her eyes went back to the pot of rice. I put him on my bed and lay down next to him, I didn't want to eat my dinner and I didn't want to sit with my mother. At the time I didn't think she could be sad. I look back and think that night I should have sat with her.

The next morning, my mother put some money into my hand.

"Give this to Old Wang."

He was standing outside his shop as usual, that nasty smile across his face. I put the money on the floor in front of him, I couldn't possibly put it in his hand, the thought of his touch made me sick.

"I know he's gone because of you! You're not a good man, Old Wang!"

The smirk disappeared from his face and I walked away. I never looked at him again, my head down every time I passed. I promised myself that one day I would go back and see him, look him in the eye and tell him what I thought but I never did. Words are wasted on someone who doesn't listen.

The canal looks beautiful as the sun sets. So far away from home but it makes me feel at home. I reach out and pick up Pang Pang, hugging him.

"I left at least, dad. They never told us where you went or what happened. The kite, I couldn't bear to keep, I put it into the hut and left it, I never went back in there again. I didn't give up though, I chased my dreams, I didn't listen to anyone else. Home has changed, you wouldn't recognise it. I don't think you would like it, it's not simple anymore. Pang Pang is still with me, we're going to go on an adventure soon, I just need to build up a bit of courage. Speak to you next year, dad."

Paddington – Toys, Hags and Pizzas

Paddington, home to a large train station and formerly home to the toy museum

"Mum, can we go and see the trains?"

"We haven't got the time to go and see them, love. Next time we're here we can stop and have a look."

"When will we be here next?"

"Soon."

"When's soon?"

"Stop asking so many questions! I'll take you soon, we're in a hurry today and we don't have time. Stop dragging your feet or we'll never be on time."

"Mum?"

"Yes?"

"Where are we going?"

"You know where we're going. We're going to the seaside."

"I don't want to go to the seaside! I just want to look at the trains."

"You'll love the seaside, now stop moaning and hurry up or we'll miss the train. You'll see some trains when we get to the station."

"But I want to stay and watch them!"

"Come on!"

This station is so big, I've not see one like this before. I just want to stay here all day and watch the trains, I don't want to go to see my nan. Her house is old and it smells and I don't like the food she makes. Cabbage, I hate it, it tastes funny but mum says I have to eat it because if I don't nan will cry and she'll be sad. I don't want her to be sad so I eat it.

After dinner she gives me a big biscuit too but I don't like it. It has this white stuff inside that's all sticky and it gets on my hands and it's all yucky. She might give me some money though, sometimes she gives me money and tells me not tell mum.

There's an old train in the station! One of them ones that has a big chimney at the front and loads of smoke comes out. It looks like a big dragon! I wish I could get on that one! Our one is a new train and I don't really like it, I want one of the old ones. I read a book about a boy who went in a wardrobe and there was a lion. He went on one of those old trains. I should look in nan's wardrobe, maybe I'll find a door and there'll be lions on the other side. It's snowing in the book though, I don't really like snow. Last year it snowed and I had a snow fight with my friends and my hands got cold and they really hurt.

There's a man dressed as a bear and he is giving people water. He must be hot in there. I know it's a man inside because bears can't talk and they wouldn't be standing at a train station giving people water. If they were in a train station they would eat everyone. If there was a bear here I'd run on to that train and I'd try to drive it away. The bear would be scared of all the smoke. It's not a bear though, it's a man. Why is he a bear giving people water?

"Mum, why is that man dressed as a bear and why is he giving people water?"

"It must be some kind of promotion, it's hot today and people should drink lots of water."

"Why is he a bear though? He looks stupid. Bears don't give people water, they eat people."

"I'm not sure why he's a bear, love."

Mum says I have an active imagination but I don't know what that means. Sometimes I have invisible friends that they can't see and I talk to them. If mum and dad are angry at me I just go and talk to my friends. I can make them look whatever I want them to look like, big, tall, fat, skinny, ugly. None of my invisible friends are ugly though. I don't tell my friends at school about my invisible friends because they'd think I was stupid and then they'd call me names and my invisible friends can't help me with that.

I don't want to get on this stupid train. If I could just walk around by myself and do what I wanted to do I'd be happy but mum says we have to go to nan's house. My friend said that he went to a museum that is near this train station and it was all toys. Everywhere there is toys. I want some new toys, some of the toys I have are old and I don't like them anymore. If nan gives me some money I'm going to go and buy some new toys. Last time she gave me twenty pounds, I dropped it on the floor on the way home though. I didn't say anything because mum didn't know I had it, she'd get angry if she knew I dropped twenty pounds.

Dad isn't talking very much. He doesn't like nan, he says she's a busybody and talks about people too much. I don't know what a busybody is but I don't think it's a nice thing. Dad said he'd rather stay at home so he could watch the football but mum told him he had to come. He looks a bit sad, I wonder if nan gives him any money? I don't think so, I don't think she likes him either. He'll just go to the pub with grandad and then they'll drink beer and come home and be silly. He'll sleep on the train on the way home.

"Dad?"

"Yes, mate?"

"Do you like nan?"

Mum is looking at dad with an angry face.

"Yes, mate, of course I do. Why are you asking a question like that?"

"I'm just asking."

"Stay here with your mum for a minute, I'm just going to buy some drinks and sandwiches for the train."

I hold mum's hand, there so many people, it's a bit frightening. When I grow up I wonder if I'll be as tall as these people? Mum said I'm like dad so I'll probably be tall. I'd like to be tall, all my friends would like me because I'm tall.

"Stay with this bag for one minute, love. I'm just going to ask that man over there where we need to go to get our train. Don't move!"

There's a loud whistle and I can see all the smoke going up to the ceiling. It must be that really old train. I want to see it but all the people are standing in front of me, I can't see anything. Mum is with the man talking, why is she taking so long? If she comes back quickly maybe she can take me to go and see it. She's still talking to him, I really want to see the train! If I go over there for two minutes, I'll be back before her, she won't know I've gone. If I was tall I'd be able to see! One minute, I'll just go for one minute and I know she won't be angry, she knows how much I want to see that train.

It really does look like a dragon! All the smoke coming from the chimney, it's making loud noises too, like a hissing sound, it sounds like a big snake. I really like the colour, it's like a dark green and some red on it. Dragons are dark green and red. There's a man on the train and he's waving at people, I wave at him and he waves back. I wonder who he is? It's making lots more hissing, it must be leaving. All the smoke is at the ceiling, it's like I am in olden times. I wish I could jump on to it!

Mum's gone, the bag's gone too! Where's dad, he went into that shop over there but I can't see him. He must have gone to try and find me, mum too. That man dressed like a bear, if I go and find him then they'll be able to see me. I can't see him though, there's too many people and they're all so big, it's like I am in a forest or something. They'll definitely be trying to find me, they won't go to nan's without me, I know that. Maybe dad ran away because he really didn't want to go and mum has gone to find him.

I can't see the man dressed as the bear, he's gone! Mum said if you get lost you need to go and find someone that's important, like the ticket man or a policeman. I can't see any policemen, the ticket man is over there but he's talking to someone and I'm to scared to talk to him, he looks like he's a bit angry. If I just stand here they'll be able to find me. There she is over there, I can see, I can see her red skirt. Oh! It's not her, it's someone else, what if I wait outside? They'll probably go outside and look for me, they might think I've run away, I wouldn't run away, why would they think that?

There's less people out here, if I just sit down on this bench they'll come along soon. There's lots of taxis and people jumping into them. What if they've got on the train without me? Maybe they're thinking I ask too many questions and they just want a quiet day without me. How will I know when they'll come to pick me up though? What if something bad has happened? Maybe dad went to the pub instead of the shop and he got drunk and then he came back and fell on to the tracks and a train ran him over. No, I don't think he'd do that would he? Dad's too clever to do that.

If they've got to nan's without me that means I can go and do something I want to do, I don't have to listen to mum or dad. I'm a big boy now anyway, I'm nearly eight years old, I should be able to do what I want and go where I want. I could go and see the trains myself and then I could go to the toy museum that my friend was talking about. I haven't got any money though, how am I going to eat something. I put one pound in my pocket before I went out! Mum told me I could have it to buy some sweets when we get to nan's, I forgot I was rich!

I'm a big boy now. I don't need people to tell me what to do. If they want to go off and enjoy themselves without me I'll go and enjoy myself too! I didn't want to go to nan's anyway, her house smells and she makes me eat cabbage and all them horrible things, and them stupid biscuits. She only gives them to me because I don't like them. She would have given me some money though, I won't be able to buy any toys now, it doesn't matter though, I can do what I want!

"Excuse me, young man? Where's your mum and dad?"

"They've gone to buy something from the shop, they'll be back in a minute."

"Are you sure?"

"Yes, we're going to my nan's house."

"Okay."

That lady was a bit funny looking, her hair was all messy and there was pink in it. She looks like a witch, maybe she is a witch, I hope she's not a witch, if she's a witch she might come back and eat me and then I'll be in trouble. I bet she has pink hair so people know she's a witch. She was asking me where my mum and dad was because she wants to take me home and then cook me. I'd better get out of here before she comes back. I don't think I'd be very tasty anyway, nan always says I'm just skin and bones, I think witches like bones though so maybe she will eat me, I'd better hide.

I can't get onto the trains because that angry looking ticket man is there, the witch lady with the pink hair is sitting down reading a newspaper but she keeps looking at me. If I can get onto one of the trains she won't be able to catch me because the ticket man will stop her. I could climb under the barriers, he won't be able to see me. I bet she's thinking about how she's going to cook me! I hope she doesn't put a spell on me! She might turn me into a frog or something.

If I was a frog I don't know what I would do. I'd only be able to jump and go in the water. What do frogs eat? Insects my teacher said, I don't really like insects. My friend at school dared me to eat a beetle once so I tried it and it tasted horrible. I don't want to be a frog, I wouldn't have any friends then, just other frogs and I don't think they can talk to each other. I have to get under the barrier before she catches me! She's got up now and she's walking towards me!

The barriers are really small but I can get underneath it, the ticket man hasn't seen me yet. The witch is running now, maybe she's just going to get the train. If I hide in there she'll never be able to find me. Running, running! Yes, I've made it inside the train. It's quiet at this part of the station, I wonder why no one else is here? There's lots of big bags on the train, there must be something important inside them. I should have a look, I don't know though, mum said I shouldn't look inside things that don't belong to me. She's not here though so it doesn't matter, she'll never find out.

The witch woman is definitely not coming, but I can see the ticket man looking along the platform. He's walking past where I am, he's not looked inside though. Now he's turned back. I bet she told the ticket man that I was her little boy and she wanted him to go and get me. Witches are clever like that. She's not as clever as me though. The ticket man has gone now, I can have a look inside some of these bags and see what's inside.

They're all big brown bags, like the ones you see that Santa has in the back of his sleigh with his reindeer. I don't think there's any toys in these ones though because all the bags smell horrible, like they are old or something. This one just has lots and lots of letters inside them. Dad told mum he lost a letter he wanted to send to the bank, I wonder if it's in here. He'd be happy if I found it. He left me here at the station though so I don't think I will look for it.

This bag has lots of big parcels in it. I shouldn't open them, but I really want to. There's got to be something nice inside them, I bet there's toys and all sorts inside. I could open just one and see what it is, I'll put it back, I just want to have a look. It's just an old book, why would anyone want that? I'll put it back and open just one more. Wow! This one has a big cake inside it. It's all white with a big red cherry on the top, it looks a bit broken though. I could try a bit, I know stealing is bad but this is broken anyway and no one will know.

It tastes nice. Better than the cakes my mum makes. She'd like this cake, I wonder if she really has left me. It's too late now, I'm having my own day to myself. Dad says that sometimes, that he wants some time to himself. I'm having some time to myself, if they can, so can I. There's a man outside, he's looking inside the train, I'd better hide behind these bags. I bet that witch has sent him, she really wants to eat me, she must be hungry, if I gave her this cake it might make her not hungry no more, no it's a trick, she put this cake here!

That old train is back again, I can see the smoke. When this man has gone I'm going to try and see if I can get inside it. If I run quickly no one will see me. He's gone inside another part of the train now, I'd better run before he comes back again. I can see the smoke and the train is hissing again, running through people's legs. Sorry! The man I bump into says something bad, dad says that sometimes when he's watching football. That man isn't very nice!

I can see her! I can see her pink hair! She's still looking for me. Oh no! She's running, she must have seen me, I have to get on that train quickly or she'll catch me. There's policemen over there but if I go and talk to them they'll just call mum and then I won't be able to have time to myself. I can see another boy in front of her, he's holding his mum's hand. She wants to eat someone else now, she doesn't want me. I should warn him, he doesn't know she's a witch, some kids are stupid like that. She's got on the same doors as them! She's definitely going to eat him now!

I can see the boy through the window and I can see the lady sitting next to him and his mum. I have to do something or he might get eaten or he'll become a frog! Tap, tap! The boy looks at me and I point at the witch.

He looks at me like I'm crazy. The doors make that funny sound they make when they're closing. The witch is standing up and she's waving and pointing at me, she knows I know! She must be getting angry! The train is moving away. At least she never caught me, but that little boy is in trouble now!

I run again, through all the legs of people. There's lots of policemen, I wonder what they are doing? I run past the first bit of the train and jump in through the door and hide between two seats, just in case she stops that train and comes back for me. Wow! This train is really old, it's like that one in the book I read. I wonder how old it is? All the seats are brown and made of wood. I hope the train doesn't leave because I don't know where it will go, I don't want to get lost! These seats are not very nice, they make my bum sore.

There's a man over there, I didn't see him when I got on. He's got one of them big hats on that they used to wear in olden times. Our teacher showed us a picture of them once. He's got all black on as well, with a big stick. Why's he on here? He looks like he's really old. He's not moving, maybe the witch put him on here and he's going to catch me!

"Come here, young man, I want to ask you something."

"Did the witch put you here?"

"Witch? There's no such things as witches my dear boy!"

"I saw one on the platform, she had pink hair and she got on another train and she's going to eat another boy but he doesn't know!"

"Pink hair?! How odd. You have quite an imagination young man! Where are you going? The train should be leaving soon. Are you evacuating?"

"Am I what?"

"Evacuating?"

"I don't know what that means, sorry!"

"The war! They're sending all the children out to the countryside. Where are they sending you? You really will love it out there, all the fresh air and the animals. You won't want to come back when this accursed war is finally over."

"I don't know what you mean?"

"Hmm, you are strange little fellow. Where are your brothers and sisters?"

"I don't have any, I'm an only child. Mum said one's enough. Where are you going?"

"I'm going to see my sister who lives in the countryside. I've not seen her for a number of years, I hurt my leg and I'm unable to fight."

"Fight who?"

"The more I talk to you, the odder you become."

"My mum and dad went to see my nan and they left me at the train station, I think they wanted some time to themselves. I'm a big boy now though so I'll be okay."

"That's terrible! You've been abandoned? We must do something about this before the train leaves."

"No! They're coming back."

"Are you sure?"

"Yes! Dad will get drunk and swear at nan and then they'll come home on the train like they always do. Mum won't talk to him for one week and then dad will buy her something and then she'll be happy."

"Well, it's been lovely talking to you young man but I have to go."

"You said you were taking this train to see your sister."

"Did I? Not today, perhaps tomorrow. Take care!"

He's walks along the train and then goes out the door. I run up to the window to see if I can see him but he's disappeared. Where did he go? Maybe he went further up the train, some people don't like children so maybe he didn't like me. He was a little bit strange but he wasn't like the witch he looked like he was a kind man. I wonder who he was going to

99

fight? I'm going to ask my teacher when we get to school on Monday, she will know, she knows everything. I want to have a look at the front of the train, just one look.

There's no one outside, just a man cleaning but he doesn't look like he cares. I run up to the front. That man isn't on the train, I looked in every window. He must have gone to get another train. It's so big! It's shiny too. I wish I had a camera but dad has got it. When I'm older I want to drive a train like this. I'll take it everywhere, all over the country, maybe take it to some other countries. I can wave at people as I pass and they'll wave back.

My friend at school said he wants to be a postman when he grows up but I told him that was a rubbish job. All they do is walk around every day putting letters in people's doors. That's not much fun. He said his dad is a postman and not to call it a rubbish job and then we had a fight but we made up the next day and he's my best friend again now. If he becomes a postman I don't think I'll be his friend anymore though. When I'm a train driver I won't have any time to be his friend I'll be too busy.

I want to go to the toy museum but I don't know how to get there, I just know it's near the station, that's what dad said. He went there when he was a little boy with his mum and dad. He told me once where it was, he said you go out of the station and then you turn right and you keep going. I'm sure that's what he said. He wouldn't lie to me. I can still see lots of policemen, maybe I should tell them that my mum and dad have left me, no if I tell them that then I won't be able to go to the museum.

If I turn left here and keep going I should get to it. I don't know what it looks like though, museums all look the same, I'll know when I get there, it'll be big and there will be lots of people outside waiting to get inside. There's a big road just down here, I hate crossing the road, I've never crossed a big road on my own, I hope I don't get run over, if I get run over then I'll never get to the museum and mum and dad will be angry at me for not looking properly. I'll cross when this man crosses, he looks like he knows how to cross the road.

The buildings all look like houses but there are shops at the bottom of them. There are lots of buses too, I'm a little bit scared of the big red buses because they're so big and I'm scared one of them will hit me.

There's a restaurant, I'm hungry but I've not got any money. Oh, my pound coin! I forgot about it! I think it's an Italian restaurant we learned that in school, I can see the flag, green, white and red. My teacher said Italian people like to eat pizza, I don't really like pizza but I can't see anywhere else to eat. There's a man standing outside and he's holding something, I think it's a menu, I can have a look, what if it's in Italian? I don't know Italian.

"Excuse me, can I see your menu please?"

"Uhmm, okay, you want to look for your mum and dad?

"No, just me. I'm hungry."

"Where's your mum and dad?"

"They're coming in a minute."

I don't like to lie but sometimes you have to tell a lie. I told the teacher once that the dog ate my homework but we don't have a dog and really I didn't do it because I couldn't be bothered. It was a boring homework, maths, I hate maths. She said I shouldn't tell lies but I said the dog really ate my homework and that he died after he ate my homework and then I started to cry so she said it doesn't matter and I could do the homework another time. This man has a moustache and nan says you can't trust a man with a moustache so I think it's okay to tell him a lie because he's probably going to lie to me.

"They'll eat with you?"

"Yes, they'll come in a minute. They are crossing the road, look..."

I pointed at a man and a lady crossing the road. I don't know who they are and they don't look nothing like my mum and dad but this man don't know.

"You want to come inside and wait for them? It's hot out here."

"Yes, okay!"

The table is big. When them people don't come in the restaurant the man is going to get angry and I think he'll throw me out, he's gone somewhere else though, maybe he'll forget about me. A lady asks me what I want and I tell her I want a big pizza even though I don't like it because I don't know what else there is to eat, all the things on the menu have funny names and I don't know what they are.

"A big pizza?"

"Yes, a big pizza."

"Where are your parents?"

"They are eating somewhere else, they'll come and pay when I've finished."

"Are you sure?"

"Yep, I promise."

"Okay, a big pizza."

On another table there is man who is really fat. He looks like he's already eaten ten pizzas. There's a lady sitting with him and she is really skinny. If they have a baby I wonder if it will be fat or skinny? It might have a fat body and skinny arms and legs then it would look really strange. The skinny lady keeps shouting at the man like she is angry and everyone keeps looking at them. I think she's telling him he is eating too much and when they have a baby it will be a strange looking baby and so she's angry. I think he should eat more because a baby like that would be funny.

There's an old man and he's drinking something from a white cup. His nose is really pointy and his fingers look funny. He is really old, like older than my nan and she's really old. If I get old like my nan and this man I think I'd try and find someone to make me look young again because when you're old you get a little bit ugly. Dad said nan is a hag, I don't know what a hag is but I think this man might be a hag as well.

"Are you sure you're parents are coming in here when you're finished because if they don't you'll be in big trouble you know?"

"Yes, they will. Why do you keep asking me? I promised you."

There's a big pizza in front of me. I won't be able to eat all of that, there's too much. I might save some and bring it to school and give some to my friends, I know they all like pizza. There's mushrooms on it, I hate mushrooms, I'm going to have to pick them all off. Maybe that fat man would like to eat my mushrooms when I'm finished. The pizza doesn't taste very nice, I only have two bites. I put the mushrooms on a plate.

"Excuse me mate, do you want some of my mushrooms? You look like you might still be hungry."

The skinny lady starts laughing but the man turns red and starts shouting so I run. I have to remember to turn left when I get out the door. Turn left, turn left. The man at the door reaches out his arm but I'm too small and he misses, he starts shouting and then he starts running. If I go down this alleyway he won't be able to find me. When we play hide and seek no one can ever find me. I need to find somewhere to hide. There's a big rubbish bin there in the corner, I'm a good climber too.

I can hear people walking about but they're not talking in English, it's just a funny sound. I want to start laughing because I know they are looking for me. This rubbish bin smells, there's loads of old food in here, now my clothes are all dirty. The voices go away and I climb back out of the bin. I think I remember which way I came from. The museum can't be that far away, dad said it was about 10 minutes down the road. That means it's about 20 minutes for me because dad has really long legs and he walks really fast.

I walk against the wall and look out onto the big road. The man isn't outside the restaurant anymore, I think it's okay for me to go. I didn't even like the pizza, the man shouldn't have got angry! There are big houses now, really big houses, not like where we live. We live in a flat and it has two bedrooms, these houses probably have a hundred bedrooms and ten kitchens and I bet they have their own cinema as well. I wish we could live in a house like these ones. I wonder who lives in them? I bet it's a really rich person.

If I had a house like that I would buy everything from the shop. We went to this big shop in Oxford Street once, I think it was Oxford Street, where all the big shops are, and all they sold was toys. Everywhere was toys, every toy you could think of. I'd buy the whole shop and then I'd put it all inside one of these big houses. I'd never get bored then, I wouldn't have to go to school either because I'd be rich and you don't need to go to school if you're rich because you've got so much money it doesn't matter.

I'd buy my mum a cleaner. Like a lady that comes and cleans up your house because she's always saying the house is messy. I don't think it's messy but she wouldn't be able to say it was messy if there was a lady who cleaned it all the time. She wouldn't have to cook anymore either because the cleaning lady could cook too. She could drink wine all day then, at night time sometimes she drinks wine and then she's happy, so if she drinks wine all the time she'd be happy all the time.

Dad says that if he had one wish in life he'd get rid of nan. So if I was rich I'd buy a robot and it'd go to nan's house and make her go away. It'd tell her, if she doesn't go away it'll shoot her and then she'd definitely run away. I think dad would be happy then. I wouldn't have to go to her house no more and eat cabbage or them stupid biscuits either and me and dad could play football in the garden all day because he'd be happy without nan and he wouldn't have to go to work no more.

Oh! I'd buy my friends loads of toys as well, whatever they wanted. They wouldn't have to go school either because on of their friends is rich and I would buy them everything they want. I wouldn't buy that little girl Sally nothing though because she pulled my hair once and said that I was an idiot. I would make her stand outside my house and watch us all play with my toys and then I'd wave to her outside and she'd be really sad because she wouldn't be able to come in and then she'd have to go to school on her own and she'd have no friends.

I don't think this museum is here because I've been walking for 20 minutes and there's no people waiting anywhere. Maybe I should go back, I think I might be lost or I went the wrong way. All I can see are big white houses. That house over there has loads of toys in the window, that might be it, maybe the museum looks like a house and not like all the other museums. There's a little boy in there playing as well. The door is shut though. If I ring on the bell someone will probably let me in, that little boy might open the door.

"Can I play with the toys as well?"

"Okay."

The room is really big and there are loads and loads of toys. The little boy is playing with a ball, I run around with him trying to catch it when he throws it in the air and he starts laughing every time I dive on the floor. I wonder where his mum and dad is? They might have gone to see his nan and left him here on his own.

"Has your mum and dad gone to see your nan as well?"

"My mum and dad are in France. The nanny looks after me when they go away. How old are you?"

"I'm eight, how old are you?"

"I'm eight too. The nanny always goes to sleep in the afternoon so we can do what we want."

His nan must live with him. My nan wouldn't be able to live with us. Mum said to dad once that she should come and live at our house but dad said 'over his dead body.' I got a bit scared because I thought they was going to kill dad. I don't want nan to come and live with us if it means that dad has to die, I'd have to eat cabbage all the time and my dad would be dead.

"How old is your nanny? My nanny is really old, she's like 57."

"My nanny is only 23."

His nanny is only 23? Wow she must have been really young when his mum and dad was born, his mum and dad must only be like 12 or something. I wish my mum and dad were only 12, then they'd be like a big brother and sister not like a mum and dad. I've always wanted a brother or sister. I wonder why his nan has taken him to the museum? My nan only takes me shopping and then spends all the time talking to her friends because she says everything is really expensive now.

"We have a swimming pool, would you like to see it?"

"Really?! I have a swimming pool but you have to blow it up with your mouth and there's a hole in it because dad fell on it once when he was drunk."

"Oh no, this is a proper swimming pool. Have you any swimming trunks?"

"No. Is this your museum? Do you own it?"

"Museum?"

"I wanted to go to the museum about toys."

"No, it's not a museum, it's my house."

Wow! His house is a museum. I think he just doesn't want to say because then it might make me jealous that he lives in a museum.

His swimming pool is massive! It's like the one that they take us too at school but there's no one else there. There's no old ladies swimming really slow and there's none of the older kids trying to push us in. He's given me some swimming trunks too. I jump into the pool and swim about and then pretend I'm drowning, the boy laughs at me.

"Don't be too loud or the nanny will wake up and she'll shout at me!"

His nanny must be worse than mine. I don't really want to meet her.

"We can play hide and seek! You have to be really quiet though."

This museum is a bit rubbish if you can't make much noise. Last time we went to a museum with the school and one of the boys in my class touched some bones and they broke. The teacher went crazy and the man that worked for the museum started crying. Then everyone else picked up some old clothes and put and them on and we all pretended that we lived in olden times. The man at the museum cried even more and shouted at the teacher. Then that weird boy that nobody likes went to the toilet in a hat and the man that worked for the museum put it on and everybody laughed and he tried to jump out the window but they called the police. We don't go to museums no more.

"Five, four, three, two, one, ready or not here I come!"

He told me to be quiet but I can hear him, he's really loud. This place is really big, there's lots of bedrooms, some people must sleep in the museum. There aren't much toys neither, most of them are downstairs where the boy was playing. I didn't ask him his name, I should ask him. I hope he doesn't have a funny name. There's a boy in school and his name is Jesus. Mum says Jesus all the time. The boy says his name ain't Jesus but that's how it's spelled. He's got long hair as well so he looks like Jesus, dad said I should I bring him around and he could turn mum's water into wine but I don't really understand what he meant, I don't think anyone can do that.

This bedroom looks like a good place to hide. There's no light on so I better turn it on, I don't want to break anything. There's all these strange things in here, they look like that time we went to London Dungeon. There's these big long things on the wall that you hit people with and there's that thing where people put their head in a hole and their arms too and then they close it and the person is stuck. There's a big black suit on the wall as well. Maybe London Dungeon lends this museum stuff sometimes. There's a box over there I could hide in that.

I think when he finds me I should go home, they might have come back from nan's already. He's taking a long time, when I'm finding someone it usually only takes a few minutes. I wonder if that witch ate that little boy and if that man caught his train? That man was a little bit strange, he looked like he might be a ghost or something. I can hear the boy opening the door, it must be the boy because there's no one else here, maybe it's his nanny.

"Are you in here?"

I jump out of the box to scare him and he jumps and starts laughing.

"You shouldn't be in here, this is mum and dad's special room, I'm not allowed in here, usually it's locked."

"I think your mum and dad went to London Dungeon and borrowed some of their stuff. Maybe they was going to give you a surprise when they come back."

"Oh, Jesus Christ! Cuthbert! What on earth are you doing in here?! And who the hell is that little boy?"

"He's my friend, he knocked on the door and I let him in."

"I've told you, you can't let strangers into the house. Get out of this room this instant, if your mother and father finds out you've been in here I'll be on the first plane home."

"What's that black thing that looks like a man?"

"It's just a toy, now come on out."

107

"Can I play with some of these toys? Please, Camilla?"

Cuthbert picks up one of them long black things you hit people with and he pretends to hit me and we both start laughing.

"No you can't play with them, Cuthbert, put it down. They're special toys and only mummy and daddy can play with them now out!"

His nanny looks really angry and she really is only 24. I don't know why he can't play with his mum and dad's toys if they're both really young, I think that's really unfair.

"Who are you little boy? Where do you live? I bet you're one of those kids who live across the road aren't you? We've told you before you're not allowed in here. Last time you came Cuthbert was traumatised and they had to put him through therapy. Now, out the door and go home, if I ever see you here again I'll be going straight over to your parents."

Cuthbert looks really sad as I leave, he waves to me through the window. I need to go back now. The museum was better than I thought it would be but some of the toys were a little bit strange. I'd better be careful when I'm walking past that restaurant in case that man is waiting outside. I hope he didn't call the police. If he called the police I'd get arrested and then mum and dad would be really, really angry with me.

I'm so hungry now, I'm tired as well, I really want to go home and lie in my bed and go to sleep. I hope when I find them they don't want to go shopping first or something because I don't think I'll be able to walk anymore or my legs will probably fall off. The man isn't outside the restaurant, I need to walk quickly so that nobody sees me. I can see the fat man is still in there, he must live in there and eat all the time. I only wanted to give him some mushrooms, I was just being kind.

When I go to school on Monday I can't wait to tell my friends all about this. They won't believe me but I will make them believe me. Some of my friends think I'm a baby because I believe in witches, but I saw one today, a real one. She had pink hair so she must be a witch and she wanted to know where my mum and dad was so she could eat me and then she followed that boy onto the train and shouted at me so she was definitely a witch, I don't care what they say, I saw one.

I wonder if Cuthbert is okay? He lives in a museum, he can be my new friend, I'll go and knock at his house again and see if he can come out to play. His nanny seemed angry but I bet next time she won't be so angry, she's like my nan when she wakes up, she gets all angry with people but she doesn't mean it, but if it's my dad then I know she means it. Cuthbert can come to my house and dad can fix the swimming pool because he broke it. I think Cuthbert would like my swimming pool.

I can see the station now. There's still lots of people about, there's lots of policemen as well, I've never seen this many policemen. I cross the road with a man and walk towards the doors of the station. One of the policemen points at me! Oh, no! They know I told a lie to the man at the restaurant and that I didn't pay for my food. I better run, but there's more policemen at the door, they're going to catch me and I'm going to get arrested. I hope they don't tell my mum and dad, what if I go to prison?

The policeman is looking at a picture and then at me.

"And where have you been young man?"

"I went to the museum, I didn't go to the restaurant, it was a boy who looked like me, I don't know his name but he told me."

"Museum? Your mum and dad are waiting for you inside the station. You have no idea the trouble you've caused today little man. Come on now, your mother's worried sick."

Something must have happened to nan. Why would they be so worried, maybe dad really did go and drink beer and then go and fall in front of the train.

"Is my dad alive?"

"What? Of course, he's waiting in here for you."

Mum is crying but when she sees me she runs over to me and hugs me, dad comes over too but he looks a bit angry.

"Where have you been? Where did you go? We've been worried sick looking for you all day."

"I went to look at the trains and then I sat on the old train with an old man that looked like he was from the olden times and then I went to museum and then I played with my friend Cuthbert whose mum and dad have some toys from London Dungeon."

"Who's Cuthbert and what museum?"

"The toy museum."

"That museum has been closed for years and years. You know you shouldn't wander off like that, we've told you so many times. I've been so, so worried about you, don't you ever do something like that again."

"Do we still have to go to nan's?"

"No, we're going home, mummy needs to drink some wine."

I don't know why they're saying the museum isn't there anymore, it is, I saw it, Cuthbert lives there. I think mum thinks Cuthbert isn't real. Dad hasn't said anything but I can tell he's angry. They shouldn't have left me on my own. I don't care, I had the best day ever and I made a new friend!

Edgware Road – Danny Boy

Edgware road, home to Church Street market and Phyllis Hogan for many years

Bacon, sausages, black pudding, white pudding, friend potatoes and the Racing Post. The smell of a Saturday morning in the flat looking over Church Street market. She looks through the horses as she pours a cup of tea. Lucky Number 13, she doesn't fancy him very much, form is poor. The Minute Man, looks like he has a chance, a couple of quid on him, that's one. Easy Goer, he looks good as well, that's two. One more for her three horses of the day. Samson's Locks, no chance. Danny Boy, 150-1, not got a chance but she can't leave him out with a name like that.

She'll have to remember to get something for the dinner tomorrow as well. They'll all be there, all four of her sons. They're the light of her life, and now some of them have moved away she looks forward to every chance she gets to be together with them. Her grandchildren too, she's always excited to see her grandchildren. She looks in her purse to see how much money she has. Enough to slip them twenty quid when their fathers aren't looking, loving see the smile on the child's face as they think about how they're going to spend their new found riches.

She wipes down the table as she waits to put the food on the table. One of her sons comes in the door with her grandson. She puts the plates of food on the table and leaves them to eat their fill. She looks out the window as she drinks her tea and smokes a Silk Cut. She's thinking of all the things she needs to get done this morning. She looks over at the table as they talk about the football. That child's clothes aren't thick enough, he'll die of hypothermia she thinks to herself.

"Will you put some more clothes on that poor child before he catches the pneumonia and you'll be taking him to the hospital."

"It's July mom! I'm taking him to play football, he'll be running around, you worry too much."

"Will you be back for dinner?"

"He's staying with us tonight so we'll be back. You going down the Admiral this afternoon? Maureen will be in there, we'll pop in there after we've been to the park."

"Will you put these horses on for me? Where did you see Maureen?"

"Just seen her down Church Street."

"What was she doing down there? Talking to people I suppose. What did she say?"

"She didn't say anything, just that she'd be down the pub later and I said I'd tell ya."

"I'll go down for a half when I've done the shopping and the racing is on. Make sure you keep that child warm, don't come complaining to me if he gets sick."

"He'll be fine! Which horses you backing?"

"Minute Man, Easy Goer and Danny Boy."

"Are you mad? Danny Boy? He's got no chance! 150-1 ain't he?"

"Just put it on, I'll buy you a pint if he wins."

"Buy me a pint? You'll be rolling in it. You'll be smoking cigars and walking down Edgware Road with a fur coat on!"

"Haha! Will you behave you fucker! Take him to the park."

She puts on her coat, not a fur coat, and heads out to do her shopping.

Saturday mornings in the market. Fruit stall owners shouting, trying to get people to buy their fruit and veg. The best fruit and veg in the market, no one else comes close. They laugh and joke with the people walking by, hoping their charm will make the punters come and have a look at their just ripe bananas and fresh strawberries.

Kids walk down the street hand in hand with their mothers, looking bemused and excited at the Saturday morning rush. Wanting to go and have a look at the toys on the stall, their mother not so keen. The child not looking where he's going knocks a punnet of strawberries to the floor and gets a clip around his head for his clumsiness. The mother reluctantly pays for strawberries she won't eat because she'd never eat anything which has been on the floor, especially that floor. The child scowls as they move off down the market.

The door to the pubs still not open. A few people wandering around eagerly check their watches, still 10 minutes to go. They don't want to look too eager but time is moving too slowly and they want to get their Saturday revelry started. One sits on the bench outside the pub, running his hand through his white hair. The only cure for his hangover from last night is another pint, the tea and breakfast he's already had just made him feel worse. The smell of the fruit and the veg lingers in the air, fresh fruit or the smell of stale beer, he knows which he prefers.

She waves at him, he waves back but he's not as full of chat as he will be later once he's had a few. Then the chat will really flow. He's been around for years but she doesn't know him well, just one of those people you see about, Sunday mornings at mass or Saturday afternoon in the pub. She always buys him a pint but he's never bought her a drink for all the years he's been around. It doesn't bother her though, buying him a pint is probably doing him more good than lighting a candle for him in the church.

The butcher is standing outside of his shop. Business isn't too good today, he waves at her. She doesn't want to go in. She had a bad bit of beef from him there last week but she likes him and she'd rather avoid him than tell him his beef was shite. She waves at him and points towards the supermarket, his face drops, wondering what he's done to earn such treatment, it'd never be because his meat is no good. Must have caught her on a bad day.

The first race is soon, the betting shop is packed but she wants to watch it. Easy Goer in the first race. Should come in, the one she's most confident about. Opening the door the smell of smoke hits, she winces, nothing worse than a betting shop on a Saturday morning for smoke. All the punters studying their newspapers intensely, looking through the form, looking for that one horse which is going to make their Saturday a better one. Their wages are burning a hole in their pockets and where better to put out that fire than the early race?

Two men are looking up at one of the screens, a dog race. They talk to each other in hushed tones, one of them has a tip, dead cert, the dog can't possibly lose. The other man has put his faith in someone he hardly knows. He watches up at the screen as the dogs fly around the track, the dead cert is in the lead, this is it, he's going to win, what a start to the day! The first man has a smug look on his face as if to say 'I told you he was going to win'. The dog starts to lose his early pace, another one begins to come around on the inside, it's going to win, the dead cert is finished, didn't have enough in him.

The self-proclaimed tipster slips out the door, he won't be back again for a while, when he does come back he'll have another dead cert, can't lose, he knows the trainer and it's one of the best dogs he's ever had. The man who put his faith in him throws the slip on the floor, he should have known, there's too many of these tipsters about, why'd he listen to him? He lights up a cigarette, pulls out his pen and begins to write something on a new slip, this one definitely won't lose, the fella in the paper said so.

Phyllis looks for the screen showing her race. Excitement is gathering, not for her, she just likes to watch the races, if it wins it's a result, if it loses, well then she's only lost a couple of quid.

"What are you backing in the race?"

"Easy Goer."

"I'll put a few quid on him too, so."

The man in the flat cap takes out a roll of notes and starts to count them in front of her, a hundred pounds. He'd better win! He writes up his slip and walks up to the counter, putting the money and slip down with the confidence of a high roller, someone who should be making a living in Vegas. He's not in Vegas though, he's in Church Street, just off the Edgware Road. The woman at the desk takes the money, not impressed, she's seen it all a million times before. There aren't any high rollers here.

A loud shout goes up, a newspaper and a pink slip thrown on the floor, a young looking man has lost his cool. You can't do that if you're going to be a high roller, he storms out of the shop, wondering how he's going to explain to his wife why the wages he got yesterday are nearly all gone. No one takes any notice, it's not an unusual sight. She watches him leave in a rage, feeling sorry for him, if only he'd put down a couple of quid like her, he could have smiled and then gone home, not having to worry how he'll eat for the rest of the week.

The race starts, shouts go up, half the shop is on the same horse. This one is definitely a dead cert, it cannot possibly lose. He has a bad start though, shakes of the head, swear words thrown about, he's letting them all down, the jockey should understand what people have riding on this one. He starts to pick up pace and he's back with the leaders, excitement builds again, pats on the back, they knew he was going to come back, they should never have doubted him, he's got it in the bag here. More people gather around. The one man who backed the outsider who's in the lead clutches his betting slip nervously.

It's the last fence, the outsider just in the lead. The commentator's voice is getting louder and more excited, he wants the outsider to win. The crowd gathered around the screen start to shout, Easy Goer is going to win, just needs to get over this fence and they're all in the money. The man who's on the outsider closes his eyes, convinced his horse is going to fall, the shouts get louder the jockey pushing Easy Goer harder and harder, the massive hurdle in front of the two horses, there's only one outcome to the race now.

Down he goes, rolling on the floor in a ball. Shouts and swear words go up through the betting shop, he's blown it! He's fallen at the last! The outsider, the longshot, the one no one would ever put money on is in the clear, passing the finish line, the winner! Phyllis laughs, it was a good race, she enjoyed it. One man walks up to the counter to collect his winnings, walking out of the shop with a big smile on his face. He did really know one of the trainers, a tip worth its weight in gold, a happy man as he walks off down the market, looking forward to enjoying his pint. The rest of them go back to their newspapers and their betting slips, the next race will be the one where they make their fortune.

The pub is packed, Saturday afternoon regulars, people who only come out once a week, those who are never out of pub and those who came for a quick one after their shopping but are still here after another three or four, shopping bags on the floor, waiting to be forgotten and put behind the bar when their pissed owner forgets them when they stagger out the door. A group of four standing underneath the television, waiting for the next race, checking the football scores and their betting slips, just need a goal in Colchester and it'll be a good afternoon.

One fella sitting up at the bar can barely pick up his pint, someone pops their head around the door and looks over at him, the woman looks at the barman and shakes her head, don't give him anymore, look at the state of him. The drunk man starts a conversation with the person next to him but loses track of what he was saying after his first few words. He looks at the barman in confusion, as if the barman has the key to his mind, knew exactly what he was going to say. The man moves himself around in his seat, almost falling off. The barman snatches away his pint and replaces it with an empty glass. He won't know the difference.

Phyllis sits down at the table in the corner, her friends already there, one of them rushing up to the bar to get her half a pint. She'll only have one she says, she doesn't want more than one, she has to go home and cook the dinner. The man returns with the half pint and she sits there sipping it, content with the company of her friends. The drunk fella at the bar falls out the door, confused that his fresh pint has suddenly disappeared, the barman not willing to serve him anymore. She feels sorry for him, being sat at a bar all day is no life for anyone.

They have their own corner, split off from the rest of the younger ones who are either watching Des Lynham on Grandstand or deep in conversation. She watches the door hoping her son and grandson will be in soon. As she sips her pint, the warm glow the lager brings on makes her wonder if she should have another, just one more after this one and then she'll go home and cook the dinner. It's early yet, there's no need to be rushing, she can watch the second race here on the television. She shouts up to the barman to get another round in.

The door opens again and she turns her head, they've arrived, her grandson holding a football and a bag of sweets. He walks over to her sits down beside her, smiling. He doesn't say much, just smiles, he's shy. Danny, her son, goes up to the bar and buys a pint, a glass of Coke and a packet of cheese and onion crisps, giving the crisps to her grandson when he sits down. He puts them on the table, more interested in the big bag of sweets he has in his hands.

"Where did you go?"

"Just went down to the park, I told you we were going down there."

"The child looks freezing! Why didn't you put a jumper on him!"

"He's fine! He's been running around, look at him, he's sweating."

"Jesus! I'd be scared he'd catch a cold or something."

"Stop worrying about him."

"Did you put those horses on for me?"

"Yeah, of course I did. I've got the slip in my pocket."

"I went into the bookies to watch the first race, he fell at the last, I thought he'd won it."

"You're joking? Unbelievable, thought he'd win that one."

"There was a fella there in the bookies, he backed the winner. He'd a nice morning out! I'd say he's at some pub getting pissed!"

"Who was he?"

"Never seen him before."

"Wanker! Should have given you the tip!"

"I've never seen the man before in my life, why would he give me the tip!?"

"I was going to back him as well and I changed my mind. Oh well, never mind, the next one is on in a minute, reckon that one will come in. You want another drink?"

"No, no, I'll be going home now in a minute once the race is done."

"What you going home for? Have another drink!"

"Go on then, I'll have another half."

The barman turns up the television as the race is about to start. Heads turn towards the T.V, people trying to look cool, calm and collected, the race doesn't mean anything to them, if the horse loses it loses. Secretly they're saying little prayers, hoping it comes in, drinks will be on them, a good night will be had by all. An old man with no interest in it laughs as he surveys the pub, which one of these will be buying him a drink in fifteen minute's time. He hopes it's not the tight fella who wins a few quid, that'd never do! He'll just slip out the door, collect his winnings and be home to the wife. He won't tell her either.

The man with the disappearing pint staggers back in the door; obviously found somewhere else where they'd serve him. He's holding a betting slip, God forbid he wins a few quid, he won't be going home tonight then, more than likely to the hospital in the back of an ambulance to get his stomach pumped. He waves the slip in the air, he wants to let everyone know he's involved in this too, no one takes any notice of him. He sits down at the bar, the barman eyeing him up, he doesn't want the hassle of throwing him out, he hasn't ordered a drink, he'll let him sit and watch the race and then send him on his way.

"Which horse do you reckon will win this one, mate? Here, have a look at this paper quickly."

The young boy looks up and down the list of horses. The numbers mean nothing, the colours the jockey wears the most important thing. He points at one of them, the jockey wearing a red top with a black stripe down the middle. His father laughs, 150-1, no chance of that winning. He tells him he'll buy him another packet of crisps if it wins, some more sweets on the way home. He could run over to the bookies quickly and put a quid on it, you never know. Nah, it won't win, no chance, it's 150-1 for a reason.

The drunk is sitting quietly, his eyes fixed on television, mesmerised by the horses, a unique way to sober someone up. He turns around to grab a drink and then realises he doesn't have one, he looks pleadingly at the barman but he shakes his head, the drunk turns back to the television, he doesn't want to drink in here even if he was allowed, once the race is over he'll be off to somewhere he's welcome. His money is as good as anyone's. A drunk person's bitterness, never wrong, it's everyone else. He's just having some fun.

The small boy starts to get excited. He doesn't understand the horse he's chosen has no chance of winning. There are 10 horses in the race, all of them have a chance of winning why wouldn't his. Some more sweets on the way home would be nice. He watches his jockey and horse as they wait to start. He's going to win, he just knows it's going to come first. He taps his dad on the shoulder.

"Did you go and put money on him?"

"Yeah, mate, put a pound on him for you." His father lies, confident the horse will either come last or not finish the race.

"You'll be sorry if it wins it!" laughs Phyllis.

"It won't win, it's got no chance."

The horses start, the jockey in red and black predictably at the back. The boy feels disappointed, he was sure the horse would win, why has he started so slowly? He was going to tell all his friends at school how he had picked a horse at the weekend and it had won. His friends wouldn't care but he'd still tell them. He stops watching the television, his dreams of having a winning horse dashed after a few seconds, he starts to read a magazine his dad bought him instead, it's far more interesting than horses.

The Minute Man takes the lead, it looks like he's going to win, he's running well. If it wins she'll give a few quid to the boy, she can see he's disappointed his horse is looking like it will come nowhere.

"Looks like he's going to win this one."

"Lucky it wasn't the 150-1 shot, you'd be paying him out of your own pocket."

A shout goes up, the drunk man is on his feet. His horse is back in the race, a jockey wearing red and black emerges at the bottom of the screen and keeps moving towards the front. He's getting more and more animated, the barman is regretting his decision to not throw him out. The horse moves closer and closer to the front, the young boy looks up, frightened, the drunk man's noise taking his thoughts away from the football magazine he's reading. The horse pulls out in front, he's going to win, the 150-1 shot is going to win!

"He's going to win! I don't believe it!"

"You should have ran over to the bookies before the race!"

"It's a freak, how was I supposed to know he was going to win!"

"You'll have to give him 150 quid now.!"

"I can't give him 150 quid, what's he going to do with 150 quid! I haven't got 150 quid to give him. I'll get him something on the way home."

The horse passes the finishing line. The drunk man celebrates, the barman holds his hands in his head. He's going to have to throw him out in a minute. The old man in the corner is hoping the drunk is allowed to stay for one more drink, enough time to get a drink out of him. A few people decide the drunk isn't *that* drunk, he's just a bit excited, maybe had a few too many earlier but it looks like he's sobered up now. The barman shouldn't throw him out, they implore the barman to 'let him stay for one more, he's harmless'. They've always like him anyway.

The drunk holds his betting slip up in the air for all to see, doing a little jig, people laugh at him, a couple throw their arms around his shoulders, they buy him a drink even though the barman hasn't quite made up his mind yet. One of them says he should go and get his winnings now, otherwise he'll have to wait until tomorrow. The old fella in the corner is suddenly alive, coming to join in the congratulations, he'll go over to the bookies with him to collect the money. The drunk man throws his arm around him and the two new friends walk out the door.

"Did my horse win?"

"Nah mate, he came last."

"I thought the horse that won was wearing black and red."

"He did mate, but that was another horse, your one come last, he's a rubbish horse. You can pick another one in the next race."

"Oh! I thought he'd won, it looked the same."

"Wasn't him mate, it was someone else."

The boy knows it was him who won the race but he leaves it, content that he chose a winner, the money doesn't mean anything. He's not sure how much he would have won anyway, it probably wouldn't be a lot. He's relieved to see the drunk man walk out the door, no more noise from him, he hopes he doesn't come back. His nan gives him a packet of peanuts, he hopes she's going to stay for another few drinks, every time she says she's going to go home he hopes dad will buy her another drink. He feels safe when she's around and she makes him laugh.

The drunk man comes back in the door, his face beaming, he's the toast of the pub after his winner, he buys a drink for everyone, even the barman, his generosity is rewarded by being allowed to stay in the pub. A winner and he's not been thrown out, it's been a good day indeed. The old man settles back into his corner, pint on the table, he'll just sit there for the evening watching the world go by, he won't get drunk, just enough that the body is warmed, when they're pissed enough he'll get one of them to get him a whiskey and then he'll go home to bed.

Danny gets another round in, his mother will stay for one more, and probably one more after that. The last race is in an hour's time, she might as well stay now. The drunk man comes over to join them but he's given a cold shoulder, curt congratulations, he thinks he's star of the show but people's patience has already started to wear thin. 'Take your congratulations and go home to your bed and sleep off the drink' is a thought shared by all. He doesn't take the hint, he can't see the hint.

The woman who popped her head around the door before does so again, she rolls her eyes when she sees him. She knows she's going to have a job getting him home. She stands at the door wondering if it's worth even trying, someone will throw him out soon and that will be easier. She goes to the bar and orders herself a drink, retiring to a small corner where he won't be able to see her. She'll watch his ejection from the pub with pleasure, she had the lunch cooked and he didn't even come home.

The boys from the market stalls come in one by one. Tired from a day of shouting and enticing customers to buy their fruits and their vegetables. The stalls are put away and tomorrow is the one day of rest, time to let their hair down. Two of them grab the drunk and walk him out the door, he doesn't protest until they push him out on the street, he's brave when they're not near him. The woman in the corner smiles to herself, he hasn't got a key and he won't be able to get in, she'll have another couple here, let him sit it out for a bit.

A man with a leather jacket walks in the door, he goes up to the bar and orders a Coke, he doesn't drink, never has done, doesn't like the taste and he doesn't like to be out of control. Besides, his motor is outside and it's full of merchandise and he can't get stopped with that. He looks around the pub, looking to see who's there he knows, who would want to buy some of his merchandise. People are fussy sometimes, you give them a good deal but they don't want it, they always reckon they know someone else who can get it for cheaper.

"See if he's got any records for sale, he had a load of them last week."

"What do you want records for? You bought a load of them the other week and you ain't listened to one of them."

"Just see what he's got!"

"I'll ask him later."

"Who's that man, dad?"

"He's a crook. We'll wait until the last race and then we'll go home."

The boy sits and listens as they talk about people he doesn't know, trying to imagine who they are. They talk about back home and their sons and daughters who are married or are getting married. People he hears about every time he's in here but has never actually seen. He wonders if they really exist, or they must be very busy. For each person he conjures an image in his head. He's glad the drunk man has gone, he can relax, there's no need to worry if he'll come back and start trouble.

"Do you want to pick a horse for the last race?"

"Okay! Let me see the paper."

The boy looks through the list of names again. He studies the names and the numbers next to them, he still doesn't know what they mean but his confidence is high, he picked the winner last time and he wants to pick the winner again. The names are all strange and he doesn't like the colours the jockeys are wearing. The last name on the list is the same name as his dad, Danny Boy. He'll choose that one, it has to win.

"I'll go and put a fiver on it for you, I'll be back in ten minutes."

His nan ruffles his hair and goes to the bar to buy him another Coke and a packet of crisps. He hopes the horse wins but even if it doesn't win they'll stay in the pub until late. He likes it in here, the people are funny and he gets to drink as much Coke as he likes and eat as many packets of crisps as he can. His nan comes back to the table, she passes him a folded up twenty pound note and he puts it into his pocket, immediately thinking about what he can do with his new found riches. You could buy the whole sweet shop with twenty pounds!

The last race is about to start, less people are taking notice, the beer and the double rum and cokes are more important now. If their horse wins it wins, if it doesn't then so be it. The jukebox is on, Des has been drowned out.

"He'll come last, it's got no chance."

The horses are off, Danny Boy at the back, the race is over before it's even started, 150-1 for a reason. Two of the leaders fall at the first fence, he's got half a chance of placing now, the table begins to shout, laughing as they do, they don't believe it will win, you have to give him some encouragement though. He starts to move up the field, closer to the front two, he's in third place now.

"He could win this you know!"

The shouts mixed with laughter turn to shouts mixed in with belief and enthusiasm, he could win this! They approach the last fence, the two out in front clear the fence easily, Danny Boy just clears it, stumbling as he lands but keeping his balance, he's lost ground, it's all over now. The whole table groans, their few minutes of belief turns into disappointment. He starts to gather pace again, closing in on the leaders, not long to go, he surely can't make up the ground now can he? The three horses cross the line, nobody can tell who's won. Photo finish!

"I don't think he's won it, should have backed him each way."

The boy sits there, waiting anxiously with everyone else, he might have picked another winner. How long does it take? The result flashes up on the screen, it's too far away, no one can see it clearly.

"Go and have a look and see who's won, I don't think he won."

The boy runs up to the screen through the crowd of people.

"He's won!"

"He's won!", shouts and cheers go up around the table. Danny Boy has won! Drinks are bought, glasses are clinked together. Danny goes across to the bookies to collect the money, when he comes back he gives his son another twenty pound note.

"Don't tell your mother."

He really is rich now, forty pounds, imagine what could be done with that!

"Go on! Stay for another one!"

"I'll stay for one more, I'll be off home after that."

They sit around talking and laughing, remembering people who are no longer around and telling stories of what the market used to be like. Just one more is forgotten and the pints and half pints flow. Saturday afternoon turns into Saturday night, nobody knows what time it is and nobody cares.

"Sing us a song, Phyllis!"

She looks out through the window, as if remembering some long forgotten time and begins to sing, they all sit there listening and smiling, the night has just begun.

In loving memory of Phyllis Hogan, loving mother and grandmother whose home was Edgware Road and heart was in Dublin.

Marylebone – Tickets Please

Marylebone, home to Marylebone Station

Ticket machines are broken again, means a day standing around, looking stern and pretending to care whether people are paying their train fares or not. Got to look stern, if you don't look stern then they'll just walk all over you, like that Michael, he looks a bit like a clown, just needs one of them red noses. Always falling for the excuses he is: 'left my ticket on the train and now I can't find it','there wasn't anyone at the station', and then there's the ones who starting quoting the law and all that bollocks, like I'm stupid and don't know what I'm doing.

It's quiet so far, just standing here, watching an advertisement board go around and around. Some woman looking all moody, selling perfume or something. Why's she looking moody? That ain't going to make people buy it is it. There's a pigeon on top of the advertisement board, it keeps running along back and forth. There's another pigeon about to fly down and attack him now. Do pigeons even fight? Oh, he don't want to fight, his chest is all puffed out, looking for a missus it looks like. It's easy for animals ain't it? They just find an animal of the opposite sex and then that's it.

"Excuse me, where's the train for Aylesbury?"

"You'll have to wait ten minutes the train's not ready yet."

"Trains are always bloody late, when are you lot going to do something about it."

"10 minutes, that's all, and then it'll be ready and you can go to Aylesbury."

I say it with a smile, it annoys them even more. She walks off in a huff and sits down on a seat, looking around to see if anyone else wants to join in in her annoyance, there's no one else about though so she's sitting there looking all moody with no audience. Not my fault though is it, I'm just collecting the tickets, I can't make them run on time. One of the pigeons lands next to her feet, she kicks out at it but he jumps back then moves towards her again, she gets up and storms off. Only a pigeon. She might be pretty but I but she's right uptight and loves herself.

I wish I'd not spoken to him like that. It was a bit out of order, I don't usually talk to people like that. Oh dear, Katie! You have made a fool of yourself, that poor man was only doing his job. If I miss this bloody interview though, I don't know what I will do. I knew I should have left a little bit earlier and got on that early train. Be there nice and early Katie I told myself all week. God, you really do make a mess of things sometimes don't you. Although, it is their fault really, how bloody difficult would it be to make the trains run on time.

I suppose it won't be the end of the world if I don't turn up, it is rather far away and I'm not sure I'll be able to afford the fares. He's still bloody looking at me. I'll just find something a bit closer to home. You've been trying to do that for the last two months, Katie and you've found nothing. You're bloody useless sometimes, all you had to do was get out of bed a little bit earlier and you'd now be sitting on a train drinking a cup of coffee thinking about how wonderful life is. Why is there no one else around to join in my face pulling and sighing?

Oh God! He's looking over at me now, I'll just pretend to be even more pissed off than I actually am, that will make him feel guilty and then he'll look away. Hmmm, this pigeon in front of me, I actually quite like pigeons, one of the few people who do but I'm sorry Mr. Pigeon, this time you're going to have to be the fall guy for my little act. Shit, he's just dodged my kick and now he's coming back for more, how stupid do I look now? I'm never going to make this interview now, I'll just go and wallow in my shame and embarrassment in some coffee shop.

Going to have to start letting people through in a minute. They all seem to come at once, like they say about the buses but it's people. Just as the train's about to leave and they all suddenly appear, tapping their feet against the floor, looking at their watches even though there's a massive clock right in front of them. Their watch will be right though, not the big one. Once had a geezer get his phone out and ring the talking clock so he could say his time was right. They edge closer and closer to the barrier, looking at me huffing and puffing as I try to look somewhere else, pretend I'm not interested. The two pigeons are dancing around a couple of chips which are on the floor.

Look at the watch, give them something. Another two minutes. Been using one of them dating apps recently, just having a laugh and all that. Not been too successful really. They have to like you and you have to like them. I like everyone, better chances that way, gotta play the old numbers game. No one seems to like me though, that's the biggest problem. See, all they see is your face, what can they tell from your face? Nothing, don't matter if I'm not the best looking geezer in the world, I've still got something to offer. Not that I'm desperate or anything, just looking for some company, that would be nice sometimes.

So yeah, these dating apps, they ain't very deep are they? I mean, they're superficial, you just see a person's face and then you decide whether you like them or not. How's that supposed to make you find the love of your life. Probably ain't supposed to be like that though is it, just another way for someone to make money. Funny thing is, that other geezer, the one who looks like a clown, he's always off meeting birds from it. How can he get so many women while I'm sitting at home bored watching rubbish on television. The world's gone mental. I've got buckets of charm, just ask all these people who see me every day at this train station. Time to open the gate and put this lot out of their misery.

"Have your tickets ready please."

They push past me, throwing their tickets up in the air and pulling them back down so quickly most of them I can't see. I'll just leave it to the geezer at the other end. As the crowd thins out a man in skinny jeans and a ripped t shirt comes running up to the gate.

"Please, I need to get this train, let me get a ticket on the train or at the other end."

"You need a valid ticket to travel sir, I'm sorry, you'll have to go and get one."

"Please, mate, I really need to get on this train."

"Ticket office is just over there sir, if you run you might still catch the train."

We both look over at the ticket office, the queue tells us that he won't be able to catch the train.

"Wanker!"

He makes an attempt at running over to the queue but it's half hearted. I'll be seeing him when the next train is ready to go in about an hours time. Not my fault he dresses like an idiot.

Fuck's sake, I want him to see me going over to the queue because I'll be trying it again in a little while and I don't want him to go telling all his mates. Why would I be going to buy a ticket and lining the pockets of a massive corporation who has never done a thing for me. Sometimes it works, sometimes it doesn't, when it doesn't work I just try again. You've got to be clever about it though which is why I'm going to blend into this queue and then slip away. I don't know who these people think they are, on their power trips. If he'd let me through, it'd make no difference to his day.

I'm annoyed at having to be surrounded by all these smelly people. None of them are clever enough to be able to live for free like me, that takes real intelligence, not running to and from an office every day, doing everything which society wants you to do. No, people like me, well not people, just me, because I'm unique, I'm the one who is sticking their fingers up and making the world stop and listen. I can't wait to put this up on my blog later, something the world wants to see, not childish and stupid videos of cats.

"Excuse me, do you mind if I buy my ticket on the train? I've got the two kids with me and their pram and we're running late as it is."

"Of course you can, madame. Do you need any help getting on to the train?"

"Yes, that would be lovely thank you."

The pram is quite heavy, poor woman has probably been dragging this around London for the last few hours while the two kids she has drive her mad. One of them, a little boy, he looks like the antichrist, just one of them looks where you know a child is naughty. I can see him watching me, he's trying to think of something he can do to the strange man holding his mum's pram. He offers me a crisp from the little bag he's holding, I smile and shake my head, don't trust the little bastard. He looks gutted. His little sister hits the bag and they fall all over the platform, the boy stamps his feet and cries while the little girl runs around crushing the crisps with her feet. I put the pram on the train and give the boy a wave, he sticks his finger up at me and then gets a clip around the head from his mother.

Poor woman, I do often wonder what it would be like to have children. I've got to be quite honest with myself, I'm not sure I want them. People love to coo, and give it all that 'they're so lovely, don't he look like you.' And then all that 'he's so angelic'. Nah! They ain't, they just cause you grief with all their running around and shouting and causing you trouble. That would be my worst nightmare what just happened, I don't think I'd be able to take it. And to think she's probably taken them on a day out to the zoo or somewhere nice and now the little fuckers are ruining her day. Poor woman!

Works every time. A couple of kids and a pram is a ticket on the train for nothing. Just gotta hope the ticket inspector doesn't come on the train, if he does I'll just give him an excuse and he'll be fine with it. Not the brightest spark that one standing at the gate, he's the one you want to be looking for, so easy. The kids are nice and quiet now too, sitting in their seats with their colouring books, I love it when they do just as I ask them to. They'll make good little actors when they grow up, I'll give them both a bag of crisps for being such darlings!

This geezer that's been hanging around the platform for the last couple of hours is starting to raise my suspicions. He looks a bit funny. One of them people you just know is up to no good. He ain't got on a train and he doesn't look like he's getting on a train either. He just keeps walking up and down, occasionally going into the shops and then coming back out again with nothing. It's the way he's walking, head down, like he don't want anyone to see him, can't blend into the crowd when I'm around. I'll watch him for another bit and see what he's doing, there's a couple of coppers over there I'll let them know.

Last year, I was the hero. There was a big gang that was hanging around the station and they was pickpocketing people. I knew it straight away when I saw them. You know what I mean? You can just tell can't you. I don't know where they was from but they weren't from around England anyway. Probably from one of them eastern European countries. Romania or Poland I reckon, I forget now because the police did tell me. But, yeah, me the big hero, loved it I did, name was in the newspaper and everything. Pickpocketing Gang Foiled Due to Vigilence of Ticket Inspector. Should put that on my dating profile.

I ain't got a problem with foreigners, don't get me wrong, I ain't racist or nothing like that, I don't judge people by how they look, I definitely ain't one of them people. It's just it annoys me that they come over here and start robbing people and then you get some of them taking away our jobs, but they ain't really their jobs are they? I just think we should look after our own people and all that. I suppose some of them work hard but a lot of 'em don't do they? I mean they just want the benefits and so little Tomasz can go to school here because their own schools ain't no good.

Looking at this geezer, he does look a bit foreign. Might be one of them gangs back again. I ain't sure though, he's got dark hair and his skin is quite dark as well. They really do take liberties, why don't they go home and rob people? They wouldn't have it that's why, we're too soft. You go to jail and you're out in a couple of months, don't even send them home I bet, then they'll be bringing their mums and dads over and getting them nice little flats. Yeah, I reckon this geezer is part of one of them gangs, I'll let them two coppers know, could be in the papers again.

I wish this guy would turn up, he said he'd be here at 11 and it's gone 1 now. Every single time I end up waiting for him, it isn't the most inconspicuous of places either is it. I'm pacing up and down the concourse like a nutcase, there's a couple of coppers over there, I'm sure they'll be watching me as I've not even attempted to get on a train. This is the last time I'm doing this, it's getting stupid now, I said it last time but it really is the last time. I need to be back by four and by this rate it isn't going to happen.

Why does he always turn his phone off as well. I don't think I'm cut out for all this, I'm the world's most nervous person. When I get a missed call on my phone I'm automatically thinking the worst. Could it be the police? Or something has happened to someone close to me? Someone is looking for money off me perhaps, they want to blackmail me. I could go into the shop over there and read a magazine for a few minutes but I've already done that about five times, they'll think I'm trying to rob the shop.

Next train is in ten minutes, he'll surely be on that one. I've said that about the last five of them. My hands are all sweaty, I keep looking over at the coppers to make sure they're not looking for me, trying not to look suspicious. I've not done anything though, I'm just standing here waiting for someone, that's what I'll say if they come up to me, what can they do?

Nothing! I'll go and get another cup of coffee, by the time I've bought that the train will be pulling in and he'll definitely be on that one.

I'm sure the man who sells the coffee was looking at me like I was up to something. It was the way he took my money, like I was handing over dirty money or something. Idiot, should just be grateful he got any money from me at all. Why is that ticket inspector talking to those two coppers, I bet it's about me. There must have been an easier way to do this, he could have just sent it for God's sake. Finally he's here. Now I can get out of this place and home.

Turns out that geezer who was waiting around was doing anything wrong. Some geezer got off a train and handed him a package, I was watching him with the two coppers. I was telling them about that gang I stopped last year, didn't seem too interested for some reason. Anyway, the geezer handed him over a package, hardly spoke to each other and then he started to leave the station. First thing that's going through my mind is drugs, it's got to be drugs. Bit of a stupid place to be handing over drugs if you ask me.

So the two coppers stop him and I'm standing there, looking well pleased because I've stopped another crime from happening. They take the package off the geezer, who looks angry at this stage, I thought he was going to do a runner. Open up the package and it's full of sausages. All sorts of sausages they said, all weird flavours. The geezer said he likes them kind of sausages and the fella who got off the train was the only person he could get them off. Checked it out with the other geezer and he's some sort of pig farmer. What's he running about getting people to meet him at train stations for? I said they should have checked the sausages because there was probably drugs inside them but they didn't.

I'm telling you, he was suspicious that geezer, I know I wasn't wrong. I asked the coppers where he was from but they said he sounded like he was English. I'm not having that, good actors some of these people, they're good at conning people, I reckon he's come over and learned the accent and it's given him some kind of cover. Him and the other fella have got some kind of drugs factory in the countryside and they're bagging them up in sausages so it looks good.

I'd make a good copper me. I should have been one really, I did try but I failed a drugs test. I don't know how it happened. Never touched drugs

131

in my life, never will do, I ain't that kind of person, anyway I reckon someone saw how much potential I have and when we was down the boozer one night slipped something into my drink. Called me for a drugs test one day and told me I failed and that was it. It's unbelievable how jealous some people get ain't it? Never been the jealous type me, I just can't understand how some people's minds work.

Oh no! It's the missus come to bring me some lunch. I've told her plenty of time that I don't want her coming to work, it shows me up don't it. I can see the bag in her hand, it's going to be something I don't like, I know it. She never does me anything I like, it's going to be ham sandwich or something. I hate ham, ever since that time I was at school and some kid put a worm in my ham sandwich, never been able to eat it since, she knows that as well, just not very bright. I bet she wants some money or something.

"You all right, love? Bringing me something to eat?"

"Yeah, thought I'd bring you something, I finished work early."

"What did you bring me? You didn't have to do that."

"A couple of beef sandwiches, you can have them when you have a break."

"Okay, love."

"See you when you get home, make sure you ain't late either because my mother's coming around and she wants to talk to you about something."

"Talk to me about what?"

"You'll see when you get home. Now, I'll leave you to it."

Not her mother, anyone but her mother. She's mental she is, craziest woman I've ever met, she's never liked me either. Reckons I ain't good enough for her daughter so she just tries to make my life a misery. What could she want to talk to me about? I bet she's been looking through my phone and see them dating apps. I bet you that's what it is. Now what am I going to do? I'll have to think up an excuse, say I put them on there by accident and I only used them because I was curious. Yeah, they'll believe that. I ain't ever cheated on her or nothing, fucking hell, there could be a bit of aggro tonight if both of them are there. I might just get on one of these trains and go up north.

I bet his head is spinning at a thousand miles an hour right now wondering what my mother wants to talk to him about. She doesn't want to talk to him about anything I just thought I'd wind him up a bit. She is coming around for dinner though. Thing is, she really likes him, always has done, don't know why he thinks she don't like him. All he does is moan about her until they're together in a room and then they don't stop talking, sometimes I think he should have married her and not me. That'd be a bit funny though because he's about 30 years younger than her and I wouldn't want him as my dad.

Was speaking to that boy he works with, the one he calls a clown even though he's always taking him out for a drink after work and looking after him when he gets into any trouble. The boy was saying when he's at work, John, my fella won't stop going on about some Romanian gang of thieves he was supposed to have foiled. He stopped some kid, from nicking a woman's purse, I don't even think the kid was Romanian, he was from just around the corner. He doesn't half get carried away sometimes.

Thing is, he's got a good heart. He talks loads and loads of rubbish and he's always slagging people off but he ain't a bad person. Last year, he done a charity run for some orphanage in Africa. I said he'd never do it but he did, went out running every morning before work running, got really fit. He don't talk about it though, I don't understand, he tells everyone he stopped a gang of thieves that never existed but he won't talk about something good he's really done. I sometimes wonder why I married him but like I said, he's got a good heart even if he is a bit stupid.

I know he's been messing about on his phone with them dating apps. I find it funny. There ain't no one that's going to go out and meet him. If they do good luck to them because they'll take him off my hands for a night. He thinks I don't know, I bet he tells all his mates, giving it Billy Big Bollocks like he's some sort of Casanova or something. I might start dropping little hints, making him sweat a bit, that'd be funny. What I might do when he gets home tonight is delete one of the apps on his phone when he's gone to sleep. He'll be panicking all day at work tomorrow then.

Starting to get a bit busy now again, you get the people going home from work, live out in some nice commuter town somewhere. I wouldn't mind a little bit of that myself really, living out in a town, it'd have to have a river, I'd be able to do a bit of fishing, I love my fishing I do. I wouldn't like it to be too small either, if it was too small I wouldn't be able to live there, too quiet, I've grown up in the city all my life, I'd end up going mad and I'd kill the wife or something. I'm only joking, I wouldn't do that. That reminds me, I better delete them apps off my phone before I get home.

Yeah, growing up in the city. I don't think I'd have wanted it any other way. We wasn't poor or anything, we had enough to live on and all that, just sometimes it was a bit of a struggle. Funny how I've ended up working at Marylebone Station, when I was a boy I used to come down here and watch the trains with one of my mates. We used to write the numbers down and everything, wish we'd had a camera, bet you could sell them pictures these days. Put it on EBo or whatever it is you call it.

I remember one day, a Saturday it was, we said we was going to go down to Gary Lineker's house on Abbey Road. We planned it all out. Mum wouldn't let me walk that far away so I told her we was going to play football down on the Lisson Green Estate. Another kid in our class had told us the address, said that Lineker definitely lived there and if you went and knocked on he's door he would give you his autograph. I even bought a bottle of water for the walk, just in case we got thirsty. My mate had got all dressed up in his England kit, we was right happy.

"If you ain't got a ticket, sir, you're going to have to pay the fine. If you talk to that gentleman over there he'll tell you what you have to do. I'm not going to argue with you, I don't have the time, you can see we're very busy."

So there we were walking along Abbey Road, past that zebra crossing where The Beatles took that photo. One of the tourists spotted him in his England kit and made him walk across the crossing with her while her mate took a photo, me following behind. We thought we was a right pair of little superstars. We get to this road which we think Lineker lives on and find the house it's supposed to be. We spent about an hour arguing about who was going to up and knock on the door. My mate said if I didn't do it then he was just going to go home so I went and knocked on the door.

Wasn't even Lineker's house was it? It was just some old woman with a big dog. I just stood there like an idiot, she got the hump and set the dog on us, jumping over fences we was, trying to get away from the dog. The dog caught my mate and bit his England shirt. Gutted he was, started crying all the way home. That made up for it a little bit because he didn't think he was a superstar no more. Still hate Lineker though, I can't watch Match of the Day, geezer's smug face does my head in, like he's looking at me saying you went to find my house and you knocked on the wrong door you idiot. Worst thing was that other kid come in on the Monday with his autograph, reckon he just sent us to the wrong place.

State of this geezer who's just got off the train. He's wearing skin tight clothes and them black leather trousers. He's got to be gay ain't he? You can't walk around like that and not be gay. I had a mate who was gay once but I don't talk to him no more. I reckon he fancied me and he couldn't take the rejection. I didn't have nothing against him, people can do what they want, but you don't have to go flaunting it in public do you? I don't know, the world's changed, you never really saw all that nonsense when I was a kid.

Don't get me started on these geezers that think they're women either. Gotta be something wrong upstairs with them. I put a dress on once when I was a little boy, one of my sister's did my face up in her make up as well. Not because I thought I was a girl or anything though, just thought it'd be funny, I was posing in the mirror and my sister walked in. She blackmailed me because of that, used to make me clean up her room and make her things to eat because she said she'd tell all my mates. But yeah, them people definitely something wrong with them.

"Sorry mate, you couldn't tell me how to get to Baker Street could you?"

"Yes mate, out the door and turn left and then straight down the road, you can't miss it. About 10 minutes away."

"Thanks."

Did he just call me mate? See, I didn't think they talked like that, I always though they talked a bit funny, that geezer I knew did anyway. One of them funny voices, like they're telling you they're gay or something. Wonder what he's going to Baker Street for? I bet he's going to one of them orgies or something. I heard they like an orgy. Wouldn't be my type of thing that, not a gay orgy, just, like a normal people's orgy. I suppose if they're keeping it behind closed doors it can't do any harm can it. An orgy hey? Things people get up to.

I can't wait to get home and get out of these stupid clothes. I knew I shouldn't have warn them home but I couldn't be bothered to get changed. Decent job though, got some good money for it. Life is pretty good at the moment and I can't complain, especially having a new flat so central. Get home, change my clothes, put my feet up, have a beer and watch the football I think. I don't think Paul will be home until late this evening he said he's got something to do in the office, be nice to have a bit of time to myself.

I do have to laugh to myself. You get these roles as a gay man, and they still get you to dress up in all these clothes as if it has to be pointed out to the world that a character in a T.V show is gay. You'd think in 2017 it wouldn't matter but obviously it still does because we're portrayed as different. Now I'm fannying around in central London in clothes I'd never wear in a million years. Not that there's anything wrong with the clothes it's just, well I'm a walking stereotype because it's what people want to see and what people expect.

Day's nearly over, another exciting one at Marylebone station. Last hour is the longest, you just want to get home and get your feet up but today I'm hoping there's an incident or something, phone the missus up and give her the old 'got to work late' story. This could turn into a right tear up, don't like having a row me, but I'll defend meself, especially if the mother is around, she'll have back up. I don't know, I'm not sure if it's all worth it, getting a divorce might be the way forward, getting a bit bored of it all now.

"You all right John? Looks like there's something up with you."

"No mate, nothing, I'm fine, just looking to get home and get me feet up for the night."

"How's the missus?"

"Yeah, she's all right, brought me some sandwiches earlier, her mother's coming around tonight."

"Get on with the mother don't you?"

"Yeah, she's all right. Going on holiday next month, all three of us together."

"Okay mate, I'm off now, have a good evening."

"See you tomorrow mate."

Always sticking his nose into other people's business him. Train driver, thinks he's all big because he drives a train, looks down on everyone else. Doesn't know I know things about him. Last month, someone reported me for being rude to a passenger. I didn't do anything wrong, it was the passenger who was being rude to me. Anyway, next day I get pulled into the office and get all sorts of grief. It could only have been him who grassed me up, he was there standing next to me, who else could it have been?

I've got no time for people like that. I'm not one for revenge but I've been thinking of ways I can get back at him. Every day he comes over to me all nice, like he's my mate or something, yet he'd gone and got me in trouble. He leaves his bag lying about in the morning when he goes to get his coffee, I've had an idea but I ain't sure whether I should do it or not. See if you got caught drinking when you're a diver that's it, your finished. I was thinking about getting a bottle of whiskey and then putting it in his bag and then grassing him up.

He'd never know it was me and he'd get another job somewhere else, I just can't handle looking at him every day after what he did. When you do something you shouldn't, people should be prepared to face the consequences. I don't know though, it might be a bit much getting him the sack. He's got a couple of kids, never stops going on about them, you wouldn't want to hurt them as well. He hurt me though, I had to go home and tell the missus I'd gotten in trouble. Yeah, do you know what I'll do it, it'll make this evening a bit easier as well, knowing I'm going to get my revenge.

I like old John, he's a nice enough fella. He can be a bit short with the customers sometimes but ain't we all? They think we're in control of everything but it ain't like that, we're just driving the trains or collecting the tickets, no need for us to put up with half the abuse we do. He had a go at one of them last month. I thought it was quite funny. The woman he was having a go at must have rang the complaints line up because he got in trouble over it. Someone said he reckons it was me that got him trouble over it but I don't believe that, he's always nice to me when I see him, surely he'd just say something if that was the case.

Looking forward to a couple of weeks off after tomorrow. The kids will be off school as well, I was thinking of surprising and taking them up to the Lake District. The youngest one loves doing a bit of walking and it isn't often I get the chance to take them away. I can't complain though, I do like my job, wouldn't change it for anything in the world. You know, I might ask him out for a drink tomorrow night before I go away on holiday, he seems a bit down recently, might be able to cheer him up a little bit.

"Sorry, mate. Do you know which platform it is for Oxford?"

"Sorry, I've finished work, go and ask one of them over there."

"What? You can't tell me the patform?"

"Finished work mate, you'll have to ask someone else."

How comes they can never understand that you've finished work? It's easy enough to go and ask someone else what platform it is you need to wherever it is you're going. They don't understand that as soon as that clock hits seven, that's me gone and they ain't my problem any more. I could understand if the geezer had an emergency but he obviously ain't got an emergency he's just being lazy, I'm walking out of the train station for fuck's sake. Don't matter, day's over now, even if I have to go home to some sort of war.

I'm not sure if I should do that to the driver. It wouldn't be a nice thing to do really would it? Bit harsh maybe, he did try and do me over though didn't he? That's not a nice thing to do either. I could have lost my job over that, how would he like it if he lost his job. I don't know, it could be the right thing to do. Some people need to be taught a lesson or they'll never know what they're doing is right or wrong. If he was in my shoes I know he'd do the same thing, he'd think of a way he could get back at me.

This girl in front of me on the bus keeps crying. I wonder what the matter with her is? I wish there was another person up here so they could say something to her. I don't know what to say to her, I ain't any good at things like that. I'd just say something stupid and she'd end up even more upset. I'll just get off at the next stop and get the next bus, it'll make the journey home a bit longer as well, bit more time to myself. She is really crying though, something bad must have happened for her to be crying on a bus like this. I don't know, maybe I should speak to her, see what's up.

What if she's one of the con artists though? I've heard a lot about them recently, saying how they've got a big problem and they ain't got any money and could you lend them a few quid to get home. They give you this big sob story, so many people fall for it. If she does then I'll just get off the bus, I'm too clever for one of them stories, you know when someone's lying. She's quite well dressed though, if it was a man I'd probably just leave it, men wouldn't be crying on a bus like that, poor woman.

"Excuse me, are you okay? I just seen you was a bit upset and thought I'd better check to see if you are okay."

"Oh, sorry, I didn't know there was someone else on the bus, I didn't see you. I'm fine, just had a bit of a bad day that's all."

"We all have bad days, love. No point getting this upset over it. What's happened to ya?"

"I lost my job. They don't need me anymore, I really need that job. I'm sorry, you're just a stranger, I shouldn't be telling you things like this."

"It's okay, say whatever you want, you'll probably never see me again."

"It's just, I need the job, I've barely enough to live on as it is and now that I don't have the job anymore I don't know how I'm going to be able to get by."

"You'll find a way, we always do. Just try and not get so upset so you can think a bit better."

"Yeah, sorry, you don't need to know all of this. I'm getting off at this next stop anyway, thank you for listening even if was just a couple of minutes."

"No problem, I hope you find yourself another job, go home and relax and try not to think about things too much."

That's a bit of rubbish advice that, 'go home and try not to think about things', of course she's going to go home and think about things. I suppose I helped her a little bit though. Not very good at talking to people me. Don't know what I'd do if I lost my job mind, she'd probably kick me out, always been funny about money, if I had none, there's no doubt I'd be out on me ear. Could be a good idea that, get myself sacked and then I'd be able to walk out no worries! Don't know where I'd go though because I ain't got anyone else.

Brace myself before I go in the door. Deep breathe! Both of them are sitting at the kitchen table, this doesn't look good, I've done something bad here. Well I know I've done something bad but it ain't as bad as she thinks it is. The mother's got up and hugged me, what's that all about, they're probably just trying to lure me into a false sense of security, yeah that's what it is. Once I'm all settled and feeling comfortable that's when they'll go on the attack.

"Good day at work?"

"Yeah, it was all right. Them sandwiches you made me were nice."

"Good. You ready for your dinner?"

"Yeah, I'm starving."

Thought they'd say something before dinner. Maybe there ain't nothing bad going to happen.

"Mum wants to ask you something."

Here we go…

"You ask him love…"

"Mum's been having a bit of hard time recently, you know that don't ya?"

"Yeah, of course I do. You feeling any better?"

"Not great, John."

"Well, she ain't got much money, you know how it is living on a pension and that. We was wondering if you could spare a bit of money for her to go on holiday for a couple of weeks."

That's all they wanted? Here was me thinking my marriage was over, planning on walking out or getting myself sacked and all they wanted was some money.

"Yeah, of course she can borrow some money. Where you going to go? Somewhere nice?"

"My friend down the bingo is going to Spain for a couple of weeks, I thought I might go with her."

"That'll be nice, mind yourself out there though, you never know who you might meet, heard that's a lot of refugees as well, looking to rob tourists."

"Don't be telling her things like that you idiot, you'll only get her worried. You'll be fine mum, you go away with your friend for a couple of weeks and have a nice holiday. It'll do you good."

"Yeah, don't mind me, I'm just giving you a bit of advice. Enjoy your holiday."

She's gone to bed now, can't believe that's all they wanted to talk to me about. Of course I wouldn't mind giving her a few quid to go on holiday. Gets her out of my hair for a couple of weeks, ain't too high a cost to pay is it? Let's have a look at a few of these apps and see if we can find someone to talk to! Fucking hell, they've gone. She must have gone on my phone and deleted them. She'll do her nut if she goes on the phone and sees I've downloaded them again. Fuck's sake, my little bit of pleasure and she's gone and taken it away from me, she knows it's only a little bit of fun. I suppose I'll just have to go to bed.

I picked up a bottle of vodka on the way out this morning, got it wrapped up in a jumper just in case someone sees it and thinks it's mine. I can't let him get away with what he did. If he loses his job it ain't my problem, he'll just have to live with it, he'll learn not to be going and grassing people up. Them apps going missing on my phone has put me in a right bad mood, who does she think she is going looking at my phone?

I've just gone and lent her mum a load of money as well, people ain't got no appreciation or respect.

"Morning, mate. Just going to grab my coffee, will be back in a minute. Was going to ask you something when I get back."

"Okay, mate. See you in a minute."

Why does everyone keep wanting to ask me something? Can't be anything important with him though, hardly know the geezer. Don't change nothing, still going to stitch him up. You know, I don't feel so good today, felt a bit dizzy when I went out this morning, must be all this stress I'm putting myself through. Fucking hell, my arm is all sore, and my chest, feels like someone is kicking me in the chest, what's going on here?

I've gone into the office and he's lying there with a bottle of vodka in his hand. I don't know what he's being up to but it looks like he's had a heart attack. I can't believe he's been drinking at work. Never looked like he was pissed, you just don't know sometimes though do you? They reckon it'll be touch and go whether he makes it or not. I hope he does make it but I don't think he'll be around here much longer if he does. How stupid can he have been to be drinking at work? I'll go and see him in the hospital later, hopefully he'll still be alive.

Baker Street

Baker Street, former home of Sherlock Holmes and current home of Madame Tussaud's

I hate museums but they've made me come. Of all the stupid things they could have me do it's write a review of a museum which doesn't need a review. I don't even get why people would come to somewhere like this, it's just models of people who you're never going to see in real life, have no meaning or relationship to you in real life. They all stand there next to them taking photographs, happy and smiling. All it is is a load of wax made to look like the person. Waste of time, yet here I am because some idiot doesn't have a better use for me.

I thought being a journalist would be fun, I'd be getting involved, making a change in people's lives, exposing corrupt politicians and using my skills for the greater good. I'd be winning awards and go on to right books on how to be a ground breaking journalist in a world their needed in. But no! Here I am wandering around this stupid museum which everyone knows, doesn't need to be reviewed because you know what you're going to get as soon as you walk in the door, pissed off with the world and pissed off with life. Wasting my talents really, and I'm telling you, tomorrow morning I'm going straight into the editors office and telling him what I really think. No more pussy footing around, changes are coming and the world had better watch out.

You know what makes it worse is all these kids. They sent me here during the school holidays and there are kids everywhere, shouting and screaming, taking photos with all these models and I bet you they don't even know who half of them are. Parents just standing there watching as their wild children climb all over John F. Kennedy and kick Albert Einstein. No appreciation at all, that's what's wrong with the world and I'm living proof of that. A little boy is punching Frank Sinatra in the balls while his mum laughs and takes a picture. Isn't he funny? No he's not, and she should be ashamed for raising such an ignorant child, Frank would have had them whacked!

My notepad is blank. There's nothing I need to write down, I know what I want to say and no note taking will change that. There's no revelations to be had, no sudden changes of heart because it's just the most superficial of places, an indictment of the celebrity obsessed world. These vacuous, self absorbed 'stars' exist because these people wandering around feed off them, they drop little scraps here and there and they all come running, hungry, needing that little scrap to survive so they can go and tell their friends.

See, I see myself as someone different, I'm not like everyone else, I'm not interested in what other people do or have to say, why would I be? I only own a phone because I have to, and it was with great reluctance I bought one. I watch people on trains and sitting outside cafes and all they do is play with those insufferable machines. No time for a good book so they might educate themselves a little, no! They must let the world know they're sitting outside a café drinking a coffee or they're sitting on a train, much like half the city, going home to a boring life.

I want to sit down but all these children are taking up the seats. There's a cupboard over there which has a stool in it. I wonder if I'd be able to get away with sitting in there for five minutes. No one would notice and if anyone asked me what I was doing I'm sure they'd be sympathetic to my situation. The door is slightly ajar, the key is on the outside which is rather negligent although I wouldn't expect anything less. I check to see there is no one watching and I slip in the door and close it. Peace at last!

The room smells musty, an old mop and a bucket sit on the floor, no wonder the key is on the outside, it isn't like there's anything worth taking. The museum will be closing soon and people will be going home, I'd like to just have a wander around with fewer people, maybe just maybe I'll see it in a different light. There's a knock at the door. I ignore it. Another and another. I don't want to open the door so I look through the keyhole. There's the face of a smiling child. Idiot. He stops knocking and I go back to resting on the stool. Oh shit! If I could see his face through the keyhole that means the key is gone! Pulling the handle of the door it doesn't open. The little bastard has locked me in here! Bang! Bang! Bang! Against the door, someone must hear me, it's a bloody museum full of people. No one comes.

A cleaner will be along soon to let me out, there's no point making a racket, it'll only attract attention and if there's one thing I don't like it's attention, besides I have my phone, they do have some uses. I can't ring anyone now though because they'll laugh at me and going back to the office tomorrow will be hell. I pull the little phone from my pocket, just to see who I might be able to call. There's the editor, but he's never available, in some meeting somewhere. There's John but John isn't around at the moment, he's jetting off to some island to review it for a feature. I could call the police but that really would be attracting attention. No I'll wait. Why do I only have five contacts in my phonebook?

It's awfully quiet outside that door, they can't all have gone home already. Surely they must clean this place up when the masses have gone home? I better give it another bang. Bang! I listen against the door but there's nothing. This really is a fucking nightmare! Locked in a cupboard by a child! I bang again, louder this time, really make some noise. BANG BANG BANG! Nothing. No one is coming to my rescue, now I'm going to have to use the bloody phone to get myself out of this mess, for God's sake, I'll never hear the end of this stupid little escapade! I can see them tomorrow morning, making stupid little jokes, laughing to themselves thinking they're oh so clever. I should just resign, I don't think I'll be able to face it!

The phone is dead! I can't even make a phone call. I bang and shout, still no sign of anyone outside. This is absolutely ridiculous, how on earth can there be no one else here! How am I going to get out? I mean, if nobody comes I'll have to sit here until the morning and they open it up again. Jesus Christ, a night stuck in a museum's broom cupboard. This must be some kind of joke, someone has set me up, it's the only thing I can think of. Looking through the keyhole I can see nothing, there's a glow but not enough to see clearly. Well, this is fucking great! I'm going to sue the museum, this is their fault.

My watch tells me I've been sitting here for three hours. For three hours I've been sitting here planning my revenge on a child I'll never find. I kick the bucket in frustration and it clatters against the wall of the cupboard, the mop falls and I kick that too. And there it is, under the bucket was a key. All this time I've been sitting here there was a key right in front of me. What a stupid place to hide a key, and why do they have two keys for a fucking broom cupboard? Not my problem now, I get to go home and no one will know of this.

I leave my prison cell, placing the key back in the door. The museum is eerily quiet, there are lights along the floor which gives the strange glow which I could see through the keyhole. The figures are intimidating in the dark, all of their eyes seem to be on me as I walk past them, wondering who this intruder to their night time world is. What am I thinking? They're just silly statues, they have no life of their own. However, it would be a good time to see the place without all those annoying children and over eager tourists. I hate people, I really do hate people.

On closer inspection I really do have to give them credit, they are rather life like, I may throw in a few good words when I write up my piece, without being overly gushing. That's another problem with society, everything is amazing or the best ever! Mediocre is a word which has been lost. I squeeze Kennedy's nose, look Boris Johnson in the eyes and tell him he's a wanker. Do you know why he's a wanker? He's a wanker because twice this week I've been late for work because they can't get trains which don't break down and I blame it solely on him. I kick him in the shins for good measure, looking around to make sure I am still alone. Ahh, now I feel better.

Here is a man after my own heart. William Shakespeare. So under appreciated in the modern age, I don't know if they still read his plays in schools but when I was at school I would learn them by heart. Such wonderful use of language, such intelligence, so far ahead of his time. I sit down beside him and gaze up as a child would when they come across someone they admire. How I wish I had lived in his times, to be able to go and see the man live, to see him for real would have been such an experience.

One creates an image in their own minds don't they? Someone you like or someone who inspires you but you know nothing much of them, nothing too deep, you build up an image of them, a perfect one, flawless. A quixotic view of the times they lived in, the ills and misfortune forgotten and ignored because they're unbecoming of your narrative. Here above me is a man I admire, a man who I would love to have seen in the flesh. I sit down beside him.

Wandering the streets of a town I don't recognise, it's far, far away from the one I know. Wooden houses, women leaning out of the windows, waste flying from the windows as I walk down a narrow street. The noise is deafening, no cars or buses, just people making noise. Shouting at each other, some arguing, some just communicating. A woman standing in a doorway looks at me and spits on the floor, looking back at me in disgust, my presence enough to anger her. How uncouth. A horse is blocking the way, eating something from the floor which is a mixture of mud and straw and rotten food, the smell is horrendous.

A man is lying outside another doorway, he barely has clothes at all, just rags, no shoes. He opens his mouth to smile a wicked smile, there's not a tooth in his head, he laughs as I recoil. A large boil on his neck is weeping, he continues to laugh as I pass on down the street, delighted in the discomfort he's causing me. There is an air of menace in the street, I hurry my pace towards the turning 30 metres away, looking back making sure the man hasn't decided to follow me, he has found new entertainment in talking to the neglected horse.

I turn into a main street. I wonder where this is? I want to ask someone but I'm too scared to open my mouth, the accent they speak in, it's as one would imagine pirates have. The buildings are tall but close together, they look lopsided and crooked, as though they could crash to the floor at any moment. I need to find out where I am and how far it is to where I went to go: the theatre, The Globe. If I can find the river then it will be easy to find but I'm not sure which way to go. A woman passes, she looks respectable, I try to open my mouth but she carries on by as if I'm invisible.

There is some kind of a tavern or a pub in front of me. I could go in there and ask, drunken people are usually much more willing to talk. I feel my pockets, there are a couple of coins inside them, of what value I have no idea, enough to buy myself a drink I don't doubt.

Inside there are not many people, just a few drinking what looks like beer. I throw the coin on the bar, the man behind the bar looks at me in amazement, he pours a drink and hands it to me, a huge smile on his face as he takes the coin. I sit down and sip my beer, wondering how I am going to get to my destination, scanning the patrons to see which of them looks approachable enough to ask. They all seem lost in their own thoughts, none have paid me any attention. Another man enters the pub, he talks to the owner, the owner points at me and they begin to have a discussion. This man seems to be reasonably well dressed, perhaps I could ask him.

He approaches me and sits down beside me, knocking his tankard against mine.

"And where are you from, sir?"

"Oh, I'm from London." He looks bemused and strains his ears as if he doesn't quite understand.

"It's okay, you can tell me you're not from around here. Fancy a tour of the city? I'll give you a good price."

"Well actually, I'd rather like to go to the theatre if that's possible."

"I'm not sure if there are any plays on, the theatre is not somewhere I go. I can take you there, but obviously for a fee. The price of a beer we'll say." He says it with a smirk.

"Well, I suppose you'll be better than no one."

"Drink up and we'll be on our way."

He drinks from the tankard and finishes it all in one go. I take a mouthful of mine and push it away, seeing I don't want it, he takes my tankard and finishes that one too. He gives a wave to the owner as we leave. I wave too but he looks at me curiously before breaking into laughter.

"It's dangerous around here you know, you shouldn't be wondering around on your own. God only knows what would have happened if I hadn't walked into that tavern. You need to be more careful sir, I still can't understand why a man dressed such as yourself would be on his own."

"Well, I'm just taking in the city."

"Taking in the city?"

"Going for a walk."

"There are far better places to be going for a walk. Come, we'll go down to the river and walk along the banks before we cross the bridge."

The river looks filthy, things floating along the top of it, black slime washing in from the tide. Men unload boxes and push them into warehouses. The smell is worse here, I've never smelled anything like it. My new companion looks at me and laughs, he can see my disgust. The road or street or path, whatever it is we're walking along is muddy, my feet stick as I lift them up to walk. The time of bards and poets is not what one would expect, I expected streets of learned men singing songs and telling tales, plays taking place in pub courtyards.

Sitting against the wall of one of the warehouses is a small child. A boy I think, but it's hair is long and face girlish. He is playing with a piece of wood, banging it against the floor, joy in his eyes as pieces splinter off and the piece of wood becomes smaller. He's surrounded by filth yet people just walk by as if he isn't there. He throws the piece of wood away and lies back on the floor before jumping up, his long hair covered in mud. He runs off down an alleyway and into the maze of streets behind the warehouses.

"How about another drink before we cross the river? I know a fine tavern nearby, The Old Swan Inn."

"Well, if we must."

"If you do not wish too we can just cross the bridge, but it's nearby and I think you will like it. I have many a friend in there too."

"I only have the price of a beer which is what you wanted to take me to the theatre."

"I'll buy you one, the price of showing you to the theatre can be the making of a new friend."

This man is well dressed yet there seems something not quite right about him. He has an air of trouble about him yet I can't seem to resist his charm. A loveable rogue would probably be how you would describe him, the odd accent accentuating his vagabond demeanour. He points the way forward to the Inn. A drink can't hurt, I'm giving up on finding this theatre anyway, I thought it would be easy but these streets are becoming hard to bare and I don't think my time left here is long.

This pub is far different from the other. There is a large fire burning, men standing around it drinking from tankards larger than the ones before. There are a few women in here too although they are gathered together and talking in hushed voices, they turn their heads as we enter, giggling and then going back to their conversations. My new friend brings over two tankards of beer, he drinks it in one go again and then orders another. I hold the tankard up, there are little bits floating around in it,

God only knows what. I might as well, I throw it back in one go and he slaps me hard on the back before ordering another for me.

There's a warm glow come over me now, sitting by the side of the fire as the men in the inn become more and more raucous, the beer flowing, the floor covered in spillages. My friend has gone away to talk to someone. A storyteller it seems, those he talks to seem to hang on his every word. He beckons me over, those around him move aside as I approach, I'm feeling confident now, not so lost, the awful beer is doing its work.

"I'd like to introduce you all to my new friend! Where he's from I am not sure, though he assures me he is from London but that I don't believe. Anyway, a toast to new friends!"

They all raise their tankards, I raise mine too. They cheer and then move away to talk and shout among themselves.

"I don't believe I asked you your name?"

"I'm Jonathan. And what might yours be?"

"I am William, and I'm delighted to meet you."

"What is it you do William?"

"Me? I wander and I wonder. I meet new people and show them the delights of this city. I get them drunk and tell them tales, then they leave, merry, head swimming but happy. You however are different. There's something not quite right about you and I can't understand what it might be. A man dressed so fine, on his own, looking for a theatre. I would love to know your story, sir."

"I have no story. I am just a man looking for entertainment. Tell me William, do you write?"

"Write!? No, I do not write, I cannot write, nor can I read. I wasn't blessed with an education which man such as yourself would have been blessed with."

"Oh, how unfortunate."

"Come let us drink some more before we move on. It'll be dark soon and a man such as yourself would not last too long on his own."

Again he buys more drinks. I'm beginning to suspect this coin in my pocket is worth far more than a drink of beer, so keen does he seem to get me drunk. There is no light from any windows so I am not aware of the time. We continue to drink even after his advice that we should leave soon. He begins to dance a jig, women flock around him, I clap my hands along with those surrounding him, encouraging his foolishness. One of the women, grabs me by the hand and pulls me into the centre of the floor. A loud cheer goes up as we dance, I have no idea what I am doing but I laugh to myself, a long time since I've felt so free and uncaring as to what people think.

She pulls me over to a corner of the inn and sits me down on a chair. William, waves over to me as he still holds court with the inn's drunkards. We talk, about what I am not sure, things which have little meaning, she laughs at everything I say, playfully hitting me and shouting over to her friends about how amusing she finds me. Centre of attention and I'm loving it.

William joins us and declares we will leave, another cheer goes up as we leave the bar. I've become a celebrity! People love me and I haven't even done anything! I wave as I leave, another tankard of beer is handed to me and I drink it in one go before going off into the darkness of the night with my new best friend.

The night is dark, very dark, hardly any light at all, in my drunkenness I trip and fall, William pulls me up with one hand and he begins to tell me the story of how he arrived in the city, a young boy who knew only the countryside. Now he is a man about town, loved and adored. There's a sadness when he talks about home and his family, people he says he doesn't think he'll ever see again, but the joy of his role as a jester and storyteller outweighs it all. I wonder how much is true and how much is just another one of his many stories.

A man approaches us with his hands out, wanting a coin or two. I reach into my pocket and throw it to him. Even in my drunken state I do not want to make contact with this wretched individual. The man's face lights up, I know now the coin is worth more than any beer. The bar man at the first inn will be celebrating tonight! William slaps me on the back, so hard it hurts and I cough. He finds it incredibly amusing. We cross the bridge and walk back towards the theatre which I can now see. Excitement, drunkenness, my new found fame, I never want to leave.

As I stare up at the theatre, it's not as big as I thought it would be. It's too late for any play to be on, a chance missed, inns and beer came first. I turn around but William has gone, it's too dark to see far but I can't feel the presence of anyone. I sit down outside of the theatre, looking much like one of the beggars I encountered earlier in the day and consider my new found fame, no more lonely nights or derision from colleagues. Ha! Who would have thought? Me, famous!

It's amazing what a person's mind can conjure up, I look up and the wax figure is still there looking down at me. I admonish myself for my lapse in concentration, escaping reality. Surely that is not what is really locked away in my own mind? A desire to be known and spoken of? No, I don't like people and I don't like attention, the last thing I would ever want is fame. I can't look up again at the figure, embarrassed at it's ability to take me off to another world. I should be going, daydreams are for fools.

There's still no sign of life as I walk through the museum looking for an exit. Someone somewhere must know I'm in here, how could none of these cameras not have picked up on my presence? They might be amused at a person wandering lost, late at night. Yes, that must be it, they know I'm here but they're just making fun of me while they watch me. I stick a finger up at one of the cameras. How difficult can it be to find a way out of here?

I try to avoid any eye contact with the models, my embarrassment at my recent daydreaming is more than my annoyance at myself for not being able to look something which isn't real in the eye. That hair, and those eyes too, my attempts at diverting my eyes are thwarted by stunning beauty. How can it possibly not be real? The blonde-haired figure in front of me, bending over slightly, her eyes locked on to mine. I can't meet her eyes and I feel my face redden as I feel the eyes follow me as I try to walk around her. How stupid can I be?

There is a chair behind her, I sit down on it to compose myself, she is looking away from me, unable to see into my soul, preying on my self-consciousness. I search the walls for a clock, there's nothing, I have no idea what time it is, it can't be too long before it opens. Maybe I could just wait here until it then, I might have to break out otherwise and then I probably would end up getting arrested. I'll sit here on this chair until someone arrives, it's as good a place as any.

Priding myself on not being superficial, I'm confused at my reaction to the woman in front of me, not a woman, a piece of wax. I never let myself get close to anyone, getting close to someone would mean opening my heart, allowing someone to look inside and that would be exposing myself, risking hurt and shame and guilt. Could you ever possibly fall in love with an inanimate object? There's no feelings, they're not real, there's nothing more than what the object looks like. I stand up to take a closer look but I can't allow myself to get too close, an irrational fear that it will suddenly come alive, turn around and be repulsed by my presence. As it is, it doesn't move nor will it, she can be whoever I want her to be. I sit back down on the chair.

I'm in a town I'm not familiar with, it's busy, the air is dirty, the people walk past me as if I'm not there, aloof, rude, they want nothing to do with this poorly dressed loser. Everywhere there is money, expensive cars, expensive clothes, but none of it is real, it's just there, I can't explain it, opulence which just descends into cheapness. Everything I hate about the world, but here I am surrounded by it with no escape.

I walk into a park which is filled with people running about in circles, men jumping up and down on the spot, flexing their muscles, look at me, look at me. They have a confidence about them which I could only ever dream of, confidence or arrogance? They're the same thing to me. I buy an ice cream at a stall, the only person buying. Someone runs past me and looks at the ice cream, rolling their eyes and scrunching their face. Who knew an ice cream would be able to cause such a reaction? I find a spot under a tree, far away from the paths of runners and the jumping men, hidden by the shadow of the large tree.

A woman walks along the path, different from the rest, striking blonde hair. The men watch as she walks by, she knows all of their eyes are upon her, they're jumping and flexing their muscles twice as much. The women running past her try to ignore her but can't help but glance back as they pass, she ignores them, keeping her eyes straight ahead. Oblivious or contemptuous to their jealous or admiring glances, I can't tell. She walks over to the ice cream stall and buys herself an ice cream and begins to eat it as she stands there. Now everyone wants an ice cream, a sudden rush taking the seller by surprise.

She walks away from the crowd, the looks of dismay on the faces of the men, offence taken at her ability to ignore the feathers they work so hard to display. Across the grass she goes, heading towards where I sit. I feel uncomfortable, I want her to come and sit near me but I don't because she might say something to me and if she says something to me I have no idea what I will say in reply, only make a fool of myself, a bumbling idiot, she would be better off talking to one of them, she'd be comfortable in their confidence, not arrogance now, just confidence, something I don't have.

She stops just in front of the shadow of the tree and sits down in the sun, her back facing me. A relief washes over my body which is suddenly replaced by a feeling of disappointment. Conflict and annoyance, I thought she'd never have noticed me sitting here on my own by the tree, away from the rest of the crowds, then hope she had seen me, a deluded idea she might want to come and sit with me, it was really me who she wanted to talk to, and then sadness and disappointment, she'd not noticed me at all.

I watch as she finishes her ice cream. The men are still jumping around, the women still running around the paths. As each of the men look at her I'm begging them not to take the chance to approach her. I have no chance, I will never approach her but if I can't even steal a couple of words with her, two minutes of her time then they too deserve nothing. It'll be heartbreak over a love that never was or never will be. If she walks away on her own, it won't be heartbreak, just satisfaction in the rejection of others.

Then she turns her head towards me and smiles and looks away again, gazing into the distance. Now my head is truly scrambled. Did she really look at me? No, she just looked to see who was behind her and smiled out of politeness, a woman as beautiful as her has no need to be polite, she was just smiling to herself, smiling at her ability to have all the attention on herself while still being able to walk away on her own. She turns again and smiles, my eyes meet hers and then look away, my face red, burning, my hands moving involuntarily looking for something to do.

"You're not going to come and join me?"

I point at myself, "me?!"

"There's no one else here is there?" she says looking around theatrically and waving her hands.

I want to tell her there are many people here and most of them far more interesting than myself. She gets up from the floor and walks over, sitting down next to me. My tongue is tied, I smile weakly, my hands playing with blades of grass as if they are the most important things in the world, they have a deeper meaning which I'm currently trying to figure out and disturbing me from this endeavour is putting me to great pain. She picks a blade of grass and throws it towards me, laughing. I feel a wide beam spread across my face.

"You want to grab something to eat?"

"Yeah, I suppose so. You sure?"

"I wouldn't be asking if I wasn't sure. Look...I could choose anyone here and they'd come with me."

Arrogance? Usually it would annoy me but I'm finding it attractive. We walk back across the grass together, I want to say something but I don't know what to say. She moves closer to me as we walk, they're all watching, envious, vindictive eyes upon me, not her, I'm the one to blame or them not getting their ego boost. None of them can understand how this non descript person can possibly have something they can't. I begin to walk with more of a swagger, just a slight swagger, but a swagger nonetheless.

Walking into a restaurant people stop and stare at her, her blonde hair bobbing up and down. They look at her and look at me. Waiters eagerly rush to our, no her, assistance. We're seated, she looks at the menu and then puts it down. I look at the menu but it's all gibberish, I can't make out what any of the words are, it's just a blur of letters which don't form any meaningful words. I start to panic but she says something to waiter and he takes away both our menus.

"Why do you think I am sitting here with you?"

"I don't know why, shouldn't you be answering that question."

"No, it's your question to answer, you know the answer."

"I don't know the answer, you're the one who brought me here."

"You're not very bright are you?"

155

"Uhm, well, I like to think of myself as reasonably intelligent."

"Perhaps you should rethink that."

Now I don't want to be here. In just a few words she's made me question the one thing I believed to have above everyone else, now I'm not so sure. Maybe I'm not as clever as I think I am.

"Before I went to sit down near you, I bought an ice cream, you know that. I walked into that park without a care in the world. People stopped and looked at me. It didn't matter what they were doing, I was the centre of attention. You envy that don't you?"

"Excuse me?"

"When we left, people were looking at both of us, you enjoyed it, at first you were uncomfortable but then you started to enjoy it, relish it. You'd got one over on other people, those people you were hiding away from underneath that tree."

The waiter appears with food. Burger and chips for both of us. I love burger and chips, a simple pleasure but not one I was expecting. I avoid answering her question, biting into the burger and picking up chips with my other hand. Making an elaborate display of enjoyment, making it obvious I was so wrapped up in my eating answering wouldn't be convenient.

"You don't have to answer."

She picks at the food, taking occasional bites, using her knife and fork to cut the burger, as if picking it up in her hands would be a bad look. She gets up from the table halfway through and walks over to a table with a solitary man eating his dinner. She sits down opposite him and begins to talk, one of the waiters looks at me in confusion, then a smile and a shake of the head. The man she is talking to turns his head and looks back at me, a look of surprise on his face and then he turns back to her and says something, she gets up and returns to the table.

"I told him I was with you and then he told me to go back to you. How does that make you feel?"

"It doesn't make me feel anything. If you'd not come back I'd have walked out the door and never have seen you again."

"You'll never see me again anyway. When he turned around and looked at you, you thought he was going to laugh or smile, make fun of you in some way. He didn't, and now I'm sitting back here with you."

"Would you like to accompany me on a walk?"

"Yes, yes I would."

"Can you not ask me anymore questions?"

"That's up to you."

We walk out the door, the surroundings are hazy. Like the menu, I can only make out the outline of buildings, some of them are smaller than they should be, some of them keep reaching into the sky as far as I can see. Behind the buildings is the sea, that I can see clearly. I still have no idea where I am. I turn to her, making sure she's still there. She is. I reach out my hand to her and she takes it with a smile, we walk hand in hand towards the sea, the outlines of people passing by take no notice, none stop and look, they just go about their business.

I feel warm and happy, I never want to let go of her hand, she squeezes it tight. We reach the water. It's the bluest colour I have ever seen, dark, blue, stretching out onto the horizon. The beach is empty, the sand the colour you only see in books. We walk along the beach, still hand in hand, in the distance I can see the beach coming to an end, I want to turn around and walk back again but as I look back I can see there's nothing behind us but sea. The buildings have disappeared too. Just two people walking on a beach which is falling away as they walk.

Then as quickly as it all disappeared it's all back again. Buildings, people, the faces are clear and no longer blurred. I want to go back, back where it was just the two of us. She smiles as she looks at me, reaching her hand up to my face and then running her hand through my hair. The most beautiful woman I have ever seen. Just the touch alone, the feeling of her soft hands on my face makes my body tingle, I feel close to someone, closer than I ever have done.

"I don't know your name?"

"My name is whatever you want it to be and I am whoever you want me to be."

"So you have no name? And when we walk off this beach you're just going to walk away."

"Maybe. Doesn't mean I'll leave you though."

"Of course you'll leave me, I'll never see you again."

She continues to stare into my eyes as I begin to get angry. Then I feel calm again, a tranquillity washing over me. I take her hand again and begin to walk, enjoying the moment, not worrying about what the immediate future will bring, it's pointless, I know what's going to happen, I might as well I enjoy what I have for the moment. We walk by the water, the sea splashing against our feet, she reaches into the water and splashes me with her hands, I reach down too and splash her, we dance about in the water, water all over each other, soaked.

Some kids begin to watch, they laugh at us, point and join in, throwing water over both of us. I want to be angry at being interrupted but I can't, I'm too happy. I throw water over the children too, one of them jumps onto my back, I throw him into the water and he laughs, I laugh along with him. For what seems like hours we splash and play with the children. Slowly they begin to disappear back to the beach, one of them jumps out of the water and turns to look at me, he reaches into a pocket and throws a key. I bend down but it's nowhere to be seen, he waves to me, I wave back at him.

Sitting down, the sun slowly reaching the horizon, hand in hand. All my life I never thought I would be in a situation like this. I never believed it, vivid, bright colours, replacing shades of grey, the sun and blue sky replacing grey clouds.

"When we leave, you were right, you'll never see me again. You still haven't given me a name?"

"How can you not have a name?"

"Give me a name, it can be any name you like."

"I don't want to give you a name. If I give you a name, it'll follow me. If you don't have a name, it's just you the person, nothing else. All my life, I've dreamed of happiness. I'm happy, a name would be meaningless. When I'm happy I'll think of you."

"Once the sun has gone, that will be it. Tomorrow it will all go back to normal. I'll just be a part of your imagination and you'll be sad, hating the rest of the world, looking down on them because they're doing something you don't see as fulfilling or is beneath you. You'll go into your little office and write a story, you won't change your mind because, if you change your mind you'll be admitting fault with yourself and you can never do that. You'll admonish yourself for being weak, it'll just be a fairy tale because you were tired. You can't ever imagine you'd be just the same as everyone else, someone with dreams. Walk with me to the sea…"

I can't answer her, the lines between reality and dreams are so blurred, something this vivid can't be a dream and if it is a dream why is it so real. We reach the water's edge.

"Goodbye."

She's there in front of me, her back still facing me. Jesus! I fell asleep on the chair. I stand up and walk over to the figure and touch the hair and then sit back down again, taking a few minutes to wake myself. I have to get out of here, I need to get out, I don't care what time it is or if anyone finds me, I'll even take getting arrested. I move quickly past all of the models, now taking no notice of them. I spot a toilet, inside I see one of the windows is left ajar, I push it out and climb out the window into an alleyway and walk out into the main road.

It's dawn, the light is just breaking through the sky, it's that strange inky blue colour with a tint of red. I keep checking to make sure I'm walking the street on my own, there's nobody beside me, I breathe a sigh of relief. I have to get to work. A woman with blonde hair appears out of a side street in front of me, my heart stops but she walks straight past me. My mind is racing, I've been locked in a museum for 12 hours and I think I may have actually gone crazy, hallucinating, probably through lack of sleep or maybe it was some chemicals they use in there. How can it all be so vivid?

The office is closed but I have a key. I unlock the door, there is no one else there. Suddenly remembering my previous inability to read I grab a newspaper from a desk, I can read it clearly. I haven't gone mad, it was all just a dream, my mind playing tricks on me. I sit down at my desk and put my feet up on it. I look in the bottom drawer, there's an unopened bottle of whiskey. I pour a drink into one of the white plastic cups I use to drink water, I drink it all in one go. I take out my pen and notepad and write the headline for my piece on the museum. My Night With William and Marylin

Regent's Park – Zoo Politics

Regent's Park, home to London Zoo

I hate them Giraffes. Long necks, long tongues, walking around like they own the place, who do they think they are coming over here and walking around like the own they place. The thing that makes me laugh is they get their own enclosure, they don't even have to worry about the lions. No, no, keep them separate, God forbid they might have to look after themselves. They even let all the people feed them, what kind of madness is that? Everything on a plate and they weren't even born in this country. Of course they wouldn't want to go back home, they'd be eaten and we can't have that can we?

I'm getting a bit bored of it all to be honest. Years ago, it wasn't like this at all, that's what my old man says anyway, he said they use to come from far and wide to see us. They'd slip us some food between the fences, a nut here, a bit of bread there, a banana if you was lucky. These days not interested. You know why? I'll tell you why, because people are only interested in exotic things these days, they don't give a shit about their own. Sorry to go off on one here but it gets my back right up it does.

I'll tell you who are the worst, if you think the giraffes are bad, them fucking pandas are even worse. They get everything they do, and they're completely useless. Did you know they can only make babies for one day a year? And even then they ain't interested. They should have been left to die off if you ask me, all they're doing is wasting resources. Ain't no one ever come and offered me a bit of bamboo or a nice place to stay in at night, I ain't got no heated room. I can't stand them but they keep sending them over, they never ask if we want 'em here though do they.

I don't think people understand what it's like to be a goat in the modern age. They go on saying we need to move with the times and zoos are multicultural places these days, but they don't understand. How would you feel if you was me? Imagine it, standing there in the freezing cold, waiting for some kid to come up and stroke you, their mum and dad take a nice photo of you, give you a carrot, but they don't do that no more. They'd rather go and stroke an alpaca or take a picture with one of them endangered species. I hate them, always moping about, moaning that their ain't many of them left and no one's doing anything about it. Be grateful for what you've got you chancers!

I went for a stroll the other day, got out the gate when one of the kids left it open, and I was talking to a few of the boys over in the Zebra cage. See, I don't mind the old zebras, they come here and they do their job, they don't need no looking after, they do a bit of galloping around, have a tear up now and again amongst each other but they don't complain, they just get on with it. If they didn't bite people I wouldn't mind them in here with me.

Anyway, they was saying that the lion enclosure looks a bit unsafe, you know, a couple of lions might be able to get through by "accident". I'm telling you now, if a couple of 'em do get through it it ain't going to be by no accident. Secretly, they want them to get out, eat a few zebras, keep the old numbers down, put a bit of fear into them as well, let them know whose boss. I've been around too long to not know how they work around here. I can't tell none of the humans what their game is either, all they do is look at me and go 'aahhhh'. I ain't cute, I'm a grumpy bastard and they're lucky I don't headbutt their little ones.

I am going on a little bit here ain't I? The missus will be back soon, you can ask her. She knows the score. She's doing one of them shows at the moment where they walk you around on a bit of rope and they get her to jump on boxes and all that bollocks, she says it pays for her keep. Tried to get me to do it but I ain't doing that, who do they think I am? I'm better than doing all them sorts of things. She does get a bit of extra food though so I suppose that is a result, kids giver her ice cream's and buns and all that sort of game. Someone give her a falafel wrap the other day, not really for me all that foreign food but I suppose whatever floats your boat.

I've been hatching a plan as it goes. Not told anyone else about it yet, don't think I will, bit of a lone wolf job. Don't know why they say lone wolf, their all together in their nice big cage, wouldn't want to mess with them. Anyway, my plan. See if I let one of the gorillas out of its cage, they'll go mental, chase a few people about maybe hurt someone, they'll shoot it. That'll give the rest of them a warning, make them know their place. I don't like the gorillas me, and there's enough of them here one dead one won't make too much of a difference.

I don't really like it here all that much, it's different from home and I don't like the other animals either, some of them don't seem too welcoming and let's be honest, they're all a bit uncivilised. Not like me. I hate the food as well. Back home they give us proper bamboo, it has flavour, the bamboo they give us here just doesn't taste right, I don't think they know how to grow it properly. They're a strange lot. I thought I'd come here, get a bit of experience and then go home but I'd go home now if I had the chance.

I've no interest in mixing with the others at all. They can't speak my language and I can't be bothered to lower myself and speak such a rough sounding language. I spent years been left to roam forests, study the movements of the world and its fauna. Days sitting around on the forest floor contemplating the meaning of life, away from the ignorant and barbaric who encroach on our habitat, attempting to impose their meaningless and violent lives upon us. Capturing and feeding us is just a ploy to make us subservient to their whims.

There is one curious animal here, not curious in that he's a rare species, curious in the way he views the world. He's not clever enough to realise I understand his mutterings, which of course I do, there's very little I don't understand. He wishes everyone would just go home, leave him here to his own little paradise. I agree with him, however the way in which he expresses such views is in an uneducated manner, he's not eloquent enough. He could come in useful at some point, help in spreading and making them all understand my superior way of living.

I do wish those petulant monkeys would shut up. Forever making a racket, sometimes I just want to take a nap in the afternoon but they go rabbiting on and on. Now if that goat is uneducated, these monkeys are at the bottom of the barrel. They do have their uses though, they make such a racket that the lions never come over here to bother me. I was told many years ago they'd wander over and roar and make a big show of themselves. Even attacked one of the Asian elephants once but they were shooed off in the end.

I do keep the monkeys on my side. They'll eat anything and they'll get up to all kinds of mischief so occasionally I'll throw them in a bit of food or I'll drop a word or two in about a rumour about how much the lions would love to eat them and they go a bit mad. It is very entertaining and it stops the lions from causing me too much bother. The old lion died recently and the new lion is a bit mad. You know what they say though, all roar and no bite. He does seem to be pissing off all the other animals as well but I don't mind that it means no one bothers me.

Back to this goat. I need to find a way that I can use him for my own means. I am rather bored in here and I would like an adventure but I need a distraction. I've been thinking about what fun it would be if the lions were released from their cage. I could sit back and watch, no need for me to go outside for an adventure. Perhaps they'd eat a person or two. As much as the monkeys are an annoying bunch I wouldn't want to see them eaten, God only knows what kind of an animal they'd put in there if they were all gone and that wouldn't do at all! I mean, what if they made the lion cage bigger! No, no, no, I can't have that.

I heard a rumour that the new lion came from somewhere far away, they didn't want him at first, half the pack didn't like him while the other half adored him. Strange animals lions, far less important than they like to think and my God are they uncivilised! If I could get rid of them my plans for domination would come to fruition. They just don't understand, I don't care what they do as long as they leave me alone, but the simple fact is they are an annoyance I can't bare and I need to find a way to deal with them. It's either the goat or the monkeys but one way or another I'll put them in their place. See? The more I talk about them the angrier I get.

My idiot of a husband has decided he's going to let the lions out of their cage. I'm sure that blasted panda has something to do with it and it seems there's no stopping him now. I suppose it's not the end of the world. I am worried about how my reputation might become tainted, I don't want to be associated with such nonsense even if I might have had a small hand in inciting him into it but we won't talk about that, if we don't talk about it it'll just go away.

I don't think he appreciates what good stock I'm from, I'm not just some ordinary goat like him. I'm the finest of finest of goats. When I was just a kid, and literally I was a kid, I was raised by the best, they taught me how to interact with the people, as much as I hold them in disdain, I must show at least that I enjoy their grubby little fingers on me. My mother, god rest her soul, told me I mustn't marry Billy, too rough she said but well, he has his uses.

Poor old Billy, he does have a rather narrow view of the world but I suppose that does come from not being educated very well. If we get rid of all the animals and all of those people we'll have no one to feed us and no one to clean up after us. Fend for ourselves? Never would I lower myself to such a thing. I've spent far too long being waited on hand and foot, whatever would I do if I had to go out into the wild and forage, I simply would not be able to do it! Could you imagine? Eating common grass, no falafel wraps or expensive ice creams. I'd die!

He's not a bad chap that old panda but he tends to hold a grudge and he thinks he's far cleverer than he actually is. I'm sure it's because, as my old mother told me, many years ago there was a panda who lived in the zoo and all the animals used to steal his food. Why hold a grudge? It's something which happened so many years ago dear boy! He thinks we are unable to realise he understands us, well Billy doesn't, but Billy is a rather special case. I told him last night, you have to be careful of him, he's not quite what he seems. Personally, as long as he keeps giving us fresh bamboo, which I am rather partial too he can do as he pleases.

I do agree with him about those accursed lions though, they really are very boorish, especially that new one which has turned up. I did go and talk to him, tell him that lions and goats have a special relationship, one which has been an open secret for generations. I mean you wouldn't think we'd get on but it's just one of those things. They protect us and in return we don't really do much, but it looks good, especially when those bloody snakes are about. I don't like them snakes at all but the lions seem to be cosying up to them and it makes me concerned, rumour has it a snake ate a goat once, you could actually see it inside! Could you imagine my poor Billy inside a snake!

I think I'll let him carry on with his plan, there'd be not much harm in shooting a lion. We need a bit of chaos now and again to make life interesting, it does get rather boring in here on occasions. I must remember to headbutt one of the children tomorrow, they'll put me inside for a little while and I won't have to mix with the common rabble.

Talking of rumours there's a rather funny one doing the rounds. I'd wandered over to the lion enclosure yesterday, there was one of them bloody children pestering me, wouldn't leave me alone so I ran off when the gate was open. Well, one of those lions told me that the new lion, the head of the pride, the one who proclaims himself the greatest lion of all time, he's impotent! Can you believe that! I thought it was rather funny.

There's no roar like my roar! I'm a special lion and the whole zoo has to know about it. If they don't know about it I'll make sure to tell them. I am such a special lion, never has there been a lion like me! I knew the moment I walked in here I had the respect of the other lions, they all told me, what an amazing lion, how could it be possible that they're graced with the presence of such greatness. I was born to lead and lead I will, the rest of the zoo will not know what's happened to them because they've never seen the likes of it before. Ooooh! Look! A bird! The greatest lion!

Those monkeys keep provoking me and I'm not going to stand for it much longer, I don't care what that stupid panda thinks. He should be solving this problem but he's not doing enough! I'm going to demand that he does something about it and if he doesn't listen then I'll do something! I don't know what I'll do about it but I will definitely do something about it and it will be the greatest thing that anything has ever been done about anything just wait until you see! I've asked the smartest lions what to do, and I only ask smart lions, and they're making a plan. My uncle was a smart lion, it's in the genes. Ooooohh! Look! There's a beetle over there, I must crush it!

Those snakes are good animals, I love snakes, they're the nicest snakes I've ever met. They keep giving me things and telling me how clever I am. They should know! What great animals, I don't know why we didn't like them before. Great animals, the best. The old head of the pride didn't like them, he said they were bad animals but they're not bad animals, I know bad animals and they're not bad animals. They keep brining me food as well, how can someone who brings you food be bad. Definitely not bad animals.

Been some trouble in the pride recently and I'm not happy about it, they need to start listening to me. One of those lions with the funny colours keeps causing trouble, telling all the other lions he should be treated like every other member of the pride. Some of the lions don't like him though, they want him gone, they say he's useless and just causes problems. Smart animals and when my smart animals say something I have to listen to them. He keeps causing me trouble though, talking about protests now, says he won't eat his food and then the humans will come along and they'll get rid of me. I'll show him, how dare he question my authority! I'll just eat the humans. Ohhhh! Look! A butterfly!

Back to them monkeys. When I've dealt with them they'll all be singing my praises telling me how great I am, and so they should, so they should, I'm a great lion, probably the greatest. They'll build statues of me, the humans that is, they'll build great statues of the greatest lion which has ever lived. Even those lions who live in Africa, they'll never be as great as me! I don't know why we haven't eaten them before, too soft that's the problem, everyone will think the lions are too easy, well it's not going to happen anymore, not with me here. Oooooh! Look, there's another bird!

I'm getting fat. It's all this food they keep giving me. They know their place though, they know they have to give me their food. I don't care that they're all looking a bit skinny, that's what happens when you have someone protect you and that person is me! I'll have them killed if they don't bring me food. See what the other animals don't understand is how special I am. They all laugh at me and call me fatboy and other silly names but they don't know my story, they have no idea how I got here.

It was a beautiful summers evening, the birds were singing, the monkeys were happy, we were all together back then you see, and a great beam shone down on that small mound over there. It's a special mound, and there I came from heaven, slowly I descended as the other monkeys felt my presence and greatness and they knew I was the one who would lead them into greatness like my father had done before. Sitting down they were crying and howling letting the rest of the zoo know that finally the great one had arrived.

Oh how they worshipped me! Food of all kinds they brought me, even though they themselves hadn't eaten. They told me they didn't need the food and if it wasn't for me and my father before me they'd be oppressed by the other monkeys. They even flew me off to a zoo in Switzerland where I learned about the world, I was kept away from the other monkeys mostly but I still learned a thing or two but mostly people learned from me.

It's actually all a load of shit but how else can I control them? Mountains and descending from heaven? Can you see any mountains? How else can I control them? They're a wild bunch these monkeys, they keep saying they're not been fed as well as the other monkeys and even some of them say they want to go and live over in that over cage, their 'cousins' they call them! I deal with those ones quickly, they have an 'accident' and fall from a great height. Never will they be reunited with their 'cousins' unless it's under my terms. Far too clever those other monkeys, never would they believe stories about mountains and falling from the heavens.

I have a problem of late and I don't know what to do. It's that bloody lion in the cage next to us. Well I say next to us, there's a big lake between us but they're still a nuisance. I can see them looking over at us licking their lips, imagining how tasty we would be. Lucky we have that panda next to us or they would get very adventurous. The panda has been a bit aloof of late though and this troubles me. He even had the temerity to tell us to shut up the other night, I thought we had an agreement but he seems to not be following it. I'll show him one day!

I keep telling the lions, if they're not careful we'll come over one day and we'll cause chaos. They have some new cubs, it wouldn't be too hard to take some of them away, that'd teach them. The thing is they'd look for revenge and then that would be the end of us. Game over. You have to put up a front though because these other monkeys might start getting uppity and thinking they'll be the ones to take charge and that's not something I'll be able to put up with!

I keep telling them the lions escape at night and that's why there's so little food, not that I hide most of it when the humans come so I really need the lions to start behaving themselves. It's this new lion though which is the problem. He's rather insane, not just a bit crazy, he's full blown nuts and he seems to think he's some kind of God. Not like me, I just tell everyone I'm a God, I'm not really, this lion actually thinks he is and there's no telling what he might do if he had the chance. I'd hope the other lions would keep him in check but it seems they've gone a bit crazy as well.

You know what she said last night? Unbelievable! She said 'Billy, you need to know your place and start listening to me, you have to be patient!'. Patient! Bloody patient! I'm always patient but I'm fed up of it now. Do you know what they've gone and done? You won't believe it! They've only brought in one of these special cows and everyone loves him. I'm fed up of this, I really am. I just want to let them lions out and they'll eat the lot of them and then there'll be none of them left. Why ain't no one paying any attention to me? It's all about them ain't it.

I've been thinking of forming a bit of a gang. You know? Go around with a few goats, we'll bleat a bit and that'll get their attention, we might rough a few of the other animals up as well while we're at it. See the thing is, and what I don't understand, there's other animals out there who were part of this zoo when it first started, when we ruled the roost and they don't give a shit. It gets on my nerves it does. They keep going on about how the other animals have a right to be here and they ain't doing no harm. I'm not having that, they don't have any pride, gone soft. That's why I need to unleash the wolves. They'll start the revolution, you know there used to be wolves in this country don't ya? Yeah, I knew you wasn't one of them stupid, gone soft types.

I'm thinking of getting rid of the wife as well. One of the wolves might 'accidently' eat her, got the wrong goat you could say. I'll tell you why, because you'll just think I'm being a cruel bastard, she ain't got no plan! She agrees with me, she wants this place to ourselves, but she don't know how to do it, all the other animals are telling her but she ain't listening because she ain't got a clue. I always thought she was clever my wife, from good stock but I've come to realise she's just an idiot who don't listen to no one.

It was the snake who give me the idea about letting the wolves out. I ain't told no one that because no one likes the snakes but they ain't so bad. I think they've got our best interests at heart, and you know the other thing about them? They don't let no one into their little cage, go in there and they'll eat you alive and they can say that as well! I can't say that, if I say that these cows shouldn't be turning up or them fucking alpacas should be back in their own country making wool everyone says 'you can't say that Billy, you might hurt their feelings'. The snake can say it though.

I'm a bit worried about this mad lion though, I thought he was all right when he first turned up but he's a bit more mental than I thought. I seen him the other day, he was talking to himself, going on about how there ain't no other lion in the world that's better than him and then the next minute he was running around his cage chasing a butterfly. Not sure about that. He ain't scared to say what he wants, I can't knock that, it's just that he's provoking them monkeys and they're evil little bastards *when they want to be. One got out once and he tore a zebra to pieces, never seen nothing like it. Leave 'em alone I say.*

When I have the wife killed I wonder if they'll give me some extra food? That'd be nice, if they do I might start thinking about getting a few more of them offed. I know it ain't nice talking about killing your own kind but sometimes you've got to do what you've got to do ain't you?

Billy's gone a bit strange in the head, I think he might be thinking about getting rid of me. He keeps telling me the time has come and we need to let the wolves out. He's so bloody insolent sometimes, it's always now, now, now with him. He doesn't understand that you have to be patient. What if he does try and get me killed? Who will look after all the other goats then? Such bloody insolence and lack of gratitude. I was born to lead and I'm not letting anyone tell me any different, how dare they think they know any better than me.

It's the lack of gratitude which gets to me. There's a few goats, you've probably seen them about, skinny little fellows, don't look after themselves properly, not from particularly good stock, we keep them around because they're useful. When we're all tired we get them to go and approach the children and pretend they're adorable and then they brings us back a bit of food. Not a single bit of gratitude from them, none at all! Do they not realise if we didn't want them around we could have them shot? All it would take would be to provoke them a little bit, rile them up and they'd go and bite one of the children and then that'd be the end of them. I'm fed up of them, I really am.

That snake has been around a bit too much lately as well. I bet he's putting ideas into Billy's head. Very easily influenced is Billy. You know, there was a time when the lions would make it clear to the snakes that they were to leave us goats be but since this new lunatic of an animal has turned up it's all gone a bit wrong. I've tried to talk to him, I really have but he doesn't listen, all he does is talk about himself for a few minutes before running off and chasing insects or butterflies, no help at all. It's a shame the wolves can't eat him.

To add to all my problems one of the goats has started telling the others that they're not getting enough food and perhaps I should be sharing! Sharing!? How dare they! Do the not think I do enough for them? They wouldn't eat at all if it wasn't for me. I've a good mind to let the wolves at him and then we'll see what happens with his ideas of 'equality'. God I despise him! The other goats seem to have become quite attached to him though and so I can't really do much, perhaps Billy is right and we should do something soon.

Oh, how I love chaos! Watching all these foolish animals running around arguing among themselves, looking to fight and eat each other. It's a thing of beauty and it's all come from my beautiful brain. Never, ever underestimate a snake. I find it amusing some of them have cottoned on to my meddling but what can they do? Most of them sound like demented madmen and most don't believe them. A zoo in chaos is how I'll be able to take back what is rightfully mine. That bird enclosure should never have been built there, and when they all go mad I'm going to sneak in and eat all of them.

There's too many Billies in this world and they're all too stupid to see it. Not just Billy but that insane lion. He does give me great pleasure. He's becoming a bit untameable though, keeps doing things which I would rather he doesn't but it all causes a distraction and for that I am grateful. See, people like Billy only want to see what is in front of them, they don't look outside of their little pen. They keep looking back to a world that's long gone, one which will never be coming back but all you have to do is dangle that carrot in front of Billy and he comes running to do your bidding.

It's the same with those lions, all it took was a bit of whispering in their ears, telling them that the funny coloured lion was the cause of all their problems and this new lion would be their saviour and we were in business. Some of them are still a bit funny but I keep my distance from them. I like giving those monkeys a bit of ammunition too, not too much but enough to keep that foolish lion occupied. They like to think they're clever but not as clever as me. I pointed them in the direction of a pile of stones which they can use to throw in the lake. They think the lions will take them seriously then.

Once all this chaos descends upon us I'll have to think of what other mischief I can get up to. I have always wondered what goat tastes like. I've been told it has a nice flavour and that Billy is a plump little goat. His wife might be quite tasty as well. Not only would I get revenge on the birds, I'd make a mockery of those goats who think so highly of themselves just because they were important some time in the past. How about a lion?

171

*That would be pushing my luck, but you never know what will happen do
you? I would like to try lion, especially that mad one.*

I've had enough of these monkeys. All night they've been throwing
stones into that stupid lake. They think a lake will be able to keep us apart.
Believe me, I know a way out of this cage. If they don't stop tonight we'll
go over there and we'll eat all of them. One of the smart lions, the
smartest lion, not as smart as me of course but I don't count because I'm
so smart said we can't go over there because the monkeys will go crazy
and start attacking the other monkeys but as I said not as smart as me.
We'll just go over there and eat all of them and that'll be it, no problem.

That god damned funny coloured lion has been causing trouble again.
He's a bad lion and bad lions need to be dealt with. My favourite lions, the
best lions tried to push him into a corner and told him he's not to come
out of there but he fought back and now some of the other lions are
starting to get a bit brave. No respect! Sad! If only I could kill the funny
coloured lion he wouldn't be a problem anymore. I should ask the snake
what to do.

I've heard some of the other animals are saying I'm impotent. How can
they believe I'm impotent? I've sired the greatest lions, lions like no one
has ever seen before, the cleverest lions. I told that stupid goat, the
female one, I don't know her name, I told her I'm not impotent. If ever
she goes to another zoo she'll see the lions I've sired and she'll know
they're the greatest lions, not as great as me but still great. I never liked
those goats, I'll see what can be done about them, maybe we can eat
them, that'd be a good plan.

Those monkeys are starting up their racket again. That's it! I'm done
with it all, we're going over there tonight and we're going to kill all of
them, I don't care if some of them are good monkeys, to me they're all
bad monkeys. I won't go, I'll stay here and send my best lions, they'll
never have seen lions like the ones I send. That fat little monkey won't be
throwing stones anymore, the head of the pride before me should have
dealt with this but he's not as clever as me. Tonight's the night, we're
going to finish it once and for all and they'll all be cheering and chanting
my name and telling me what a great lion I am! How dare they call me
impotent!

I'm letting the wolves out tonight! I've had enough of it all, it is finally time. It's the only solution to this problem! I can't wait to watch as they finally rid our great zoo of all these foreign animals. There won't be no more oooohhhs and ahhhs! I'll be the one getting all the rubs and the food and all the acclaim, all the praise. Me the great Billy who finally liberated our fair zoo! I've managed to get some of the skinny goats involved, not all of them want to be part of it but we'll manage it, don't you worry!

I've decided she has to go. I was going to save her, I was going to let her know of my plan but I can't do it. I don't want someone who flip flops, who doesn't believe in what she does. I'll miss her, there's no doubt about that. A long time we've been together and the kids will miss her too but that's how it goes sometimes ain't it?

I've got a special plan for that one which keeps stirring up trouble, the one that keeps telling all the other goats that we're equal. I'm going to make sure his death is going to be a painful one, special plans for him. There's no place in this world for people who don't know their rightful position. If only he'd been quiet he could have lived a bit longer, I'd have probably had him killed at some point because he annoys me, but he'd have got a few more months. He better not try anything funny before tonight or there'll be trouble.

I'm letting the wolves out tonight. I've decided Billy has to go. He has ideas far above his station and I can't be having that. I loved him once but that love has long since gone. Once the wolves have dealt with him we can go back to being how we were. He never understood that you can't rock the boat, that we all have our levels in our society of goats. I'll be sad to see him go but it's for the best. Poor Billy, he was an idealist but you simply can't have people around who are a liability.

I'm not going to kill the agitator though, I don't want him gone, he has his uses. You have to give the others hope that something might change because when they don't have hope they can start to get a bit uppity and then we'll have problems. At least he provides them with hope even though not enough of them like him for him to actually do something. Can you believe he was actually saying that some of the skinny goats should be given some of the straw I sleep in at night? Shocking! Once they see what happens to Billy I'll be able to keep the threat of the wolves hanging over them.

I do believe that snake is up to something and I hope he doesn't interfere with my plans for tonight. He's been talking to that lion a lot and those bloody monkeys won't shut up. They had better not be planning something because that stupid lion has no idea what kind of madness he'll unleash if they go over to those monkeys. I hate them, they're a nuisance but the chaos they can cause is the likes of which we've not seen before.

So, the lions are going to come over tonight! I the Great Leader of the monkeys is going to finally take control and unite us all! I thought they never had the balls to actually do it. There's not much left for me to do but to tell the other monkeys to attack their 'cousins'. They'll be free to kill as they please, they can eat all the food they like over there. That stupid panda has been telling me not to do anything 'stupid' as though he has any control over me. If they're going to eat me I'll make sure the rest of them pay for it.

I told them, I told all of the pandas that the lions were arrogant, ignorant and foolish. Some of them said they envied the freedom the lions had but they just couldn't see it. They worship an insane dotard who will bring them to their death. Perhaps I should have reigned the monkeys in a little bit, but they have gone insane too, they just don't listen! I don't know how all this will end but I do know it's because of the absolute stupidity of the rest of the animal kingdom. If only they had the intelligence of the panda.

The monkey asked me if we'd come to help but I declined. I no longer wish to be involved, let them all kill themselves and then when the dust has settled it'll be a much nicer and orderly place for us, the pandas to rule. There'll be no lions left. I have plans for that snake too, he seems to think we like him but he couldn't be more wrong. He's useful, everyone is useful to us. Friends? We have no friends, friends are for the weak and foolish.

I should probably make sure there's no way for them monkeys to get in here or they will just come and cause trouble. They all look so hungry and there is no way we are feeding them. We have enough for ourselves and that will do. Never mind that they're uncultured fools who will pollute our pens with their idiocy.

It's chaos, chaos everywhere! Billy released the wolves and they ate him! He didn't stand a chance, I know I was going to have him killed but to see him finished off like that, I don't think I'll ever forgive myself! The whole zoo has gone insane! The monkeys are killing the other monkeys, the lions have gone mad and are eating the monkeys too, the panda broke out of his cage and killed a lion, the snake is eating all of the birds, it's all gone mad! I don't know what to do, there'll be none of us left! How could it have come to this!

We were warned, we were told it would happen. They said you're all too interested in yourselves, you don't care about the others who are sharing your space. I never wanted to do this anyway, it was Billy, he pushed me into this, I'd never have gone through with it if it was for that foolish old goat! Now what? We have nothing! There's only a couple of goats left, the wolves have gone mad, the lions have gone mad, the snakes are sitting back and watching. It was inevitable though, we wouldn't listen, we never listen. Our zoo is ruined and nothing will ever be the same again!

Oxford Circus

Oxford Circus, home to London's most famous shopping street which is illuminated each Christmas

The calendar is at the end of my bed. Every morning when I wake up it's the first thing I see. The twenty five little doors, seventeen of them already open. Each one has a small piece of chocolate inside. I am not bothered about the chocolate, each door that's opened means it's a day closer to Christmas. One more door and there's no more school! I have to do one more thing at school though before it's done with. The thing that is making me the most nervous! Once that is over I can really really look forward to Christmas.

The school play, I only have one three words but I'm scared. I asked the teacher if I could not be in it but she said it was too late and she couldn't find someone else now. I didn't want to be in it in the first place they just chose me! It wasn't fair! Each evening when school has finished we go into the hall and go over the play again and again. I wait nervously each time for my three lines, when I have to run out onto the stage, dressed all in green, a little green hat and big red circles painted onto my cheeks. I so want it to be all over!

The radio is on in the kitchen, Capital Gold, playing Christmas songs. It's foggy outside and it's not quite bright yet. Mum comes into the room with a plate of toast and some cereal, she looks surprised to see that I am already awake. I sit down on my bed and eat it as I think about the play. How many people are there going to be there? What if I make a mistake and everything goes wrong and I make the whole play wrong. People will laugh at me and then I'll never be able to go back to school because they'll all make fun of me.

One of the other kids has a big part, she's Father Christmas' wife, she doesn't care though. When we're practicing she always says her lines right and the teacher is always telling her that she's doing really well. She talks to everyone at school and all the teachers love her. Sometimes I wish I could be like that but I'm not, I'm really shy. Now I have to stand in front of the whole school and all their mums and dads. It's just three words though, I'm sure I can do it, mum keeps telling me I'll be fine, if she says I'll be fine then I should be!

I know how many days it is until Christmas and I know how many it is until I finish school but I count all the doors left on the calendar again, just to make sure. I open today's one and take out the small chocolate and eat it, making sure mum isn't there, she says you shouldn't eat chocolate in the mornings. Now only seven doors left. I wish I could hide inside tomorrow's door! Then I wouldn't have to go to the play. It's too small though! The man on the radio says it's eight o'clock, still half an hour left before I have to go to school.

The calendar is a picture of a house. There's a big snowman in front of the house. It never snows at Christmas here though, I wish I could make a snowman one day. I'd make it big and fat, I'd give him a coat too so that he doesn't get cold. There's a cartoon that I saw last Christmas, a little boy who makes a snowman and the snowman comes inside his house and they fly away together over the town. I wonder if I build a snowman will it come alive and then I can go and fly with him! Maybe he'll take me to Oxford Street and I can see all the lights! I really want to go there!

There's a catalogue by my bed. I quickly put on my school uniform and then sit waiting for mum, looking through the toys. All the things that I'd love to have. I can't have all of them though, that would be too expensive. I just want one or two. There's a big castle made from Lego, I really want that but it is so expensive. I don't think mum'll be able to get that for me. One of my friends said they were going to get a bike for Christmas but I can't get a bike, I'm not allowed to go out on my own and mum says all the kids downstairs are naughty so I wouldn't be able to ride it anywhere. I would love a bike though.

"Time to go! Hurry up or we'll be late!"

It's so cold outside! When I breathe and blow out I can see my own breath. None of the trees have any leaves on them. The sky is really grey as well, it looks like it's going to fall down. We walk slowly down the street because it's slippery, there's little patches of white on the ground, every time I step on one I feel my feet slip forward. If mum wasn't with me I'd try and slide down the street but I can't while she's here because she'd get angry and tell me it's dangerous, maybe if they let us in the playground I'll be able to do it later!

177

There's lights outside some of the houses, one man has put a big Christmas tree in his garden. There's all different coloured lights and underneath the Christmas tree there's a Santa Claus pulling some reindeer. One of my friends said that in Australia Christmas is summer time but I don't believe him. How can you have Christmas in summer time? That's definitely impossible. The High road is busy even though it's in the morning. Everyone looks excited and people are smiling more than they usually do.

"I'm getting five hundred pounds for Christmas and my dad is getting me a bike and my mum is going to take me to America!"

"So?! My dad is giving me a thousand pounds!"

"Our Christmas tree is massive too, it's so big that we can't even fit in the house, we have to leave it outside the house, and it's got lots and lots of lights. I bet it's bigger than your tree."

"No! My dad said he's going to go to Lapland and get a tree from there and it's going to be so big that there'll be no tree bigger than it. He said he's going to get my Christmas presents from Father Christmas early as well. I bet your dad can't do that."

We have a nice Christmas tree. I don't know why they want such a big Christmas tree, I like our little one. There aren't many presents underneath it yet, even if there isn't any I won't care, I just want it to be Christmas. I don't believe them anyway! The teacher wants us to write a story about Christmas, I hope I can write a good one, the person with the best story will get some sweets tomorrow after the play is over. Maybe if I know I'm going to get some sweets it'll make the play go quicker!

One day there was a boy. The boy was only seven years old. Every Christmas he wanted it to snow but he still hadn't seen it snow at Christmas. When he wakes up in the morning he looks out the window and at the sky hoping that just one little snowflake will fall from the sky. On Christmas Eve, he thought he saw a snowflake. Only a little one! He ran down the stairs and out of his front door and looked up at the sky trying to find the snowflake but there was no snowflake. The boy was sad, he really thought it was going to snow.

One of his friends saw him standing there and came and asked him what he was doing. The boy said 'I'm trying to catch a snowflake!' His friend stood there with him and they both looked up at the sky trying to see if they could see one but there weren't any. His friend got bored and went home leaving the boy alone. The sky became dark and the clouds went away. All he could see were stars and the moon. His mum shouted to him through the window to come inside otherwise he'd catch a cold. The boy looked up one more time and he saw a star moving across the sky. In his head he wished for it to snow, just a little bit.

The boy's mum cooked him his dinner, but he was excited because tomorrow was Christmas day. He looked at the big Christmas tree in the corner. Under the tree there were big boxes, red ones, yellow ones and blue ones. All of them had big red ribbons on them and a big bow at the top. When the boy's mum went to wash dishes he sneaked up to the boxes. He looked at the door to see if his mum was coming, she wasn't. He tapped the boxes with his finger, then he picked one up and shook it a little bit to see if he could find out what was inside. Then he heard his mum so he put the box down and pretended to watch the television.

His mum told him he had to go to bed. He lay on his bed trying to go to sleep. His friend told him that if he counted sheep he would be able to go to sleep quickly. He counted one hundred sheep in his head but he still couldn't sleep. He heard his mum go to bed, all the lights in their house were off. There were no noises outside, still he couldn't sleep. I just want to go to sleep so I can wake up in the morning and open all my presents he said to himself. He climbed down from his bed and opened the curtain a little bit so he could look outside, maybe he would be able to see Father Christmas!

In the sky he saw a light moving and flashing. Maybe that's Father Christmas! I wonder where he has been tonight already! He must have been to so many places. I hope he doesn't forget about me, mum says he gives me one present every year but the rest of them are the presents that she gives to me. The light moves away and then it disappears. Maybe he has forgotten me. The stars slowly started to disappear too, if it's clouds maybe it really will snow! The boy finally fell asleep sitting next to his window.

When the boy woke up it was still dark. He went into the kitchen to see what time it was, it's still only five o'clock! He can't wake his mum yet, she will say it's too early and he needs to go back to bed! He goes quietly into the living room, it's so dark! The boy is a little bit scared, he doesn't like the dark but he is excited too! He looks out the window but there is no snow, maybe next year it will snow, I can wait one year for snow he says to himself. He sits by the window again, there's nobody outside, no cars driving in the street, no one walking. There is a light on in the house across the road, he can see a boy jumping up and down. Why isn't his mum angry?

At the bottom of his house the boy sees a strange shape. It's big and round, it's really white too. It looks like a snowman! It really is a snowman! He has a hat, and his nose is a carrot, he has a black coat on too. Where did he come from? It hasn't snowed! The snowman waves at him. The boy looks over to the other house with the light but the light is off now, maybe his mum was angry! The snowman waves again, telling him to come down the stairs. The boy doesn't know if he should go or not, he's a little bit frightened, then the snowman smiles and the boy smiles back. He walks down the stairs slowly and quietly.

When he walks out of the door the snowman takes his hand and they walk down the street. The snowman can't talk, he just smiles. He walks with the boy through the streets, pointing at the windows as the lights come on in each house, little children playing with their new toys. The boy is worried he will be late and his mum will be angry that he has gone outside on his own. The snowman turns around and takes the boy back home. When they get to the door, the snowman points to the sky and smiles, then he walks away. The boy climbs the stairs, his mum is still not awake. He looks out the window and can see that it's snowing! He finally gets Christmas present that he has always wanted!

I hope the teacher likes it!

"That boy over there, he's not going to get any Christmas presents. His mum and dad haven't got a job and are poor. That's what my mum said."

"What's the point in Christmas if you don't get any presents?!"

"I don't care, my dad has lots of money and he's going to buy me all the best presents."

The little boy is called Mark. I don't ever talk to him, he doesn't talk to anyone, he's very quiet. I told my mum that the other kids say bad things about him and mum said that I should just ignore them. He's drawing a picture, it looks like it's a tree and some presents. I think I should talk to him, he must be lonely if no one ever talks to him.

"What are you drawing?"

"A tree, and some presents."

"Is it your house?"

"No, we have a tree but there won't be many presents."

"Oh, why not?"

"My dad lost his job and he doesn't have much money. It's okay though, I don't mind, my nanny is coming for Christmas and she always makes me laugh."

"Why don't you talk to people?"

"They all make fun of me, they say I'm poor so I don't want to talk to them. I'm not poor we just don't have much money."

"You should just ignore them."

He carries on drawing his picture. It's like other people aren't here, he's just drawing his picture, as though he's the only person in the classroom. At the top of his picture he is drawing lights, they are all different shapes, stars and Christmas trees and angels. I wish I could draw like that, I can't even draw a man properly. I wonder what it's like to have no friends? What does he tell his mum about when he goes home from school? He puts down his pens and folds the piece of paper into four and puts it in his pocket.

"What are you going to do with that?"

"I'm going to take it home and give it to my mum. I saw some lights on the television, it was on a big street, there were lots of Christmas trees and angels, I wanted to draw it for her. She'll like that I think."

The teacher in charge of the play is in the room. I forgot about the play! Why did she have to come into the room? I wouldn't have to think about it then.

"Remember everyone who is in the play, you come here straight after lunch so we can get ready. Everyone will have to be on their best behaviour, all of your parents are going to be there watching and we want to put on the best play we can for them."

I'm not sure if my mum is going to be able to make it. She has to work, she said she will try and get away early but I am not sure. If she doesn't come it doesn't matter, I don't really care, I only have a tiny part anyway.

"Why were you talking to Mark? He's weird."

"He's okay, I think he's just lonely."

"If he wasn't so weird then he'd have some friends. If other people see you talking to him they might make fun of you too."

"I don't care, I was only asking him what he was drawing."

"My mum is taking you home with us tonight."

"I know, my mum has to work."

Mark is in front of us kicking a stone, just him and his stone, like when he was drawing the picture, as if nobody else is on the street with him. I wonder what he is thinking? I wonder how his holidays will be? He doesn't have a part in the play, I wish I could be him, he doesn't care about anyone else. He goes into a doorway, the door opens and he goes inside, as we pass his house I look in the window. There's a small Christmas tree in the window, there's a lady looking out the window, she smiles as we walk past, I put my hand up to wave at her and she waves back.

It's cold and dark outside when mum picks me up from John's house. She talks to John's mum for ages, I don't know what they are talking about, they keep whispering and then laughing, sometimes mum rolls her eyes. I just want to go home now, I'm tired. John's mum gives mum a drink and they close the door and sit down. I know we won't be going home for a long time yet. They laugh and talk about people. John is asleep on the sofa so I have no one to play with. Finally mum puts her coat on and we go home.

It's so cold outside, even colder than this morning. I blow out, it looks like a big puff of smoke, it makes me think of my favourite book about a purple dragon that had a thorn stuck in his foot and no one would help him to take it out. Puff was his name! I hold mum's hand as we walk slowly down the road, I think she's enjoying the walk.

"Are you looking forward to your play tomorrow?"

"No! I don't want to do it! Can you write me a note?"

"I can't write you a note now, it's too late, they won't be able to find anyone else."

"Pllleeeaaasseee?"

"No! You'll be fine, I don't know why you're so worried about it. All you have to do is say a couple of words and then it's over, you won't even feel it."

"Will you be coming?"

"Yes, I'll be able to finish at lunchtime tomorrow so I can come and see you. Your nan is coming as well."

Nanny usually gives me some money.

"Okay."

"I have a surprise for you tomorrow night as well. When the play is over you'll see what it is."

A surprise? I wonder what kind of surprise it'll be? It can't be a present because she wouldn't give that to me until it's Christmas day.

"What is it?"

"It's a surprise, you'll see tomorrow night. You can bring one of your friends with you if you like."

"So we're going somewhere?"

"You'll see tomorrow!"

Where will we be going? I just want it to be tomorrow after the play already, I don't want to have to wait another day.

We pass a man in the street who is drunk, he has fallen over. I think he is talking to himself, I hold mum's hand tighter but she doesn't seem to be worried. Another man is shouting at the drunk man but the drunk man is just laughing. I feel a little bit scared.

"Don't worry, he's just had too much to drink."

I wonder if the drunk man will sleep outside all night? If he does won't he be cold? The man shouting at him walks away, the drunk man starts singing 'silent night'. I know that song because we sing it in school sometimes. I keep looking back to see if he's okay, he just keeps singing, people walk past him looking scared. He doesn't look scary, he's just a little bit loud.

"Will that man be okay?"

"He'll be fine love, he's just a bit drunk."

"Why is he singing a song?"

"He's probably just happy."

"Won't he be cold if he sleeps outside?"

"He'll find his way home."

"Why do people get drunk?"

"It makes them happy and they can sing songs."

Why do you need to have something to make you happy? I sing songs to myself when there is no one else around, I don't need anything to help me. I hope the man will be okay.

We climb the stairs to our flat. I am really tired now.

"Time to go to bed! It's late and you've got a long day tomorrow."

"Can I look out the window? Just for five minutes."

"Five minutes and then it's bed, if you're tired in the morning you've only yourself to blame."

Every night before I go to bed I like to look out the window. In front of where we live is a bus station. The driver makes the name of the place on the front of the bus change before he drives away. Some places I've never heard of, I try to imagine what they would be like. One bus has 'World's End' on the front. What's at World's End? Where is World's End? Do they have Christmas at World's End? Everyone has Christmas! The driver is about to go, then he stops. I see the drunk, he's still singing, he jumps onto the bus and sits down at the back, his head against the glass.

"Bed! Now!"

Mum kisses me on the head and turns off the light in my room. I can feel butterflies in my stomach, I'm so tired but I don't want to go to sleep because I know if I go to sleep tomorrow will be here and then I will have to be in the play. I know tomorrow morning is going to go so fast, I want it to go slowly. What if I make a mistake and then everyone laughs at me? I'll be like Mark, no one will talk to me and then I'll have no friends. I wonder if he is a good person? He doesn't seem like a bad kid, he's never naughty.

The lady waving to me through the window, was that his mum? She looked a little bit like him. All the other kids said that his mum is a bad lady because she never comes and picks him up from school. I think it's because he only lives two minutes away from the school, she doesn't need to come and pick him up. I wonder if that drunk man went to World's End? Maybe the driver threw him off the bus. I don't want to do this stupid play...

When I want something to happen the time always goes slowly. When I don't want something to happen the clock moves really quickly. It's the last day and everyone has brought toys to class and we can do whatever we like. Every time I look at the clock it has moved forward half an hour! Some of the other kids keep talking about the play and it is making me more nervous. Now I just wish it was over. I forgot that mum has a surprise for me. I still don't know what it is, I can't even guess. It's nearly lunch time now, I really don't want to do this!

"I can't wait for the play! They said it will be really good this year, there's elves and Father Christmas and they said that at the end everyone is able to get a present."

"Miss!! He took my toys from me and he won't give it back."

"I'm telling my mum, you're not allowed to bring that to school. She'll tell the headmistress and then you're going to get expelled!"

"No I won't!"

"Miss! Whose story was the best one? I bet it was mine! When are you going to give me all the sweets?"

"I asked my mum if you could come to my house at Christmas and she said yes but you need to ask your mum first."

"I'll ask her after school."

Why is everyone so noisy today? Some of them are running about and some of them are jumping up and down. The teacher doesn't care, she's just talking to one of the kids. They're all so excited! Mark is sitting by himself reading a book, no one else is playing with him. Five minutes until lunchtime! My stomach feels funny, I wish I could run away!

"What book are you reading?"

"It's about a dragon."

"That's my favourite book!"

"Are you going to be in the play today?"

"Yeah, but I don't want to be. Do you want to do it for me?"

"I'm not allowed to do that. It'll be okay."

"My mum and my nan are coming, is your mum coming? I think she waved at me yesterday."

"No she can't come, she doesn't like to go outside. She says it makes her frightened."

"Oh! What about your dad?"

"He went to a new job today. It doesn't matter, I'm not in the play anyway."

The bells rings and Mark puts the book back on the shelf and walks out, everyone else pushes past him. Today is school's Christmas dinner. There'll be turkey and roast potatoes and gravy and some vegetables. Most people won't eat the vegetables though. I have to eat mine quickly so we can get changed and get ready for the play.

"Miss! I feel sick! I think I need to go and see the nurse!"

"You look fine, you don't have a temperature either."

"But I have a headache, and my belly hurts."

"Really? That means you won't be able to have the sweets I was going to give you for having the best story then. Don't worry about the play, you only have a small part and it will be over in seconds, now hurry up and go and get your Christmas dinner before it's all gone."

"When can I have my sweets?"

"You can have them when the play is over. Don't go running to any of the other teachers telling them you're sick either because I'll let them know you're not."

"Okay, Miss!"

I'm not even hungry, it doesn't taste nice. Mum's turkey will be much better than this. What if I ran away out the door. No one would miss me. Mum would see I'm not there, the teacher would probably come and look for me too. I throw away the dinner, I don't want it.

"Everyone who's in the play make sure you come to the hall in 10 minutes."

The hall is full of kids and teachers. The kids are all excited. I think I am the only one who is nervous, everyone else is running around while the teachers try and catch them to try and put their costumes on. They tell us all to move into a corner where there's a curtain. The teacher gives me my green costume and my hat. I put it on. One of the older kids comes over and puts red lipstick where my cheeks are, I look in the mirror and see I have big, red, rosy cheeks. I think I look stupid, everyone else looks stupid too.

"Remember everyone, I will tell you when you need to go on stage, don't worry, don't be nervous, everything will be fine."

There's a big, fat kid sat next to me in the same costume as me but his doesn't fit properly and he looks even more stupid than I do. He keeps talking to himself but I don't know what he's saying. He looks at me, his big round face looks yellow even though he has lots of makeup on.

"I think I'm going to be sick!"

He runs off into the corner and I hear him throw up. All the other kids laugh and make noises, some of the girls start screaming. The teachers run about even more trying to tell everyone to be quiet. The fat kid comes back and sits down next to me and starts to talk to himself again, one of the teachers has a mop and bucket and is cleaning up his Christmas dinner.

"There's turkey in it!"

Someone comes through the curtain, the curtain doesn't close properly and I can see outside. There are so many people. Oh no! I didn't think there would be this many people. I look to see if I can see my mum and my nan but I can't see them. What if she couldn't make it? What if I am not going to be able to get my surprise now! She might have had to work late and she won't be able to see the play!

The girl who everyone likes is wearing her costume, everyone is telling her how nice she looks. She just smiles and doesn't say anything. All of the teachers look worried.

"Five minutes!"

I want to be sick like that boy! Through the curtain I can see Mark, he waves at me. I look around me to see if anyone is watching and then I wave back at him, he laughs and pulls a face, I laugh too. The fat kid sitting next to me runs away again but this time he runs through the door. A teacher runs after him trying to catch him. Where's he going?!

Everybody goes quiet and the lights go dark apart from the big one on the stage. The girl goes on to the stage and starts to sing. Some of the teachers are smiling. The teacher who chased the fat boy comes back in the door with her hands in the air, she looks at the other teachers and shakes her head. I wish I had thought of that! Now he doesn't have to do the play. How can I make myself sick? I try to pretend I want to get sick but I don't feel anything. The girl stops singing and the people start clapping.

I watch all the other people run on and off the stage to say their words or sing their songs. I still can't see mum through the curtain. I don't think she has made it. Mark keeps making faces at me. I laugh at him and one of the teachers sees me and tells me to be quiet and stop messing about, I feel my face go red but I know she can't see it because of all the makeup. The teacher holds up her hands showing two fingers. I think she means two minutes but I'm not sure, she didn't do that when we were doing the rehearsals.

I feel a little bit dizzy, the other kids that have finished their parts are all laughing and playing, they don't have to worry anymore. The teacher is waving her hands up and down at me but I just look at her. I don't want to get up. I can't even move if I want to, I feel so heavy! Another teacher grabs me and lifts me up. They both hold me by the curtain and then I hear them both start counting to three, when they say 'three' both of them push me forward.

I run onto the middle of the stage next to the girl who has just been singing again. I can't see mum, I can just see lots and lots of people but they all look the same. I look down and I can see Mark and he is still making faces at me. I don't want to laugh though. I am shaking, I know I have to say my words or else everyone will be laughing at me and then I'll have no friends and all of Christmas will be ruined and mum will be angry at me.

"What about Ready Express?"

My voice sounds stupid, it doesn't sound like my voice. I look on both sides again but I still can't see mum. The girl pushes me and I run off the stage. It's over! It's over! It only took a few seconds, mum was right! The teacher smiles at me and tells me I was good. I don't think I was good, it's over, that's all I care about. I look through the curtain and I make a face at Mark and he laughs, one of the teachers outside tells him to be quiet. I laugh while he gets told off. In the corner at the back I see mum and nanny sitting next to each other. They can't see me but they're here!

The play is nearly over, the girl is singing another song. We all have to go onto the stage at the end but I don't care about that because I don't have to say anything and everyone else is there. Everyone walks onto the stage, the girl is standing on a box, she tries to get off the box but she falls over. Everyone starts laughing. The teacher picks her up and shouts at everyone to shut up but they keep laughing. Some of the parents are laughing too. The girl starts to cry and runs off the stage. At least I never fell over, I didn't like her anyway so I don't feel bad for her. The curtain closes on the stage, the teacher keeps shouting at people but we all run through the curtains to our mums and dads.

"I told you it would be easy! You were brilliant!"

"I tried to get sick but it wouldn't work."

"What did you do that for?"

"I didn't want to do it."

Her eyes roll around and she ruffles my hair. What's my surprise?

"Here's your sweets for your story, I told you it would be fine!"

"Thank you Miss! Mum? What's my surprise?"

"You'll see in a bit, did you ask John if he wanted to come?"

"Can I take someone else?"

"Take whoever you like, love but they need to ask their mum or dad first."

"Okay, I'll be back in two minutes."

If his mum wasn't here I think he might have gone home already. I run over to where he was sitting but he isn't there. I go back to the classroom to see if he has gone to get his bag. He is there, reading the rest of the book he was reading earlier.

"I wanted to finish it in case it isn't here after Christmas."

"My mum wants to take me somewhere, it's a surprise and she says I can bring one of my friends. Do you want to come with me?"

190

He looks a little bit sad, then he smiles.

"Yes, but you have to come to my house first so I can ask my mum."

"Okay, let's go."

Mark's mum looks like she is a bit frightened but she tells mum and nanny to come in for a cup of tea. We go inside and sit down, mum goes to the kitchen with his mum and I can hear them talking. They come back with some tea and some biscuits. I take one of the biscuits but it doesn't taste very nice.

Their Christmas tree is small and there aren't many decorations. Their television is really small too. It feels like an old house. In the corner of the room there are lots of books in a pile. His mum sees me looking at them.

"Have a look through them, if you like them you can take one."

"He's enough books of his own at home."

"Mark, make sure you behave yourself when you're out."

"I will! Where are we going?"

"You'll find out soon enough."

"It won't be too late by the time we get home."

"It doesn't matter, they don't have school tomorrow."

"Mum? Why can't Mark's mum come with us?"

"She's tired love, maybe she'll come with us another time."

We sit upstairs on the bus. So many people are outside shopping, it's like day time but it's almost night time. They all have big bags full of things. The bus is moving slowly because there are lots of cars. Mark stares out the window too, he doesn't say anything, he looks happy. I looked at the front of the bus to see where it was going but it's to a place that I have never heard of.

The bus turns and I know where we are! We're in Oxford Street! I can see all the lights hanging over the street. They're all different colours, there's lots of stars and angels and Christmas trees, there's Father

Christmas with his reindeers and presents. Mum moves us to the front of the bus so we can see better. They all look so close. I look at Mark but his eyes are wide open and so is his mouth, he looks back at my mum and smiles at her. We pass all the shops, they have trees and presents in all of their windows, I want to go inside, it looks real, like they are really Father Christmas' house!

We get off the bus, mum holds both of our hands. There are so many people, pushing past each other, all of them with big bags, none of them say sorry, I think that's a bit rude! I look up at the lights as we walk along the street. They go the whole way across the road, all the way down the road, how many are there? How long did it take them? How did they make all of them? Mum takes us along the road, both of us are staring upwards.

It's cold but I don't feel cold, I feel really warm. Some people stop to take a picture of me, I forgot! I am still wearing my green costume and I still have big, red, rosy cheeks! They don't speak English but they laugh and smile at me as they take a picture.

We stop in front of a big shop. Nan bends down gives me a twenty pound note, I put it into my pocket. Wow! What can I buy with a twenty pound note! Inside the shop it's filled with kids and toys, there are toys everywhere. I wish I could buy all of them. There are so many colours too, things I've never seen, there's a little helicopter flying around with kids running after it trying to catch it. There's a man dressed as Father Christmas and he has lots of elves, kids are waiting to see him. I can tell him what I want for Christmas!

Mark is looking at some Lego, it's not big, just a small thing you can make. He puts it down again and comes over and plays table football with me. He's quite good, he beats me three times. He goes back to the Lego toy and looks at it again, he reads the back of the box and then puts it back.

"How much is it?"

"It's £15, I just like the look of it but it's too expensive, I don't want it anyway."

"I can buy it for you."

"No, it's okay, I don't want it. One day I can get it, you can buy yourself a present for Christmas."

"No, I want to buy it for you!"

"Why?"

"I don't know, I just thought you might like it."

"It's okay, I don't want it, it's good just to see it. What are you going to buy with your money?"

"I don't know, there's too much here, I want everything."

I really wanted to buy it for him but he wouldn't let me. Maybe he's shy. He doesn't seem to be unhappy, he keeps laughing and smiling as we look at all the other toys. Mum calls us both over and tells us it's time to go home. As we sit on the bus on the way home, I look out at one of the stars and make a wish. I wish that the snowman doesn't come to visit me, I wish he goes to visit Mark and his mum and they can go out together.

Piccadilly Circus

Piccadilly Circus, famous for its iconic advertising boards and tourists

Tourists, you always know the tourists. It isn't just the camera or the bright yellow raincoat, it's the way they walk, they never really know where they're going, they're just walking, hoping to find something as interesting as the last thing they saw. It's a bit like a drug that way, not much is going to top the first thing you saw, it's all disappointment after that. By the end of the holiday, they're walking around as if they want to enjoy what they're doing but they're not really sure they are, just going through the motions, the magic and mystery has worn off. Inside they're probably cursing the stupid English and their weird ways, longing for pushing into queues and a little less passive aggressiveness.

You know which countries they are from as well. The Americans, you just know, there ain't no explanation, you just know it's them. The Europeans, they look around with an air of aloofness, moodily smoking a cigarette, it's nice to see the quaint little English people and their strange ways but they're still better than them and God forbid one would have to live amongst them. The Chinese, they have money but they're not quite sure how to pull it off yet, they look frightened having been regaled with tales of murderers and rapists aplenty, stalking them as they walk the streets of London, not a gentleman in sight.

Piccadilly Circus. Circus is apt. There's all sorts wandering around, putting a show on as I sit here. I'm part of that show too, a major part or a minor part? I'm probably the small pony that's paraded around for the kids to see and touch before they bring the big animals out, the lions and the tigers. Maybe I'm the strongman, you think he's interesting in a perverse way but you soon grow tired of his antics, he's a one trick pony that you don't take much notice of the more you see him. He too is tired of all the people, but the people are all he has, his eyes imploring you to give him the adulation he needs to keep going. My adulation is money. That's all I want, just a pound, 50p, whatever you've got.

The sleeping bag my legs are inside is starting to smell and there are holes in it, I need a new one. It's one of them things that I'm really fussy about, I can't have a sleeping bag that looks tatty. You'd think that was a bit picky when you're in my position but not having somewhere to live doesn't mean you can't be fussy. I always keep where I sleep tidy as well, everyone knows it's my spot. I don't care what you do a few metres away, you can piss all over the floor for all I care, just don't invade my space and make it messy.

Crossing the road is a geezer with a map, he's holding it up as he crosses, a black taxi nearly takes him out but he's oblivious. He isn't bothered by the tutting either as men in suits tut and mutter their way past the stupid tourist and his almost life size map. He stops just in front of me but I don't think he's noticed me. I keep my eyes on him, I want him to turn and look my way, he'll probably ignore me but you never know. I'm not sure where he's from, that's odd. He definitely ain't a Yank, and he's not European. He takes an age to fold his map up and put it in his pocket. He looks straight at me, his forehead is ruffled, he's got mad curly hair as well, he looks a bit like a mad scientist.

"My friend! Which is quickest way to Oxford Circus?"

'My friend' means he's probably from the Middle East or South Asia. Got to be Middle Eastern, he doesn't look like he's from South Asia.

"Straight up that street there mate, Regent's street. Keep following it and you'll know when you're there."

"Thank you. 5 minutes?"

"About ten if you walk quickly."

He nods his head then starts rummaging around in his jean pocket. He takes out his wallet and then pulls a twenty pound note from it and puts it down on the sleeping bag, walking off towards Regent's Street. I slip the note into my pocket. I'll be able to get something decent to eat tonight. Might treat myself to a kebab or something. It's been a long time since I've been able to get a kebab for myself, a mixed grill, lamb, chicken, beef. I'll stay here another hour and then I'll head off to get something to eat.

A couple of fellas in suits stop just by the doorway I'm sitting in. They pull out a packet of cigarettes, light them and then start talking away. They're talking about people in the office they work at, slagging whoever these people are off. One of them is going on and on, the other fella is holding his phone, looking at it as if it's the most important source of information in the world. He nods his head, smiles and occasionally laughs, allowing the other geezer to keep talking about shite he doesn't care about but he's got to show he's interested. Probably his boss or something like that.

The one that's talking looks down at me as he rabbits on, he mustn't have noticed I was there before. I smile up at him, a bit of a gummy smile as I've a few Hampsteads missing. He frowns, moving away, looking at me as if he's just found out his missus is cheating on him with me.

"Any spare change mate?"

"No, I have no money."

"Wanker."

"You should be bloody grateful you don't live in a country where people like you are taken out and shot."

"Fuck off, mate."

"I really wish they'd do something about all these undesirables around here."

I laugh as they walk off, people look at me, they probably think I'm some sort of lunatic. I'm not a lunatic, I'm just an average person. The only difference is that I live outside while they live in nice houses and flats. You get used to the abuse, you've just got to shake it off. If I took it to heart, I'd have thrown myself off Waterloo bridge a long time ago.

I don't want to get up and go. For all the years that I've been sitting here, waiting for people to drop a few coins onto my sleeping bag, the bit I love the most is the people watching. You have to do something to make the time pass. It's one of the most famous pictures in the world, the big neon adverts above my head, the old red buses. People see that and think 'wow!' I really want to go there. They get here and they stand around taking photos of each other, posing, laughing and smiling. I often ask myself the question, do I envy them? Nah, not really, I made my choices.

I pick my sleeping bag up, fold it and put inside a plastic bag. I cross over the road walking towards Leicester Square. It's busy, there are all them performers in the square, dancing, trying to get people involved, pretending they're your friends, wanting you to dance with them but really they're not your friends, they just want what's inside your pocket. I stop and watch as one guy twirls around on his head to the beat of his ghetto blaster. There's only a couple of people standing and watching him, they don't seem too impressed either, they're just watching because now they feel for the guy, if they walk away they'll hurt his feelings.

He finishes his performance, stands up and bows to his audience. He doesn't acknowledge me, he knows I'm no good for what he wants. The two tourists look at each other realising that they should be giving him something for the dance, a dance they thought wasn't particularly impressive. He's got them, play on people's emotions, their need to feel like they're doing the right thing. His eyes plead, he looks around, emphasising that they're the only ones watching and they should be paying for that privilege. The man wants to walk away but his girlfriend taps him on the back and he reluctantly pulls a note out of his pocket and puts it in the dancer's hat. The dancer thanks him. Off they go to enjoy a meal in China town while the man broods over his stupidity and the girlfriend posts on Facebook about her amazingly charitable boyfriend.

I'm starting to wonder about my choice of dinner. I mean I'd love a kebab but this geezer has given me a right touch with this £20. Could do with spreading it out a bit. It's been going around that people begging on the streets are taking home thousands and thousands of pounds a month. I ain't seeing any of that money if they are. Some days are good, some days ain't too good and some days I get next to nothing. Thing is though, people listen to all these reports and then they don't give you nothing because they reckon you're going home to a four bedroom house out in the suburbs somewhere. Only place I'm going home to is a little spot on the Charing Cross road.

The security guard in the supermarket is watching me. I only want to get myself a drink. I hold up some change and show it to him, he still looks at me with suspicion so I walk around every single aisle, picking things up, looking like I'm debating whether or not I should buy it. I see a roast chicken, lemon and thyme it says on the package.

"This any good mate?"

He just looks at me, he wants me gone out of the shop.

"My cooker's broken anyway, ain't much good to me. Maybe next week, hey?"

"Just buy what you want and go."

"I fancy an iced coffee. I've never had one so I can't really fancy one can I? You've got to have had something before in order to fancy it. Ever had one? Are they nice?"

He shakes his head and slopes back off to the door of the shop. I pick up an iced coffee and pay for it at the counter. The girl at the counter smiles as she takes the money and calls me sir. I wonder to myself if she saw him following me around. Half the people in the world you hate and the other half you love. There's no in between.

Pall Mall is empty, it's always empty at night. I'm hungry but I don't want to eat yet, it's like the anticipation is better than the actual meal. I know I'm going to eat well and I want to make that feeling last as long as possible. Once I've eaten the anticipation will be gone and I won't know when I'll be able to treat myself again, there ain't always Middle Eastern fellas knocking about handing out £20 notes. There's a few coppers knocking about on The Mall but they take no notice of me. There's still a few tourists around taking photos, standing outside the palace, waiting for something exciting to happen. I want to tell them nothing's going to happen but it's like me, it's the anticipation, it doesn't matter if nothing happens.

Each night when I decide to go home I take this route. It's completely backwards but it kills time. I walk up The Mall to the palace, laugh to myself about the tourists, look up at the windows and see if I'll ever catch a glimpse of the woman herself. I can't really laugh at them can I? I'm just as bad, I'm never going to see her. Some people resent her, I don't resent her. If anyone should resent her it's me, I ain't got somewhere to live and she's living in a gaff like this. What's the point though? There ain't one, there's no point wasting my time hating someone.

The kebab tastes good. You've got to treat yourself sometimes. I throw the paper wrapping in the bin as I walk down Charing Cross Road, my nightly lap done. I nod my head at a few of the people sitting in the doorways, some nod back others don't notice and some just ignore me. I put the sleeping bag down on the floor, right on my spot and sit down on it. There's two old boys a few metres away, they move when they see me, they know it's mine and I ain't letting anyone encroach on that.

Pissed people walk pass as the pubs start to empty. It's as good as sitting at Piccadilly Circus. Geezers arguing with their girlfriends because they're too drunk to walk. People singing as they walk down the road. Sometimes you get the idiot who thinks he's hard and wants to have a go, they only pick on the people that won't fight back though. All you have to do is stand up, when you're tall it's usually enough to frighten people, if not, start searching in your pocket and they'll think you're going for a blade. Once midnight passes it begins to calm down a bit, just the odd shout from some of the old boys who've got pissed and are fighting with each other.

I'm feeling satisfied tonight. My stomach is full, the evening is clear but it's warm. A geezer walks past and hands me a bottle of beer. Says he doesn't want it, he's had enough already. When he's walked away I walk over and give it to one of the old boys. Not my thing beer, I don't like it, never have done. Some people use it to cope but I don't want to do that. I have my own ways of coping. They ask me how do I cope? I cope by normalising it. This is my life, this is the way it is and at the moment I can't change it. Maybe by normalising it means I won't change.

Don't get me wrong. If you come up to me tomorrow and said to me, here's the keys to a flat, here's 50 grand I'd take your hand off, of course I would. It ain't going to happen though is it? So what else am I supposed to do? It's like the old girl in the palace, I should hate her, but I don't, there's no point. When I do eventually go out, I don't want to go out all bitter and twisted. Maybe there's something wrong with me, maybe I should be bitter and twisted and hate the world but I just can't do it. Oh well, enough of the philosophical stuff for tonight, I'll get a good kip while my stomach is full.

The street cleaner with his machine wakes me. It's still early, no one else about on the streets, I pack away my sleeping bag. The air is cool, much cooler than it was last night. The lights still haven't turned themselves off on the bridge, it gives it a strange glow in the early morning sky. On the other side I can see him sitting down by the river, in his usual spot. He waves to me, I don't know how he can spot it's me from down there but he does, every morning without fail he waves up as I walk across Waterloo Bridge.

"It's my birthday today you know."

"I didn't know that, how comes you never told me? I would have got you something."

"Nah, I don't want anything. Sitting here of a morning is good enough, you can get me a coffee though if you're good for it."

"I'll get you a coffee."

He has the bluest eyes I've ever seen, they're so blue you would think they're not real. His hair is black but white is starting to show through. We have the same ritual every morning, meeting by the side of the river, putting the world to rights.

"Here's your coffee. Doing anything special for your birthday?"

"Haha, nah, nothing planned. You going to take me somewhere special?"

"I would if I could mate, but you know how it is, bit down on my luck!"

He laughs, running his hand through his thick hair, gulping down his coffee.

"If you could do anything for your birthday what would it be?"

"Anything?"

"Yeah anything, money's no object."

"The obvious would be to have somewhere to live but I think that would be a waste of an opportunity. One day I'll find somewhere to live of my own. You know what I'd really fucking love to do?"

"Go on..."

"Have a nice meal and then go to The Trocadero and play on the arcade machines."

"You can do anything you want and you want to go to The Trocadero and play computer games? I mean you could go and spend it somewhere on the beach or you could get a room in the Ritz for a night and have a load of beautiful women. The fucking Trocadero?"

"Simple things my friend, simple things."

"Go on, I'll humour you. Why the Trocadero?"

"Used to go there when I was a teenager with my mates. They were happy times, the happiest of my life. If I had a room in the Ritz with a load of beautiful women I'd just want to go to sleep on the bed, waste of a Genie's wish mate."

People going to work are walking past us. Most ignore us but a couple of people stare and then avert their gaze as I look back at them.

"It's your birthday, I can't take you to the Trocadero but I can get you a couple of cans. Meet me back here tonight and I'll sit with you while you have them. Can't be on your own for your birthday."

"I'll be back for eight. Enjoy your day!"

A boat passes by on the walk back to the bridge. There's tourists on it already, snapping away at everything and anything they can see, pointing at different things. When the boats pass by I wonder if they see the people that are out there or do they just see the buildings. You only see what you want to see. If I was dressed in a pink suit with a big pink top hat they'd notice me. You've got to stand out from the crowd otherwise we all just look the same. I wave, nobody from the boat waves back.

I sit down back on my spot, preparing to look as sad and as dejected as I can. A policeman walks by, tells me I can't sit there. I get up and walk down the backstreets in a circle and come back to the same spot, no sign of the copper, I sit back down. I wonder if there'll be any rich people giving me £20 notes today?

I've never taken much notice of my birthday, it's just another day. Some years it's passed and I ain't even remembered, it's only a few days later that I've suddenly thought I'm a year older. A man passes by and throws 20p on to the sleeping bag. When you don't really care about it you forget that other people do care about it. A tourist stops in front of the traffic lights and looks back at me, his phone is in his hand, he's trying to take a photo without me knowing. I'll get him a six pack of beer, it ain't much but at least it's something. The tourist looks at his phone and frowns, the picture must have been shit. Lucky I never charged him.

There's a geezer next to me arguing with his missus on the phone, well I think it's his missus anyway.

"I know I didn't come home last night but I was really busy at work and I ended up sleeping on my desk, I was so tired I just fell asleep. I couldn't ring you because there was a power cut...I bought some candles at the shop...of course I ain't lying to you? Why would I do that? You know your my one and only...which slut from the office?...Of course not babe, she wasn't there, she went home, you know I don't like her anyway... what do you mean you've cut my fucking clothes up?...All of them?"

She's hung up. He rests his head against the wall.

"Problems at home mate?"

"Can I come and live with you?"

"I would but my gaff is a bit small."

"I might be your next-door neighbour later on tonight."

"Fantastic, we'll have a party! Give me the money now and I'll go and get a few cans."

He smirks and gives me a fiver.

"Look after yourself mate."

"Remember, you're welcome round mine anytime you like!"

There's a lady screaming over by the fountain. People are surrounding her trying to find out what's wrong. People start rushing about looking for someone, her child must be missing. A copper walks over and starts talking into his radio. The woman isn't making any sense, it don't look like she can speak English, no one knows what she's saying. I get up and walk towards the crowd, it's drawing me in, it's a scene I see every day but today I want to help.

A girl appears from one of the shops selling tat and runs towards the woman, the woman grabs her and hugs her. Another one who's lost their child, their world collapsing and coming together again in a few seconds. My sleeping bag is gone, the little bit of change was on top of it. Why did I leave it? Why would anyone be so fucking heartless as to take it? I've still some money in my pocket, that'll get me by but I want my fucking sleeping bag back.

One of the street sweepers might have taken it. They don't usually. Up the back streets and have a look around there, the person who's taken it is probably just wanting to use it for themselves. A fucking sleeping bag and someone has nicked it!

Each person I pass I check to see what they're carrying. They clutch their belongings closer to them and try to avoid eye contact. I must look like a lunatic. I look back and see a woman approaching a policeman, she points in my direction. I turn into a side street and then another, I can't be dealing with coppers at the moment, they're only going to give me grief. I turn a corner and the copper is standing there. I've lost my mind, ended up going back on myself without realising. It doesn't matter I ain't done nothing wrong.

"Can I have a word please, sir."

"Okay."

"We've had reports of a person acting suspiciously. Can I ask what you're doing?"

"I know it was that lady who told you, I saw her. I wasn't try to rob her or anything. I've lost something and I'm trying to find it."

He's looking at me as if I'm stupid, one of them 'yeah, yeah, I've heard it all before' looks.

"What have you lost?"

"I've lost my sleeping bag. I'm homeless, it's what I sleep in at night."

"Where did you lose it?"

"Down in Piccadilly, someone nicked it."

He looks even more incredulous.

"What's your name sir?"

"William, William French."

He starts talking on his radio, giving them my name and date of birth. The woman at the other end comes back to him, he nods his head as he talks.

"Go on, go and find your sleeping bag."

I don't acknowledge his last words, I just walk off. I was sure he would at least search me, make me feel as inferior as possible but no he's just let me go. Wherever it's gone, I ain't going to be able find it now. Whoever has it will be long gone. I suppose I could check tonight when I get back to see if anyone there has it. They'll just say it's theirs, they've always had it, why would they nick my sleeping bag. The money as well, I was going to buy the few cans with that money, don't look like there's going to be any party by the river tonight, I don't even want to go now but I promised him.

I'm angry at myself for being so stupid as to leave it there. It's only a small thing though, it doesn't really matter, you'll be able to get another one. It ain't that one though is it. Stupid woman, how could you not be aware enough to know where your child is. It's her fault I've lost it. You can't blame the woman, she lost her child for fuck's sake, imagine how you'd feel if you lost a child, all you've lost is a fucking sleeping bag.

I'm hungry and tired. I sit down outside one of the theatres and watch as a few of the performers stand outside smoking and talking to each other. They speak loudly in one of those look at me voices. I suppose that's what they do though ain't it? They want everyone to look at them, they want to stand out from the crowd. Two of them throw their cigarettes on the floor and start dancing in the middle of the pavement, the others start clapping as they dance. They all look happy and I hate them for it. What a difference a few hours make? This morning I'd have had something cynical, something sarcastic to say about them then I'd never think of them again. Right now I hate them, I wish they'd just fuck off and let me sit in peace.

"Excuse me? Would you like to accompany me for a cup of coffee?"

"What?"

"I really need someone to talk to and I thought you'd appreciate a cup of coffee. I don't know you and so it's easier for me to talk to someone I don't know."

He's a small guy with mad professor hair. There's a scarf which looks like a handkerchief around his neck, he's wearing a white suit, he kind of looks like he should be living out here with me but he obviously isn't.

"What's you name?"

"Phillip. And yours?"

"William. You often invite strangers for cups of coffe?"

"No, never! You're the first."

I wait outside while he goes in to order two cups of coffee. Today is a bit surreal. I mean most days are odd but today has been particularly strange. I'm dreading what this fella wants to talk to about, it's going to be about his girlfriend or his boyfriend and how his world is about to collapse around him. It can only be that, why else would you take a random homeless man for a cup of coffee to talk about your problems. This'll be fun. He clumsily comes out of the door, barely managing to keep hold of the two cups. I take one of them off him before they're all over the floor.

"Thank you for accompanying me in having a cup of coffee, William. You most likely think I am a complete lunatic but I can assure you I'm not."

"No not all, thank you for the coffee, it's very kind of you."

I want him to get round to what he wants to spill out but he's gazing over the road now, almost like he's forgotten why he's sitting outside a coffee shop with a homeless man.

"10 years of my life! 10 years I've wasted and it's all been for nothing!"

"Problems at home?"

"At home? No, no, no! Problems in the theatre, dear!"

"You're an actor?"

"Oh no! I always wanted to be an actor but I never quite had the talent for it. I was the little boy who auditioned for every part in every play and ended up playing the tree. My biggest role was when I played a rock in the local production of Robin Hood and His Merry Men. Sometimes you have to recognise your limitations and give up. No, dear, I'm a playwright!"

"That must be interesting! Anything I've ever heard of?"

"No, no. Not yet anyway. See that's the problem, I can't seem to get the break I need. 10 years I've been writing this bloody play, it's absolute genius if you don't mind me saying so myself! It just seems no one else can appreciate it!"

"I take it you've had some kind of rejection today then?"

"Yes! I went to pitch it to some producers and they weren't in the least interested. They said it'd have no appeal to the mainstream, it's too much of a risk and people like the tried and tested, they've got no time for innovation. If I'd had a gun I would have shot them right there and then! I've never been so angry in my whole life!"

His face has turned bright red, he's becoming more animated as he talks, moving his arms about, huffing and puffing. For all his threats of violence towards these producers I've no doubt that this man wouldn't be capable of violence. Bravado or frustration. Maybe he thinks I'm violent. Amazingly, I feel sorry for him. Most people I don't really have much time for, their problems aren't mine and I have enough to concern myself with but this seems like someone on the edge. Maybe the sleeping bag and the few quid aren't so important. I'll go back to my spot and sleep tonight, might be uncomfortable but I'll sleep, one day I'll get a new sleeping bag and live happily ever after. This guy looks like he could go home and top himself.

"What's your play about?"

"It's about a boy growing up in London, but it's not a story exactly, it's just how it is. There aren't any high dramas or twists or any of that nonsense. It's simply a play about a normal person living a normal life but people don't really want to see that. People fail to see the exceptional in what they perceive to be normal."

"You're not from London are you?"

"Me? Don't let appearances deceive you, I'm actually a Cockney, born within the sounds of Bow Bells."

"Someone will pick your play up one day."

"What's your story William? I assume you're living rough, however I just told you not to make assumptions and I've made one about you!"

"Your assumption was right."

"You must think what I'm telling you is incredibly boring and pretty inconsequential in the grand scheme of things."

"No, I feel for you. Just because your own life isn't the greatest doesn't mean you should dismiss other people."

He looks uncomfortable as I say this. He thinks I'm just humouring him, trying to make him feel better because he feels guilty. The coffee shop worker is wiping down the tables and listening in to our conversation, it don't take that long to wipe something down. He gives Phillip a strange look as he walks past and back in the shop door.

"I don't think I'd be able to survive."

"Survive what?"

"Survive living out on the streets. I think I'd just give up."

"Your still trying to get your play out there aren't you? You'd survive, most people would. Not that it's easy, of course it isn't but you always find a way. Sometimes I think to myself I don't know if I could go back to living an ordinary life, a nine to five job. What's your most prized possession, Phillip?"

He looks surprised at the question, then he turns his head to gaze across the road again, thinking about the most important thing he owns.

"You see all these tourists walking about the streets. They come and go from the theatres, they go home and they tell their friends and families about the amazing play they saw in London. I sit here at this coffee shop often, watching them and wishing it was my play that they were going back home to talk about. I look up at all the billboards and dream of having my play in bright lights over one of the theatres. My most prized possession would be my pen. A simple thing, but without it I'd not be able to dream."

He takes his pen from his front pocket and holds it up. It isn't anything special, it's just a pen you'd buy in any shop. He laughs to himself and puts it back in his pocket.

"What about you William? I feel rude asking this question because perhaps you don't own much, and I don't mean that in a horrible way so please don't take offence."

"No offence taken. I don't own much, but it would be my sleeping bag."

"Why your sleeping bag or is that too obvious?"

"It keeps me warm, it's my bed, it goes with me everywhere. It's not the most amazing of objects but it's been with me wherever I've been."

"Would you like another cup of coffee?"

"Yeah, go on. I'll have another one."

Two Chinese kids standing in front of me are trying to take a picture together but they can't get the angle right. Holding up the phone, moving it around, holding up two of their fingers.

"Do you want me to take the picture for you?"

"Thank you! Thank you!"

Press the button on the phone, two Chinese kids having the time of their lives laughing and joking with each other.

"Please, can we take picture with you?"

"Uh, okay, if you like!"

I become self conscious, they don't seem to have taken any notice of the way I'm dressed, the way I look.

"We huddle together and they take a picture."

"Maybe I can send it to you, can I have your email address?"

"No, it's okay, it doesn't matter."

The girl looks disappointed I don't want the picture of the three of us. I shrug my shoulders, what else can I say. They walk off down to Piccadilly, still trying to take photos as they go. I would have liked to have had that photo.

"Here's you coffee. I'm not keeping you from anything am I? I'm sure you'll be wanting to get away from the crazy man who's nabbed you off the street for a chat soon!"

"No, thank you. I've enjoyed sitting here."

"Can I ask you a question?"

"Go for it..."

"How'd did you get into the situation you're in?"

"I wish I could give you a sob story, you could feel sorry for me and I'd be able to go back to Charing Cross Road tonight knowing that there's someone who sympathised with me. But, I don't. There's a lot of people out here that have fallen on misfortune, different problems that've led them to be living out on the streets, some of them horrific stories that I'd never wish upon anyone. I think that's why I keep myself to myself, I feel almost guilty."

"Guilty about?"

"For throwing it all away. I had a decent job, I had my own place. I wasn't married but I had a girlfriend. It was a good relationship and we were planning on getting married. I worked as an electrician. One day, I'd had a bad day at work, nothing was going right. I'd saved up some money, someone at work gave me a tip for a horse, said it was a dead cert and all that bollocks. I left work early, went down the bookies and put my savings on the horse. It was just impulse, I'd never gambled before that."

"I take it the horse didn't win?"

"It won. Doubled the money I'd put down on it. Thing is, I didn't feel happy, it was like I'd wanted it to lose. You always hear people down the pub talking about dead certs and they never come in. I had enough money now to pay for a wedding, go on a nice honeymoon somewhere and start a family. So I picked another horse in the next race, Broken Dreams it was called, 66-1. I put the lot on it. The geezer in the shop even asked me if I was sure. I told him I was. The horse come in last. That was it, all of it gone."

"Must have been a hard thing to take."

"Not really, I was relieved. That's going to sound ridiculous because right now I have nothing but I walked out of that betting shop with a smile. I went home, the missus hadn't finished work yet, I picked up a carrier bag, a few clothes and a sleeping bag and walked out. I never even left her a note, I just left the world I'd been living in. Here I am, 20 years later."

"Did she ever try to find you?"

"I guess so. I thought I saw her a few years back but she wouldn't have ever guessed that I'd leave to go live on the streets."

"Wasn't there anyone else that would have looked for you? Your parents?"

"My dad left home when I was a kid and I never really knew him. My mum died not long before I left, she'd not been well for quite a long time so it wasn't really a surprise."

"Do you regret it?"

"I could say I do and that I wished I never did what I did. The honest truth is that no, I don't regret it. It's probably hard for you to rationalise that."

"You obviously weren't as happy as you thought you were."

"Maybe, a world with rules and boundaries, the happy married life scared me. I don't have any boundaries now, I can go where I want."

"You ever thought about finding her?"

"No, I wouldn't be able to look her in the face. That's the only thing I regret, hurting her."

"Perhaps she's living a happier life than what she would have had if you'd stayed. You would have left her at some point I'm sure."

"Yeah, wherever she is I hope she's done well for herself. Like I said, I feel guilty because I chose this life. It might've been an impulsive decision but it was a decision I made. A lot of people don't have any choice in it."

"Have you ever been to see a play William?"

"Nope, never have been to the theatre. Sat around here all these years and it's never really interested me."

"How would you like to go and see a play?"

"I can't. I'm supposed to be meeting someone this evening. It's a good friend of mines birthday, I said I'd get him a few cans and we'd sit by the river. My sleeping bag is probably well gone by now as well."

"Sorry?"

"Oh, when you came up to me I'd just been wandering around looking for my sleeping bag. I went to help some lady that'd lost her little girl and when I got back it'd gone."

"Oh dear! It might be a strange request but would you mind if I joined you and your friend? Perhaps you might think I'm being voyeuristic and trying to intrude in your world for some bizarre pleasure but really and truly William, I find you good company."

"If you don't mind sitting by the river for a few hours and you don't mind getting a few cans in then you're more than welcome Phillip. You could run that play by us, my friend likes the arts, fancies himself as a bit of a playwright himself!"

"No problem! We'll finish this cup of coffee and we can go down to the supermarket."

In the supermarket he picks up some extra strong beer. I tell him to put it back down and choose another one. He looks like a glass of wine would leave him on the floor, I hardly ever drink and Geoff drinks once a year on his birthday. He looks embarrassed. My friend the security guard is following us both around, Phillip looks uncomfortable, making a big gesture of putting the beer into his basket and making sure the security guard sees it. I wave at the security guard, he just looks back at me without expression. How can you dislike someone that's never caused you any bother?

We pass my spot, the place where I live, my dwelling. Does it have to be a building to be a dwelling? I point it out to Phillip, he wants to say something but he doesn't know what to say. Not much you can say really. He looks forward hoping not to catch anyone's eye as he walks past the misfortunate of Charing Cross. I can't remember what I ever felt when I used to walk past homeless people. A sense of guilt? Guilt for what I don't know. Not everyone can save the world, you can feel for people without thinking you've done something wrong.

"You know if you ever want somewhere to stay…"

"I don't want anywhere to stay, I'll be fine, you don't have to worry about me."

"You are sure I'm not intruding aren't you? I wouldn't want your friend to be angry that you've brought me along."

"Don't worry, he won't mind. You can see him there sitting on that bench."

He waves up at me, even through all the evening crowds he can see me, there must be something he could do with that kind of talent.

"Geoff, this is Phillip, he's a friend of mine."

"Nice to meet you Phillip, come to join in my little party."

"Yes! I hope you don't mind?"

"Nah, the more the merrier mate."

"Phillip writes plays."

"Yeah? I'd love to write a play myself. Always have had lots of ideas up in my head but never put them down on paper."

"You should do!"

"I doubt that's ever going to happen. What sort of plays do you write? Ever done anything famous?"

"If he'd done anything famous do you think he'd be sitting here with us two?"

"You never know. He might be getting ideas for his new play. Imagine that hey, William. Me and you the stars of the West End? You'd let us come to the first night wouldn't you Phillip? I mean you'd have to give us some money and that!"

"Shut up you nutcase, he ain't going to be making any plays about us two let alone giving us money."

Phillip hands us both a can of beer. We knock them together and Phillip starts to sing happy birthday, even I'm feeling a bit self conscious as he sings away, people looking over at us. He gets up and does a little jig at the end. Geoff loves it. I can see why he never made it as an actor. The two of them talk away together, hatching plans to write plays and become famous. I don't think I've seen an odder combination of people get on so well just after meeting each other. A failed actor, playwright and a homeless man sitting under Waterloo Bridge.

"You can come round to my house when you have some time, we can see about writing something, you'll have to excuse the mess though, it is rather messy. You know they say that genius' are messy?"

I wonder what she has done with her life? If she did get married and found the happy family she'd always wanted. It's funny, all these years and I've hardly ever thought about it. Even that time I thought I seen her, I never thought about what she might have become.

"You must have loads of money and that though?"

"Oh no! I'm rather poor. Well, I mean you know I'm not rich, I don't have that much money, but I survive. Poor was probably the wrong choice of words there, I am sorry, I really would have no idea what it's like to be poor or have no home."

I take a swig of beer and swallow it grimacing, I hate the taste of the stuff, I'm glad he didn't buy any of that strong stuff or we'd end up swimming in the river naked or something stupid like that. I wonder if she ever had any kids? That's one thing I regret a little bit, not having any kids, I'd like to have a little daughter or son, well they'd be older by now.

"You must go to some right mad parties and that? I heard them West End types get up to all sorts of madness. I bet there's mountains of cocaine and women and all that game. You reckon when we've written a play together I'd be able to come to one of them parties?"

Broken Dreams hey? Couldn't have stuck the money on a better horse. Why did I decide to lose it all. I could have just given it all to charity or something. What would I do if I had that kind of money in my hands right now? I don't know that'd I'd trust myself, I'd probably be back down the bookies and put it on a 100-1 shot.

"No, no! I've never been to one of them kind of parties! You must think we're all debauched! I'm a quiet man who lives a quiet life. I live for the art of writing, I have no other time for other indulgences."

Geoff looks gutted that he isn't going to be going to parties full of cocaine and hookers. I can tell that Phillip is secretly loving the idea that Geoff thinks he's some kind of famous writer. They open another beer, I'm only halfway through my first one and I'm thinking of throwing it away.

"So when can I come around and we can start then? I'm right excited! I can't believe you had a friend like this William and you never introduced him to me."

"Anytime you like Geoffrey! It'd be an absolute pleasure to have you around for dinner. Perhaps you could bring a few friends around too!"

I look up at the sky but don't say anything. The man's naivety is endearing but he'll get himself in a whole world of trouble. I lose track of their conversation. A couple of middle aged women are walking beside each other. I wonder what she looks like now? It was a few years since I thought I'd seen her. One of these two women could be her for all I know. Did I walk away because I never loved her or because I was too scared. I ain't sure. There's no point bringing it all up now. The sleeping bag's gone, it was the only thing I had left from that place.

"I'm off you two, I'm tired, fancy a stroll to wake myself up a bit. Phillip, lovely to meet you mate, thank you for the coffee and you be careful out there. Geoff, I'll see you in the morning mate, happy birthday, you two enjoy yourselves."

I walk off before either can reply, especially Phillip, I don't want him saying he'd come and find me or whatever, I don't need that. Walking up the steps I hear them laughing, grand plans that ain't ever going to come to any fruition. Good luck to them, ain't no harm in dreaming. I walk slowly over the bridge, I can't help but look at anyone I think might look slightly like her. I'll end up getting stopped again. I look back down over the bridge, Geoff and Phillip are happily talking away. I wave down at them but they don't see me. Time to move on I reckon, find myself a new spot somewhere else, I could do with a change.

Charing Cross

Charing Cross, home to Trafalgar Square and the National Portrait Gallery

There she sits, the pigeons flocking around her, throwing the seeds on the grey paving stones. Nelson's Column towering over them, the National Art gallery in the background. To anyone else looking down upon them they'd see her, the pigeons and swarms of people. Red buses passing by, tourists taking photos, policemen watching, waiting. To her, there's nobody else, just her and her pigeons, happily watching as they peck away at the seeds and the grey stones, feeling for any little scrap which has been left over. You'd feel sorry for her if you didn't know her, birds and crazy women, they go hand in hand.

She throws the last of the bird seed on the floor, the birds go into a frenzy, eating what they can, she'll be gone in a minute and they'll be back to harassing ice cream eating Germans, who might kick them. One pigeon lands on her shoulder, she pulls something from her coat pocket and hands it up to him, he eats it in one go. He pecks her shoulder and then flies off to wherever it is that pigeons go. Rats with wings, diseased, how could you ever let one of them near you the passers-by will be thinking to themselves.

Off she walks, across the square, head up, held high, chuckling to herself. The crowds move away from her, there's nothing which will move people quicker than a nutter, especially ones who feed birds, they're the ones you have to look out for. The crowd forms behind her again as she passes, more photos taken, the odd comment, the knowing looks as some of them watch her make her exit. She's crazy but she can hold an audience, if you or me were to walk across Trafalgar Square we'd be barged out of the way, anonymous, insignificant among all the going ons.

Attention turns to a man dressed all in silver, like a statue, he moves suddenly, kids gasp and tap the shoulders of their parents, they want their photo taken with the silver man. He moves again and more kids rush around, is he real or is it just a statue? Their parents laugh with each other, the innocence of the children is amusing. They slip notes to the silver man as the children stand next to him, cameras flashing. Another anonymous person who's famous, his picture on fireplaces and living rooms across the world.

She's back again. Thoughts of her exit were premature, there's no bird seed in her hand but the pigeons rush down expectantly. Stupid birds, or perhaps not. She sits down on the steps in front of the gallery, her favourite bird lands again on her shoulder. His head moving in that strange way, a fluid motion which looks unnatural, protecting her. They won't go near her while I'm here he says to himself. She scratches his purple, blue breast, he coos contentedly, neither caring for those around them.

For months she tried to decide on a name for him. First, she thought perhaps Nelson, after the column and the man who won wars but she hates war and all it entails. Then she thought she was being foolish and Nelson would be a good name but the bird ignored her when she called. How about Trafalgar? Still he ignored her as they sat together in the mornings when the square was empty. Perhaps Picasso? He liked Picasso, the gallery was his home, where he slept at night and when she called Picasso he would come and sit on her shoulder.

That was when their pact truly began. She would bring food and he would perch on her shoulder, she'd give the other pigeons the seed but for Picasso she always brought something special. A piece of cake she had baked the night before, a bite of the biscuits she had bought for him specially. She wondered to herself, does he only come and sit on my shoulder because I give him something special so one day she brought nothing and still he came and sat on her shoulder. Unconditional love for the crazy woman who feeds the birds.

That's how they see her, crazy, lonely, without anyone else in the world but her birds. Never do they ask her if she's okay, or if she would like to sit down and talk for five minutes. Naïve perhaps, to think in a city of millions where people only care for themselves to think they may ask her for a chat. Why not? There'd be no harm done, only the harm to the ego as people look at them curiously sitting with the mad woman. People they'll never see again, people who care nothing for them, not out of spite or malice but because why should they?

Picasso continues to coo, she strokes his breast and whispers soothing words to him. A man passes by and smiles, she smiles back at him, he goes on his way happy, a skip in his step because he did something nice and it was reciprocated, the simplest of things. A smile, an acknowledgement of existence. Not just for her but for him too, his bad day has turned good. Picasso flies off again, she doesn't watch him, she doesn't care much for where he goes, only caring that he'll be there when she arrives.

A woman sits down beside her and looks at her curiously. She takes no notice, the woman starts to say something, her mouth opening but it closes again, she wants to say something but it's not coming out. The pigeon lands on her shoulder again and the woman moves away slightly, contact with the pigeon is a boundary she won't cross. Picasso doesn't care for her, he has no interest in going near her. The woman gets up and walks away, walking aimlessly, going in one direction and then another, not straying too far from Picasso and Mary.

Again she sits down next to her. This time she turns and looks at her, the pigeon still uninterested moves his neck, surveying his square. She takes the woman's hand, she wants to walk away but there's something comforting about her touch. Her hands are warm, not as she would expect, she expected cold hands, rough but they're smooth.

"What's your pigeon's name?"

"Picasso."

"Like the painter?"

"Yes, like the painter."

"Why did you call him Picasso?"

"That's a long story. Why did you sit down next to me? What is it you want to say?"

"Nothing. I have nothing to say, I want to say something but I don't know what. I'm here in this city on my own, sometimes you just want to say something, anything to someone."

"You've said something," she smiles. "I think Picasso likes you."

"Could you tell me the story of Picasso?"

"Picasso is a bird who lives in a big city, he eats what I give him and then he flies happily home at night to sleep."

"I'd like to know why he's called Picasso."

Mary doesn't answer, she sits there as the woman waits for an answer. It begins to rain, and still she sits there not moving, the woman doesn't know if she's thinking or if she's ignoring her. The air is heavy and damp, the smell of wetness in the city. Umbrellas go up, people rush for the station entrance, a little staircase, pushing and shoving, getting wet is as bad as being near a pigeon, you never know which illness might get you.

"Let's go and sit up there under the shelter, you'll get wet. I'll tell you some of the story."

Together they walk up to the shelter in front of the gallery. The onlookers watch the strange couple, nothing else to do, the rain ruining their day, curiosity needing to be satisfied. They sit down on a step, both looking out of the rain.

"Do you think rain is sad?"

"Sad?"

"Yes, I think rain makes me feel sad."

"Rain doesn't make you sad. I love the rain. Breathe in. Already the air is lighter, cleaner. It's sad because you're sad, if you were happy you'd enjoy the rain like I do."

"You're happy?"

"Why wouldn't I be? You see a crazy lady who feeds birds. I'm not crazy and I feed birds because I like them. Such simplicity is hard to understand, people always want reason and complexity. There's nothing complex about me."

"And Picasso?"

"Picasso? Picasso is simple too."

When I was a student I would come here and I'd watch the people as they wandered around. I'd watch the birds too, but I never fed them. I was too scared, all these people and me with a bag of bird seed, they'd think I was crazy. Why is this young lady spending her time feeding birds when she must have better things to do? I'd just watch as they pecked the ground and annoyed people. They didn't care though, they just did what they had to do, everything else was inconsequential to them. My friends would invite me to go for dinner or go to a party but I wasn't interested, I was happy with my own company sitting in the square.

I was an art student, I'd go home at night and I'd paint from memory. Everything I had seen that day, the birds and the people, the buses, that column. My memories all down on a piece of canvas. My messy little room was filled with paints and pictures. I'd fall asleep with a brush in my hand, waking up with hands of all colours. I could hardly move in the room, there were paintings everywhere. Friends would come and visit and they'd say you only paint the same thing. They weren't the same though, each day you could see something different.

I thought I was different, that the world didn't understand me, and never would understand me. I hated and loved the world I lived in. I loved it because I could draw and paint it, I hate it because the drawings and paintings were the world I lived in. It wasn't real, it was pieces of canvas, when I sat in the square I could watch but I couldn't reach out and touch. I wanted something but I didn't know what, it confused me and I began to be spiteful and angry that no one would listen. I was different, but like the world around me I hated and loved being different.

One day I was sitting in the square and I saw a lady feeding the birds, much the same as I do now. Just as I had thought, people avoided her, they didn't want to get to close, their imaginations running wild as to what this woman might do to them. She didn't care though, she just went about her business, feeding the birds. Some would take photos of her and they'd laugh as they did, still she wouldn't care, to her, she lived outside of their world, they were just people passing by, she'd never see them again, why should she care that she was just a form of amusement?

So the next day I brought some bird feed as well. I fed the birds, they came closer and closer, while people moved further and further away from me. What was important to me was that I was happy, I didn't care much for other people, it was that lady who taught me that. If I'd never seen her I wonder if I would be as care free as I am. Would I have gone down to the square the following day and did what I did. A small thing, but for me it

220

was a sense of liberation. After that, it was what I would do every day, I'd still go home and paint but I was there in the middle of those paintings, me and the birds, standing out in the blurry crowds.

That is when I met my friend. The lady who will always be the best friend I ever had. She walked across the square with such confidence. Look in front of you now, everyone looks the same, there's nothing which makes them stand out, but she was different, you just knew by the way she held herself. She asked me if she could take some of the seeds and she stood there with me in silence as the birds ate. I went home that night and when I painted there were three things which stood out in the picture, not just me and the birds.

The next day she came again. In the evening we sat there and we talked, we talked as if we had known each other our entire lives, she wasn't just a stranger who had suddenly entered my life but someone who listened and talked and smiled and laughed and didn't care what anyone thought of her. She wanted to take me somewhere she told me. I was shy, I had always been shy but I trusted her, I knew she wouldn't harm me. I wanted someone who would listen to me and I knew she would, I didn't care where she took me, I just wanted to be with her.

The next morning came, I was supposed to be going to class but I had promised her I would meet her and I knew I couldn't let her down. She was there standing in the middle of the square, waiting with a smile. She took my hand and we began to walk. She said she was going to take me somewhere far away. She led me through the square to the train station, she was silent but it was a nice silence. I knew she understood me, she knew I was different and she was different to, and when you're different the only people who understand are different too.

We sat on the train and I looked out the window. I was imagining what adventures we would be having. I could see streams and trees and foxes and rabbits. I was living a fairy tale, my imagination running wild. The greyness of the city was replaced by the dark green of the countryside, the blues of rivers and streams and lakes. Purple, yellows and reds of flowers which grew wild in fields. Each time the train stopped I waited in anticipation for her to make a sign it was our turn to get off. Finally she stood up and I followed.

I didn't know where we were, I didn't really care either. I had escaped, I was outside the bubble I had lived in my whole life. The greys and blacks were no longer there, the world was colourful and bright, I wanted to reach out and touch it all, when I reached out I felt I could grasp it, I could pluck the flowers or pick up a blade of grass and throw it in the air, the dark green freshness against the sky blue, the dots of purple, yellow and red. It is what I had been looking for, it was colour. We sat in the grass and we talked.

She told me how she was well known, perhaps even famous. I had never seen nor heard of her before but why would I? My life was one of solitude, I had abandoned my friends because they didn't understand me, my life was going to school and then sitting in a square or standing in a square and feeding birds. How could I possibly have known who she was. I didn't ask her what her name was, and she never did tell me.

"You still don't know who she is?"

"No, I don't know."

The rain has stopped, both of them still sat there as the sun breaks throw the clouds and shines off the paving stones, the puddles little specks of white. Those around them carrying on with their photo taking, the silver man back in his spot. They've been sitting there too long for them be interesting to anymore.

"Where did she take you?"

"I don't know that either, I just went."

She told me how she had grown up in a wealthy family, they had money and they lived well, she never wanted for anything. She went to the best schools and her father knew the right people, she told me she was talented but her own talent wasn't enough, you had to know who the right people were. There wasn't any sadness or regret in any of her words. She told me she came to this place when she wanted to be alone and away from the world. No one would recognise her because the animals don't know and don't care.

People were fleeting she told me, they came and went. They wanted to know her because of who she was and what she could do to help them, never was it what they could do to help her. They never think you need help when everyone knows you. They see your world as one of perfection, it's what they want, they want to know how to achieve that perfection but there is no perfection. Flawed, just like everyone else. She knew she was flawed, but no one else wanted to believe she was flawed. They wouldn't listen to what she had to say.

She had wanted to be famous she told me. She didn't regret it, it was a life she had chosen and one which she'd never be able to change. It was missing something though, she was surrounded by people who always wanted and never gave. She had no one she could talk to. That's why she chose me. I was a person no one wanted to talk to, standing there in the middle of the city, throwing seeds to birds, she heard people talking about me, saying I was crazy and there must be something wrong with me.

She'd walked the streets for months, looking for the right person and it was me who she chose. You don't have to believe me and you don't have to speak to me ever again when we go back but for the short time we have together I am grateful because my burden will be lighter. Just words but words are heavy and when you carry them around for years they get heavier. The world becomes darker and you can't see the colours because you're no longer looking for them, you only want to see the blacks and the greys, the red, yellow, blue and greens are an inconvenience, reminding you that grey and black isn't all that exists.

"Your friend like to speak in riddles, I think."

"No, it will become clearer."

As we sat on the train home she was silent but this time the silence wasn't so comfortable. She was going home, back to the life she chose but had no escape from. I sat there wanting to say something but not knowing what to say, much like yourself when you first sat next to me. I questioned myself, was I so different? All those people I paint, I've been blurring out, me at the centre, but are they really so different to me. If I had seen this woman doing what it is she does, I would look at her and I would think I am so different from her, but really I am not. She, like me is just looking for something. Something which is clear to neither of us.

At the station we parted ways, I realised now why people would look at her. They knew who she was and they wondered why this woman who could have any friend in the world was with someone such as myself.

223

People judge, I judged too, I was different and they were just normal, boring, without any depth. No different to myself because that's what they would say about me. I watched as she walked down the street, her green dress moving among the grey suits and black dresses of people on their way home.

From the corner of the road over there, where it goes down to the Strand I looked over at the square and could see the pigeons, they were being fed by someone else. Happily pecking away. Tonight I'd just leave them, they'd found someone else, they didn't want me there. It was a dark evening, one of those just before a storm where everywhere is grey, there is almost a tension in the air and everyone is just waiting for it to break so they can breathe again, the thick air gone.

The next day I went back in the afternoon and she didn't turn up. I wanted to see her but I was conflicted, she had confused me. I didn't want to be confused, now I was sure I had been happy thinking I was different and the rest of the world was the problem. If I never saw her again then I wouldn't have to think about it. Yet, I wanted to talk to someone, I wanted to let those words out like she had said, let some of the weight from inside be released. I stay with my pigeons, the only things in the world that comfort me.

When the pigeons were happy and fed and had flown away I decided to go for a walk. Usually I went home, my room and the square, and the journey to the square were my life. I had given up on school because I didn't think I was good enough, my confidence had been lost but I didn't know why. Just one day it disappeared. I looked at the canvases in my room and decided they were rubbish, I was foolish to paint them in the first place, no one in their right mind would ever buy such a thing. I couldn't bear to look at them because I was embarrassed.

I walked in no particular direction, I wanted to get lost because I thought if I got lost then I'd never be able to find my way back. The foolishness of youth. The happiness and colour I'd seen and felt the other day had completely gone. I hated her, why did she choose me to talk to? Was it because she felt sorry for me? I was just a tool for her to make her feel better about herself, to make herself feel normal. I thought she was a friend but she wasn't she'd tricked me, made me feel special only to take it all away and confuse my mind.

As I walked over Westminster Bridge I started to take notice of people. Before they had been blurs, they were transient, they meant nothing. If I hadn't seen them they didn't exist and when I couldn't see them anymore they no longer existed. Now I was looking at them and seeing more than just the word 'people'. A man standing on the bridge, looking down at the boats as they passed in the summer evening. That was his pleasure, he enjoyed it. He looked happy, he turned to point at something but realised he was on his own and then laughed to himself.

I stood next to him, at first he looked surprised but then he pointed again, I looked down at one of the boats and there, standing on the deck of the boat was a man waving at everyone. I looked at him with a smile and carried on walking across the bridge. I looked back and I could see faces of all kinds, different coloured hair, tall and short, fat and slim. Colours stood out, the orange glow of the lights, the yellow of the taxis crossing the bridge, even the black didn't look dark anymore, there was a shine to it.

"Did you ever see her again?"

"Yes, I saw her again. I have to go now, I want to go home, I'm tired."

"Will you be here tomorrow?"

"Yes, I'll be here tomorrow."

"Can I come and listen to you tomorrow."

"If you like."

Both of them stood up and went their separate ways. Mary walking towards the back of the square, the young lady ascending the stairs to the underground station. Standing on the platform she wonders to herself where the woman was going, was her home still that little room. She hadn't told her why the bird was called Picasso either. Perhaps she is crazy and it would be better if she didn't go tomorrow to listen to her. A man bumps into her as she pushes onto the train, he says sorry and she smiles to herself as she accepts his apology with a nod.

The people on the train are all lost in their own world. Some of them looking at their phones, probably wondering what their friends are doing that evening, no doubt something far more exciting than they are doing.

Others looking at newspapers, handed to them for free, which scream headlines about the coming end of the world, death, destruction, torment, sadness, and of course there is nothing you can do about it. Just go about your day as you usually do and wait. They wearily depart the train as it pulls into their station, sighs and heavy legs.

She opens the door to her flat, her dog jumping on her as soon as he can get through the crack in the door. She rubs his head and calms him down, taking a bone she'd bought for him during her lunch break. The dog chews contentedly on the floor as she sits down and sighs. Just her and her dog. She loves the dog and she'd never go anywhere without him but it would be nice just to have some friends, even a boyfriend. She does have friends, just they're all back home and home is in another country.

Closing the curtains before she climbs into bed she takes one more look out the window, the dog joins her, resting his paws on the windowsill. The dog is looking for threats, she is looking for comfort. She remembers what the mad woman was saying about colours. It's too dark for there to be any colour, it's just dark. Opposite the window is a small tree, one she sees every night, she stares at it intensely, forcing her eyes to see something just a glimpse of brightness. Nothing, the woman is crazy, I'm her in the story and she's the famous woman, it's all just a game.

Picasso lands on her shoulder as usual. Today she's happy. Last night she went home and she painted a picture. It was a picture of a bird, in the background was a woman with a green dress. She would put it on her wall one day soon and it would remind her of times gone by. One day Picasso won't turn up, she knew that. Hopefully it will be a long time before it happens. A kid with a ball kicks it too hard and it frightens the pigeons. He looks at her with wide eyes, petrified she might look for retribution for scaring her beloved birds.

"It's okay, they'll come back."

The boy runs to the ball, picks it up and runs off to his father. He points at her, the father looks and turns away with a wave of the hand. Don't worry about her, she's just crazy, she won't do anything to you, not with me around.

Will that young lady come back again today? I doubt it, she probably went home, embarrassed with herself that she'd resorted to such measures as talking to strangers in Trafalgar Square. She was a nice young girl, shy but there's more to her than meets the eye. She wants to finish off the story she was telling, she's not sure if the girl was enjoying it but she was enjoying it. Perhaps strange to some, sad to others but without sadness there can't be happiness because we wouldn't know what happiness was.

"You came back?"

"Yes, I told you I would. I enjoyed sitting with you yesterday. Last night I went home, me and my dog we sat and looked out the window looking for colours in the trees, like you said you did, but I didn't see any, I'm not sure about the dog, maybe he saw some."

"Ha, ha! If it was dark you wouldn't be able to see any colours."

The girl looks at her confused, she shoudn't have changed her mind, she have just gone straight home from work and sat with the dog for the evening.

"You don't talk much do you?"

"No, I don't say much. It's just my way."

"You look tired and heavy."

"Tired, yes. Heavy, perhaps. You didn't tell me why Picasso is called Picasso yet."

"Well if you stay, I'll tell you."

She did come back. A few weeks later, I was stood there with the birds, the same place you can usually find me. I could see her coming as soon as she entered the square. She didn't have a green dress on this time. This time she had black trousers and a black shirt. As she approached I feared she would just keep on walking, I didn't know whether to wave or not. Strange, because usually I didn't care. She came over to me and took my hand, this time her grip was so sure, there was doubt in it but still I went with her.

We didn't get on any trains that time. We just walked, through the city. Some people stopped to look at her, pointing and staring. On we walked, she took no notice, or she pretended to take no notice. Like my own walk the night before, there was no direction, we were just walking. We stopped outside a building, it looked abandoned. She pushed the door and it opened. We explored the empty building, there was nothing in it, holes where there used to be walls, even holes in the floor. The stairs creaked as we walked up them, all the way to the top we went until we reached an attic.

The attic was completely different to the rest of the house, there was a rocking horse in the middle of the floor, painted all in white, it had a brown mane. She walked over to it and began to rock it back and forwards, her joy visible in her eyes. On the floor was a carpet, soft even with shoes on, it was a deep blue colour. The walls were covered in stars and crescent moons. I sat against the wall as she continued to rock back and forward, this grown woman lost in another world as she played with a child's toy.

It was as though she was in a trance, if I'd left she wouldn't have noticed. Time passed, I sat there looking at the walls wondering what I was doing there. She came out of her trance suddenly, getting off the horse and coming to sit down next to me. She asked me if I thought she would come back again. I told her I didn't know, I hoped she would and at the same time hoped she wouldn't. She laughed as if she knew that was what the answer was going to be. You're my friend of course I was going to come back. A friend who I had only met once, yet I had enjoyed her company more than I'd enjoyed the company of anyone else.

Then she asked me about myself, the first time since we had met that she had asked me anything. I gazed up at the stars and the moons on the wall, they felt real, as though I was lying in a field at night and looking up at the real stars in the sky. Often I would look up out of my window at night and wonder what was up there. In a universe so large we're just insignificant. She laughed as I told her. There's probably someone out by one of those stars looking towards us and saying the same thing, if none of us are significant then there is no point in the world.

So I told her about myself. How I had two brothers and two sisters, all of them were clever, not like me, a simple art student who floated her way through life with no direction, happy that there was no direction. A foolish dreamer is what my father would call me, no chance of ever achieving anything because it's all inside your head and none of it is here, existing. I hated him, I knew I shouldn't hate him, he was a man who was from a *different time but I couldn't make myself not hate him, it was too difficult so I ignored it.*

It was then I began to paint. I could put everything which was going on in my head down, I could visualise it, it would be there in the canvas and I had proof that I was different. When I showed other people they would just look at the canvas in confusion. They couldn't see what I wanted them to see, all they saw was dashes of paint and colours, there was no picture they told me, why would anyone want to buy that. You should give it up follow your brothers and your sisters and make your father proud of you. It's not that he doesn't love you, it's because he wants what is best for you.

One day I left, I took my paints and my clothes and put them all into a bag and I walked out the door. I haven't seen him since. She looked at me and told me sometimes she wished she had done the same. I thought she had wanted to be famous that's what she told me when we were sitting on the grass. No, she didn't want to be famous she only thought she did, it was someone else's dream and not hers. If she could go back and change it she would. Time which should have been spent being a child was time spent being an adult when she wasn't.

Tell me about your other friends, tell me what you do. I hadn't any other friends left, I'd moved away from them, I didn't think they were people who understood me. Sometimes we would go out and we would drink or we would go to a restaurant and have something to eat. Other times we would just walk and talk, much the same as we're doing now. We never did anything special except enjoy each other's company. You should have appreciated what you had.

She stood up and looked down at me, when you go home tonight you can paint this house, you could even put me in it if you want to. I like the stars and the moon on the walls. Two friends sitting there and enjoying each other's company, the moon and the stars looking down on them, neither of them wanting any more than what they have. Of course I could paint it and I would give it to her. She didn't look me in the eye, a faint smile across her face. She walked to the window and looked out then sighed, it was time to go.

We walked back down to the square and the place where we first met. We said goodbye and I walked home, slowly through the streets. I smiled at people as I passed them, they looked at me stranger than when I was with the birds. I am her door to the world she doesn't know, a world she'd always wanted to see and live in but never had the chance. I hoped she was happy. I was happy, I had told someone that I hated him and I no longer felt heavy, my steps were light even though I moved slowly.

When I looked at my old canvases, all shades of grey and black and white, there was no happiness in the pictures. I had wanted to paint happiness but it wouldn't shine through because I was not happy. Even my birds hadn't made me happy, I just thought they did, but now I had a friend and I had told them, talked them, released the burden I had always been holding. She had done what she didn't want to do, I should be happy that I walked away and did what I wanted to do. I began to paint the picture.

Two people, one in green and one in red, they were sat under a night sky, but the sky wasn't black, it was blue, the stars were a bright yellow, the moon an even brighter yellow. Both of them had smiles on their faces, one pointing up at the sky. The grass they were sitting on was a beautiful green, like an emerald and next to them ran a river which was the colour of a morning sky. I laughed as I painted, the sun slowly rose and peered in through the window and shining down on to the canvas. I fell asleep below it.

The next day, I went to class. I said hello to friends I'd not seen in weeks, we made plans, they were happy to see me. I am different but it doesn't matter because we all are. You'll never be understood because there's too much to understand I told myself. Each evening after my classes I would go to the square and feed the birds, I'd wait until the sun had set, hoping that she would come. She never came. I never hated her for it. She was fleeting, a friend I only ever met twice but she was the best friend I'd ever had because she'd shown me something different. Different, always something different.

"And Picasso?"

"There have been many Picassos, not just this one."

One day when I was sitting there waiting a bird came and landed on my shoulder. I'd never let one touch me before, he looked happy and content, why should I move him. I looked at his feathers, grey and white but there in the middle of his chest was a bright purple. He reminded me *of her, before her there was the grey and darkness and after it was colour. Since that day, I always come to feed them, I don't care what people think, there has always been a Picasso, I don't know how many but there's always one who comes and sits on my shoulder.*

"I have to go home, it's getting late and I will miss the last train."

They both look up, not realising how much time has passed as she told her tale of the famous woman whose name she never knew, how she changed her life. The young lady stands up and waves goodbye, and goes down into the station. Mary sits there silent, Picasso has gone but she doesn't want to leave just yet, she wants to enjoy the warm evening.

Sitting at the window with her dog the young lady points up to the sky. She can see the colours, the bright yellow of the stars and the moon. It's not all bad she thinks to herself.

Embankment – Wine, Society and Conversation

Home to Gordon's Wine Bar, London's oldest wine bar, occupying its place in Villiers Street since 1890

1890 – Slum Adventures

"Have you been past the bridge recently? It looks as though it's coming on nicely."

"Yes, I went past it the other day, I'm not sure what it's going to look like when it's done but it sure is a grand old thing. So tell me, how did your adventures go? I'm dying to hear."

"It all went very well although I'm not sure I'd recommend it to you, you are very faint of heart and I'm not sure you'd last very long out there."

"Where exactly did you go?"

"I went to Whitechapel; a good friend had done as I did and told me it was the best place to see how they live and he wasn't far wrong."

"I do admire your bravery! It can't be easy living among such debauchery and filth. I suppose my interest was piqued when I saw that wretched man on the street. He moved something in my heart and I thought the best way to understand how a man could live like that would be to go and live it myself. I do agree with you though, I think perhaps I might not have the constitution for it. Do go on and tell me how it all went and I'll be able to make a decision if I should go or not."

"Well, I suppose in a way I felt a bit voyeuristic, going to see the lower classes and living among them. Nothing can really prepare you. You hear so many stories and of course the murders. To actually see it with your own eyes it moves you to want to do something about it but quite what I don't know."

"Yes, indeed! I've thought for many years that it's a problem but, really what can we do about it? These people are of a different nature."

"The morning I left I donned my common clothes and walked down to Whitechapel; I'm sure they could tell I was not one of them, people of different classes carry themselves in different ways, it's difficult to suddenly behave as if you own nothing."

"Too true and this is something I worry about myself, were they to discover who I really were how would they behave?"

"I'm sure you would be fine. One tends to think of them as savages but that does them an injustice, one thing my trip taught me is that they are indeed just people who are trying to get by from day to day."

"Did you go to the workhouse?"

"Yes. A terrible place I must say. Men and women, old and young with barely a break during the day. They receive a piece of bread in the morning and one at night and some tea if they're lucky. The old men are not even allowed a smoke. Such a simple thing for me or you but to them it is a great pleasure that they are denied, even as their days come to a close."

"Awful!"

"I stayed with a family. Obviously they knew who I was but they took little notice, I paid them and that was all they were really interested in. Seeing such conditions in that workhouse really moved me, I would even say, much like yourself, that I would like to do something but I really don't know what."

"It's a difficult question indeed. One often wonders if they themselves are to blame or is it us and our ignorance and lack of empathy?"

"I find that people now see them as a curiosity, the East End has become a bizarre kind of zoo where we go to look at people as if they were animals. They aren't animals, as I said, they're just people much like ourselves but due to misfortune in circumstance they've not been afforded the privilege we have."

"I tend to agree although I do think they sometimes don't help themselves. Do you not think they pity themselves and this self-pity leaves them wallowing in their own debauchery and misery?"

"Are you happy?"

"Whatever does that have to do with it?"

"I take you as a man who is not happy. You often complain and while I sometimes admire your desire to help those less fortunate I wonder if that is to make yourself feel better or if it's a desire to actually help those who are struggling."

"I wish to help of course."

"Let me tell you a story, you can make up your own mind then if your charity is self-serving or not."

"Please, tell me."

"At night, the streets are dark, the gas lights barely work. As you walk the streets in pitch darkness, only the occasional glow of light from a working light or a candle from a window, you pass all sorts of misfortunates and miscreants. You could look down upon them and think perhaps this is their own fault, their half empty bottle of gin by their sides, talking away to themselves in some incomprehensible language, lying in filth which no one cares to clean up. If one does nothing for themselves then surely no one else should help?"

"But..."

"It's a rhetorical question. As I walked through the streets, I came across a woman. She looked old, her eyes were sunken and black. She looked up at me with hatred, my existence insulted her, me a man free to walk the streets, unburdened by worries of the kind she has. By her side there was an empty bottle. That was her comfort, her way to pass the lonely nights as she sat homeless, cold and uncared for. What desire or motivation would she have to do better for herself when she indeed has no opportunity?

"Does she go to the workhouse and work every single hour possible, sleep and then wake the next morning to eat an old piece of bread and do as she did the previous day? A fate she'll be held to until the day she finally passes away. Yet all we do is pity her or in some cases blame her. She moved me unlike anyone I have met before. I sat down beside her, I didn't care for the fact I was going to get dirty myself, such things are trivial."

"And? Did she talk to you? Give you some idea of her plight?"

"What words could she give me of her plight? It is something I don't understand. I was born a man who was given opportunity at every corner. She said nothing, perhaps it was my own fear to talk to her, I did not want to know her story or where she had come from and what had damned her to live her life sitting in the streets. What could she tell me which I would truly understand anyway? To see her was enough. It brought upon me a guilt which I had not felt before."

"Yes, I agree, something should be done."

"No, you misunderstand me. It was a guilt that I was here, I had dressed up as a common man, walked the streets pretending to be one. For what purpose? Solely for my own curiosity! We have an obsession with the poor but it is not because we want to help but because we want to look and then to tell our friends and family. They too wish to hear stories of depravation and sadness. We have a cruel fixation with them. No doubt there are good people who go and help and give money and try to better the lives of those less fortunate than us, but they do not tell anyone. Unlike myself who is sitting here drinking wine while regaling you with stories of my adventures to a slum."

"I have the impression that it has quite changed you."

"Yes, it has changed me. It was only two days and one night but I saw things which I never wish to see again. And that my good friend is why I advise you to think about what you want to do."

"And you? Is it not hypocritical of you to have done the same thing I wish to do but to advise me not to go?"

"My experience changed my thinking , so no, it is not hypocritical. If you truly wish to change something then go ahead but if you wish to do it so you can tell stories in wine bars and taverns across the city then, please don't. There are other places where stories can be found and they do not have to take advantage of the misery of others. My words are honest, I believe I'm an honest man."

"I will think about it, but your tale has made more interested not less."

"That is always the case when it comes to danger and adventure, it is however a long way from the picture you are now sitting there with in your head."

1912 – Give Them the Vote? Don't be Preposterous!

"What do you think of this awful business of these women smashing windows in Oxford Circus? I was starting to come around to some of their ideas but not after this insanity! Who do they think they are?"

"Terrible! They wish to persuade us of their right to have a vote and then they go and do this. If anything it proves that they should be forever deprived of it. It's emotions you see George, they simply can't handle them. Imagine if they were having a say in how the country was run? We'd be in a perpetual state of war."

"I completely agree with you. I do think a good war would sort the country out though. Women have to stand behind their men when they're out there fighting the good fight, there'd be no more smashing of windows and there certainly would be no more talk of votes."

"Yes, a war would be good! We'd get rid of some this tension. My daughter supports them you know? I've never told anyone, you're the first. I'm quite embarrassed she has such thoughts but what can you do with the naivety of youth. She'll grow out of it once she gets married and realises that women have responsibilities which differ from men."

"It's caused quite the disturbance. Putting these ideas into young people's minds, I don't know why they can't spend their energies elsewhere. One can only wonder what kind of a nation we will have in another fifty year's time, it's quite frightening."

"Both crews sank in the boat race last weekend, I think that shows us what we're dealing with when it comes to the young people of today."

"They'll lose us the Empire if it carries on in such a way. How can a country project strength when it is seen to be giving in so easily? This is my worry."

"You see, I'll just say it straight, women should be at home and looking after the children and taking care of the house. There's no room for emotions in politics, these are decisions which affect the whole country and can't be taken when in the midst of a personal crisis, of which women seem to have many."

"Food on the table and my clothes washed are all I want, it's not too much to ask is it?"

"It's not too much to ask. My daughter said to me, there's no difference between men and women, if women are looking after men then why shouldn't they have some say in how the country is run? I told her that they do have some say, it's just through their husbands and brothers and fathers. It might not be a direct input but it might as well be."

"I quite agree about needing a war. It'll show the young men and women of this country of what it means to truly love one's country. Nothing like seeing people wounded and killed to make them understand the realities of life."

1940 – Scolded in the Air Raid Shelter

"You were in the train station last night? What's it like down there, it all seems terribly exciting."

"Exciting? Are you mad? It's full of people and it's smelly and dirty."

"Oh come on! You must have had some good fun down there. The bombs won't reach down that far, I've head they have a right good party."

"I wasn't down there by intention, I had nowhere else to go."

"I don't believe you, I'd say you went down there because you wanted to. You are rather transparent sometimes. What do you think of this wine?"

"It's good, not as good as the stuff they used to get."

"It's the war isn't it? I'm sure when it's over we'll be able to go back to drinking that other stuff, I've forgotten the name of it. Anyway, do tell, what did you get up to down in the depths of Archway station?"

"Why are you so curious? It's an underground station filled with people, rats and train tracks."

"Look, Robert, I know you. You didn't go down there because you had no choice, you went down there on purpose. I bet it was for a woman or some such thing."

"What are you implying?"

"I'm implying nothing, I'm just telling you how I see it."

"Well yes, you're right. I suppose there was an ulterior motive."

"Go on then, tell me! Who is she?"

"Why do you assume it has to be a woman?"

"What else would it be?"

"It is a woman but I'm not entirely sure about her. She works in one of the factories, which one I'm not quite sure. I've not said this to anyone before but I feel quite inferior. Me sitting around with my bad leg, unable to go off and fight and there she is doing her bit. It shouldn't really be like that should it?"

"I suppose it depends on how you look at it. I imagine once the war is over things will change quite a lot. You have to move with the times as they say."

"True, perhaps I'm just old fashioned."

"Tell me more, what happened?"

"Nothing of note happened! I knew she often sheltered in Archway station and I just happened to be nearby..."

"You mean you were waiting around for the sirens to go off..."

"No!Honestly, I was just nearby!"

"Yes, yes! I believe you!"

"Will you ever shut up and listen?"

"Sorry, I'm just a bit excitable today that's all, I think this wine is going straight to my head."

"Once I was down there I honestly thought I wouldn't be able to find her. I sat down on the platform, and I'll tell you it was all rather raucous. Being so late in the evening I thought the children would be all sleeping but they were all running around the platforms playing games and being a nuisance if I'm quite honest. You know how much I dislike children."

"I remember when we were on the train last year going to Brighton and that child kept annoying you while you were trying to talk to that woman. I've never wanted to laugh so much in my whole life. You should lighten up sometimes Robert, you're far too serious."

"I'm not serious at all! Besides you see life as one big joke and that my good friend will not see you in good stead."

"Robert, I've been unable to walk properly since I was a child. If I were to take life too seriously I would be walking around with a frown all the time and lamenting my own bad luck and the hand I've been dealt, but there's no need for that."

"Yes well, maybe I should try to be a bit more humorous at times."

"Yes, yes you should! You'll never woo this woman with that look you're sitting there with at the moment. Carry on with your tale, I'm looking forward to hearing how you made a fool of yourself."

"I was trying to get my head down, I had an early start in the morning and I can't tell you hard the floor is on those platforms. One of those bloody children..."

"Just children, Robert, remember what I just said..."

"One of those *CHILDREN* was running about backwards and forwards, making an awful racket, his mother and father were nowhere to be seen. Well I thought to myself I need to do something here or I'll never get a wink of sleep. I stood up and I told him he needs to quieten down and learn some manners. He looked at me with a terrible fright on his face and to tell you the truth, I was quite pleased with myself."

"I'm sure you were. Did the child cry?"

"He did cry, and I'm telling you now, I don't feel one bit of remorse for telling him."

"So this is your story? You told a child off for being too noisy?"

"No, the most terrible thing happened."

"Oh good, this should make it more interesting…"

"I turned around and who was there standing behind me but that woman."

"This woman, does she have a name because I've not hear you refer to her as anything other than 'the woman' or 'that woman'?"

"Her name is Dorothy although I don't think that quite matters anymore."

"Dorothy the factory worker, does your mother know?"

"Do behave yourself."

"What did she say?"

"She was quite angry."

"Quite?"

"She was very angry! She told me that it wasn't my place to be scolding another person's child and that the child was only playing. In such times we should be more patient. The poor child had ran off and was crying she told me. Then, she had the cheek to tell me I should move on somewhere else on the platform because the child would be too scared to come back."

"That was you told!"

"I see you've no sympathy for me!"

"Why should I have any sympathy for you?"

"Well, I mean you don't think she was out of order? It was hardly her place to be telling me I shouldn't be scolding a naughty child."

"Why shouldn't she scold you? For God's sake, you were telling of a child for being a child. Let me ask you a question. Had it have been a man who told you off, would you have quite the same reaction? I very much doubt it. It's little wonder you don't have much success with the ladies."

"If it was a man, well I would have told him where to go."

"No you wouldn't have, you'd have picked up your belongings and you'd have moved along the platform."

"Well, yes! I would have! You're right. I just felt as though I shouldn't be shouted at by a woman. If she was an older lady then perhaps it wouldn't have been so bad, it would be much like being told off by your mother but she's not young at all."

"You've had your manliness questioned my friend and you've taken it quite badly! I think you need to realise that's the way things are going. Besides what does it really matter? She was only protecting the child. Did she say anything to you afterwards? I bet you were too scared to approach her."

"Well, no she didn't say anything to me but that's beside the point."

"Hold on a minute. You don't actually know this woman do you? You've been hanging around waiting for air raid sirens so you could go down to the same underground station as a woman you don't know. Didn't you just say she never told you which factory she works in? It's not because she's not told you is it? It's because you've never even spoke to her! Oh dear!"

"You know how shy I get!"

"Hold on a minute, how do you know her name is Dorothy?"

"I don't. I plucked the name out of the air, you didn't give me much time to think."

"Fantastic! You've just told me the story of Dorothy the factory worker, who you've never even met and you've followed her down to an air raid shelter. Does she actually exist?"

"Yes, of course she does! She did tell me off, it's just I'd never gotten around to speaking to her before that."

"Let me give you a bit of advice. Following women you don't know around might be perceived as being a bit strange. You really are a strange fellow sometimes, I do wonder if when you injured your leg you injured your brain too."

"You're just jealous. Besides I want nothing more to do with her, I can't possibly be civil to a woman who spoke to me in such a way. Let's order another bottle of wine, I need to forget this incident ever happened and I regret telling you at all."

1969 – What am I supposed to do?

"I'm not sure what you can do. What are your options?"

"I don't have many options. Either I go through with it or I end up a social outcast. There's no way I'd be able to tell my father, he'd go fucking mad and end up killing me."

"I know that. Surely there has to be some sort of compromise though? Can't you marry him?"

"I don't want to marry him! It's the last thing I want. I don't have any feelings for him and then what happens in a few year's time? It'd just cause more and more problems. I can't believe I've managed to get myself into this mess."

"There's no point beating yourself up over it, what's done is done, you just have to try and do what's best for you and for it."

"Don't call it 'it'."

"Sorry, that was insensitive of me."

"It's okay, I know you're just trying to help. So, what do I do?"

"Well, what are your options?"

"Marry him and live a life of unhappiness. I can't believe I ever let myself get involved with him, he's an ignorant bastard. Loneliness does these things I suppose."

"I don't understand why you say you're so lonely though. You have me, you have your sister too. Does he know?"

"No, she doesn't know, she'd go running to dad as quick as she could. I love her to death but she can't keep anything to herself and she'd just worry. For some reason she thinks dad is able to solve everything and is completely blind to his faults."

"Well, why wouldn't he be able to help?"

"He's from a different time, the shock would kill him and he'd be sure to tell me to marry him. I wouldn't listen to him and it would cause problems which, right now would not help in anyway at all. I'm not near home, I know I have you and I have my sister when she's not cavorting around town with some bohemian she's fallen in love with."

"She is a bit odd your sister, I do like her but she is prone to impulsiveness."

"That's why I can't tell her. You know when I came down here I did it to get away, start afresh, find a job and live my life relatively free from any other pressures and now I've gone and ruined it all."

"You can't blame yourself, you're not the only one who's in your situation."

"That doesn't make me feel any better, I'm sure other people would be able to handle it far better than I have."

"I very much doubt that. The girl downstairs, a local girl, she met some man when she was out one night. Bright girl as well, well a couple of months later and she finds out she's pregnant and she's decided she's going to get the boat to America and start a new life."

"With the baby?"

"Yes, with the baby. I'm not sure how she'll fare though, she's not the most streetwise of people."

"How much is the boat? I have some money saved up."

"Don't be ridiculous! What about your friends and family?"

"They're not helping much at the moment are they?"

"They don't know so they can't help!"

"If I went over there what would I do? I heard it's pretty easy to get a job there. Would they even let me in? I don't know anything about it. It does sound like an intriguing prospect though. Has she gone already? Could you ask her for me?"

"You're not getting the boat over to America, it's a foolish idea. You wouldn't know anybody, you'd be completely on your own and you never know what kind of savages you might meet out there."

"It's America, not the middle of the jungle, I'd expect it wouldn't be too much different to what it is like here."

"I won't let you."

"You wouldn't be able to stop me. I'd pack my bags and leave in the middle of the night and you'd be none the wiser. I would send you a letter when I got there though, just to let you know I was doing fine."

"Your ability to make light of serious situations makes me incredibly envious at times."

"If you've not got your humour you're left with very little else at times like this. I am partly serious though, if I could go I would, it'd solve an awful lot of problems."

"You'd end up regretting it. I know your father can be a pain but you'd miss him."

"It's not so much him that I'm worried about, he'd get over it, he has my sister and for all her stupidness she'll settle down with a nice man and have babies and a nice little family and he will be delighted. I don't ever see myself doing that and I'll only be an embarrassment to him."

"Don't say things like that, you won't be an embarrassment to him whatever you do. Besides, I don't want you to go, what would I do without you? I'd be sat here in this wine bar drinking and feeling sorry for myself and you wouldn't want that would you?"

"With all due respect, at this current moment in time, you feeling sorry for yourself is the least of my worries."

"So, what are we going to do?"

"There more I think about the less I want to give her or him up. Why should I? Just because people think you're some kind of whore because you've made a silly mistake?"

"You do realise how difficult it'll be don't you? I don't just mean what people say, I mean looking after the child. You'll not have the same life you had before."

"That's something I'll have to take on the chin, besides if I gave away the child, where's it going to go? I'd give it to the nuns and God only knows where it would end up. I even heard a rumour they send the children to America. I might as well go myself if they're going to do that."

"You're strong enough without having to leave. You're not seriously entertaining that idea are you? I wish I hadn't mentioned it now."

"Of course I'm not. You have to admit, you can see why she would run away though, it's an attractive prospect, far better than being labelled some kind of outcast."

"Half of them had children out of wedlock anyway, that's the reason they're all married and unhappy. Hypocrites!"

"I'm sure not all of them are. All I want is for the child to have a good life and if I can give it to him myself then why not give it a go?"

"You'll have difficult questions when he grows up, you'll have to think about what the other kids at school will think of it as well."

"That's something I'd deal with at the time. Tell me, honestly, what do you think I should do? What would you do?"

"What I would do and what I think you should do are two different things. It's not quite the same when you're in the situation is it?"

"What do you *THINK* I should do then?"

"You won't like it but I think you should give it away."

"I thought you would say that."

"I'm trying to think rationally. I know how difficult this all going to be for you and I'll be honest, I'm not sure you'll be able to look after a child on your own."

"Why not?"

"It's just not something you're prepared for. Tell me honestly, when you're walking down the street and there are people looking at you and pointing and whispering and talking about you, the single mother with no morals, would you be able to handle that? I don't think you would and that's why I think you should give it up. Besides, do you want your life to be over before it's already begun?"

"Why would it be over?"

"You won't be sitting here drinking wine with me for a start, you'll hardly see your friends. Your father will probably never talk to you again, are you honestly prepared for the repercussions?"

"I'll ask you a question. Are you talking for me or are you talking for yourself? Is it you who would be upset that they won't have a friend to be going out with?"

"No! Of course not!"

"I know you're right, well in some ways you are. I'm not sure if I am strong enough to do it, I don't want to be a social outcast, but I don't want to give the child away either, it's mine and I don't want someone else bringing them up. I've made a mistake and I just have to live with it but I don't want the child to think it's a mistake, I want it to be loved and have the best life it possibly can."

"It's your choice. If it was me, I would give it up, but then I enjoy my life too much and I'm not sure if I ever want any children anyway."

"You always were very different, Claire."

"What are you going to do?"

"I don't know. Perhaps that boat really is an option."

1990 – Squatters Rights

"This place is a bit posh isn't it?"

"It isn't that posh, you can treat yourself sometimes you know."

"I feel a bit guilty, the others are back at home and I'm sitting here drinking wine with you. It's all a bit clandestine."

"It's not really is it?"

" Some of them are not sure about you, one of them thinks you're a reporter and a couple of others have said you're probably nothing more than a jumped-up toff."

"Nice."

"Don't take them so seriously."

"It's difficult not to take them so seriously, I'll never fit in with them, that much I can tell."

"They will accept you one day, you just need to be persistent."

"They think I'm doing this because it's all a big adventure don't they? I can assure you I'm not, I feel passionately about it and I hope you understand."

"I do understand, I wouldn't be here with you otherwise would I?"

"What is their problem then?"

"You're just not one of them, you never will be properly. They know you have money, most of them have nothing. While I know you won't, you have to understand that they see you as someone who can just run away, you've got something to fall back on. If they get evicted, they have nothing, a lot of them will be living on the streets."

"I know that, and I do understand why they would think that way. I suppose I just want to fit in, that's all."

"What's your obsession with fitting in? Just be yourself and things would be a lot easier."

"Why do you do it?"

"Shouldn't I be asking you that question. It's obvious why I do it."

"No need to be short with me, I'm just asking a question."

"I do it because it's something I feel passionate about. Our country is falling apart, if you've not got money then you're pretty much worthless, they built all of this housing and then they've gone and left it all to ruin. People are living in their flats with damp on the walls, they've got no heating and the winter is coming, they've got children who they can just about feed and yet we still have the cheek to call ourselves a developed country."

"We are a first world country. No matter how much people like to dismiss it, it's the basic truth. We have a welfare state, you are free to walk into a hospital if you're sick, if you're unemployed you can get money to help you survive."

"What experience do you have of any form of poverty?"

"I could ask the same question of you."

"Really? You actually think you can throw that question back at me."

"You like to think you're poor but you're not really are you? I mean, you're living on the bare minimum of that there's no doubt, but poor? I wouldn't say you're poor at all."

"Fuck you! How dare you question my belief in what I do! After everything I have done for you?"

"I'm not questioning your belief in what you do."

"I'm sorry, tensions are a bit high at the moment and I'm a bit all over the place. They're talking about trying to evict us and I'm sat here sipping wine with you."

"What's wrong with sipping wine? What's wrong with being here, in fact?"

"Well, it doesn't sit very well with the cause does it?"

"Why not?"

"Stop being so bloody petty. You know exactly what I mean."

"If I told you I completely believe in what you stand for and I believe in the way you are going about it, but I don't believe in the people you are surrounding yourself with, what would you say?"

"I'd say that they're probably right and there is something not quite right with you. Are you sure you're not a copper?"

"I'm not a policeman."

"Then why the fuck are you doing this? They are right, there's no motivation for you to be living in a squat, pretending to stick up for those who have been oppressed."

"Oppressed? Do you have any idea what the word oppressed means? If you were anywhere else you'd have been thrown out of them flats by now and you'd all be doing time in jail or some forced labour camp. That's oppression."

"Oppression is relative. Just because somewhere else they have it worse, it doesn't mean you can't be oppressed relative to other people's conditions."

"I agree with that but just look at those places. They're absolute tips, the walls are falling apart, it's cold, it's damp, it's no place to bring up any child. You do realise that you can't win? We can't win, they'll throw us out and then that'll be the end of that. They'll sell them all off to developers in a few year's time and then they'll be a trendy spot to live in. That's the reality of the world we live in and I don't quite think you understand that do you?"

"Wait, hold on a minute! What exactly are you doing living with us then? You've practically just admitted to me you don't believe in what we're doing and that it's a complete waste of time. I've defended you so much! A whole year, non stop they've been telling me there's something not quite right about you and I said no, you're fine. I'm leaving, please don't follow me or come back tonight, you're not welcome."

"Wait, just hear me out. There's better ways to go about this, I'm worried for your safety, I'm concerned that something bad will happen to you. You don't have to keep fighting like this, life isn't some kind of eternal struggle, you're a bright person, you could do so much more than be locked up in some shitty squat fighting for the rights of people who don't even care about you anyway. You say you can relate to them but you can't, they're not your people."

"I can't believe I am hearing this. Let me tell you something, I fully believe in what I am trying to achieve, so does everyone in the flat. We don't want them flats to go to ruin and we don't want the people who live in them, legally or not, to end up homeless."

"Listen, I have to tell you something, in fact, it's why I took you here tonight. I am a journalist."

"Please, please, don't tell me that! You can't be!"

"I am, I'm a journalist, I work for a newspaper who wanted an investigation into squatters and what motivates them. I've come to the conclusion that most are troublemakers who are out for their own ends; I don't think you are, but I also don't think this a path you should be pursuing. They're going to be coming tomorrow morning to evict you all. I shouldn't be telling you that but it's the truth, this time tomorrow it'll all be over and you'll all be living on the streets."

"Why are you telling me this?"

"I've fallen in love with you."

"Oh for fuck's sake!"

"I care about you, I don't want you to go back there, I know what some of them are like, they're troublemakers and I don't want any harm to come to you. I'm not going back tonight, that's why I brought you here, I want you to leave with me. I have a place to live in and you can stay with me. They'd never find you there."

"This is insane! I trusted you, I actually thought you believed in the same things as I did, yet all you're doing is using me and using my friends as some vehicle. It's voyeurism! I hope you fucking die! You can write that in your shitty newspaper report as well. I hope they paid you well for this."

"Please don't go! You don't understand, all I'm doing is trying to make a living, I'm not different to you and I do believe in some things, this year has taught me that but I can't just throw away my life for a cause which is never going to come to fruition."

"Goodbye! And you've obviously learned nothing!"

2017 – It's Terrible, isn't it?

"It's terrible, I'm thinking of moving away, I don't know how I've lived here for so long. What about you? You must be growing tired of it all by now?"

"I was reading something yesterday, it was on Facebook, one of my friends had posted it and they were saying that we'll be going to war soon."

"I think I read the same thing. Usually I would be a bit suspect about something like that but I'm starting to believe that World War Three isn't that far away."

"What would you do if there was a war? Would you fight or would you be a pacifist?"

"I don't know, I suppose I'd be a pacifist, do you have that option? They can't make you can they?"

"I'm not sure. I don't think I would fight, too much chance of not coming back and I can't take that risk. There are so many things I want to do with my life, I'm not having it taken away by some war I want no part of."

"Did I tell you I've been offered the chance to go to Africa and help some poor children?"

"No! How did that come about? Are you going to go? That would be wonderful! I've always wanted to help poor people. I should have done it when I left uni but I was too focused on my career. You'll have to put pictures up on Facebook if you do go, everyone would love to see it."

"An old friend of mine, he set up some kind of an orphanage out there. He gets gap year students to come over for a few weeks. I shouldn't say this, but he makes quite a lot of money out of it. I know it's a bit unethical but I suppose you have to make money somehow."

"It is a bit unethical but I doubt he's the only person doing it and if he's helping people out, I don't really see the problem."

"Oh, you always get some do gooder who'd find a problem with it. You know? One of those save the world types."

"I had a friend like that, you had to be careful what you said around her because she'd go off on one."

"Not like in the old days, hey?"

"You sound like my father but I'm inclined to agree with you even if I wasn't around in the 'old days'. What are you doing this weekend?"

"I've not got any plans at the moment."

"David's found this great new bar down in Peckham, said we should go and check it out, if you're up for it you could come along with us on Saturday."

"Is it safe there? Do you remember Sandy? The guy who works in finance, he came out with us one night? He went to some place in Hackney and someone pulled a knife on him. Frightened the life out of him, can't even get him out for a couple of pints anymore."

"No! It's quite safe. You don't really get any of the locals going into the bar we'll be going to."

"That sounds cool then, I'd love to come along. You are sure it's safe though? You hear a lot of stories."

"I'm sure it's safe, he wouldn't take me there if he thought it was unsafe."

"I suppose. I've stopped taking the tube to work by the way. I decided it's easier and safer to walk."

"Safer?"

"Yes, you never know what might happen with all these terrorists running about everywhere, it's out of control. They can't get me if I'm not there. You should think about it too, it's not like you'd have far to walk."

"I hate walking! I might think about it though, you're right."

"Be careful if you're out after dark though, you never know who might be walking around."

"Don't worry, I will! You shouldn't worry too much though, we'll be packing our bags to go off to war soon!"

"Yes! We'll probably be all dead next week anyway! Let's have one for the road! I'll only be going home to spend the night looking at my laptop."

"Cheers!"

Waterloo – View From the Bridge

Home to Waterloo Station and Waterloo Bridge

What a beautiful evening! The perfect day to finally get this finished, it surely won't rain today. Six months of work and I'll finally be able to give it to her tonight. I'm quite proud of it, it really is one of the best pieces of work I've done. The idea came to me when I was walking across Waterloo Bridge with her one evening, we both stopped and looked out at the view: The City of London, St Paul's, the sun setting in the background, the sky that incredible red colour which brings a warmth and feeling of optimism. I said to myself that evening, 'I'm going to paint it for her!'.

I'm what you would call a shy artist. I paint, I've always painted but I've never let people see what I paint, well people I know anyway. It causes all sorts of suspicion because my girlfriend does wonder where I get off to when I disappear to paint. It's therapeutic, I don't usually care much for the quality of what I paint, it doesn't really matter because no one will ever see them, but this one is different, it's not for me. I'm excited because I know it's beautiful but there's always a nagging doubt in your mind when you do something that it's not quite good enough.

I walk across the bridge several times when I come, nervous, self-conscious, people are curious as to what you are going to be doing. They want to see what's on that easel. Some nod their heads, others complement me on my work, while others try to offer advice. Those who offer advice are always the worst. It's my painting and I will be the judge of it! Well she will too, but a random stranger certainly won't be!

I know she'll be delighted when I bring it home tonight, finally compete, she'll know where I've been disappearing off to in the evenings as well, no more secrets! It is looking very good, it'd win a competition if I had the balls to enter one. I did think about doing it but it would be too much trouble, they'd want the painting and I wouldn't be able to give it to her until it's been judged, never mind that they might think it's rubbish and then I probably wouldn't give it to her because my pride would be destroyed.

Once I've given it to her, I'm going to ask her to marry me. I know she won't say no to that question, but I wanted to make it special. We've been together for four years now and my friends have said she's waiting for me to ask the question. If she did say no I would have a big problem! She won't say no though, I know for sure she won't say no. I've even got the honeymoon planned out. She's always wanted to go to the Caribbean and I've seen a nice little villa on a quiet island, she'll absolutely love it.

This man standing behind me has been there for a about ten minutes now, surely the painting isn't that interesting to him. He keeps moving then looking at me and nodding his head as though he's directing me. I don't need any direction, thank you very much! Perhaps he can't speak English which is why he hasn't said anything. I'm getting a bit uncomfortable now though, I wish I could tell him to move on, he's distracting me. I'll give him a smile. No, that hasn't worked, he's standing there looking even more maniacally at me. Oh! He's going now, thank God for that!

I should have it done within the next couple of hours. I'll miss coming here in the evening, even though I'm surrounded by people, there's something soothing about standing here. I think it's the river, water always makes a person feel relaxed. Not that I'd want to fall in there, I don't think I'd get out again, God knows what kind of diseases you'd pick up in there. I'm not sure about this red, I don't know if it quite captures the sunset. I have to have it finished tonight, I can't wait any longer!

I'll go and get a coffee, coffee always makes me think better. What will I do with the painting though? I don't want to leave it here, someone might take it. That man could have had a use, he would have been able to watch it for me. Everyone crossing the bridge looks in such a hurry, I daren't ask one of them to look after it, they'd probably shout at me for bothering them. I'm going to have to take the risk, the coffee shop is only at the end of the bridge and I'll be able to see until I go inside, it'll only take two minutes.

I keep looking back to see if it's still there, stopping every ten paces and checking. No one will take it, why would they want it? It's a personal thing, it'd be no good to anyone. It's okay, just go and get your coffee, come back, finish the painting off and then you can go home and present it to the love of your life. Then you have to propose as well, I mustn't forget that! Deep breath, no one's going to take it, if you keep stopping it's only going to take much longer to buy the coffee. Come on Sam! Stop being a dithering idiot!

The queue is really long! I knew this would happen. I'll wait, the painting will be there when I get back, I'm sure of that. I'm sure I recognise that guy standing at the front of the queue. Oh yes! It's John from work! I wonder if he'd like to come and see it, I don't normally show people my work but I do like John, he's a nice guy and he's always asking about Jennifer and me.

"John! Have you got a minute? Would you like to come and see a painting I've been doing?"

It's so fucking boring around here, there ain't anything to do. All these lot keep talking about how they're making money but none of them have got any money. It's always tomorrow or the day after when they're getting money and it never comes. All we do is stand around pretending to look hard, staring at people. Some of the people who live here have started complaining as well, saying we're a menace and the police have been coming around bothering us. It ain't like we really do anything, it's all just a front.

I keep saying to them we should go out, have a walk about, do something different but all they say is 'what do you want to go out for?'. No ambition, man. We don't even play football anymore, I used to like coming out to play football, at least you were doing something. My mum is on my case all the time as well telling me I need to find better friends, the ones I've got ain't any good for me and how they're all a bad influence. They might be boring but they're still my friends, I can't drop them out just like that.

At college they were going on about some art course that we could do. My teacher was saying that I'm good at art and I should get involved, you don't know where it might lead and all that. I don't know though, I'm worried what people might think, they'll say I'm some kind of nerd and they'll be the ones who'll be dropping me out. I don't know why I worry so much about what they think, it's just like that, people don't understand when you're my age it's all about image and no one cares about anything else.

I haven't really got anyone to look up to though, that's the problem. The only people that are making any money around here are doing it illegally, everyone else is just working shit jobs for hardly anything. I shouldn't say things like that because that's what my mum and dad are

256

doing, working hard, but I don't want that life. They're always arguing with each other about money and then I feel guilty because I think I'm part of the problem. I don't want to spend half my life in jail either, that'd just be a waste. How come they say being a kid is easy?

"You lot want to go up Waterloo Station? See who's about?"

"What do you want to go up there for?"

"Just look innit!"

"There's nothing to do up there!"

"Come on man, let's just go for a walk somewhere, sitting around here all day is fucking boring, you never do anything."

"Come then, you're buying me something from the shop though."

"I ain't got any money."

"Rob it then."

"You rob it."

"You're such a pussy."

Darryl, my best friend. We've been friends since we were about three years old, always together. Recently I ain't been that sure about him, he seems to be getting involved with some stupid people. I ain't no angel but for me there's a limit but with him there ain't none. If he thinks he can do something that'll make people look at him with 'respect', he'll do it. I tried telling him that he's going to end up getting himself into trouble but he's one of them mad people that don't listen to what you're saying. He knows what's best and there ain't no other way.

"Take your hood down, man. Too many people looking at us."

"No! Why should I take my hood down?"

"Everyone's looking at us like we're going to rob them or something."

"We ain't robbing no one, why do you care what they think about us?"

"I don't care, but I don't like walking the streets when everyone is looking at us, it makes me feel uncomfortable."

"Fucking hell, man! You need to chill out, bruv! Who cares what anyone thinks?"

He's right but it don't make me feel any more comfortable. When I go out the door, I honestly ain't looking to rob anyone or anything like that. It's just that you dress in a certain way and people start staring at you or they cross the road or when you go in the shop, the security man starts following you around. It kind of makes you want to steal something just to say, 'yeah, you was right.' Sounds stupid don't it? That's how I feel though.

"Let's go to the bridge, I want to have a look."

"What do you want to look at? There's nothing there."

"I just want to have a look, I was thinking about painting a picture, I reckon it'd make a nice scene."

"Haha! Whatever, don't be there for long though, I got things to do."

"You ain't got nothing to do! What you lying for? We'll only be ten minutes anyway."

There's loads of people on the bridge, all going home from work, up to the train station. I reckon that'd make a good picture. You could paint all the people on the bridge, with the city in the background with the church. I want to paint something deep, like, all these people are like ants, going back and forward to work. The sun setting in the background would show that's the end of their day, and all they do is work. Yeah, I might talk to my teacher about it, I reckon he might help me.

"There's a painting over there, whose is it?"

"I don't know, let's have a look at it, it looks good."

"It does look good actually. Why have they just left it? Do you reckon we could sell it? I heard you can make loads of money from paintings."

"From famous paintings! You can't steal it anyway, someone's taken loads of time to do this. Look at it, it's good."

John didn't want to see my painting, he said was very busy and had to get home, I'm a bit disappointed. I wish this bloody woman at the counter would hurry up, she's taking forever and I need to get back. Finally! This coffee tastes good. I think the red looks quite good actually, it's just me being too much of a perfectionist. Half my problem, always looking for everything to be just right.

Who are these two looking at my painting? They look like they might be a bit confrontational. What if they try to steal it? Do I try to stop them? Look at me I'm a skinny weakling, they'll kick the shit out of me. Oh Jesus! Please don't take the painting. I could give them some money to make them go away, yes that will work, me giving them money will be worth far more than the actually painting. It means far too much to me for it to get robbed.

What if one of them has a knife? I'm going to get killed aren't I? This is it, my last day on earth and I had such wonderful plans for this evening. What will Jennifer think? She'll think I'm useless! I will be useless because I'm about to get stabbed and instead of having a wedding they'll be burying me six feet under the ground. I knew I shouldn't have left it there, I am such a fool! Oh God! One of them is touching it! He's going to ruin it. I could throw the coffee in his face, it'll burn him and he'll run away for sure, but then his friend will probably stab me!

Now they're discussing something and I'm standing here like an idiot trying to decide what I should do. It looks as though they are arguing. They want to take it, I know they do! I have to intervene, this is an important piece of work. Come on! Be courageous! What's the worse they can do to you? There's too many people about for them to do something terrible. What if they throw me over the bridge into the river? That doesn't bare thinking about. One of them has walked away, he might be going to get reinforcements. I have to put a stop to this!

"Excuse me? May I ask what you are doing to my painting?"

"Oh, sorry! I didn't know it was yours. I was just admiring it, I'd like to do one myself one day, I had the idea of painting it on this bridge."

He seems quite well spoken but I'm not sure I can trust him, he certainly doesn't look like someone who likes to paint. It's a trap, he's keeping me occupied before his friend comes back with a feral gang of youths and they're going to steal it.

"Yes, I'm quite proud of it. Where did your friend go?"

"He went home, he doesn't like art. You thought we was going to nick it didn't you?"

"No! No! Of course I didn't, I was just wondering why you were looking at it, I had gone to get a coffee."

"Is there a special reason you're painting it?"

"No, not at all, I just like painting."

"Yeah, me too. I don't get much chance to do it though, some of the stuff is pretty expensive."

"It's not all very expensive. What made you want to paint the bridge?"

Perhaps I've had him all wrong, he didn't want to take it and he's actually admiring it, it's very good for the ego I must say.

"I just thought it'd be a good place to paint a picture of, you know, people walking across it, they're like ants. I think people work too much, don't take enough time for themselves and it'd be a good way of showing it if I managed to get it right."

"You should give it a go."

"I'd like to be but I don't have any paints or brushes or an easel, nothing like that."

"That's a shame."

"It looks like it's going to rain in a minute, you'd better get it packed away or you'll end up ruining it."

"It looked so nice just an hour ago. You're right, I'll have to wait until tomorrow. Good luck with your painting, I hope you have some success out of it!"

"Thank you, I hope whoever you're painting it for likes it."

How does he know I'm painting it for someone, is it that obvious? I suppose we just give off an air sometimes which leads people to know exactly what our intentions are. He's right, I'd better go or it will get ruined, what a nuisance, all that build up and I never managed to finish it. It'll have to wait until tomorrow. The excitement inside me is bursting! I'd better hurry up, I'll still be able to catch the earlier train.

That boy standing over there is the one who was with the other boy who was talking to me. I'm sure it's him. Why is he looking at me? This street is a bit quiet, there's no one around. I could go into that shop over there, he wouldn't follow me in, he might just wait though. No, just be a man and continue on your way to the station, he won't do anything to you and if he does tell him sternly that you'll go straight to the police. I shouldn't expect that would bother him all that much though. He's just put his hood up! Oh shit! I think he's going to rob me!

"Give me the picture! Hurry up and I won't hurt you."

"I'm not giving it to you! It's very special to me and I won't give it up for anyone. I'll call the police!"

"I don't give a fuck about the police just give me the picture and I'll just go."

"No!"

He's grabbed it, I couldn't stop him. He's running too fast for me to catch him, there must be a policeman around here somewhere. What will they do though? All these months of work and now it's all been for nothing. There must be a way I can find him, he must live close. That's just stupid, there's no way I'd be able to find him. I want to cry, I really do!

"Why did you rob him for?"

"You liked the painting, innit, I robbed it to give to you."

"Shut up! You didn't rob it for me, you ain't even got it on you. You know you won't be able to sell that, right? No one's going to buy it off you, it ain't worth anything, it's just some geezer's painting."

"Shut up, man! I'll get rid of it, don't worry about that."

"So you wasn't going to give it to me then?"

261

"You've turned proper weak you know that? You ain't no fun anymore, I used to think you was a cool guy to be around, you'd be up for anything but lately you just don't want to do anything. It's just a painting anyway, he'll go and paint another one! I don't know why you're so worried about it. You saw him, he looked like a proper nerd."

"What does it matter what he looked like? He's just some guy that done a painting, he likes painting, it's his hobby and then you've come along and taken it. It probably took him months to do that. You're a fucking prick, man! I don't know why I waste my time with you anymore."

"Yeah, yeah! Go and find him then and tell him you're sorry like the little idiot you are. I don't care, you're a fool! I don't want nothing to do with you anymore! You better watch your back, people will be after you, you know!"

When we were standing on the bridge and the man wasn't there, I told him not to take it, you can't just take someone's stuff like that. The man clearly put a lot of effort into that painting and I could tell he was doing it for someone, I don't know how I knew, just a feeling I had. Then Darryl started getting all aggressive saying that he was going to take it and all that but I managed to persuade him not to, well I thought I did. I don't even know who that man was or where he lives or nothing, it's not like I can give it back to him.

I've had enough of all this. He might have been my best friend for years but I don't want nothing to do with him now. I ain't one of these people who think they can guide people on to a right path and all that shit, that's personal responsibility and he ain't got none. He won't listen to me. I kind of wish I'd just punched him but that would just cause even more trouble, I don't want to be scared to be walking out the door because someone might be waiting for me, I ain't got any time for that. Friendship? I thought it was supposed to last forever.

I feel like I should try and get the picture back. I don't know how though, Darryl ain't going to give it to me and he ain't going to tell me where it is. Even if I can't give it back to the man, I could at least keep it for myself and then it's on somebody's wall, might not be the person he wanted but it's better than it getting thrown in the bin because that's what's going to happen when he realises that no one is going to want to buy it. This is one stupid situation! I was saying I was bored earlier, I'd *rather be bored than involved in this. I feel guilty and I ain't even done anything!*

I reckon that man will go back to the bridge. He might try and start again or something, that's the only way I'd be able to find him. I could try and explain to him what happened, even if he doesn't want to listen I'd know I tried. I'll go tomorrow, see if he's there. I need to try and get the painting back first though, if I could go back with the painting then that would make things better. He might even have thrown it away already. I know! I'll try and ring that geezer he hangs around with, hopefully they ain't together.

"Yes, Darren! What you up to?"

"Nothin' man, just at home innit. You seen Darryl?"

"Yeah, I seen him earlier."

"He's got some painting that he stole of some man on Waterloo Bridge and he's trying to sell it. I told him I'd give him 20p for it and he got all mad. You need to tell your friend to calm down a bit man, he keeps doing stupid things."

"Yeah, yeah, I don't know what's wrong with him lately. Does he have the painting on him?"

"Why? You going to buy it?"

"Nah, just wondering."

"I don't know man. Those flats across the way, you know the ones that girl lives in, the one who's always looking for Darryl?"

"Yeah, I know them."

"Last time he stole something he couldn't sell he hid them in the bins at the bottom of those flats."

"Yeah, yeah. I just want to have a look at it, see if it's worth anything. Don't tell him though, you know what he's like."

"Nah, I won't tell him. If you sell it though let me in, I'm broke, I need some cash."

"Yeah, I'll ring you later, innit."

I'll go and have a look and see if it's there. I don't think it will be, he's most likely thrown it away if he knows it ain't worth nothing. If I find it though, I'm going to see if I can track this man down.

I'm going to give up the painting, I don't want to do it anymore. That piece was my pride and joy and now it's gone. I don't even know why he'd want to rob it from me, it wouldn't be worth a single penny, the only thing it was worth is in my heart and that's no good to anyone. Oh God! I'm getting emotional and soppy now. I hope no one is looking at me. I could just propose anyway but it wouldn't feel right, it wouldn't have that extra touch I wanted to give it. I'm fucking angry and I'm going to do something about it!

Tomorrow, after work. I'm going to go and hunt this boy down and I'm going to get it back. I'm not letting some kid take away my pride and joy. I'll wander the streets of South London until I find him, he won't be that hard to find, all they do is hang about on the streets. I don't care if there's twenty of them, I'm getting it back. I'd better bring some form of protection with me as well. This could be a little bit dangerous. No! You can't back out now, you need to defend your honour and your pride and you need to defend Jennifer!

It appears she's not at home yet. That's good, I'll need to plan what I'm going to do tomorrow and she'd only distract me. What kind of a weapon could I take with me? I'll have a look in the kitchen drawer and see what we have. I won't use it, it'll just be for show, make him a little bit scared when I do find him, and I'm definitely going to find him. What if he has one too? It'll be a stalemate, I'd rather not die but I need to get that picture back. I'll use it if I have to, I must, I can't let someone treat me the way he has.

Oh God! She's home, she'll know I'm angry, she always knows when there's something wrong. I'd better put on my happy face or else I'll face an endless barrage of questions.

"What's the matter? You look like you've had a rough day."

"No, not at all! Just a bit tired, work was busy and I went for a drink with John when it was finished."

"You seem to be seeing John a lot recently. Good friend is he?"

"Well, he's a good work friend, I wouldn't say a good friend as such but he's a nice enough bloke."

"What about tomorrow? Will you be going for another drink with John?"

She thinks I'm lying to her. I should just tell her but that will spoil the surprise, I can't get this far and then reveal it all to her without having the painting.

"Yes, probably. We've important things about work to discuss. I'm sorry I'm out every night, I will make it up to you. I have a surprise for you tomorrow night too."

"Oh? Really? What kind of surprise?"

"I'm not telling you, you'll find out when I get home tomorrow."

"Okay, well if you're going to be like that I'll just wait."

Why is she looking in the kitchen drawer?

"Have you seen that knife my mother bought me for Christmas, the big one."

"No, I haven't seen it. What do you need it for?"

"Nothing, I just noticed it wasn't there."

"Why were you looking in the drawer."

"You're acting very strange lately. It's my home and I wanted to find something in the drawer."

"I haven't seen it."

She's on to me, she knows I've taken the knife. Why the hell was the first thing she did is to look in the bloody drawer? This is probably a really, really stupid idea, maybe I should just leave it, there's no point in getting myself killed over a silly painting. It did take me a long time though and it'd all be for nothing! Imagine that, all them hours and you have nothing to show for it, you have to go and find that boy and get your painting back. Show the world you're not a wimp!

The painting's there, I can see it! At least I've found it, now all I've got to do is find that geezer. I reckon there's little chance of that happening but I'll wait on the bridge for him tomorrow, if he turns up, he turns up. If he doesn't I'll keep it and put it up on my wall. It's a good painting. It looks even better than when I saw it the first time, this guy has some talent. I wish I could paint like that, I wonder if I gave it back to him would he be able to give me some lessons or something. Nah! That would be a bit too cheeky.

I saw Darryl hanging around outside the shop when I was on my way over here but he never saw me. He ain't going to care about this now, he must have just tried to throw it away. I hope he don't come knocking at my door later, that's what he does when we fall out, he comes knocking like nothing's ever happened. I'll tell my mum to say I ain't there, she doesn't really like him anyway so she'll probably be pleased.

It hurts though, you know? He might be an idiot but he's been my friend for years and now he ain't no more. Not just because of what happened today but I've had that feeling for ages. I suppose people change, just because you're friends when you were kids, doesn't mean you'll still get on when you're older. I mean we're still kids, sort of but not proper kids. I just wish he'd listen to me, the mad thing is he's a really good football player. If he'd put all of his energy into that then he would probably be able to make it. I don't even know why he's changed so much, I can't see one thing where I can say 'yeah, that happened and that's why he's like he is now'. It's weird.

Looks like my mum is waiting outside the door, she don't usually do that, I hope there ain't nothing wrong.

"Where you been?"

"I was out."

"You been hanging around with Darryl, getting into mischief? What's that thing under your arm?"

"It's just a painting I found, it's rubbish."

266

"If it's rubbish, why are you bringing it home?"

"I mean, I like it but most people would think it was rubbish. Why you waiting outside the door?"

"There was some madness going on outside, I was watching to see what happened."

"What happened?"

"Some kid got stabbed. That's why I don't want you hanging around out there late at night. I ain't having you ending up stabbed."

"Who got stabbed?"

"How am I supposed to know!"

See, that's what happens when you get involved in foolishness. It's all this big front, one kid says something to another and then instead of having a fight or just taking no notice they have to go around stabbing each other. Now someone else will get stabbed because that kid just got stabbed. He probably ain't much older than me either, what's the point? I don't get it. Oh shit! It can't have been Darryl. I don't think it would have been him but you never know. I'd better ring him.

"Yeah?"

"I was just ringing to see if you was okay innit?"

"Why wouldn't I be okay?"

"Some kid got stabbed, I was just making sure it weren't nothing involving you."

"Why do you care? I'm too clever to get stabbed, you know that."

"Ain't no one too clever to get stabbed."

"I threw that painting away. Darren tried to give me 20p for it so I just dashed it in the bins."

"Yeah, it weren't worth nothing man. Seriously though, I'm still angry about that, you shouldn't have done it, that geezer didn't do nothing to you."

"Forget about that geezer man. He'll just do another one, you need to care more about your friends than people you don't even know."

"I ain't getting into this again."

"I'm sorry, all right? I'll go with you tomorrow and we can go to the bridge and that. You can see what you want to paint."

"I ain't got nothing to paint with."

"I got you something, innit. Like a peace offering or whatever you call it."

"What kind of peace offering?"

"You'll see tomorrow."

"I'll see, I might have something to do."

"That how it is? I offer you something and you turn me down! This is what I'm sayin!"

"Okay, okay! I need to go Waterloo tomorrow evening, need to sort something out. Come around seven and I should be finished. Don't come before then though because you won't be able to find me."

"Who you going to see?"

"No one. Just come at seven."

What kind of peace offering has he got me. Now I'm all conflicted. I should have just said no because he's probably gone and robbed someone or somewhere and he's going to give whatever it is he's robbed to me. Every time there has to be a foolishness with him. He better not turn up before seven because if he does and that geezer does go to the bridge then there could be problems, it wouldn't surprise me if he called the police. I need to go to bed, today has just been stupid.

I've put the knife down the front of my trousers. I thought that's how people carry them but it feels a bit uncomfortable, the blade is nicking my leg. I'm going to go home tonight and look like I've been in a fight with a load of angry cats. I have to say though, I feel quite brave with it down my pants. Like no one can fuck with me, because if they do, I'll pull out my knife! You could even say there's a bit of a swagger in my walk. I bet this kid will be surprised to see such a different man tonight when I track him down.

Six o'clock. Time to go hunting. I'll start at the bridge and then walk down to the station, there's some housing estates further along that road too, I could have a look in there. This little bastard is going to regret ever taking my painting. Jennifer will be so proud of me for standing up for myself! If I find him I might ruffle his feathers a bit, play with him, make him really believe I'm going to do him some damage, that way he'll never do it to anyone ever again.

I was thinking last night. I bet his friend was in on it too, all that talk was just to distract me, make me fall off guard. A double act. I hope I find both of them, scare the shit out of both of them! I actually quite liked the kid who said he was admiring my painting and that makes it all even worse. I'll make him pay for ruining my night.

The sky is clear, I would have been able to finish it off if I'd still had it. Tonight would have been the night. Now I have to go looking for it, hope it doesn't rain tomorrow night and then go finish it then. Another couple of days before I'll be in any position to make my proposal. That crazy, grinning man that was looking at me yesterday is standing in the same spot. He must be a mad man. He's looking at me. I'll give him a little glimpse of the knife, that'll show him not to annoy strangers on the street. Look at this! You lunatic!

The smile dropped from his face and he's run off. For the first time in my life, I have a feeling of power. I don't care who I'm frightening, it doesn't matter, they're all scared of me and I can control them. I've never seen anyone run so fast! That was a buzz! I can't wait now for the real show to start. Hold on a minute, this is making me quite crazy, I think I'm losing my mind! Keep level headed and everything will go according to plan, you'll get your painting back. You'll propose, give her the painting and this whole thing will never be thought of again.

Rather oddly, Jennifer didn't kiss me when I left the house this morning. She always does, I wonder what was the matter with her? I'm sure she thinks I'm cheating on her. I would never do such a thing but I suppose my behaviour has been rather odd. I think that's him ahead of me. I'm sure it's him, he's standing at the end of the bridge, it's the one who said he liked to paint! I've got him, it is a bit public though, I'll need to get him somewhere I can use this knife. Hold on a minute, what's he holding in his hand?

"Oi, you! Where's your friend and where's my painting?"

"Your painting is here. I'm sorry, my friend, he's an idiot, I told him not to take it but he don't listen to me."

"What made you think I'd be back here today? I think you're lying to me."

"Why would I lie to you? Listen, your painting ain't really worth nothing to anyone but yourself. I come here because I thought if you was going to look for it, this would be the place you'd come."

"I still don't believe you."

"Just take the painting. Here..."

"What makes you think you can take something from someone? Do you know how long it took me to paint that? Do you have any idea what I wanted to do with it? I'll tell you, I was going to propose to my girlfriend tonight and this picture was her present. You and your little friend completely fucked it up and now I'm angry and to be honest I want revenge!"

"I don't care if you want revenge. What are you going to do to me? Just take the picture, go home and propose to your wife. Why are you getting so excited?"

"So excited? So excited? Are you stupid?"

"Take the painting man, I'm going. I thought I was doing you a favour but by the looks of it, you're completely crazy."

"You're coming with me."

This has got even more stupid now. The guy has a fucking massive knife! All I wanted to do was give him his painting back and now he's marched me to this little park. I need to get out of this. I'm just going to have take a chance and hit him, hope he goes down and run. He don't look like he'll be able to use the knife but you never know. Of all the stupid fucking situations I could get myself into this one has to be the craziest.

I don't know what to do now I've got him here. I mean, I'm not really going to stab him or anything. It was all just bravado before, I'm quite frightened and I don't know how I'm going to get myself out of this. I should just walk away right now but I'm scared he might have something on him and then he'll stab me while I'm walking away. Jesus Christ! I really do need to have a look at the way I handle stressful situations, I went completely mad and now I'm in this ridiculous situation.

I'm just going to run, fuck it, he ain't going to catch me and by the looks of it, he's shitting himself and doesn't know what to do. I need to give him some way out of this. That painting must really, really mean something to him. Oh shit! Why is Darryl here!? Now the geezer has that mad look back in his eyes, I thought he'd calmed down. Darryl's got a knife in his hand as well. I should have left that stupid fucking painting in the bin.

"Put the knife away, Darryl. The geezer is about to go home, he don't want any trouble."

"Shut up! Both of you! You set me up yesterday and now I want revenge!"

"What kind of revenge are you going to get? Just take the fucking painting and walk away, that's it over with, none of us will ever see each other again. Darryl, just leave the park man, I can sort this out."

This Darryl is coming towards me with a knife, I don't know what to do. I should never have come here, why didn't I just leave it, start the painting again or even just proposed to her without the painting. He's moving quickly, I need to do something or I'm going to end up dead. I'm not dying for anyone!

Fuck! He's stabbed Darryl! He's stabbed my friend! Shit! Shit! I don't know what to do! The geezer's ran off, the painting is on the floor. There's blood all over Darryl's jeans. What am I supposed to do? He's smiling, why's he smiling? He's just been stabbed.

"Yesterday, after I threw the painting away, I went to the shop and I bought you this paintbrush, it's just a little thing man, but I know you'd

appreciate it. Sorry, man. I ain't been the best friend recently. Make sure you use the paintbrush."

Don't go on me man! Please, don't die on me! All this over a fucking painting!

Lambeth North

Lambeth North, home to London's Imperial War Museum. A reminder of the futility of war and those who have lost their lives.

He's been whistling for ten minutes, but no one's stopped him. It's a lull, a break from the madness, the simple sound everyone takes for granted brings joy, thoughts of home, a cooked dinner, fresh air free from the smell of death. Keep going, keep going. I keep telling myself I need to keep going, it'll finish some day and then I can go home and see my mother and father, my Gracie if she still wants me. The whistling brings the smell of home cooked food, you never thought potatoes had a smell before but I'd recognise them in an instant now.

The whistling stops and the silence is back. It's not the silence you have at night when you're lying in your bed waiting for sleep, or the silence at the beginning of a performance when you're waiting for the singer to open her mouth. It's thick, you're waiting for it to break but you know what breaks it won't be a dream or a beautiful voice. It'll be more bangs and flashes and screams and shouting and then it'll go silent again, if you're still there to listen to it. I sometimes wonder if death would be better than the silence, an endless dream with no more screams.

I wonder what they're doing back home? I'm sure mum will be cooking something for dinner, dad will be sitting at the table smoking his pipe and reading the newspaper, a small fire burning. The steam coming off the pans. How many times I sat in that room, impatient, waiting for the food to come, sighing and huffing, my father staring at me with that look of 'mind your manners'. I'd happily take being there with him scolding me, the food arriving on the table, a hot mouthful, the feeling in your stomach as you feel the warmth travel down with the food.

I was going to be a hero, all dressed smart in khaki, Gracie standing there admiring me, I'd be home in a few months and we'd get married, have a big party. A hero, that's the words that always stick in my head. What's a hero? Someone who goes off to a land across the sea to die? Men with families leaving them with smiles on their faces, never to see them again because it's your duty to fight an enemy you'd never seen or met before? Called heroes by those who have no idea what it's really like, I'm not a hero, I'm just a boy who did what he thought was right.

The wall of the trench is hard against my back, a wall made of mud and God only knows what else. I don't like to think, I'm probably leaning against a part of a friend. His reward for being a hero was becoming part of the thing that killed him. My feet are sore and wet but I daren't take off my boots for fear of what I might find. They're not bad enough to be sent home but they're bad enough, I don't want to see them, maybe I should make them bad enough to be sent home. They wouldn't believe me though, I wouldn't be a hero anymore, I'd be a traitor.

My friend Billy Watson, he went last week. We signed up together, walking back as happy as could be, we were off to war. Billy was getting married too, I wonder if she knows yet? She was a nice girl. She could be a bit moody but Billy was a silly bastard and he needed someone who would have put him straight. Oh! She would have put him straight! He never stopped talking about her, every day it's all he would take about, oblivious to everything that was going on around him, he was sure he'd be going home.

It's cloudy tonight, I wonder if it's going to rain? It just makes it worse when it rains, the mud gets everywhere, you're scared to look down at the floor for fear of what you might see. It looked like rain last night but it never so we might be lucky tonight. Nothing has happened for days, you know it's coming but none of us ever know when. A bit of sun would be nice, you don't realise what a little ray of sun hitting your face can do, it brings just the smallest bit of hope. Poor Billy, hey? He'd love to be able to see the sun one more time.

You see them sometimes when they pop their heads up over the trench. I don't want to see a person, I want to see the devil. If it was a devil, it'd make it easy to hate. I can't hate them though, they can't be any different to what we are. Just a load of kids who've left their families and they don't know when they'll see them again. There's a German me over there, and he's dreaming of a German Gracie who'll be waiting for him when he gets home. They're supposed to be your enemy but the longer it goes on the longer you realise we're all just the same.

I've been saving this cigarette, Billy had it in his pocket. I shouldn't have taken it but I said to myself if anything happened to him I'd have it for him. I knew he was saving it for a special occasion. When it's over he said, we'd share it with each other, celebrate going home. You were a good man Billy, this one's for you mate. A hero. The smoke feels good as it hits the back of my throat, small pleasures where there are few to be found. Staring at the orange glow of the cigarette I think of the sun, yeah, maybe it won't rain and it'll be sunny tomorrow.

Dear Gracie,

I hope this letter finds you well! The first thing you will probably want to know is if I'm well and I am. I am very well. My feet were a bit sore the last few days but they're feeling better now. It's a bit boring to be honest because we don't do very much, they're saying that we should be home by Christmas because those bastards over in those other trenches are on the verge of giving up which is good. It's taken a bit longer than we expected but at least we're winning! One day I'll take you to France, I think you'd like it here.

I was thinking that when I get back and when we get married we'll have to live with my mum and dad for a little while because I don't have much money but I'll get work and we'll soon have a place to ourselves. I'll buy you that dress that you like too! Have you seen much of mum and dad? I've written to them but I ain't got any replies. I hope they're well, mum said she was having a bit of trouble with her back so I hope that isn't still playing her up. It'd be nice if you went around to see her, she'd like that.

How is Billy's girl? He don't stop talking about her. He reckons when he gets home and they get married they'll have ten babies. Imagine! Ten Billy's running around Lambeth! I hope she knows what she's let herself in for! Billy is well too, he keeps me going when I'm not feeling so good, he talks about home and we laugh about when we was kids and used to knock on people's doors and run away. That time old Mrs Jones caught him and gave him a clip around the ear! Didn't stop hearing about that story for months after!

You know what darling, I've never told him this because he'd think I was being a right soppy bastard but I don't know what I'd do without him. You don't get much that reminds you of home here but I have him. I know that Billy would do anything for me and he would you too because he knows how much I love you. He's definitely going to be my best man at the wedding. He keeps a cigarette in his pocket, says he's saving it for when we get the boat home. Each morning, he's there whistling away, nothing bothers him. I wish I could be like that sometimes.

Anyway, enough about me, I haven't asked you about yourself. How are you and what are you doing with yourself while I'm away? I hope you haven't forgotten about me already! How's your mother? We'll take her down the market when I get back and she can get some nice veg and she can cook something nice, I know she likes cooking. She does like me doesn't she? Sometimes I'm not sure, she looks at me a bit funny. I hope I'm a good enough man for you, Gracie. I promise you I'll do whatever it takes when we're married to make you happy.

Some of the boys have been able to get leave recently so I'm hoping that'll come up for me. If I do get it perhaps we can go to the theatre or something like that? I know you said you've always wanted to go to the theatre. You'll have to think of something we can go and see because I don't really know much about all that stuff. We could walk down there from home, it'd be nice to go for a stroll seen as I haven't been home for a year. Next time I write I'll let you know if I can come home and you can make preparations.

Love you my sweetheart

Alfie.

Some of the boys tell their people back home what it's really like here but I don't want to do that. I'll only worry Gracie and my mother would be forever panicking, her heart's not very good as it is. One of them can't write to well so he asked me to write his letter for him. He was crying while I was writing it, he wanted to tell his mum that his friend had died but I didn't write it for him, I just pretended to write. He'd think I was a bad person if he really knew but I was just trying to do him and his family a favour.

They must know what it's like. The boys go home on leave and they say that the women in London follow them around. I'm not interested in that, the only one I want to see is Gracie. They must tell people and I'm sure Billy's mum will tell my mum but I suppose when I write the letter, he can still be alive for me. They'll probably think I've gone mad. A piece of paper with words on it, which I don't know if they ever see is the only connection I have with them. There's no point making it miserable. I hope she does get the letters, she might think I'm dead and gone and found herself another fella.

We'll be leaving to go back to the billet for a bit soon, time away from the front, less chance of being killed. A week I've been here and it feels like a year. The silence will be broken soon, it has gone on too long. The walls feel like they are getting closer and closer together, like a vice which is taking its time to slowly crush you, taunting you as you consider your own sanity. A wisp of smoke passes my face, the smell of tobacco, an orange glow only a few metres away but I can't see the face. I wonder what he's thinking.

The walls keep taunting me, even in the pitch black. Staring at it I can see faces starting to appear in the dark mud. Faces of the enemy taunting you, faces of friends you've lost, the faces of people from home, their delight in your heroic act for king and country. If only they knew, war is tragic and there's nothing that I can do about it, a simple man who signed up because he felt it his duty, surely it's my duty to let the rest of the world know? Stop, now Alfie, you're upset, upset Billy has gone, upset that you've not seen Gracie in so long. Stop, calm down, you're still a hero.

A flash, another flash and a dull thud, someone diving to the floor, he gets up and sticks his head slowly over the sandbags. I wait for another flash and another thud, hoping the thud is the bag and not the head of the boy. Nothing comes, he gets braver, his head rising more, still no flash. I close my eyes. I wonder what Gracie is doing now? I bet she's sitting at home doing some knitting, yeah, she likes knitting. Thud! I open my eyes, he's still moving, he raises his own rifle and fires back at the flash. Eyes closed. I bet she's knitting something nice, it might be for me when I get back home, keep me warm. Thud! The body of the boy slumps to the floor. Another one gone.

Yeah, she'll be waiting for me. When I get off the train, she'll definitely be there, arms open waiting to give me a big hug. How I could do with a big hug now. I'm not the big man who left, the one who swaggered down the road with Billy, I'm scared. The boy's body stays there, another boy is holding him and stroking his hair, tears coming from his eyes. He's me and the dead boy is Billy, I'm looking at myself. Gracie, Gracie, Gracie, I wish you were here for me now. Please don't ever leave me like I left you. The sky lights up, an explosion further down the trench, mud hits me in the face.

The boy puts his friends head back on the floor. There's a madness in his eyes, even in the dark it shines through. He grabs his rifle and begins to shout. I don't know what he's shouting I can't understand, it's just noise, shouts, screams all mixed together into a sound you'd never heard before you came here but now it's too familiar. His head goes up above the sandbags, he looks at me, I shake my head but there is no reason in war. He pulls himself over the trench and begins to run. Two steps, just two steps and he slumps down to the floor. He died for his Billy, I'm no hero.

More flashes and more explosions, the noise, madness surrounds me as people run back and forwards shouting. No one knows what they are doing, someone grabs me and pulls me up and I move with him. In front of us a bang and fire and brightness, we both fall backwards. Where do we go? There's nowhere to go, if we go over we're dead, if we stay here we're dead. Trapped, the walls will get you somehow, still taunting you, begging you to go over them, begging you to flee to your death. Run, the only thing to do is run.

There's mum still sitting by the fire, dad's still smoking his pipe. The food is all eaten, they've had their fill and now they're happy and content. There's arms on the floor, arms but no body. I can feel a tear running down my face but I'm not crying. Dad will be going out for his evening stroll in a minute. He normally walks down to Waterloo and then along the embankment. Different kinds of walls. Another hand grabs me and pushes me down, my face against the wet mud, the smell of death and decay forced into my nose.

I can't do it anymore, I can't do it. I'm going to go over, I don't want to be here, I want to go home, I want to be by the fire with mum and dad and Gracie and we'd be talking about how we were going to arrange the wedding. I just can't stay down here, those bastards over there, I said they were no different to me but they are different they are devils. I'm going over to finish them off, they took Billy and they took that kid! I reach my hand up to the wall and I can see Billy's face, I push the arm off me, I'm going over, I'm going to kill those bastards!

My Dearest Billy,

How silly of you, of course I still want to get married to you! Don't think too much about my mother, she can just be a little queer sometimes. If she

278

didn't like you she would just tell you so I'm sure that she approves. I'm so madly in love with you Alfie that I really don't care if she approves or not, we'll run away if she doesn't! I am joking, but yes, don't worry about my mother. I am so looking forward to you coming home. Do you really think you'll be getting leave soon? That would be wonderful! I would love to go to the theatre, I know you don't care for it much but you'd have such a fun time!

Your mother is fine. I accompanied her yesterday for a walk, her back is sore but the doctor says she must get out more. She's spending a lot of time at home and I don't wish to worry you but if you do write to her please tell she must go for a walk each day. She worries about you Alfie, we all do, but she does far more. I told her you're a hero for going and doing what you're doing but she says she'd rather have a son than a hero. I hope she doesn't say that to everyone or she could find herself getting in trouble.

I saw some of the boys home on leave when I was passing the station last week. They all look so handsome in their uniforms but don't worry I'm not interested in any of them, there's only one man in uniform who I am interested in! I must tell you my friend, Hetty, I think you met her once but I can't remember. She's only gone and fallen in love with a Canadian and then they went and got married, she's only known the chap for five minutes, imagine that? I told her she was foolish and that he would be on the first boat back to Canada when the war is over but she thinks he'll be staying here with her and they'll have lots of babies.

I am sorry to hear about Billy, Alfie. There was no date on your last letter, oddly it had been torn out so I must assume you wrote it before Billy's death. I do understand how much he meant to you and I hope you are coping. You must look after yourself out there, I want you to come back in one piece because I don't know what I'd do without you. Billy's mum has gone rather mad and it's so sad to see, she walks the streets in the evening and talks to herself. I should tell you the girl he was in love with hasn't been seen for weeks, I do hope it is because of grief.

Well, I shan't bore you anymore with my ramblings. Remember to please look after yourself, Alfie and don't forget to write again soon. I'll be waiting for you when you get off the train in London when you get that leave,

Your Dearest Gracie.

Each time I'm passing the station I look at the faces of the soldiers in the hope Alfie has come home to surprise me. Some of them look so tired, and the mud and dirt on them, they must be living in the most awful of conditions. The other girls of course go mad for them, the soldiers show them their caps with bullet holes in them and they follow them around. I shouldn't complain because they are defending the country but I suppose it brings the danger closer to home, especially when you have someone out there. I hope Alfie doesn't have any bullet holes in his cap.

I'm a bit lost without him, I thought we'd be able to get married before he went but he said it would be better if we waited until he come back again. Sometimes I do wonder if he will come back. You hear stories from people, not everyone wants to talk about it but you can't help but think. I see those young girls that are running around after the soldiers and I think to myself, they don't know what they are letting themselves in for. You keep telling yourself not to worry and that he'll be home soon but well, really, who knows?

Him leaving was the hardest thing, I think about that day all the time. The evening before he left we went for a walk together, along the river, he bought me a flower, I've put it inside a book and now it's all dry but it's still a memory. We walked and he talked about how he'd be home in a few months and when he got home we'd be married and we could start a family. My head was dizzy with all the things he was saying. When he left the next day, getting on the train, I've never told anyone this, but I did wonder if I would ever see him again. My hero, off to fight the war.

I wonder what it's really like out there for him? I don't think he tells me the truth when he writes his letters, certainly not from what I've heard anyway. It was a bit strange him talking about Billy like that as well. I know the letters do take quite a long time to get back and they cut bits out but I think Billy was already dead when he wrote that last letter. Why would he pretend he was still alive? Very strange. I suppose I don't know what it's like out there and you don't know what it does to a person's mind.

This jumper I'm knitting for him should do him good, it'll keep him warm in the winter and he likes blue as well. Mum keeps looking at me funny, like she knows something is on my mind. She don't say much my old mum, she just looks at you funny, likes she's trying to say don't be thinking them silly things. Poor Alfie, I bet he's cold and wet. I'll have to have a good think about what we'll go and see when he gets back. It'll have to be something nice because he gets a bit fidgety when he's not interested in something.

I was just thinking there, I remember when them two was little boys, I was a little girl as well obviously. They used to get up to right mischief, always laughing and joking, they was the two kids that your mum and dad used to tell you not to hang around with but they always made us laugh, especially Alfie. I don't know where he gets his cheek from because his old man is a bit fierce if I'm telling the truth, I wouldn't like to get on the wrong side of him. I should go and have a look for wedding dresses, that would be a nice surprise for him when he gets back.

That poor Billy's mother was out in the street again tonight, she just wanders around talking to herself. I don't know what anyone can do, when you talk to her she just walks past you like you're not even there. I said something to mum but she didn't say nothing. Poor Billy, he was a good man but I wasn't sure about that girl he was hanging about with, I don't think she was that interested in him and no one's seen her since. I didn't say nothing to Alfie in the letter but the rumour is she's gone off with one of them soldiers that was on leave and he's gone AWOL. Serve her right if he gets arrested.

If Alfie died I don't know what I would do, it doesn't even bear thinking about. I think I'd just live a life on my own, I wouldn't be able to look at another man without thinking about Alfie, it wouldn't feel right. I shouldn't be thinking like that, I really shouldn't but I can't help it, you worry about the people you love and he's over there in a dangerous place. I wish it would all just end, I've never said it to anyone but I wish it'd never happened. Please come back in one piece Alfie, and don't be bringing no hats home with bullet holes in them because I won't be sewing them up for you.

Dear Gracie,

Thank you for sending me your letter, I was beginning to wonder if you'd already forgotten about me. I don't know when they will give us leave, there are only rumours and we won't know until it actually happens.

I will write to my mother and tell her to go for a walk, I know she can be stubborn sometimes.

Gracie, I am a bit scared. Last time I wrote I tried to tell you everything was okay but really I am scared. I don't want to tell you because I don't want to worry you but the day I get on the train home from this place will be the happiest day of my life.

Have you decided what you want us to go and see when I come home? I think a good trip to the theatre would do me good, it'd get my mind off things. I'm sorry I don't have much to write about this time. Hope to hear from you soon.

Alfie.

Sam is sitting next to me, his shoulder against mine. I didn't know his name until last night. I tried to go over, my hand was on the sandbag and my legs were ready to jump. I'd pushed him away, he was on the floor, I could see him, as I went to jump his hand caught my leg and I fell back down, face first into the mud again. I just lay there, I couldn't smell that horrible smell, the sounds were gone, I just lay there and I don't know how long I lay there for. The explosions stopped and the silence returned. Sammy picked me up, lit a cigarette and we shared it as if nothing had happened.

"When you go home, Sammy, what's the first thing you want to do?"

"I want to lie in a bed, a nice soft bed. I don't know if I'll be able to sleep though because all I'm used to now are these hard floors. What about you?"

"I want to hug my Gracie. That's all I want, I'd sleep on hard floors for the rest of my life for just being able to have that one moment with her."

"What's your Gracie look like, Alfie?"

"The most beautiful woman in the world. Do you have a girlfriend Sammy?"

"Aye, I have a woman back home. Wouldn't surprise me if she's ran off with someone by now though, never received a single letter from him since I left."

"Have you written to her?"

"No, truth be told, I joined up because I couldn't get rid of her and now I'm sitting here, caked in mud, my legs are destroyed, my hearing is going and I've seen more dead men than a mortician will see in his lifetime."

For the first time since Billy went I smiled a real smile. The silence wasn't so oppressive when there was someone there with you. Rumours were still floating about that we'd be able take some leave soon. I'd stopped believing them, not until I was in London would I believe them. I can just imagine now getting to the boat and a hand reaching out, turning me around and telling me that I can't go, something has come up and you're to go back to the front. Getting sent to the boat was just a tease, give you back a little bit of the hope that you lost.

I wonder where Billy is now? I don't believe much in God, even less so now. If there was a God how could he let all of this happen? No being who had a conscience would allow all this destruction, the loss of life, the families ruined because fathers wouldn't be coming home. Why would someone create something just to let it go ahead and destroy everything. No, I can't rightly say I believe there's a God because the things I've seen tell me otherwise. The faces appear back in the walls, I'm getting angry again. Calm yourself, Alfie.

I want there to be a God. I want Billy to be in a place where he's happy. I want to go somewhere I am happy. Some days I'm resigned to it, I know it's coming. The chances of me getting out of here without dying aren't going to be big. I'd just want to be able to go back to Gracie and tell her she needs to find someone else to love her. I wouldn't mind that, she can't live the whole of her life alone. Heart drops, I'm never leaving this place am I? It's going to be my final resting place and there's nothing I can do about it.

Sammy has left, I didn't even notice, I could still feel the warmth in my shoulder, his against mine but I was imagining it. Please take us away from here soon, just for a couple of days, a couple of days of respite. I rub my hands together and blow on them, for a couple of seconds I can feel them again. Tapping my foot against the ground, trying to find a rhythm, a song I'd heard before I'd left. The whistling starts up again, I close my eyes and listen, travelling away with the sound as it cuts through the silence.

A squirrel runs along the top of the sandbags, stops just in front of me, looking down as it holds something in his mouth. Thud! The squirrel runs off, away from the battlefield, free from all the burdens we carry. They're even trying to shoot the animals, they've done nothing but be unfortunate to call this place home and here we all are destroying it. I can't even watch it run away, to look over would be my own death. Not even able to appreciate the beauty of an animal. A chuckle to myself, I hate squirrels, I used to chase them around the park, teasing and taunting them, now I wish this one would come back.

"Watts? Alfie Watts?"

"Yes, sir."

"You're going home Alfie. Three days leave. You're to report to the billet and they'll get you to the port."

"Yes, sir."

Home, I'm going home. I'm going home! I can't believe it. Sammy had returned, he patted me on the back but said nothing. We're all the same we all want to go home, both envy and happiness, happiness because how could you hate someone who could die lying next to you. My rifle and bayonet and my kit bag, moving along the walls, men sat there bored, the twists and turns, an endless line of sadness and I could finally leave. Gracie! I'll finally be able to see Gracie, but I can't tell her, she won't be able to meet me at the station. Not to worry, we're going to get married, I'm not waiting any longer.

Green fields. I've lived in green fields for the past two years but they're not green fields anymore, not like these ones. The beautiful green with the white of the frost on top. Undisturbed, left to its own devices, there'd be no bombs falling on them this morning. The smell too, the air is fresh and clean, it smells of home, there's no smell like it. From the moment I left the boat I felt free, even if it's only for two days, I'm free to do as I pleased. A train full of soldiers, horrors that can't be described fill their minds but today and tomorrow they'll be gone, home cooked food and the women they left behind are all that fills their minds.

My stomach is full of butterflies, the train pulling into the station, waiting for it to stop. The doors already open, most can't wait, jumping off the train as it slows. Their movements are slowed, in front of us is

284

another group of lads, clean uniforms, not muddy and torn like ours. Newly sewed patches, the khaki colour visible. Their eyes meet ours, some nods. Their leave is over, they're going back, eyes different to those disembarking the train, the bright eyes are dead again, they know what they're going back to.

"Enjoy it, you'll be us in a few days."

Heads down until we're passed them and out into the street. Waterloo road. I could get home with my eyes closed from here. A Scottish lad waves goodbye, his journey nowhere near complete, just for a few hours at home. Do I walk or do I take a taxi? My rush to get home and my need to enjoy these few moments fighting against each other. A walk will do me good, I don't know what I'll say to them when I get in the door. There'll be questions, mum could never help herself when it came to questions.

I knew it was her as soon as she turned the corner. She was dressed all in black, as she walked down the road she'd look up and shout and then look back down at the floor, her conversation with herself continuing, people stepping aside or crossing the road. What do I say to her? What can I say to her? If I say nothing I'll regret it and Billy would never forgive me. Drawing closer I can see her face, it's old, she has gotten so old, her eyes are dark, dead, no recognition as she looks at me. The head going up again and another shout, incomprehensible, like the screams in the trenches.

I reach out to her, I want to say something but I don't know. She brushes past my hand, I'm not here, nor is anyone else on the street. Grief has killed her, walking the streets by herself, oblivious to all around her. She stops by the green and stoops down, there's a daffodil, very early for daffodils, perhaps it's been warm here. She plucks it and twirls it between her fingers, watching as it spins. I can see her close her eyes, as though she's gone to sleep there on the spot. She throws the daffodil down to the floor and continues her walk of lament. Life taken too early.

From sadness to joy, tap tap at the door, mum holding her back as she opens the door, the pain magically disappearing as she holds me tightly. The neighbours standing on their doorsteps, pretending they have business to attend to. Some of them weeping, mothers of others who won't be coming home to knock at the door. Holding me tight, I don't

285

want to let go, I thought I was a man when I left but now I'm just a boy who has seen things most men will never see. Pushing me into the doorway, a look out at the neighbours and a proud smile. The door shuts and locks out the rest of the world for the next few hours.

"It's good to have you home Alfie, how long are you here for?"

"It's good to be home, mum. Two days and then I have to get back, took me a day to get here."

"Alfie, while you're here can you promise me one thing?"

"Anything you want."

"Don't talk about the war. I don't want to know what happens over there."

"I won't talk about it, I don't want to talk about it either."

"Good lad."

The pan starts to sizzle, the smell of fat and fish. There's not much around she tells me, wishes she could cook me something nicer but that's all there is. I'd eat anything that's not bully beef. Nice and hot, be able to sit back when the meal is finish and enjoy the feeling of being full. She holds her back as she tosses the frying pan, grimacing, my homecoming only enough to hold back the pain for a few minutes. Every few minutes she looks around at me, smiling but not saying anything, I look down at the floor uncomfortable in her gaze. I shouldn't be, but I am.

The front door bangs shut and I jump, mum looks at me in alarm. I take a deep breath and sit back down, I'm not there anymore, I'm home. My father opens the kitchen door, sees me sitting down, he doesn't know what to do. I can see in his eyes he wants to hug me, but that would be giving too much away for him. He pats me on the shoulder, good to have me home. Lighting his pipe he gazes at me too, wanting to say something but not knowing what. Finally he sits down and opens his newspaper, you'd think I'd only popped out for some sugar and it'd taken a year to get back.

Eating in silence, a comfortable silence. I don't know what to say. She said don't talk about the war and I don't want to talk about it, but what

286

else do I have to talk about? Between them they talk about the woman down the road or the price of bread and how hard it is to find. Someone was making bread from turnips my mother laughs. This isn't my world anymore, I can't connect with anything they say, it all seems so pointless. I can't say that to them though, it's not fair, their world and my world are different places.

"I'm going to ask Gracie to marry me while I'm home."

"I thought you was already going to get married."

"No, we'll get married while I'm here."

"That'd be nice, I shouldn't expect you'll be out there much longer anyway. They said it'll be over soon."

I nod, but say nothing. I'm not sure it'll ever end.

"Has she been around lately?"

"She came around yesterday. I wish we'd have known you was coming home, we could have made some preparations."

"There's no need mum, I only want something simple. We ain't got much time either."

"I'll go up to the church in the morning and see what I can do. You'd better go around there and ask her though."

"Of course I will. I saw Billy's mum today."

"I'm sorry, love. I know how close you was to Billy. Poor old Ethel, she loved that boy so much, she's completely lost it since she found out. It's best to leave her be, Alfie, she don't really recognise anyone anymore, it's the shock and the grief."

"I know, but I wish I could do something to help her."

"There's nothing you can do, love."

"I'll go around to Gracie's then, if you don't mind, I'll be back in a bit."

"Get that uniform off you before you go, it's filthy and you smell."

I hope she's there, she might be busy or have gone off somewhere. What if she doesn't want to get married? I don't know what I'll do, I don't think I can wait much longer. A girl and a soldier pass me, hand in hand, the girl is holding a flower. I knock at the door, her mother opens it, I'm sure I can see a small smile on her face as she holds the door open for me. No words, just a nod towards the back.

"Who is it mum?"

"It's me."

She turns around, her hands wet from the clothes she's washing. How long I've waited for this day. She's more beautiful than I ever remembered. She jumps into my arms and I hold her tight. I can feel the wetness of her tears against my cheek, I try to hold back my own tears but it's futile, they pour down my face, a release of emotion, I'm safe now, safe and I don't ever want to leave. We stand there, holding each other for what seems like hours. Finally we both let go and we sit down, she just sits there smiling at me, me smiling back, awkward, like when you were just a boy and the girl you liked sat next to you.

"Gracie I want to ask you something but I'm not sure if you'll say yes."

"You've already asked me to marry you silly, what else can I say no to!"

"I'm home for two days, will you marry me tomorrow. Mum said she'd go to the church and she'd be able to arrange it. If you did it would mean so much to me, I know it's a bit of a surprise and that but..."

"Stop waffling on, of course I will."

"What about your mother?"

"Make sure you look after her and you can marry her." Standing there the whole time she'd been watching us. The smile on her face is more pronounced now, you might even say she looked happy, maybe she isn't the old dragon I thought she was.

"Let's go for a walk, Alfie."

By the river hand in hand. I used to think it was dirty but it looks clean, I'd go for a swim in it if I could. Couples walking along just like us, happy to have their few moments together, not wanting it to end because they're not sure the happiness they have now will ever be bettered.

"When you come back Alife, we'll have a good life, I know we will. I hope it's over soon."

"I hope so too. I hate it Gracie, you're the only person I've ever said these words too but I don't want to go back. You'll never know what it's like over there. I shouldn't be telling you this but I have to tell someone or I'll go mad. Seeing Billy's mum has made me realise that it ain't just us out there who's affected, it's everyone."

"I know. I hate thinking of you out there but you can't not go back, you'd have to run away and then how would we be together? I can't leave my mum on her own and your mum and dad would only worry, although I think your mum would agree. She don't like you being out there, it's like she knows more than she lets on."

"She knows. She's cleverer than most my mum."

"Just think Alfie, it'll be over and then you'll come back for good. You'll be able to get yourself a nice little job and we can get ourselves somewhere to live. We'll have a couple of kids. I want two boys, we can call them Alfie and Billy. They'll just be like you two when you was kids, mischievous little so and so's. You've got to go back Alfie, you're a survivor, you'll be okay."

"Come on, let's not talk about it now, we're wasting our time together."

We walked and talked for hours, plans for the future, what kind of house she'd like and how she was going to dress the kids when we had them. I want to get excited but I can't, there's still something hanging over it, I can't let go until I know it's all over and I never have to go back again. She's right though, I am a survivor, I'll get through it.

Just me, my mum and her dad standing outside the church. I'm nervous, the old man looking at me, that look in his eye as if to say you sure you know what you're letting yourself in for. I know, I'm marrying the love of my life and I'm never going to let her go. We walk back to the house, just the five of us. Mum cooks something to eat while dad and her mother talk about Billy's mum. She's been standing over on Waterloo Bridge, looking down at the water.

"Can we not talk about this today, please."

"Sorry, Alfie."

I want to go and see her before I go, I have to see her, even if she doesn't know who I am anymore. Gracie smiles at me and strokes my hand. Tomorrow I'll be off on that train again, I'll be the one looking at those getting off it in envy. She said she's coming to the station with me, I didn't want her to because I'm not sure I'll be able to hold it together, I can't let the rest of them see me crying.

"We didn't go to the theatre Alfie."

"We didn't have enough time, not with getting married. We'll go next time, next time I should be back for good anyway."

We spent the rest of the evening playing cards, mum sang a few songs, me sitting in the chair with Gracie in my lap. All of us laughing, dad even getting up and doing a jig. There was joy in his eyes, even getting carried away and spinning mum around, her back pain forgotten. We walked Gracie's mum back home and slowly walked back, knowing this would be the last carefree moments we'd have for a long time. Dad was still sitting in the kitchen, Gracie went up to bed, exhausted. The old man handed me a cigarette and he lit his pipe, we sat there in the kitchen, smoking in silence. I rose to go to bed, he stood up to, throwing his arms around me and hugging me tight. There was no awkwardness, his repressed love all coming out at once.

"Make sure you come home, son. I know I don't say much but I love you and you've made me so proud today."

Nothing I can say back.

Mum holds me tight, she doesn't want to let me go. The old man waves and even gives me another hug. The journey to the station always seems shorter when you're going somewhere you don't want to go to. At the entrance I pick up and kiss Gracie, holding her against me. Her tears flowing down both our cheeks. Goodbye Gracie, my love. I will back soon and we'll be a proper family then. She holds my hand not letting go as I walk towards the train. She lets me loose, I turn and wave, kissing my hand and blowing it to her. It'll be over soon.

The Elephant and Castle

The Elephant and Castle, formerly home to a large, pink shopping centre and last stop on the Bakerloo line

It's all fuzzy, everything looks like it's made of plasticine, if I reached out and touched it I'd be able to mould it into beautiful shapes, butterflies, birds, balloons or an elephant. An elephant would be nice, if I had an elephant I'd just spend all day riding it, around the streets of London, imagine the faces of the people walking the streets? Me on my big elephant waving as I passed them. Have you ever ridden an elephant? I've never had one, I might make one out of that bed side table over there, a massive one, even bigger than the ones they have in Africa.

I keep thinking that geezer over there keeps looking at me but I'm sure he's nice. I don't know him, I don't think I know anyone here, all their faces are blurry, I can't make out who they are, just the way their heads move to look around. They're talking about something but I've no idea what. I can't even move, it's like I've lost all ability, I can just sit up and I'm stuck like that. I want to say something, anything, just to let people know I'm still here but I can't, my mouth won't open, only my eyes are able to move.

I'm floating, up towards the ceiling, I'm looking down on myself, I can see myself sitting there, no idea what's going on. Have I died? Is this what it's like when you die? I feel calm, I'm not panicking but I've left my body and I don't know where I am going. I reach out to touch myself but I'm too far away. No one else can see me floating here, they're laughing, I can see their faces now, some of them look happy and soothing but some of them look harsh and as if they want to do some harm. I'm safe up here on my own, they can't get me, they can't even see me.

I'm back, back inside my own body. I rub my hands together and touch my legs, make sure they're still there, make sure that I'm alive. They all turn and laugh at me, welcome back to reality. How long was I gone for? Was it nearly the end? Could I have died? Fuck! I reach for a cigarette, inhaling deeply and slowly blowing out the smoke, watching it as it rises, it's making patterns, I can see dragons and castles merging into one another, crashing against the ceiling, fading away to nothing. I don't want to talk, I ignore their laughter and their questions.

Crisis of conscience always come at inopportune times, you doubt when you should be happy or doing something you previously thought you enjoyed. Why now? Why couldn't it have been 24 hours ago and I might not even have ended up here. Do I want to be here? I think so, I'm not sure. They reckon when you doubt something it's because you really know what you want to do but you don't like the answer so you just pretend you're not sure to reassure yourself. So, do I really want to be here? I really don't know.

We're always questioning ourselves though, right? I mean it's natural, you do something and more often than not you're thinking am I doing the right thing. That's usually when you're doing the right thing though, when you're doing something you shouldn't do it's more impulsive. I'm sitting here now and I'm wondering if the whole of my life has been a complete waste and what if I'd done something different, all them paths you have to choose from and if at one of them paths you'd taken a different turn you wouldn't be where you are now.

All these people sitting here with me, they're my friends, well at least I think they're my friends. We do everything together, everywhere I go, there's usually one of them with me. We've been through everything together, since we was kids, we've seen each other grow up and now I'm wondering if they're really my friends. If they thought I was doing something wrong in life would they say listen you need to sort yourself out or would they just let me go along with it and let me because they're choosing the same fucked up path along a never-ending road of madness.

This weekend ain't any different from any other, why am I contemplating the deeper meaning of life and the values of my friendships? Jesus Christ, something's gone wrong somewhere for me to be sitting here. I need to knock it all on the head, go on the straight, take one of them paths when I walk out the door. Where'll that path go though, that's what I worry about, the path I'm on is getting old and boring but at least I know where it's all taking me. I don't know where the other path will go and I don't know where I'll end up and that's the thing that frightens me. How the fuck did I end up here?

Friday evenings are the worst and best of the week. You're just sitting there waiting for the clock to reach five and then you can go. It's the excitement, knowing that in a couple of hours' time you'll be enjoying yourself, but fuck me does that clock tick slowly. It reaches five and then that's it, out the door, through them doors is like being liberated from prison, you don't have to see the rest of the wankers in that office for another three days and they're out of your mind until you're back on the tube on Monday morning.

There's this big, pink shopping centre where I live. I don't know who decided pink would be a good colour to paint a shopping centre. It's like this massive pink blob in the middle of London. When I stand on my balcony in the morning having a fag it's all I can see. Masses of people making their way to work, a big pink stain in the background. It's almost as though it's taunting you, look at me, look at me! I don't know what it's got to taunt me about though, It's not like I want to be a massive pink blob.

It's the moment of calmness, that period of time after work and before it all begins. The weekend, where everything is let go, it's what I live for, my whole reason of existence. The week of typing shitty numbers into a database, being told what to do by some guy who doesn't know what he's doing himself, just so I can enjoy two days a week. The thousands of other people in the streets below, jumping on buses home. Some of them will be going off to nice big houses to spend the weekend with their families or go to the park with their kids. Some of them'll sit at home on their own, bored and questioning their own existence. Fuck that, I ain't about that kind of life.

If you've got your big house in Dulwich and you've got your three kids and they've got three bicycles that you take to the park every weekend, what's that all about? I mean, fair play and all that, if that's what they really want but how comes when you see a geezer down the park with his kids he always looks harassed, he wants to kill them. You can see it in his eyes, he's thinking what the fuck have I done? Then his missus starts shouting at him because one of the kids has fucked off on an adventure somewhere and they can't find him. Then the dog starts shagging his leg while he's looking for the missing kid while the other two kids start battering each other. You're mad if you think that's the life for me, nah, filling numbers into a database and getting wrecked at the weekend is what it's all about.

You know what gets to me as well? Those people that always ask you when you're going to sort yourself out, and when you going to find yourself a nice girlfriend, get married. What's it got to do with them? I'm happy doing what I do, why do they always have to be asking questions. I go around my mum's on a Sunday evening and that's all I hear, telling me how I'm wasting my life and Tommy who lived next door when I was a kid has a nice girlfriend and they're having a baby soon. I'm delighted for Tommy, I really am but I ain't Tommy.

That feels better, let it all out! Someone at work said to me the other day that I'm going through an existential crisis. I told him to fuck off but I've been thinking about it, maybe he's right. Anyway enough of that. Time to get ready and go out.

The pubs are all full, Friday night in the centre of the city, madness. You get every kind of person out and about. The city people in their suits, laughing loudly, wanting everyone to look at them. There's the kids outside with their fake IDs trying to con the geezers on the door but they're not having any of it. Those that are just old enough to be able to drink in a pub and think they're hard, hanging around the pool table or by the bar looking moody and staring at everyone who walks past them. Then you've got the old geezers sitting down moaning about the kids in the pub and how they'd bar them all if they could.

I order a pint, drinking it quickly, watching all the goings on in the pub. I love people watching. It kind of sums this place up. You've got all these social classes mixing with each other, well not mixing because they don't have anything to do with each other but they're all in the same place. Resentment from those that have always lived here, the new people that have suddenly turned up delighted they've got a nice pad 10 minutes from Westminster but still a bit scared to mix with the locals, not wanting to make eye contact until they've had a few. When they've had a few there's a bit of mingling going on but they're all weary of each other, sizing each other up.

It's a bit of a strange area this really. I grew up here and I love the place but I've seen the change. It used to be one of them places where you'd say you was from The Elephant and they'd go 'ooo, bit dodgy around there, I heard loads of people get stabbed.' It weren't that bad, when somewhere's your home is just that ain't it? Your home, you don't worry about what other people say about it. I've never seen anything too bad anyway, I mean I saw a geezer get robbed once and someone get stabbed another time but I wouldn't say it was dangerous.

It's changed though in recent years, they've knocked down all the old estates, and that big one, the poster child for brutalist, sink estates is standing there, an empty shell. The people who say it's dodgy have never been there, probably couldn't tell you where it was but in their mind it was a shithole where everyone ran around stabbing and shooting each other and if you weren't stabbing or shooting someone you'd be sat at home banging up smack while laughing at the rest of the country for giving you benefits. Being right on the edge of central London don't help either, prime real estate means money and that's all people give a fuck about these days ain't it?

Most of my mates have moved away, they can't afford to live here no more. That's what my problem with it all is. Make an area safe, build shops and restaurants and whatever it is you do to make an area nice but don't price the people that have always lived here out of it. Build all these nice flats next to the tube station because some wanker from a village in Surrey doesn't want to walk to far to the train station and fuck all the undesirables off because they ain't the ones that are going to be making you money are they? They don't get it though, or I should say they do get it but they don't give a fuck.

I should be a social David Attenborough. Watch as the cap wearing thug surveys his territory, there are invaders on his turf, he's not quite sure what to make of them. His instinct is to attack but he also sees opportunity to sell his wears. The chino wearing man from Cheam is wary too, he knows he's taking a risk but he believes his wit and his charm will be enough for the cap wearing thug to allow him to stay in his territory. Perhaps they can come to some arrangement whereby Chino from Cheam can purchase copious amounts of cocaine in order to keep the thug from stabbing him.

My mate walks in, looking around him to see if he can see anyone he knows. I wave other to him and he walks over with a big smile on his face.

"I don't know anyone in this gaff anymore, lucky you're here or I'd be standing around drinking on my own."

"Take you long to get down here?"

"Na, just got the train to London Bridge and jumped on the bus. Good to be back in town. What you having?"

"Double vodka and Red Bull."

"You trying to bankrupt me?"

"There's a party over in West London later, we'll go to that if you want."

"Yeah, I'm up for that. Can't go on too mad a one this weekend though, I've got to be at work early Monday morning and I ain't going in there like I did after last weekend."

"You always say that you nutcase."

The bus is empty as it takes its time going through the streets of South London. Paul is quieter than normal, usually he's the type that doesn't shut up but he hasn't said a word since we got on the bus. He ain't even on anything yet either.

"How comes you're so quiet?"

"Just thinking."

"Thinking about what?"

"The missus was talking about getting married."

"You? Get married? You won't be doing any of this if you do that."

"I know that. I'm not sure I want to be doing it anymore mate. It's time to grow up and all that. She's getting the hump because I'm out every weekend, can't blame her really. Anyway, I'm getting bored of it. It's the same thing every week."

"It's up to you. I don't think you're ready for the settled life though, you'd end up going mad."

"That's you talking for yourself though ain't it? Drugs and booze and getting wasted every weekend, there's got to come a point where you think it ain't worth it anymore."

"It ain't like you're a smackhead or anything."

"I know that, but that's just a false equivalency."

"What the fuck's that?"

"You're saying that things ain't that bad because I'm not a smackhead."

"Well they ain't are they?"

"No, they ain't but it's not about whether they're bad or not, it's just getting fucking boring. I'm fed up of feeling like shit for three days after the weekend. I don't think you get it."

"I do get it, but I don't want to be going living like average Joe."

"That's up to you then ain't it. I'm done after this weekend, take some time off."

"You'll be wearing a flat cap next time I see you."

He shuts up again. The bus stops outside a supermarket, I watch the people going in and out, carrying bags of shopping, geezers with their girlfriends holding hands. Probably going home to make a nice meal or something. Can't remember the last time I didn't have something that I didn't just shove in the microwave, never mind have someone around to have a meal with me. The bus pulls off again but there's something drawing my eyes to the couple walking down the street together with their carrier bags full of food. I pass Paul one of the round pills in my pocket. He looks at it before he puts it into his mouth, never seen him hesitate before, there's definitely something up with him.

We get off the bus and walk down the leafy street, old Victorian houses, no mistaking where the party is coming from, the bass from the speakers can be heard from the bottom of the road. I'm starting to feel good now, I like to have a beer but nothing beats the feeling of coming up on a pill. There ain't no worries anymore and the geezer with his shopping bag is just another mug who's chosen a life he probably doesn't want.

He's a nice mug though, not saying he's a bad geezer, in fact he's probably a really nice fella.

All my fears and worries wash away as I step into the house, I can feel the music moving through my body, my stomach feels as though it's going to jump out of my mouth, it's a sensation that should feel horrible but it's not, I love it. This is my world, away from the offices and the dreariness of everyday life, where people come together to dance and talk. I knock back a shot of vodka, the warmth running through my body, I'm on my way now and there's no one or no thoughts that's going to be getting in the way of it.

Standing in the kitchen, there's a geezer I never met before telling me his theory of life and how we're all just pawns in a big game of chess. I nod my head and agree with him, I'm not really sure what it's all about, what he's saying, but it sounds good. Halfway through telling me about the game of life he starts talking about his dog and how much he loves it and if anything ever happened to the dog it'd kill him. Some people shouldn't be allowed out. He wanders off and starts talking to another random person, they do the same thing as me just nod their head, you can tolerate people talking shit when you're off your nut.

I can see my friend across the room, chatting up some bird. She doesn't look too impressed with whatever it is he's telling her. I say he's my friend but he's just someone I know, not like Oliver who I've known since I was a kid. If I met him out on the street on a Wednesday afternoon we'd nod at each other say hello, ask questions to avoid silences and then go on or way, glad that the awkward encounter is over. Not here though, here we're best mates, like we are every weekend. It's a friendship of convenience, someone who understands, until Monday morning when it's all over and you're full of regrets and fear.

The girl makes her excuses, back to her friends with a roll of the eyes, Jack, I think his name is Jack, delighted with himself because he's just validated to himself that he's a Casanova, the smoothest man in town and no woman could ever spurn his advances, her moving away is because she can't handle him, not because he's boring and only talks about himself.

"You know what Johnny, I'm struggling a bit mate."

"What's the matter mate? Never thought I'd hear them words from you son, what's happened to all them plans you was telling me about last week, new business and all that?"

"Fell through didn't it. Didn't trust the geezer I was supposed to be doing it with, you know what it's like."

"Yeah, yeah. You want to get yourself a proper job."

"Jobs are for mugs mate, I'm an entrepreneur, the world ain't ready for what I'm going to bring to it."

"Yeah, I know what you mean. What's the matter with you then?"

"I don't know, man. It's a bit deep."

"Go on then, we're all friends here."

"I'm fucking depressed man, I mean, I wake up in the morning and I feel like I don't want to get out of bed, I'm tired, I don't want to go out the door because I don't want to see no one. I can't go out unless it's the weekend and I'm on something, it's all I'm doing, living for the weekend. During the week it's just a filler, you know what I mean? There's no substance to it."

"You want to knock whatever you're taking on the head mate, it can't be doing you no good if you're thinking like that."

"I know, I know but if I ain't got the weekend then what have I got? Most of my friends, no offence, my proper friends, they've moved away or they're doing something with their lives. Me, I'm just sitting around hatching plans in my head which I know are never, ever going to happen. I know people laugh at them, I suppose it's an escape for me mate, just the thought that there might be something better than what I've got, it keeps me going in a way."

"I know what you mean but there comes a time when you've got to realise it's just not worth it."

"Do you know what does me as well? It's not like it's my home no more. That sounds stupid because I've lived here all my life and I do know people and that but it's just not home no more, it's just same place I live.

The geezer who lives next door to me, I don't know who he is, I don't know what he's job is, I don't even know the geezer's name."

"Why don't you ask him then?"

"I never see him and even if I do ask him he probably ain't going to tell me, most people don't want nothing to do with each other anymore. I'm fucking anonymous Johnny and I hate it. I'm not talking like I want to be famous or anything like that, I'm just saying it'd be nice if someone stopped me when I was walking through my block of flats and said 'hello, how you doing mate?'. "

"That's your fault though ain't it? You've got to go out and meet people when you're not off your nut. Look at me and you, yeah we're talking now, we're going pretty deep and that, but I've seen you on the street during the week and we barely say a word to each other. I like you Jack but we're not real mates are we?"

"Yeah, yeah, I understand that, but that's all there is these days, acquaintances, just people that have their uses innit? I don't know man, maybe it's me, I must be losing it or something. My mum rang me up yesterday and said I need to grow up. I don't think I'm ready to grow up though Johnny, I'm like you, I just want to live like this forever."

"None of us will live like this forever mate, it'll catch up on us at some point or we'll get bored with it."

"You know what, if I had the money I'd go and do one of them backpacking things. Go and see the world and all that. I might do it you know. You coming to the club later?"

He'll no more go backpacking than I'll be getting married on Monday morning before work. We all have a lot of dreams but not many of us go out there and get them. It's like looking in a mirror, everything he's saying I've said myself but here I am trying to tell him everything will be all right and giving him advice. Who the fuck am I to be giving this geezer advice? I've no more of an idea where I'm going with my life than he has. I get what he's saying though, It's a crisis of identity or whatever they call it.

"Just going to go and see where Oliver is mate, I'll catch you later."

"I don't know what to do Johnny, I really don't."

I leave him to grab someone else who he can spill his heart out to, I'm not in the mood for this, this is my weekend and I ain't spending it playing therapist. I pull the packet of white powder from my pocket and go into the toilets, it goes straight to my brain, my face numb but now I'm invincible, he should have caught me ten minutes later and I'd have been able to solve all of his problems. I can solve my own now anyway, I'm just a cog in the wheel of life but right now I'm the biggest one, the most important one.

That girl over there, I'm sure I was talking to her last week, I wonder if she'll remember me, yeah she'll definitely remember me, how could anyone forget me? The power of confidence, a few minutes ago you're questioning all your life choices and now you're the wisest man on the planet.

"Hey, I thought you'd forgotten me."

She's not even English, sounds American.

"How could I have forgotten you. You look nice tonight."

"Thank you. You disappeared last weekend, I couldn't find you, where did you go?"

"Went back to my mates house I think, I can't remember to be honest, you know how it is."

"Do you remember what you promised me?"

Oh shit, What the fuck did I promise her?

"You were telling me about where you lived. Said you'd show me around one time, give me a proper tour, places the tourists don't get to see."

"Yeah, of course I remember."

What the fuck did I say that for?

"Let's go then."

"What now? It's the middle of the night."

"I like looking at things in the middle of the night, there's an atmosphere about it."

"Let's go then, I'll have to warn you, I might have exaggerated a little bit though."

I must have been a right mess if I was promising her to be a tour guide around The Elephant. What am I supposed to show her? Here's a building that used to be here but it's not anymore. There's a pink shopping centre, I never go there but it's quite a sight! Here's an underground station as well, I'm sure you've seen plenty of them while you've been living here.

The bus is empty, just me and her sat upstairs, the driver looks pissed off, I'd be pissed off if I had to drive this thing around all night as well. What do you do? You see the same thing every night, hardly anyway gets on the bus, must be a shite job.

"I'd like to have his job."

"Who? The bus driver?"

"Yeah, I think it'd be pretty cool."

"It'd be a shite job, it must be one of the most boring jobs going."

"Why? I mean, he gets to drive around this city at night when there's no one on the streets. City's are always different during the night. There's a glow, you know? Like all the energy from the day is rising up and leaving it."

Fucking hell, she's a hippy or thinks she's a poet or something.

"I suppose so, I just think it'd be boring, you'd see the same thing all the time. Wouldn't be for me."

"What's your favourite place in the city?"

"I don't know, I've never really thought about it, when you live somewhere you just take it for granted don't you?"

"Yeah, but you must have somewhere."

"There's a park, down the Old Kent Road, my dad used to take me there when I was a kid to feed the ducks and then we'd play football. It's not one of the big attractions and you wouldn't know about it if you don't live here but yeah, I suppose that's my favourite place. What about you?"

It's a long time since I've been down there. I should go for a walk down there one night after work. He used to stand by the edge of the lake and pretend to fall in, I'd be panicking, thinking I don't know how to swim, if he does go over, how am I going to rescue him. Bit of an idiot my dad, a joker. I've not kicked a ball about for years either, would be good to get a bit of exercise.

"There's so many but I suppose if I had to choose The London Eye..."

"The Eye? It's a waste of money that thing."

"Hey, I don't live here, we see things differently."

"I suppose, but don't you think it's all just a bit commercialised. You go up on this big wheel to look out at the city and pay a fortune for the privilege. I've lived here all my life, why should I go and pay to see it."

"Why shouldn't you pay?"

"We get off here."

I'm a tour guide on a Friday night to some American woman in the middle of The Elephant and Castle, life doesn't get much more surreal than this. There's no one around, I'm not even sure what time it is, the battery on my phone is gone, the train station shut.

"Where do you want to go?"

"I don't know, you're the tour guide."

Where the fuck am I supposed to take her?

"See this building here, this thing that looks like a shopping centre? It used to be pink, like a bright pink."

"They should have left it pink, it could do with some colour."

"I'm sure they'll turn it into something else soon enough."

"Why did they paint it pink?"

"Who knows? 'Add colour to the place' is what they'd probably say. When I was a kid, I used to look down at it from our window up there. I'd pretend it was a castle, and I'd be imagining what it would be like to be inside there if it was really a castle. My dad thought I was gay because I liked pink."

"Are you gay?"

"No! I'm not gay."

"It'd be cool if you were."

"Honestly I'm not gay, I just liked the building! Anyway, one time my mum took me shopping in there, when you go inside it's just one of them dull and dark shopping centres, she gave me a couple of quid and told me to go and buy something for myself. Instead of buying something I went and sat in the middle of the shopping centre and pretended I was in a castle."

"You had quite the imagination."

"My mum came and found me and I was sitting there with my eyes closed. I think she thought I'd gone mad."

Past the old cinema, I remember going there when I was a kid, I saved up all the money I'd made doing a paper round and I was delighted with myself that I had enough to go on my own. I can't even remember what it was I went to see, I think it was Karate Kid or something like that.

"See these buildings in front of us, they're knocking them down soon. No one lives in them anymore, I had a few mates that lived in there but they've all moved away now."

"Wow! That's sad. Why are they knocking them down?"

"Said they're too dangerous, too much crime. They'll just build expensive places on top of them. It's right next to the centre of London, people will pay a fortune to come and live somewhere like this but they need to get rid of the locals first, wouldn't want them mixing with the local riff raff would they. Some bent councillor is probably getting his cut as well."

305

"Can we go inside?"

"It's all boarded up."

"Come on! We'll just jump over the fence, no one will see us, it'll be interesting!"

Fuck am I letting myself into here.

"Go on then, make sure you're careful though, not sure what we'll find in there."

She's enjoying this, maybe I should become a tour guide. I'd be like Oliver but a proper Casanova, showing all these foreign women around abandoned parts of London. Like an adventure guide or something. I give her a leg up and she disappears over the blue boards, I jump up and grab the top and pull myself over. It's quiet, the boards keeping the sounds of the cars and buses out, it's eerie. These will be all gone soon, it'll be weird without them, I associate this part of The Elephant with these buildings, it's like it's ingrained in my head.

The drugs are starting to wear off but I feel strangely happy wondering about abandoned building sites with a woman I don't know. I feel in my pocket to make sure the wrap is still there, it is, if I had a line it'd make the experience all the better, give me an extra buzz. Nah, fuck it, I'll have some later. I'll need to go back and find Oliver, he's probably got the hump because I've left him on his own, bit rude of me really but fuck it, you got to take your chances when they come along.

We climb over another wall and up the staircase. Used to come up here when I went to knock for my mate. I bet kids don't do that no more, go to their mate's house and ask their mum if they're allowed out to play and then if they wasn't you'd walk back home with the hump because you had no one to play with. Just give someone a ring or a text, I didn't even know my mate's phone number! I'm going to be one of those miserable bastards who's always talking about the old days in a few years.

All the doors to the flats have iron gates on them, there's no way you're getting through any of them. I pull it but it doesn't shift at all, the window is covered with a metal plate. All the way down the landing you can see the metal gates and boarded up windows. People used to live here, a couple of years back they'd be going about their business, now they're probably living in some place they've no connection to and know nothing about. All about the money though ain't it?

"You used to come here when you were a kid?"

"Yeah, my friend lived in that door over there. Used to come on Saturday afternoons when I was coming back from the park with my dad. I'd knock for him and then we'd go to the shop and steal penny sweets."

"So you were a thief as well as mad?"

"You've not lived if you've not stole penny sweets from the corner shop."

"Want to see if we can open the door?"

"There's no chance that's opening, it's solid metal."

"Try anyway."

I pull the door but it's the same as the other one, shut fast, there's nothing moving that. She taps on the boarded up window and then puts her hand underneath the metal, she pulls hard and it comes off, falling to the floor with a loud bang. We both duck down behind the balcony, I look over the top to see if anyone is there, there has to be security somewhere. No one, streets are empty and no one from the buses would notice or even care, you just go about your business, fuck what anyone else is doing.

There's no glass in the window, she's already climbed in, standing in the flat, I climb in after her, a bit apprehensive, not because I'm doing something I shouldn't be but because it's like going back in time. The kitchen is bare, the units have all been ripped out, there's paper and rubble all over the floor. I remember standing in this kitchen, his mum lecturing us on being careful when we're out and about. She was strict her, much stricter than my mum. I can see us now, two little eight year old boys staring at the ground trying not to giggle.

The living room isn't completely empty, there's an old sofa, I don't recognise it, someone else lived here after they had. In the corner there's an old television, one of them small ones, I doubt it's a colour one, not worth anything, there'd be no point in anyone taking it, that's what their possessions have come to, whether they're valuable enough to nick or not. She sits down on the sofa, a cloud of dust jumps up. Sat in this room a few times, watching the football with his old man, both of us excited all day, waiting for the match to start. I can see him in the room now, pretending he had a ball, kicking it about. I thought he was a nutter playing with an imaginary ball, forgetting my time in the pink castle.

"What are you thinking?"

"Just thinking about the times I used to spend in here. It's weird, this was someone's house and now it's all empty, there's no life left in it. When someone lives in a home there's a feeling, you know someone is living there but this place just feels empty, like they've completely sucked the life out of it."

"Yeah, it is a strange feeling. What's that over there?"

There's an old book on the floor. I pick it up, someone has written a diary but the pages are all stuck together, I try to open it but they tear as I pull it apart. The little bit of writing I can see is illegible. This is some poor fucker's memories. I wonder where they are now? I hand it to her, but she can't make any sense of it either. I sit down on the sofa with her.

"When you're a kid, you think everything around you is going to be there forever. You don't think it'll ever change but you forget that everyone else older than you has seen it all change, what you think is how it's always been, they think is change, they don't like it. I never thought I'd see this place go. I used to think of the pair of us as old men, living next to each other, we'd pop into each other's flats. Ain't going to happen now is it?"

"Change isn't always bad though. You said it was dangerous."

"It wasn't that dangerous. This was someone's house, and the flat next door was someone else's house. They were just people living in the only place they knew. Is the only way to make something not dangerous is to tear it down? People are always telling you what the place you live in is like when they haven't got the slightest idea. Who the fuck are they to tell me that my home is a shithole and should be knocked down?"

"Surely it's for the better though, it'll help people."

"It'll help people who have money and want to come and live somewhere close to work. It don't help the people who're living some place miles away from where they grew up because they didn't have the money. Don't get me wrong, sometimes things should change but why do they always have to fuck with people's lives when they're doing it?"

"I don't know, it's just the way it goes sometimes. I mean, where you live is still there isn't it."

"I'm sure they'll find a way soon, when something doesn't fit in with its surroundings, it has to go at some point."

"You shouldn't be so bitter."

"It's hard when you don't recognise your home no more and you ain't sure if you fit in or not. I can't be the only person who feels like that."

She nods her head but doesn't say anything. I'm getting angry but I shouldn't, maybe she's right, change is good and I'm just a miserable bastard who doesn't want to embrace it. I look inside one of the bedrooms, I'd always wanted to look inside that bedroom it was the only part of the flat I had never seen, it was his mum and dad's room. It's empty, I feel disappointed, I don't know what I expected to see.

"Come on let's go, I'm worried there's security here and you don't know who might be hanging around anyway."

"Where we going to go?"

"Don't know, where do you want to go?"

"You're the guide."

I just want to go back and find my mates and get fucked. Seeing the flat has brought up too many memories for me. I don't think she does though. We climb back out of the flats and onto the main road. There's a bus coming, I could jump on that and be back at the house in half an hour. She can see me looking at the bus, she knows what's going through my head. I didn't realise how pretty she is. She wants to go home with me. We could just go home now, five minutes away, spend the weekend in bed, I'd wake up Monday morning feeling fresh and perky.

She reaches up and touches my face and then kisses me. The bus pulls up at the bus stop, the driver looks even more pissed off than the other one. I can't just leave her here. I don't want a girlfriend, what if she wants to be my girlfriend. Fuck this. I take twenty quid out of my pocket and put it in her hand, I give her a forced smile.

"Get a taxi home, I need to go somewhere. Sorry."

I jump on the bus.

"Johnny, I've been thinking about what I said earlier to you and I think I've come up with a solution, I'm going to start my own business, but it's going to be proper this time. I'm going to sell ice cream. I'm a fucking genius Johnny."

"Go away, mate, I'm not interested."

Not in the mood for the nonsense ramblings of some wanker I don't really know. The whole trip back I was angry at myself, angry for leaving her there, angry I didn't decide to take a different route and fuck all of this silliness off. But here I am back at the house again.

"Where did you go?"

"Just went off for a while. You all right? You look a bit fucked?"

"Yeah, I'm good. We're going to some other geezer's gaff soon, you coming?"

"Yeah, I'm coming."

"Where's that bird gone?"

"She's gone home."

"You fucking idiot."

Sat in some random person's house, there's white lines all over his coffee table, I'm not sure what I'm taking, it ain't cocaine anyway, I think it's ketamine, I'm tripping my balls of here, I feel like I'm having an outer body experience, part of my body has left me. Like my mind has gone for a walk and left a little bit left to sit there and worry whether I've died or not.

These people, sitting here with me, why would they let me get like this, they must be able to see me but they don't stop me, it's all just a laugh. I shouldn't have left that girl. I went back to the past and now I feel more alone and confused. I'm going, I'm going and I ain't coming back, these people aren't real, they're just figures who accompany you along the road, falling by the wayside, disappearing at different crossroads, never to be heard from again. I have to get out, I can't breathe properly in here. I can hear their laughter as I push open the door, no care just amusement.

The park is empty, not a soul, the sun rising up above my head. Saturday morning, if I'd stayed I'd be getting ready to go somewhere else, waste a day at the pub, get wrecked, spend the night at some other random's house, talk shit with strangers. Is it it shit though? A lot of what we say sounds like nonsense but there's some truth to it. None of us really know what we're doing here or where we're going. You can call it cliched as much as you want but things change and you don't recognise them anymore, it hurts, things are taken away from you and it's out of your control. It's always for the better but no one ever asks you if it's for the better, you're just told and if you say otherwise, well you just don't 'understand'.

I kick a pebble along the side of the lake, pretending I'm a footballer, enough drugs in my system for there not to be any self consciousness, the only thing that would see me are the ducks anyway. I kick it into the lake, watch as the ripples spread out and then disappear. There's nothing wrong with being deep is there? I don't think I'm a philosopher, I'm just trying to understand the lack of control I have in my life, I can choose a path but somewhere along the ling something will drag me in another direction and it ain't always the direction I want to go.

Almost home, now what do I do? Go to bed? When I wake up what am I going to do? For years my weekends have been dominated by madness, some fun, some not so much. I suppose I could go for a walk. I might even go and look at the Eye, a half arsed attempt to embrace the change. It's not all bad, I'm just seeing the bad, perhaps it's my problem, why are there so many people out there like me though? We can't all be pessimistic and miserable.

The empty flats on my left as I near The Elephant. When they built them, they were a symbol of hope, somewhere people could live with all the amenities they wanted, hot water, central heating. Then they let them decay and blamed the people who was living in them so they're knocking them down, put new people here, people that've always had a chance in life, people that won't give a second thought to who they're replacing. That place was a symbol of my childhood, it was a constant, I knew the people who lived in there, now they're all gone and I'm left on my own.

The pink castle isn't there anymore either, it's blue now. Not that it's a bad thing, it fascinated me but it looked terrible. I'll give them that one. I open the door and throw myself down on the bed, I'm exhausted. Through the gap in the curtains I can see the old shopping centre. A pink castle, I'll go and wander around my pink castle, at least that won't have changed because they can't change it, it's all up here in my head. What a world hey? I've not got a fucking clue where I'm going and no one listen because I don't understand.

Thank you for reading! I have two other books which are available at the following links:

https://www.amazon.co.uk/Unwashed-Se%C3%A1n-Hogan/dp/1537391216/ref=sr_1_1?ie=UTF8&qid=1507830588&sr=8-1&keywords=the+unwashed+sean+hogan

https://www.amazon.co.uk/Liar-Se%C3%A1n-Hogan-ebook/dp/B01LYLWXNH/ref=tmm_kin_swatch_0?_encoding=UTF8&qid=&sr=

28955815R00173

Printed in Great Britain
by Amazon